HOW TO TRAIN YOUR VISCOUNT

BOOK ONE IN THE ASTLEY CHRONICLES

COURTNEY MCCASKILL

HAZEL GROVE BOOKS

THE ASTLEY CHRONICLES

Book 1: How to Train Your Viscount

∼

Coming Soon:

Book 2: What's an Earl Gotta Do?

Book 3: The Sea Siren of Broadwater Bottom

∼

For more information, visit www.courtneymccaskill.com.

THE ASTLEYS OF HARRINGTON HALL

Edward Astley IV, Earl of Cheltenham
Georgiana Astley, Countess of Cheltenham

Edward Astley V, Viscount Fauconbridge, age 26
Harrington Astley, age 25
Anne Northcote (née Astley), Countess of Wynters, age 23
Lady Caroline Astley, age 19
Lady Lucy Astley, age 17
Lady Isabella Astley, age 17
John Astley, deceased at age 2
Frederick Astley, age 13

First published in 2021 by Hazel Grove Books.

How to Train Your Viscount, Copyright © Courtney McCaskill, 2021.

Excerpt from *What's an Earl Gotta Do?* Copyright © Courtney McCaskill, 2021.

Paperback ISBN: 978-1-63915-000-7

Kindle ISBN: 978-1-63915-001-4

eBook ISBN: 978-1-63915-002-1

This is a work of fiction. Names, principal characters, events, and incidents are the products of the author's imagination. A few real historical figures make cameo appearances. Although I attempted to make these cameos consistent with the general personality traits of these characters when those traits were known, these are fictionalized portrayals, and, other than Thomas Hope's rout debuting his Duchess Street mansion (which really did take place on May 7, 1802), the scenes in which these characters appear have no factual basis. Any other resemblance to actual persons, living or dead, or actual events is purely coincidental.

HOW TO TRAIN YOUR VISCOUNT

CHAPTER 1

ondon, England
April 1802

Lady Caroline Astley slipped inside the dark, silent room. At the sight of the naked man across the gallery, she recoiled, choking back a shriek as she sloshed hot candle wax all over her kid leather glove.

The unclothed man did not so much as blink, nor did he attempt to cover himself with the length of cloth draped behind his back. She exhaled, realizing it was a statue. Of course it was a statue—the mansion she was skulking about belonged to Mr. Thomas Hope, heir to one of the richest banking families in Europe and a renowned collector of art and antiquities.

This happened to be the reason she had stolen away from the dinner party she was supposed to be attending and was now creeping through darkened parts of the house that were ostensibly closed to visitors—because the new acquisition

Mr. Hope had described to her sounded very much like something she had lost.

Or, more accurately, something that had been stolen from her.

She peered around the shadowy room. Dear lord, Mr. Hope had told her his new interiors were going to cause a sensation when he debuted them two weeks hence, and he hadn't been exaggerating. For someone who had spent the better part of three hours lecturing her on the paramount importance of classical simplicity in both dress and interior design, Mr. Hope had been rather liberal in his use of blood-orange satin curtains. Throw in the floor-to-ceiling mirrors and the gold gilt covering every single piece of furniture, and the room was threatening to give her a megrim, even by the light of the candelabra she had commandeered from the ladies' retiring room. It had to be spectacularly atrocious when fully lit.

Caro managed to locate the only thing in the room that interested her, *the door*, which was buried amongst the curtains. She hastened through it.

The next room was some sort of Turkish salon, with low crimson sofas, even more gold gilt, and... She sniffed the air suspiciously, hoping that lingering, spicy aroma was nothing worse than incense. Not that she had any firsthand experience with opium, but she imagined this was precisely the sort of room someone with that particular proclivity might design.

The doorknob to the third room creaked loudly enough that she flinched, spilling more hot wax on her gloves. Once she was through the door, she sagged with relief, though, because she had finally found the Egyptian Room.

Caro shuddered as she noticed a miniature mummy case in the center of the room, its painted colors still bright after thousands of years. She wondered if a tiny mummified body still rested within the coffin. For the life of her, she could not understand this recent fashion for decorating not just in the Egyptian style but with actual sarcophagi. This was someone's final resting place—a child's, by the look of it. To regard it merely as the pièce de résistance to complete one's parlor was sickening.

She found that her hands were trembling, and she placed the candelabra on a black lacquered table. Truly, she wasn't cut out for... for any of this. She was the daughter of an earl; she did not skulk through opium dens and mummies' chambers, contemplating larceny.

She drew in a breath and reminded herself why she was here. *Anne. She had to do this for Anne.* She needed to find that necklace, and she needed to hurry. Her absence from the party would be noticed soon. Now, where would someone stash a pendant?

Then she spotted it—a small leather box on the side table. She hurried over, her hands shaking as she struggled with the lid. If the box contained her sister's necklace, she didn't know what she would do. The possibility of recovery hadn't even occurred to her until Mr. Hope mentioned that he had purchased a new Egyptian necklace in the shape of the Eye of Ra that very morning. Should she... Surely she shouldn't steal it? She had never stolen anything in her life. Although it was rightfully Anne's, and how else could she get it back?

The lid gave way, and her shoulders sagged. It was a moot point, because this was not the pendant her sister had suggested Caro borrow for an Egyptian costume party two nights ago, the one that had then been stolen from around her neck by a cutpurse posing as a flower seller. The shape was the same—the Eye of Ra so frequently seen in Egyptian design. But this one was turquoise instead of lapis blue, and it lacked the beautiful gold detailing of her sister's piece.

Well, that settled that. Caro shut the lid. As disappointed

as she was, at least now she could return to the party. She had experienced quite enough clandestine wanderings for one lifetime—

She froze at a familiar sound—the creak of the doorknob. She watched in horror as the door began to inch open.

She scoured the room for a hiding place. There was *nothing*. What if it was a servant? What was she going to say? Oh, God—what if it was Mr. Hope? If she was caught alone in the dark with a rich, eccentric bachelor, she would be *ruined…*

A man slipped through the door, illuminated by his own candle.

It was not a servant, nor was it Thomas Hope.

It was infinitely worse.

Really, this had to be the most terrible luck anyone had ever experienced, save perhaps Achilles, when that craven halfwit Paris had somehow managed to train his arrow on the one and only inch of flesh where he was vulnerable.

The vilest man on the face of the earth (for that was who had entered the room), blinked at her incredulously. "Lady Caroline? What on earth are you doing here?"

Four years ago, this man had humiliated her, completely and utterly.

To this day, she closed her prayers with a plea to the Almighty that she would never have to see Henry Greville ever again.

Yet here he was.

Her very own Achilles' heel.

CHAPTER 2

*C*aro regarded him in the candlelight. Truly, there was no justice in this world, because the vilest man on the face of the earth remained appallingly handsome. He was wearing his golden-brown hair short these days, cut à la Brutus, which should have looked ridiculous, as his hair was stick-straight, and that style called for windswept waves. Yet somehow it suited him marvelously. (Did anything not suit this man?) His wide-set brown eyes were just as she remembered, which was perhaps unsurprising. Once upon a time, she had spent an alarming number of hours daydreaming about gazing into those eyes. And he was every bit as broad of shoulder and trim of waist as he'd been four years ago, athletically lithe, muscular without being bulky. She would wager that underneath his impeccable black evening kit, he was even more perfectly sculpted than the naked man two rooms over.

Good God... this was *not* the line of thought she needed to pursue right now.

He was crossing the room toward her. She felt her throat constrict. Suddenly she was fifteen years old all over again, standing on that balcony and wondering if it was possible to die of humiliation as she watched the subject of her schoolgirl infatuation mock her to a pack of his friends. She was terrified to even open her mouth, because she had absolutely no idea what she was going to do—rage and scream? Be cold and dismissive? Burst into tears?

She had the most terrible feeling the answer was burst into tears.

She lifted her chin. She was *not* going to let Henry Greville see her cry. "What I am doing is leaving." She seized her candelabra. "If you will excuse me—"

He stepped in front of her, blocking her way. "Wait—please wait."

"Although you have shown yourself to be unacquainted with the finer points of decent behavior, even you must appreciate that I cannot remain. If we are discovered here together, I will be ruined." She laughed blackly. "And as you made inescapably clear four years ago, it is not as if *you* are going to marry me."

"No, I mean, yes, I mean… I understand. But I need to speak with you—"

"How unfortunate for you, because I never want to speak to you ever again." She gathered her skirts and made to step around him.

He grabbed her by the forearm. "I only need one minute."

It was the first time he had ever touched her. During his visit all those years ago, there had never been an occasion when he had offered her his arm or handed her down from a carriage. The one time she had poured him his tea, his fingers had not brushed hers as he accepted his cup.

And, needless to say, he had never asked her for a dance.

She *hated* that she knew this, but not as much as she hated the tremor that ran through her in the instant his hand touched her arm.

She took a steadying breath, then drew herself up to her full height, which was a half a head shorter than he was, but never mind that. She reminded herself that she was every inch the earl's daughter and that she had inherited her mother's condescending glower. She now employed it in all of its fury. "I will thank you not to manhandle me." He had the grace to look shamefaced as he slid his hand down her wrist to press her hand.

"Please, Caro."

His voice was soft, and the raw emotion in his eyes, the sincerity, the longing… It was precisely the way she used to dream Henry Greville would look at her.

But that was back when she had been a naive little fool. She was not so *stupid* anymore.

That was not love in his eyes. Only pity.

Lady Caroline Astley did not require any man's pity.

She jerked her hand from his. "I did not give you leave to call me that," she said, proud that her voice quavered only the tiniest bit. She strode through the door with her chin up, not looking back.

THANKFULLY HE DID NOT FOLLOW. She hurried back through the darkened rooms and found a tiny alcove filled with strange statues. She ducked inside and slumped onto a plush bench, not trusting her trembling legs to take her any farther. Deep down, she had always known this day would come, the day she would have to face him again. They were part of the same world—their fathers were both earls, and he was her brother's best friend to boot. But was avoiding him for her first few weeks in London too much to ask?

She closed her eyes. She could picture the moment it had all started, the moment he'd come riding up to the house…

Although that wasn't quite right. Really, it had started years before that.

In his first letter home from Eton, Harrington described how the senior boys had challenged the newcomers to "borrow" a goat from a local farm and sneak it into the headmaster's rooms. Most of them balked (not Harrington, obviously, as there was no form of mischief he wouldn't try at least once). But there was one other boy who was game: Henry Greville, the young Viscount Thetford and heir to the Earl of Ardingly. The two of them were successful in liberating the goat and getting it up the stairs and into the headmaster's rooms (it turned out that Lord Thetford was a dab hand at picking a lock). But before they managed to quit the room, the headmaster, Mr. Davies, walked through the door, in the very moment the goat took a bite out of his copy of Xenophon's *Anabasis*.

Edward is in despair, Harrington wrote, *because he's never been flogged, not even once, and his little brother got twenty strokes on his first day. But everyone else says Thetford and I are regular swells. We shared a feast of sausages with the older boys to celebrate, and Thetford and I tried our first cheroots. I've been here six days and Thetford and I have both been flogged six times. School is brilliant.*

Every letter that followed was filled with tales of Harrington's misadventures with "Thetford," with whom he became inseparable. Through Harrington's letters, Caro felt as if she got to know Lord Thetford, too. She knew that Harrington was the better shot, but Thetford was the better horseman; even at the age of twelve, there was no rail he would not take. She knew of his love of any variety of pickled food, from vegetables and fruits to eggs and meats, and how he delighted in disgusting his schoolmates by putting them on everything. And she knew that he always made an excuse when his friends wanted to go bathing in the river, because he had a terror of leeches he thought no one else knew about.

But most of all, Caro enjoyed the young viscount's sense of humor, which was every bit as caustic as her own. How many hundreds of times had she laughed aloud at one of his witticisms, which Harrington took care to include in his letters because he knew how much she enjoyed them?

Caro had therefore been thrilled nine years later, when Harrington, who by then was attending Oxford, had asked to bring a few friends home during the April break between terms. She had wanted to meet Lord Thetford for years, after all. She recalled standing on the portico with her family, waiting to greet Harrington and his party, thinking to herself that although she and Lord Thetford were not yet friends, they were going to be. They would have the best conversations, just the way Harrington described in his letters.

But then Harrington and his friends rounded the bend, and she saw him for the first time. And she could recall the roaring in her ears, and the racing of her heart, as his face came into view. She grabbed her mother's wrist and whispered, "Mama, who is the gentleman on the black horse?"

Her mother raised an eyebrow. "That, my dear, is Lord Thetford."

And in an instant, Caro fell horribly in love with Henry Greville, in that very particular way one can only fall in love at the age of fifteen. He consumed her every thought, both waking and sleeping. When she was in his presence, she was simultaneously desperate for him to notice her and terrified that he would, because at fifteen, Caro had been able to see nothing but her own flaws, so she was convinced that all he would see were the spots on her face, the embarrassing things she said, and how awkward and horrible she was.

Alas, even friendship proved a bridge too far. On the handful of occasions she had the opportunity to speak with him, she was tongue-tied with nerves and nothing like her usual self. Meanwhile, he didn't seem to notice her at all.

She knew full well he didn't feel the same way, and she honestly didn't mind. No matter how much you might wish otherwise, you couldn't force someone to return your feelings.

What she did mind was the fact that he had made sport of her to all his friends. It was one thing to have a sad case of unrequited love; it was something else entirely to be made into a laughingstock for it.

She had thought she knew Henry Greville through the stories in Harrington's letters. She had been wrong. The boy she'd been drawn to, the one with the irrepressible spirit and wry sense of humor, had never even existed. He was—

From a few rooms away, she heard that dratted doorknob creak.

He was *coming*.

CARO SEARCHED the room for a place to hide. The alcove was tiny, little more than a closet, and there was only one entrance. If Lord Thetford cornered her here, there would be no escaping. Fortunately, Mr. Hope being Mr. Hope, the room was lined with bright red curtains. Caro scurried behind them. Scorch marks blackened her ruined gloves as she snuffed out all but one of her candles, which she shielded behind a cupped hand.

She heard the door to the adjacent room open, and she held her breath…

… only to hear his footsteps pass and see the glow of his own candle fade to nothingness. He had headed back toward the main stairs, not the sculpture gallery where the rest of the party was gathered.

She was rid of him at last.

She exhaled and let her head fall back in relief. Strange, the curtains extended overhead, and—no, wait—this couldn't be a—

A burst of laughter emerged from Caro's throat, surprising her, as she realized that Mr. Hope had constructed a tent inside of a closet, in order to house his idols in a befitting style. A red tent, with gold fringe (naturally). Suddenly her evening crossed some indelible line and went from being merely horrible to being comedically horrible. She had known that adventures would await her in London, and here she was sneaking by candlelight through rooms that either were or were not opium dens, searching for the Eye of Ra amongst the mummies, and hiding from her first love and current nemesis in a Bedouin tent.

She smoothed her skirts, preparing to rejoin the party. Really, it was for the best that she ran into him tonight, like this. She could not have spoken a tenth so frankly had she encountered him in a crowded ballroom. Tonight she had told him plainly that she never wished to speak to him again. Her message was inescapable. So when their paths crossed in the future, she would never have to do more than nod and smile. That much she could bear. But he would avoid her, and she would avoid him, and everything was going to be all right.

CHAPTER 3

*T*he following day, Henry Greville made the short drive from his bachelor apartments to his parents' town house on Hanover Square.

As he entered, he came within a hairsbreadth of bumping into the gigantic alabaster sarcophagus that dominated the foyer. You would think by now he would know better. The sarcophagus had been in its current location since he was six years old, after all. But he somehow always forgot how completely it filled the room.

He glanced at the sandstone bas-reliefs that lined the hallway leading to the library. It was jarring coming here. One minute you were driving along in your high-flyer, the wind in your cravat, past the queue of carriages waiting to get an ice at Gunter's Tea Shop, the smells of coal smoke and manure competing for predominance as your pair trotted through the meticulously planned squares of Mayfair, with every sight and smell and sound proclaiming that you were in the most modern, most prosperous city in the world.

And then you stepped through the door to the Greville family town house and could be forgiven for fancying that you had travelled two thousand years back in time and were now inside the pyramid of Cheops.

A pair of columns carved with hieroglyphs announced the library. Most of the Egyptian items in the house were genuine antiquities his father had brought back from his grand tour. But the furnishings in the library were modern pieces in the Egyptian style. Other than that crumbling sphinx in the corner. And the canopic jars on the mantelpiece...

Henry noticed something new by his father's desk and wandered over to investigate. It was a piece of black granite that had once been part of a much larger statue. This must be the recent acquisition his father had mentioned, which he had described as a torso fragment from a statue of Anubis.

Henry supposed the description was correct in the strictest sense. Yet how unfortunate that the only portion of the statue to survive the ravages of Father Time was Anubis's impressively taut buttocks.

Henry settled into a chair to await his father. Last night he had thought Thomas Hope a bit cracked to keep a mummy in his drawing room. But glancing around his own family's town house in the harsh light of day, it occurred to him that there was a famous saying about those in glass houses that probably applied to anyone who had the Arse of Anubis in their library.

And to think that the mummy had only been the second most surprising thing he had found in Thomas Hope's Egyptian Room.

What in blazes had Caroline Astley been doing there? That had been the first thought to cross his mind. But coming right on its heels was the realization that he didn't give a damn. The only thing that mattered was that she was there. She was there, he was there, and finally, *finally*, he would get his chance to apologize.

That he owed her an apology was beyond question. He would never forget the look on her face as she stood on that terrace, utterly crushed, struggling not to cry.

He didn't manage to apologize last night, but he would find another chance. Now that he knew she was in Town, it would be simple enough. The first thing he did this morning was send his manservant round to Astley House, where he learned that the ladies were at home to callers on Monday mornings.

Tomorrow was Monday. And so tomorrow, at long last, he would make Lady Caroline a proper apology.

HENRY'S REVERIE was interrupted by a sharp voice behind him.

"Did Thomas Hope show you his new Eye of Ra?"

"Good afternoon to you, too, Father," Henry said, standing. "I would not say precisely that he showed it to me." When he asked Mr. Hope for permission to view it, the man had refused, blathering on about his intention to show his Egyptian Room only once the decorations were complete. Not that Henry was the type to let that deter him, hence his sneaking around in the dark. "But," he continued, "I managed to have a look at it, nonetheless. I've been admiring your new acquisition. Dare I ask how much you paid for the Arse of Anubis?"

His father sat behind the desk, glaring down his nose. "Why must you always be so crass? Returning to Thomas Hope's Eye of Ra—what did it look like?"

Henry sank into his chair. "It's made of faience porcelain, around this size," he said, holding up his pocket watch for comparison.

"What color of faience?"

"The usual turquoise."

"Did it have any other materials? Any gold inlay?"

Henry paused, thinking. "There was no gold. It had a dark stone for the eye—onyx, perhaps. It was a very standard Eye of Ra amulet, nothing special. I would wager you've seen dozens like it over the years."

His father's shoulders slumped. "I see. Well, thank you for going to investigate."

"You seem rather curious about Thomas Hope's antiquities. May I ask why you didn't attend the dinner yourself? Mother mentioned that you received an invitation."

His father snorted. "I will have nothing to do with Thomas Hope. Not after what he said about my collection."

Henry suppressed a groan. *Not this again.* "Father, have you considered that you might be overreacting—"

"'A few minor pieces,' was how he characterized it!" the earl said, ignoring him. "I ask you, is there anything 'minor' about the sarcophagus of Mycerinus?"

"Indeed, there is not," Henry said. "As it happens, I've been meaning to speak to you about that. Do you really think the entryway the absolute best location for it?"

"For a man who knows nothing about antiquities, you have some strong opinions about where best to display them. First it was my canopic jars—"

"You had them in the dining room, Father!"

"I still do not see anything wrong with that."

"The purpose of canopic jars is to hold mummified entrails, a fact you were all too eager to explain to your dinner guests—"

"My antiquities are fascinating. People enjoy hearing about them."

"Not while they're trying to eat. Mother had to keep smelling salts in the sideboard. Those jars are much better off here in the library. But returning to the sarcophagus, do you not think having someone's coffin in the foyer is a bit... macabre?"

His father shook his head. "I wouldn't expect you to understand, but it conveys a powerful message. 'Memento mori,' as the ancients say. It means—"

"'Remember that you will die.' Are thoughts of their impending death the first ones we wish to inspire in our guests?"

"I'm surprised you even recognize the quotation."

Henry sucked in a breath through gritted teeth. "I do have a basic grasp of Latin, Father."

"Not of Greek, I'll warrant," the earl muttered.

Henry sighed. His father was not wrong. In defiance of his erudite father's hopes, he had been an indifferent student at Eton, and even worse at Oxford. This wasn't a distinction, as most noblemen made little effort at university, and few took a degree. Henry had spent his days then much as he spent them now—on horseback. Many fathers would be proud to have such a son, a true Corinthian, who hadn't lost a horse race, in the saddle or at the whip, in more than five years.

Henry wasn't a complete wastrel. To be sure, he liked a fast horse, a willing woman, a strong drink, and a game of cards as well as the next man. But he also had pursuits, serious ones. He had started a breeding stable at his family's estate, and although he had only been at it for three years, he was already turning a modest profit.

But Henry's activities were not the sort to impress his scholarly father.

"Well," Henry said, "I think you should extend an olive branch to Mr. Hope. He is from Amsterdam. English is not his first language. He likely meant no offense. And given your common interests, I wager you would find much to discuss."

His father huffed in response. Henry waited a few beats, then rose from his seat. "If that was all you wanted to speak to me about—"

"Sit down, son," his father said. Henry complied. After a moment, his father muttered a curse and reached for the decanter on the credenza behind his desk. Henry's eyebrows shot up. He had never seen his father indulge himself at—he glanced at the clock on the mantel —half two.

Henry took a small sip from the glass his father handed him; the earl downed half his drink in one swallow. "What I'm about to tell you," his father said, "is not to be repeated to anybody. In particular, you are to say nothing to your mother."

Oh, dear God. It was common enough for a nobleman to keep a mistress, not that Henry had ever found evidence of the earl doing so. But this was the last topic he wanted to discuss with his father.

"We're experiencing some financial difficulties," the earl said.

"We are?" Henry furrowed his brow. "That's odd—I thought rents were up in Brighton." His mother's dowry had consisted of dozens of terrace houses in Brighton. Farming could go up and down, but in recent years, Brighton had boomed in popularity thanks to the patronage of the Prince of Wales, causing rents to rise and, with them, the Greville fortunes.

It had never even occurred to Henry to worry about money. His family was envied because not only was their income significant, it was stable. What on earth could have—

"The Brighton terraces are gone," his father said.

"Gone? What do you mean, gone?"

"I sold them."

Henry's entire body jerked, launching a cascade of brandy

into the air, most of which rained down upon the Arse of Anubis. "You *what?*"

"Henry!" His father hurried around the desk and began sponging the statue clean with his handkerchief. "You must be more careful. This is a priceless piece from the tomb of Ptolemy—"

"Who cares? You sold the terraces? Why did you— When was this?"

"Four years ago."

"Four years ago! What have we been living on?"

"Savings." Giving Anubis's left buttock one final swipe, his father returned to his seat. "But those have been used up, so the time has come to enact a new plan."

It struck Henry that the time to enact a new plan had long passed. As this was not the type of sentiment a son was permitted to express to his father, he drew in a deep breath, struggling to remain calm. "I should say so. What necessitated the sale of the terrace houses?"

His father's jaw locked. "I needed to buy a ship."

"A ship? What on earth did you need a ship for?"

"To transport some, er, items."

"But why *buy* a ship? Why could you not pay someone who owned a ship to transport them for you?"

"No one was running this route, due to the situation in the Mediterranean."

Four years ago, the situation in the Mediterranean had been fraught indeed. All of Britain had waited with bated breath while Admiral Nelson combed the Mediterranean, searching for the French fleet that had disappeared without a trace. In August, he found them in Egypt, and the Battle of the Nile ensued. Henry had a terrible feeling in the pit of his stomach. "The Mediterranean, you say. Where exactly in the Mediterranean were these 'items' coming from?"

The earl said nothing.

"Father?" Henry pressed.

"Egypt," the earl snapped.

Henry sagged in his chair, disbelieving. "You sold the *terraces*. An asset that would have supported our family for generations. All for a few crumbling stones and dusty trinkets—"

"These were not crumbling stones and dusty trinkets! My agent in Cairo had found the most magnificent treasures—a painted cedarwood sarcophagus, several large statues, including a rare one of the winged goddess Isis, bejeweled scarabs, a sandstone obelisk covered with hieroglyphs—"

"All of which you already have! And none of which could possibly justify risking the estate."

"I did not expect you to understand. You have no appreciation for art or history."

Henry was only half attending, his mind scrambling for a solution. "The terraces are gone, but what about the assets you purchased? We can sell this ship, and—"

"It was captured. The captain was unsuccessful in running the French blockade." His father shook his head. "All of my priceless treasures, in the hands of those bourgeoisie scum."

Henry was unable to contain a hint of acid in his voice. "To say nothing of the men who lost their lives attempting to run the French blockade."

"There's no need to be melodramatic, Henry. The sailors were taken alive. I understand they were impressed into the French Navy."

"So, they were forced to commit treason before dying in the Battle of the Nile. How reassuring." Henry drew another deep breath. "I know the conversation will be difficult, but we've got to tell Mother."

"She is not to know."

"She needs to know. She deserves to. Those terraces were her dowry!"

His father's look of derision was one he had seen many times over the years. It stung, as it always did. "Have you absorbed nothing I have tried to teach you about what it means to be a man?" The earl rose and began to pace the length of the library as he recited the speech Henry must have heard a hundred times. "A man is strong. A man is stoic. A man is steadfast."

Henry had to bite the inside of his cheek to keep himself from adding his own s-word to the list: *spendthrift*.

The earl continued, "A man does not burden those around him by whining about his problems. And the last person he should complain to is his wife. Women are *emotional*." His father accompanied this pronouncement with a scowl. "Emotions, needless to say, must be restrained at all times. A man must present a strong face to the world, never show any weakness. Besides, women lack the faculties of reason to do anything in the face of financial troubles. Telling your mother would have no effect but to cause her anguish." His father settled back into his chair. "No, a man should bear his troubles stoically and leave his wife out of them."

"But... is Mother not planning a rout? We need to economize. How can she do that if she doesn't even know?"

"There is no need to economize."

Henry blinked. "No need to economize? I thought we had run through our savings."

His father made a dismissive gesture. "We can still throw the rout. Those are tradesmen's bills. We can default on those. It's not as though they are a debt of honor."

An image sprang unbidden to Henry's mind of his washerwoman, a stooped old woman named Mrs. Dakers who had all of four teeth. Although his valet, Gibson, tried to shoo her from Henry's bachelor apartments whenever she came to deliver the wash, Mrs. Dakers was impervious to his hints and insisted on greeting her employer. Henry found Mrs. Dakers, and the distress she induced in his very proper valet, amusing. He always took a few minutes to converse with her. Last week, Mrs. Dakers had been uncharacteristically silent when she came to drop off his linen, causing Henry to set aside the letter he had been working on and ask what was wrong. Tears spilled down her cheeks as she informed him that she had the care of her four orphaned grandchildren. They lived together in a single room in Wapping, down by the Thames. Last week her youngest grandson had succumbed to a fever that had swept through the neighborhood, and there was no money for his burial. She had no choice but to keep the body in the room they all shared, while his siblings played on the floor beside the little coffin. Henry remembered how she had sobbed when he pressed three two-guinea coins into her hand, and how she had sobbed even harder when he handed her one of his clean handkerchiefs to blow her nose.

Henry could not see anything honorable in failing to pay Mrs. Dakers, or anyone else, simply because they were tradesmen.

"We can have an auction," Henry said. "There is a great interest in all things Egyptian right now, due to the artifacts that were seized from Napoleon's army. We will get a good price for your collection, and we can—"

"Henry!" His father looked affronted. "We will do no such thing. There's no need to worry. I have a plan."

Henry's patience was fraying. He struggled to summon his last few shreds of filial piety. "Do you, Father? Because from what I can see, we are on the brink of disaster, and you have done nothing to remedy it. To the contrary, you went out and bought the Arse of Anubis! Well, please enlighten me —what is this plan of yours?"

"You need not know the details—"

"I most certainly do—"

"Why? You think you have something to add?" The earl snorted. "That's rich. *You*. Who has the barest grasp of Latin, and no Greek. The man who didn't attend a single lecture in four years at Oxford. What do *you* have to contribute?"

Henry bristled. "The fact that I do not read Sophocles for leisure is beside the point. What this situation requires is some common sense—"

"Which you are also lacking. I don't think a single week went by when I didn't get a letter from the headmaster at Eton, detailing your abominable misbehavior. First it was that goat—"

"I was twelve years old, Father. That has no bearing on the man I am today."

"The man you are today divides his time between drinking, gambling, and womanizing. When was the last time you rose before noon?"

"This very morning. I was up before dawn."

His father arched an eyebrow. "Really. What was the occasion?"

Henry sighed. "I had a horse race—"

"A *horse race*. Well, there is the mark of a man of letters." His father shook his head. "No, Henry, you have no head for business. The planning will fall to me."

Henry wanted to protest. Whatever his faults, he couldn't possibly do worse than the man who had driven a profitable estate into ruin in order to buy a second sarcophagus.

But the truth was, Henry knew nothing about running an estate, about choosing investments, or about managing money. He knew these were topics he would need to learn someday. He had thought he had plenty of time.

Little did he know he was already too late.

He sighed. "Then why did you tell me this, Father?"

"Because I will need a small amount of assistance in order to enact my plan. Your going to Thomas Hope's party last night was the first such task. There will be others in the coming days. I need you to perform them without fail."

"I will do my best. So, what did Thomas Hope's new amulet have to do with all of this?"

"You recall my little Egyptian box, the one in the shape of the Eye of Ra?"

"I recall it well."

"It is… no longer in my possession. I have reason to believe it has been stolen."

The box was made of dark blue faience, an early form of porcelain, with gold inlay outlining the Eye of Ra and a touch of ivory for the white of the eye. The workmanship was exquisite and the condition of the box remarkable. It did not look anywhere close to its age. It was one of the most valuable pieces in his father's collection, worth more perhaps than even the alabaster sarcophagus that graced the entryway.

"That is bad news indeed," Henry said.

"There is more. I had to take out a loan to get us through recent months. For five thousand pounds. I offered the box as security on the loan."

Henry leaned forward, tightness building in his chest. "And who is the holder of this loan?"

His father fell silent for a moment, then said, "Suffice to say, it is a debt of honor. This loan must be repaid. And it is due in two weeks."

Henry sagged back in his chair. "So, what you're saying is, we have two weeks to either recover your Eye of Ra box or come up with five thousand pounds, or we will be well and truly ruined."

"Precisely."

"Have we run through the full five thousand?"

"No, there's a bit left. But it won't last long." His father cleared his throat. "I would expect that those who stole my box will be looking to sell. So, if you should hear anything about a newly acquired cosmetics box, or anything about the Eye of Ra—"

"Look into it. I understand."

"Phillip, there you are," a feminine voice trilled from the doorway.

Henry rose and forced a smile to his lips. "Good afternoon, Mother." He bent to give her a kiss on the cheek.

"Henry! I didn't realize you were here. What a treat." She turned to his father, who had risen from his position behind the desk and was making for the door. "Did you find the missing invoice I mentioned, Phillip? The one from the vintner?"

"I did not," the earl replied.

The countess wrung her hands. "Shall I send a footman 'round to Clarke and Sons to request another copy?"

The earl was already halfway out the door. "No, no, I'll take care of it."

"But my rout is the week after next, and—" She sighed, watching her husband retreat down the hall. "Oh, bother."

"What is it, Mother?" Henry asked.

The countess rubbed her forehead. "Oh… there's been some sort of mix-up with the vintner. A missing bill that has gone unpaid. I've explained that it's a simple mistake, but they are refusing to send us any wine. And with my rout coming up, I don't know what I'll do."

Henry did his best to maintain a neutral expression, but inside he was groaning. It would appear that his father's plan to save money by defaulting on tradesmen's bills was already in effect.

And now his poor mother was about to be humiliated before the *haute ton*.

He dug into his pocket, pulling out a handful of bank notes. "I happen to have won a horse race this morning," he explained, handing them to his mother. "Will this cover it?"

She flipped through the notes. "Oh, yes—the amount is nowhere near fifty pounds," she said, trying to hand a few of the notes back.

He curled his mother's fingers around them. "Why don't you keep them? Just in case. That way you won't have to worry about a thing."

She beamed up at him. "Thank you, Henry. You are the best son in the whole entire world."

It was nice that one of his parents thought so, Henry mused as he stepped outside. He found he was in no mood to stand amongst his father's antiquities while he waited for his phaeton to be brought around. He glanced at the elegant townhouses lining Hanover Square. He had grown up without a doubt in his mind that he belonged in this world. He was rich, and he was titled, which meant that he was envied by most everyone he met. He had never once questioned his worth, until now. He had not realized that his familial wealth played such a significant role in his identity until it was gone.

But as soon as it became public knowledge that the Greville family didn't have a farthing to their name, he wouldn't be that envied young man any longer. In an instant he would become the man everyone laughed at behind his back, the one matchmaking mamas steered their daughters away from, the one whose company was no longer welcome. And as furious as he was with his father, Henry felt every bit as angry with himself. He should have taken more of an interest in the estate. If he had, not only would he have some idea how to fix their current problems, but he might have noticed them years ago, when there was still a chance to get things back on course.

Instead, he had been playing cards and racing horses. He was worse than useless.

If he wasn't the young man he had thought he was, the rich future earl without a care in the world, then who was he?

Henry had no idea. But it appeared he had two weeks to figure it out.

CHAPTER 4

The instant Caro crossed the threshold of her sister's building in St. Giles, she was enveloped in a flock of excited children. The first thing Anne had done upon marrying the Earl of Wynters at the age of eighteen was to found her very own charitable organization, the Ladies' Society for the Relief of the Destitute. Its core mission was to establish model lodging houses for widows with young children, charging them a fair rent for a safe, clean room. As Caro had only arrived in London a few weeks ago, this was her first time visiting her sister's establishment.

"Caro!" She turned to see her sister approaching. Anne's husband had died in his sleep last summer, and she wore black from her slippers all the way up to the stylish capote bonnet that topped her brown hair. But her sister somehow managed to look radiant in mourning. Anne had dreamed of founding her own charity ever since she was fourteen, and here at her building, she was truly in her element, glowing with joy and enthusiasm.

The sisters hugged and kissed each other on the cheek. "I'm so excited to finally see your lodging house," Caro said.

"I cannot wait to show it to you." Anne gestured to the children, who looked to be around six years old. "The little ones have been practicing a song for you. And then it will be time for the midday meal—I thought you might join us."

"I would love to," Caro said.

The song was "Lord, How Delightful," and the performance was indeed delightful, no less so for being a bit out of tune. Caro applauded, then they made their way to the dining hall.

She accepted a bowl of beef stew and joined a group of children at one of the long tables. She turned to the girl seated to her left, who had a long brown plait. "So, Agnes— do I have that right?" Agnes nodded. "How do you like it here?"

"'Tis wonderful, m'lady, like a paradise."

"Agnes lived on *Hopkins Street* before," an older boy with dark hair said, as if this clarified everything.

"Hopkins Street?" Caro asked.

"'Tis by the pig house," he offered by way of explanation.

"The… the pig house?"

"They've cows, too," he confirmed.

"Pigs and cows, I see. I'm sorry, I did not catch your name—"

"I'm John, m'lady."

"Aye," Agnes said. "The trouble was, the houses sunk over the years, so they were below ground level, ya see? So when it rained, it washed out the stockyard, and everything would come pouring straight through the front door. You ended up with this great flood of—"

"Oh, my gracious!" Caro cried, comprehending. She gave a nervous laugh. "Well, I'm glad you're no longer living there, Agnes."

"Me, too, m'lady. Although me aunt Beth and three of me

cousins moved into those rooms. 'Twas better than their old place."

Caro did not dare imagine what their previous rooms must have been like if a room that flooded with pig excrement was a step up in the world. "How I wish your cousins could come live here, too."

"Lady Wynters is trying to find a place for them," Agnes said, slurping a bite of soup.

Caro shook her head and turned to a little boy with blond curls. "And what is your name?"

"Timothy, m'lady."

"It's nice to meet you, Timothy. How long have you been living here?"

"Two weeks."

"How do you like it so far?"

"I mean, I do like it here. I don't mean to complain." He squeezed his eyes shut. "If ye'll excuse me, I think I'll see if there's any more bread."

Once Timothy was gone, John leaned forward. "Timmy don't mean to sound ungrateful. His father died the month before last, and he hasn't adjusted yet."

"Oh, dear!" Caro said. "How I wish I had not questioned him. I did not realize his wound was so recent."

John made a dismissive sound. "You couldn't have known. 'Tis hard for Timmy to think about his father, on account of his death being a bit"—he stared off into space, as if searching for the right word—"gruesome."

"You—you don't say."

"Aye, he worked in the mill. His sleeve snagged on the buckle of one of the straps. Ripped his left arm clean off at the shoulder, and he bled to death right there on the floor." John shook his head. "You know, the usual sort of thing."

Caro found she was quite incapable of saying anything in return. She was having difficulty comprehending a world in

29

which having your arm ripped off was "the usual sort of thing." "How terrible," she finally managed.

John nodded. "Aye. Lady Wynters don't want none of us children working in the mills. We go to school during the day, and not just to learn reading—writing, too, and maths. She got my big brother apprenticed to a shipwright, and I mean to follow him in a few years. You make a good living as a shipwright, you do."

"I think you have the makings of a fine shipwright, John."

"Thank you, m'lady. She'll find something good for Timmy in a few years, too," John said, taking a spoonful of his soup.

And so the luncheon proceeded. Caro discovered that each of Anne's little charges had a horrible story to share, about how their fathers were killed in action against the French, or pulled into some sort of machine at work, or had succumbed to their taste for gin. She came to understand that their mothers had been unable to earn enough to feed and shelter their children, in spite of working themselves to the bone. Most of the children told these stories unflinchingly, even though every one made Caroline want to cry.

How trivial her own problems—a stolen bauble and a man who had once insulted her—now seemed. Caro vowed to speak to her sister about ways she could help. Now that she understood the trials these children had faced, she could not stand idly by.

AFTER LUNCH, Anne took Caro on a tour of the building, which concluded in her office, where a pot of tea was waiting. "So," Anne said as they settled in, "what do you think?"

"Your lodging house is wonderful, Anne. It is—" Caro raised a hand to her mouth, startled to hear her voice break, as the shock and sorrow she had been holding in for the past hour came bursting out.

Her sister set aside the tea service and reached forward to take her hands. "You are not used to it."

"I knew the children would not be here unless something dreadful had happened to them. But I was unprepared for it. I think it was the matter-of-fact way they told their stories. As if those horrible things were the way of the world, rather than a tragedy."

"You have hit upon it precisely," Anne said. "One man's tragedy is another's lot in life. And the need is boundless. I am proud of the work we do here, but it is never enough. There are a hundred deserving applicants for every one I can accept. Although I have some good news on that front." Anne gave Caro's hands a squeeze and sat back in her chair. "Let's speak of something else for a few minutes. I can tell how hard this has been for you, and besides, I want to hear all about my little sister's first season."

Because Anne was in full mourning, it was considered improper for her to attend large parties. She had made an exception for Caro's debut ball, which she couldn't bear to miss. But other than that, the sisters had been able to attend few events together.

"How was Lady Spencer's ball?" Anne asked, handing Caro a teacup.

"It was lovely."

Anne's brown eyes sparkled. "Did a certain marquess ask you to dance again?"

Caro could not suppress a smile. Anne was referring to Marcus Latimer, the current Marquess Graverley and future Duke of Trevissick, who was regarded as the most eligible man in all of England. In addition to being a future duke, his estate generated an income rumored to be well north of a hundred thousand pounds a year. "He did," Caro said.

Anne squealed. "He never dances with anyone. He just stands to the side of the ballroom and watches, looking bored. But now he's danced with you *twice*. What do you think of him?"

Caro pictured the marquess, with his elegant fencer's physique, pale blond hair, ice-blue eyes, and features almost too beautiful to belong to a man. "He is every bit as handsome as everyone says he is," she said. "And he has been… attentive."

"Is that so? What constitutes attentiveness?"

Caro paused. "He asked what day I receive callers—"

"I knew it—he's courting you!"

"He is not," Caro said, even though she knew few would agree. The marquess who did not dance had not only attended Caro's debut ball, he had led her out for the first set, causing the gossips to declare them to be all but betrothed. Which was ridiculous. Two dances meant absolutely nothing, and Caro for one was trying not to get carried away.

That had never resulted in anything good, she thought, picturing Lord Thetford.

Anne ignored her protests. "My little sister is going to be a *duchess*."

"I haven't even decided if I want to set my cap for Lord Graverley," Caro said.

"Which is sensible," Anne hastened to say. "But if nothing else, being the sole recipient of the attentions of the most eligible, most aloof man in London should do wonders for your popularity. And I know that's what you've wanted these past four years. Ever since *Lord Thetford*." Anne said his name as if it were the vilest blasphemy in the English language, her eyebrow giving a violent twitch. Her elder sister was one of the few people Caro had told about the incident, along with her maid, Fanny, and her best friend, Cecilia Chenoweth. The rest of her family remained ignorant.

"I cannot tell you," Anne said, "how hard it has been, seeing him around town these past four years and having to pretend nothing is amiss. I swear, Caro, I have never given the cut direct to anybody in my life—"

"I should think not." Her sister, the kindest, most charitable woman in all of England, had the temperament of a sunbeam, shining upon a rainbow.

"—but I would cut him *dead* if you would let me."

"I appreciate that, more than I can say. But don't. Please."

Anne huffed. "If you insist. In any case, I'm so happy for you, Caro, about Lord Graverley and all your other beaux. You have earned it."

She truly had. Her recent popularity was no accident. Ever since she caught that horrible Henry Greville mocking her to his friends, she had been determined to become the most sought-after girl in London when she made her bow. Her goal was simple: to show him what an idiot he had been. She wanted him to feel absolutely sick to think that he had stood a chance with the likes of her, and he had thrown it all away.

And so Caro had embarked upon a relentless beauty regimen. She studied her fashion magazines until they fell apart, then spent hours closeted with Fanny, trying every hairstyle and dress silhouette, until she understood exactly how to flatter her face and figure. She spent an alarming sum on Olympian Dew facial tonic and used it religiously. It was worth every penny, as the spots that had plagued her for years had finally cleared. And she and Fanny spent hours practicing the art of applying rouge to her face so that it didn't *look* as if she were rouging her face. She arrived at every event in smoggy London glowing as if she had frolicked through a meadow to get there.

Much of her transformation she could claim no credit for. She was her mother's daughter, after all, and Georgiana

Astley, Countess of Cheltenham, was considered one of the most beautiful women of her own generation. Caro favored her mother, having the same honey-blonde hair and blue eyes. The Astley eyes, they had come to be called, for Lady Cheltenham had passed them down to five of her seven children. Only Anne and Harrington did not have them. The Astley eyes were famously huge and sparkling, and they were a startlingly intense shade of blue. So even at the age of fifteen, when she was gangly and awkward and had spots on her face, Caro hadn't been entirely without her charms.

But it was only after her sixteenth birthday that Caro had shown signs of having inherited her mother's very fine figure, too.

Her next step had been to test out her charms upon the local gentlemen. Most of the techniques she had postulated would be successful in attracting a man (flattery, feebleness, and flirtation) had been highly so. She had thought that perhaps her wit and sense of humor would prove to be assets as well but had been disappointed on that count. Caro soon discovered that nothing terrified a man more than a woman who appeared to be more intelligent than himself, and she found that she had much more success attracting a large flock of gentlemen admirers when she pretended to be empty-headed.

Anne interrupted her reverie. "I also want to hear about the Egyptian costume party."

This was it, the moment for Caro to confess that she had lost her sister's necklace. She drew up her courage. "In truth, there is something I've been meaning to tell you about that night. Oh, Anne, it's about your Egyptian necklace—"

"How did it look with your white lawn gown? I was surprised you sent it back so soon. I thought you might keep it for a while."

A sliver of hope dawned in her heart. Was it possible she

was wrong about the cutpurse? That she had dropped the necklace at the party, and someone had returned it to Anne? "You have it, then?"

"Of course I do, silly." Anne laughed, pulling a velvet pouch out of her desk drawer and opening it to reveal a string of lapis lazuli beads. "I brought it with me today. Why don't you keep it for the Season? I'll be in mourning for months; it's not as if I can wear it. And you look so beautiful in blue because of your eyes."

That was when Caro understood that Anne had never meant for her to borrow the Eye of Ra pendant. That when Anne had told her to grab the "Egyptian necklace" off of her dressing table, she had been thinking of her lapis beads.

"Speaking of things Egyptian," Anne said, "I must tell you my good news. Do you recall the pendant I showed you the other day? In the shape of the Eye of Ra?"

"I remember it well." Caro's voice sounded a bit strangled to her own ears.

"I had an appraiser look at it last week, and this morning I received his report. It turns out that it is not a 'pendant' at all —it is an amulet and thousands of years old."

"An—an amulet? How is that possible? It doesn't look that old."

"I thought the same. But I received his estimate today, and you will never believe it—he thinks the amulet will fetch five thousand pounds at auction!"

"Five thousand pounds! That is—"

"Marvelous, it's absolutely marvelous! And that leads me to my good news—with five thousand pounds, I can open a second lodging house."

Caro's heart lurched downward to approximately the level of her navel. The amulet was the key to her sister being able to open a second lodging house. To being able to save hundreds of women and children like little Agnes and Timothy from their wretched circumstances.

And she had lost it.

CARO COULD HARDLY BREATHE, let alone speak. She struggled to find some appropriate words. "Oh, Anne, that is… that is…"

Anne misinterpreted her stilted response. "Do you think it wrong of me to sell it? Because it was my husband's final gift to me?"

"Of course I don't." Caro leaned forward and took her sister's hands. The death of Lord Wynters had come as a shock. It had happened just two days prior to Anne's birthday. She had handled her loss stoically. She had gotten on well with Lord Wynters, but it had never been a love match. The earl had been their father's age, after all. The amulet had been found in his dressing table along with an amethyst necklace and matching pair of ear bobs. Lord Wynters's valet had tearfully confirmed that the items in that drawer were to be Anne's birthday presents.

"It will fetch such a good price right now," Anne said, "with all the excitement about the new Egyptian artifacts at the British Museum. And I know he intended it to be a gift, but Wynters knew how much my charity means to me. To be able to help so many women and children…" Anne placed a hand over her heart. "It means everything to me. Do you think I am absolutely awful to sell it?"

"No, Anne. You are the least awful person I know," Caro said.

The awful one, she added silently, *is me.*

And she knew this was the moment, that she needed to tell her sister the truth. But Anne was rhapsodizing about her plans for her new lodging house, and every time Caro opened her mouth, her tongue felt thick and foreign to her, as if speech were an impossible skill she had not yet mastered. And she couldn't bring herself to do it.

There was a knock at the office door, and one of Anne's footmen appeared. "My lady, you asked me to knock at half two."

"Thank you, Hugh," Anne said, rising from her chair. "I must leave for a fundraising call."

Somehow Caro found herself walking out the door without having told her sister the truth. Outside, two little girls were rolling hoops along the pavement with sticks. One of them perked up. It proved to be young Agnes. "That's her," she said to her companion. "'Tis Lady Caroline."

The two girls approached. "This is my cousin Eliza, m'lady. She's one of the ones I was telling you about. Who lives on Hopkins Street."

Caro thought she might be ill right there in the middle of the street, as Eliza made her a charming curtsey. Young Eliza who, unbeknownst to her, was condemned to continue living in a room that flooded with pig excrement, thanks to Caro's negligence. She forced a smile to her lips. "Eliza, it is a pleasure," she said in a strangled voice.

Caro sagged into the cushions as soon as the carriage door closed.

She needed to tell her sister the truth. She knew this.

The problem was that the truth was unbearable.

And suddenly, Caroline felt angry. That she had been so gullible was humiliating. That she had gone out of her way to help the old woman who did it, giving her three pence for a rotting posy not even worth a ha'penny, was galling. But most of all, the living conditions of the women and children who could not be helped without that amulet were unacceptable.

That was precisely the word. Unacceptable. The entire situation was unacceptable.

And by God, she was not going to accept it.

Now the only thing that remained was to figure out what she was going to do instead.

CHAPTER 5

*T*he following morning, Henry set out for the Astley town house, a peace offering of pink primroses in hand.

He was in no mood for this call. In addition to the devastating news he had received the previous day, he avoided the sorts of activities that brought him into close proximity with young, unmarried ladies—balls, social calls, and the like. In the back of his mind, he knew that one day he was going to have to marry one of those girls. He had never been able to muster much enthusiasm for it. Some of them were pretty enough, he supposed. But on the rare occasion he attended a ball or a dinner party, the conversations he had with proper young ladies were just so... vapid. All they wanted to discuss was Miss So and So's new fan, or what Lady Such and Such had been overheard saying about the Countess of Who Cares, or whether it would rain on the day of Lady Featherbrain's upcoming picnic.

Of course it was going to rain on the day of the bloody picnic. This was England, for God's sake.

It wasn't that Henry minded small talk. But did nobody

have any wit? Perhaps a sense of humor? Was he truly expected to endure these inane conversations with his future wife every day for the rest of his life?

All he wanted was a pretty girl who could bear up under his lacerating wit and give as good as she got. With God as his witness, if he could find a girl who wouldn't reach for her smelling salts every time he made a joke about the Arse of Anubis, he would marry her on the spot.

But in his experience, such girls were thin on the ground.

He probably now needed to add "an enormous dowry" to the list of traits he required in his future wife. Which all but ensured he was never going to find her.

He would have better luck finding a unicorn, no doubt.

He sighed. He was only in a bad mood because he was about to be publicly humiliated, then watch everyone he loved sink into poverty and wretchedness.

Which, when put that way, was a fairly reasonable justification for a bad mood. He shook his head to clear it. He couldn't indulge himself in such feelings today. Right now the only thing that mattered was that he make things right with Lady Caroline. He owed her this apology.

HENRY HAD BEEN twenty-one years old in the spring of 1798, and in his second-to-last year at Oxford. Every April there was a two-week break between Hilary Term and Easter Term. Henry couldn't make it home and back in two weeks. But his best friend, Harrington Astley, was from Cheltenham, a mere half-day's ride from Oxford, and that year Harrington had invited Henry and a handful of their friends for a visit.

It was a topping good time. They were left to their own devices, and they rode to the hounds every single day, enjoyed an excellent meal each evening, then stayed up late into the night, drinking Lord Cheltenham's best brandy and playing cards until the sun rose. Sleep until midafternoon, rise, and repeat.

They dined with Harrington's family each evening, and those suppers included two of his best friend's younger sisters. Lady Caroline was fifteen years old, and the infatuation she developed with Henry was both subtle and completely obvious. It was subtle in that she did nothing to seek him out or try to gain his attention. But she couldn't hide the way her eyes would light up whenever he entered the room, nor how her gaze would follow him wherever he went. If he happened to catch her eye, she would smile, then glance down, then glance back up again in a pantomime of shy interest that would surely be understood in any place in the world, at any time throughout history.

Once he wound up sitting next to her at dinner, where she made a bashful yet eager attempt to engage him in polite conversation. Someone must have drilled her in the topics that were appropriate for a young lady to discuss. After exhausting every possible observation that could be made about the weather, she asked him what he was studying at Oxford (a difficult question, considering he had not opened a single book since matriculating three years prior), his thoughts regarding the rector's sermon that morning (another challenge, as he had slept through the entirety of the service), and about his home in Sussex.

Henry was bored out of his skull, but she hung on his every answer. He remembered being glad when the ladies withdrew, leaving the gentlemen to their port.

Lady Cheltenham did ask the young gentlemen to indulge her in one thing—an evening of dancing, to take place on the last night before they headed back to school. One of Harrington's other sisters, Lady Anne, would be making her

London debut in a few weeks, and this was a good opportunity for her to gain a little polish.

And so they put on their evening kit and gathered on the back terrace, Henry and Harrington and their friends Arthur Nichols, Jacob Cartwright, and Peter Ferguson. Harrington produced a decanter and some glasses, and soon they had drained it of brandy.

"A toast," Arthur Nichols said, "to Thetford's big night."

"My what?" Henry asked.

"You know," Nichols said.

In truth, Henry did not, but beside Nichols, Cartwright was nodding. What was he missing? He shook his head to clear it. The way it was swimming, you would think he had overindulged in the brandy, but he'd only had three glasses. Or was it four? In addition to the rum punch the Cheltenham butler had brought round to the stables earlier—Henry had been so parched after a full day of chasing the hounds, he had downed three glasses of that in quick succession.

Perhaps he should slow down. He had drunk… well, he wasn't entirely sure how much, but more than he ought to have had before dinner even began. "You'll have to enlighten me," he said to Nichols.

"You'll get to dance with your not-so-secret admirer," Nichols said.

A few guffaws followed, and Harrington intervened. "Come on, Nichols, that's my sister you're talking about. Besides, Caro's all right."

"Is she?" Henry asked.

"She is," Harrington said, slinging an arm around his shoulders. "She's not been acting much like herself these past two weeks, but she's quite funny. Sarcastic, even." Harrington paused, staring into his glass with a faraway expression. "I've sometimes wondered if you two…"

Henry gaped at his best friend. "If we two... what?"

Harrington jerked to attention, realizing he had committed the grave faux pas of saying something sincere in front of his young, male friends. "Nothing. Just... Caro's a good sort, and if you got to know her, you would like her. Gad," he said, holding up the empty decanter, "listen to me. What was in here? And how much did I drink?"

"Too much? Or not enough?" Peter Ferguson said.

"Not enough to stop me from fetching us another bottle," Harrington said. "You scoundrels talk about something else and leave my little sister out of it." He made for a side door leading to the library, singing an enthusiastic, if not very tuneful, rendition of the "Four Drunken Maidens."

"So," Henry said, "cards tonight? After the dancing, that is."

Nichols waited for the click of the door, then grinned. "How about blind man's bluff? I believe I can recruit one of Harrington's sisters to join us. At least when you're having a turn with the blindfold, Thetford."

"Very funny," Henry said. "I believe I'll pass."

"Well, you'll have no such luck getting out of your impending dance with her," Cartwright said.

"Your impending nuptials, if Harrington has anything to do with it," Nichols added, causing the two of them to snigger.

"Now cut it out, the both of you," Ferguson said. "Lady Caroline is a nice girl."

"Nice, is she?" Cartwright asked. "Watch out, Thetford, you have competition."

"Do neither of you have any sisters?" Ferguson asked. Ferguson was a newer addition to their circle, whom Henry and Harrington had met at Oxford. His father had joined the East India Company and fallen hopelessly in love with a local girl as soon as he arrived. He had married her, and it was to his mother whom Ferguson owed his dark hair and russet complexion (his lanky frame and the Scottish burr that emerged when he was in his cups were thanks to his father.) It turned out that Ferguson's maternal grandfather was a wealthy textile merchant, and Ferguson's father soon abandoned the East India Company to take up the family business.

Ferguson fit in with Henry and Harrington's circle at Oxford well enough, but he'd only been in England for three years, and sometimes it showed. He was a bit more strait-laced than most of Henry's reprobate friends from Eton.

Ferguson continued, "It pains me to think of some galoot speaking of my little sister this way—"

"It pains me!" Nichols cried in a falsetto voice, clutching his heart. "Have we offended your tender sensibilities, Ferguson?"

"Quick," Cartwright added, "someone fetch him a vinaigrette."

Henry grimaced. Even if Ferguson had the right of it, he should've known better. The surest path to mockery at the hands of one's friends was to talk about your *feelings*. It was as his father had taught him—a man should be strong. Stoic. Steadfast.

And when it came to your feelings, especially your painful feelings, *silent*.

"You're fools, the both of you," Ferguson said. "And I daresay in a few years, you'll be eating those words."

"Is that so?" Nichols asked.

"Have you seen Astley's mother?" Ferguson said. "Because that's who Lady Caroline favors. Mark my words, that girl is a swan, and someday you'll regret having squandered this chance to charm her."

"What do you think, Thetford?" Cartwright asked. "Will Lady Caroline bring London to its knees?"

Henry suppressed a groan. He'd been trying to stay out of the line of fire. "Hell if I know."

Cartwright peered at him. "Wait… are you blushing?"

Henry didn't think he'd been, but now he could feel heat rising in his cheeks. "No—"

"You are blushing!" Nichols cried. "You like her! I knew it."

"I don't. I—"

"Shall we have them call the banns this Sunday?" Cartwright asked.

"Better send for a special license," Nichols said.

"Caroline Greville, Lady Thetford," Cartwright said. "It has a ring to it."

In retrospect, Henry could see that he had been at a crossroads. That he should have followed Ferguson's example and spoken in Lady Caroline's defense. It need not have been anything elaborate. Even *Don't be such a jackass* would have sufficed.

But all he had cared about was getting his friends to stop ribbing him. And so what he said was, "No, I most certainly do not like her. I don't even want to dance with her. I'll have to. We'll all have to, at a party this small. But I'm dreading it. She is a naive little child, she is as dull as ditchwater, and if she has any charms, they have escaped my notice."

Ferguson was shaking his head, but Cartwright and Nichols were hooting encouragement, so Henry continued, "You know my tastes, gentlemen, and they don't run to a girl as flat as the Salisbury Plains. And don't even get me started on those hideous spots—"

"Look what I found," Harrington said, bounding onto the terrace, a bottle in hand. "This is the *really* good stuff—oh, good evening, Caro."

The four of them froze. Henry remembered feeling

confused, his brain refusing to process Harrington's words. Caro? What did Harrington mean, Caro? She wasn't there.

She... she couldn't be.

But when he turned around, there was Lady Caroline, standing on the far side of the balcony, next to the pair of doors opposite the ones Harrington had used, the ones that led into the drawing room. One look at her face told him there was no need to ask the obvious question, which was whether she had overheard.

She had heard, all right. She had heard *everything*.

If he lived to be as old as Noah, he would never forget her expression. It was that horrible face you make when the whole world is falling apart, but you have to pretend that everything is fine, that everything is *splendid*.

His friends, who had been half-drunk and rowdy seconds ago, had fallen silent. "So, what brings you out here?" Harrington asked his sister.

To say that the smile Lady Caroline gave her brother did not reach her eyes was a gross understatement; it barely reached her lips. But even from across the balcony, Henry could tell how hard she was trying. "Mama asked me to fetch you in to dinner."

As Lady Caroline spoke, her eyes, the ones that could not go for a space of more than three or four seconds without darting to Henry, remained fixed on the ground.

Harrington frowned. "I say, Caro, is everything all right?"

Nobody on the terrace drew a breath. Because although Lady Caroline was down, the truth was, she held all the trump cards in her hand. All she had to do was tell her brother what Henry had said, and he would be disgraced. His friendship with Harrington would never recover. You could not say something like that about a man's little sister and expect him to shrug it off. All at once it struck him that Harrington had played a part in every single one of his best memories. That he was the person whose company Henry preferred over anyone else on the face of this earth.

Until that second, he hadn't realized how much Harrington's friendship meant to him. Not until it was about to be snatched away. All Lady Caroline had to do was tell her brother the truth.

What she did instead was even worse.

For one second, she looked Henry square in the eye. Underneath the humiliation, her eyes held a spark of anger, and Henry was sure it was all over. But then she looked at her brother, and her shoulders slumped. "Yes, I... No. I'm feeling unwell. I have this, this headache. I think it must be a megrim."

"You don't get megrims," Harrington said.

"No, I never have before, but we've all heard Mrs. Carruthers describe hers, and that's how it feels."

Harrington's frown deepened. "How so?"

"That it hurts so badly you wonder if you're going to die," she whispered, a tear streaking across her cheek.

"I say, Caro... if it's that bad we'd better fetch the physician—"

"No! I—I only want to lie down. If you would please tell Mama I'm unwell. My apologies, gentlemen." She dropped the briefest of curtseys and was through the French doors before Harrington had the chance to call after her.

She had covered for him. After he had treated her in the most abominable way possible, she had lied to protect him.

It was so... sporting of her.

To say that he didn't deserve it was the grossest sort of understatement.

"Poor Caro," Harrington said, seeming not to notice the unnatural silence from his four friends. "It must be awful if she's going to skip the dancing. She's been allowed to attend a few local assemblies, but tonight was going to be the

47

closest she's ever gotten to a proper ball. She was so excited."

They made their way to the dinner table, and the rest of the evening passed in a blur. Henry was certain he danced with Lady Anne and with the other young ladies who had been the lucky recipients of such a coveted invitation. But he remembered none of it. He could picture nothing in his mind's eye except Lady Caroline's misery.

He rose at dawn the next morning—hardly an inconvenience, considering he had been unable to sleep. He had never felt so wretched in his life. He had to see her, had to apologize. But she didn't come down for breakfast.

By one o'clock, his friends were ready to head back to Oxford, but Lady Caroline hadn't left her room.

He appealed to Harrington's mother for assistance. "I was hoping to speak with Lady Caroline. Is she well enough to come down?"

Lady Cheltenham dispatched a maid to check. She soon returned with the news that Lady Caroline was suffering horribly and couldn't rise from the bed.

"Poor dear," Lady Cheltenham said. "I knew her headache had to be very bad for Caro to miss the dancing. This confirms it. My apologies, Lord Thetford."

"Might I leave her a note?" Henry asked.

The countess raised a haughty eyebrow. "What do you have to say to my daughter in this note?"

The countess's supercilious glower was terrifying. Henry scrambled for a plausible explanation. "It is a personal matter of great importance. That is to say, well, it's important to me." He swallowed, then said in a rush, "Would it be impertinent to ask that it be for Lady Caroline's eyes only?"

Lady Cheltenham maintained her hawk-like glare, and Henry knew how that sounded. It sounded as if he was going to make a declaration. Oh, but this was horrible—he was fairly certain he was blushing. *Again*.

But then Lady Cheltenham surprised him. Her face softened, a genuine smile easing over her features. "Why, Lord Thetford, I did not have the slightest inkling. Caro will be delighted." The countess rose and gave him a firm look. "This one time, we will allow it."

And so he sat at Lady Cheltenham's own writing desk and filled three sheets with a disjointed, rambling apology. He begged Lady Caroline to send him a reply so he could at least know she had read it.

She never did. And so he sent her another letter a week later, and two more after that. She did not respond to any of them.

HENRY HAD NEVER BLAMED her for not replying. He craved her forgiveness, but he could not pretend he deserved it. Nevertheless, he wanted to make her a proper apology. He owed her that much, at least.

He had arrived at Astley House. Traffic was normally sparse at this hour of midmorning, but a queue of carriages stretched around the block. What was going on?

He made his way up the front steps. Inside the foyer there was a crush of humanity. Why the devil were so many people here? Did the Astley ladies host a salon?

That was when Henry noticed the common denominator between the people crowding the entryway. Every last one was a gentleman. An unmarried gentleman, based on those whom Henry recognized.

And they were all carrying flowers.

CHAPTER 6

*H*enry squeezed inside the morning room, which was packed with young men. He was surprised to see his friend Peter Ferguson.

"Ferguson? What on earth are you doing here?" he asked.

Peter's expression was all innocence. "What? I can't call upon an eligible young lady?"

"You never have before," Henry noted.

"True. But you see, I was right."

"You were right about what?"

"Lady Caroline. I told you she was a swan."

Henry glanced across the room and found her seated on a settee, surrounded by a flock of admirers. Of course, he had seen her in Thomas Hope's Egyptian Room, but it had been dark and their encounter had been brief.

She managed to look the same as he remembered, with blonde hair and big blue eyes, and completely different, all at the same time. In the intervening years, Caroline Astley had... ripened. Her figure was his personal ideal, full and curvy in all the right places and slim and lithe everywhere else. God, her breasts would completely fill his hands, but her waist was so tiny, he wondered if he could span it…

Henry shook his head to clear it. Upon further reflection, this was not the right time to dwell upon her figure. No, this line of thought was having a predictable effect upon certain parts of his anatomy, which was unfortunate in that he was in a crowded room, wearing the sort of breeches that left nothing to the imagination.

He would dwell on her figure later. Specifically, he was going to think about it while he completed the last task he performed for himself every night before falling asleep.

"You see?" Peter said.

Henry grunted. "She's pretty enough, I suppose."

"Pretty enough—that's rich. She's the most beautiful woman I've ever seen."

Henry cast his friend a pitying look. "Don't be ridiculous." Caroline Astley wasn't the most beautiful woman he'd ever seen, not even close. After all, there was…

He combed his memory. There must be someone—an opera singer or a ballet dancer or… or…

Well, just because he couldn't think of someone *right at this particular moment* didn't make it true.

She smiled at one of her admirers, and Henry forgot how to breathe.

The door opened, and Harrington squeezed in. "Thetford. Ferguson," he said.

"What in blazes are you doing here, Astley?" Henry said. "You can't call on your own sister."

Harrington chuckled. "No. I'm here for the spectacle," he said, gesturing to the packed room. "You won't see a farce this good on Drury Lane."

Indeed, glancing around the room, Henry saw that many of the young men were employing some rather… novel techniques, in their attempts to gain Lady Caroline's attention.

There were the poets, of course, with their sheaves of paper and florid waistcoats. He recognized Tristan Bassingth-waighte, who was mid-recitation, kneeling before Lady Caroline and gesticulating passionately, with little regard for the nearby tea service. One young man appeared to be sketching a portrait, which Henry didn't mind. At least sketching was silent. But what in God's name was that hideous bellowing sound?

"What is that noise?" Henry asked, scanning the room.

"Over there," Peter said, inclining his head. "Archibald Nettlethorpe-Ogilvy has brought his famous contrabassoon." Mr. Nettlethorpe-Ogilvy was the grandson of a wealthy industrialist and would one day inherit an iron-making empire. He was probably the richest man in the room, but if this was his notion of how to impress a pretty girl, Henry didn't think much of his chances.

"Contrabassoon doesn't seem like the most romantic instrument," Henry said.

"In his defense, he's playing 'The Blue Bells of Scotland,'" Harrington said.

"How can you possibly tell?" Henry asked.

Harrington laughed. "The point is, my sister—my mischievous, underhanded little sister—is the toast of London. Look—there are six peers here to court her—seven including you, Thetford—and all the richest men in England to boot." Here Harrington gestured toward Peter, whose family fortunes had done nothing but rise, as the English could not get enough Indian muslins and Kashmiri shawls.

"In addition to Ferguson and Nettlethorpe-Ogilvy," Harrington continued, "there's Thomas Hope." Harrington nodded toward Mr. Hope, who hovered over Lady Caroline's shoulder. "And I wouldn't be surprised if Lord Graverley turns up. He's danced with her twice, and he never dances with anyone, from what my mother tells me. But don't you two feel discouraged by Graverley, with his impending dukedom and his hundred thousand a year. I'd much rather see her married to one of you louts. I'll even put in a good word for you. I think…" Harrington paused, and although he was ostensibly speaking to them both, he was looking at Henry. "I think you really stand a chance."

Henry tugged at his cravat, which suddenly felt a tad tight. Harrington had no idea how wrong he was, on so many counts. Even Lady Caroline didn't know the worst of it. God, if she knew the truth of his financial situation, she would be thanking her lucky stars he had spurned her all those years ago. Yesterday morning he would have felt that he belonged in this room, that were it not for the incident four years ago, he could have been vying with Lord Graverley for this beautiful girl's hand.

But in light of the news his father had told him yesterday, he felt like a fraud.

Beside him, Peter snorted. "I doubt it."

Henry knew Peter was referring to his blunder on the balcony, but Harrington, who still knew nothing of the incident, misunderstood. "Don't sell yourself short, Ferguson. Not only are you bloody rich, isn't your family connected to the Earl of Darrow?"

Peter raised an eyebrow. "I'm not sure that being Lord Darrow's third cousin twice removed constitutes a 'connection.'"

Lady Cheltenham spied Henry from across the room. She smiled and spoke in a voice that somehow rose above the poets, the din, and even the contrabassoon. "Caro, darling, look who is here to call on you—it is *Lord Thetford.*"

Lady Caroline froze mid-sentence. She swallowed, then turned and found him in the crowd. The smile on her lips he would have described as bright and welcoming.

The look in her eyes suggested that she would have liked

nothing better than to tear out his heart and feed it to a pack of wild dogs.

Her mother continued, oblivious. "Won't you please join us over here, my lord? You"—she pointed her fan at the man seated on Lady Caroline's left—"move aside for Lord Thetford." The man looked displeased but did not dare disobey.

"Astley," Henry said under his breath, "are all the women in your family so uncommonly bossy?"

Peter regarded him with interest. "You don't have any sisters, do you, Thetford?"

"That's right. Four brothers, no sisters," Henry replied.

Harrington and Peter exchanged a grin. "He doesn't know," Harrington said.

"I don't know what?"

Harrington grabbed him by the shoulders and spun him to face the settee. "Never mind, old chap. You'll find out soon enough." He gave Henry a friendly shove. "Off you go!"

HENRY APPROACHED the settee with a feeling of dread and presented his primroses. "Lady Caroline, how lovely to see you again."

"Lord Thetford. An absolute *delight*."

He sat beside her. After a moment, she leaned in conspiratorially and whispered, "Pray tell me, my lord, which part of *I never want to speak to you ever again* taxed your understanding?"

"I'm here to apologize."

"You chose an excellent venue for it, while I am in the midst of entertaining forty-three gentlemen callers."

"How was I to know there'd be such a crush?"

"So, you expected I would be unpopular. How flattering."

Well, that had come out wrong. *Again*. Fortunately, yet

also *very* unfortunately, he was saved from having to reply by a young man with a shock of orange hair, who rose to his feet. "If I may," he began, blushing as he peered at Lady Caroline over the top of the papers he clutched with white knuckles, "I would like to recite an original poem. It is entitled 'Caroline.'"

He cleared his throat.

CAROLINE, *oh, Caroline!*
 With eyes like stars and lips so fine,
 What can I do to make you mine?
 Oh, Caroline!

MY HEART WILL EVER BEAT *for thine,*
 To hold you, Oh! Would be divine!
 You are my intoxicating wine,
 Oh, Caroline!

"THAT DOESN'T EVEN SCAN," Henry muttered.

"And I suppose you could do better?" Lady Caroline said.

"Indeed no, which is why I am wise enough to keep my mouth shut."

"Trying something new, are you?"

Henry felt a grin spread across his face. "Touché, my lady."

Tragically, the aspiring poet was not done.

WHY MUST *you my heart decline?*
 Your defenses—labyrinthine!
 So cruel, my prickly porcupine,

Oh, Caroline!

"IT WILL ONLY GET WORSE," he murmured, unable to resist. "With this limited rhyme scheme, soon he will be on to *swine*."

"Try not to be so charming, my lord. I am like to swoon, and Archibald Nettlethorpe-Ogilvy is occupying my favorite fainting couch."

"And then *bovine*," he mused.

"*Asinine* is the word you bring to mind."

"Ah, but that rhymes with your name, not mine."

"Nothing rhymes with Henry. It would appear that you are proof against poetry. In so very many ways."

Lady Caroline's serene smile was belied by her eyes, which were full of poison as she delivered this riposte. But Henry's grin was genuine. What was this? The bland girl who had discussed the weather as if the fate of the British Empire depended upon it had an acid wit? That was... delightful, and Henry didn't mind one bit that her slights were directed at him.

They were spared from the further effusions of the redheaded poet by her mother. "Thank you, sir," the countess said. "Pray sit and be rested. Your heroic efforts to break through my daughter's *labyrinthine* defenses during the six days you have known of her existence appear to have exhausted your poetical capabilities."

The next poet launched into a Shakespearean sonnet, which was fortunate, as Henry wasn't sure how much more original verse he could stand. He tilted his head toward Lady Caroline's ear. "*Lovely* I suppose I cannot argue, but *temperate*? This man doesn't know you at all."

"What an outstanding apology you are making, my lord.

What lady would not be moved in the face of such sincere remorse?"

"You have me there. Allow me to select something more appropriate from Shakespeare—forgive me, Lady Caroline. After all, 'Sweet mercy is nobility's true badge.'"

"Much to the contrary, I find that 'Nothing emboldens sin so much as mercy.'"

"I know you despise me, but it is worse than I thought if you have taken *Timon of Athens* as your moral guide."

"This from the man who just quoted *Titus Andronicus*."

"In *Timon of Athens*, the title character vows to destroy all of his former friends, and then everyone wanders around the wilderness until they all die of venereal disease."

"That your mention of venereal disease ranks as only the second most offensive thing you have ever said to me speaks volumes. Besides, *Titus Andronicus* is far worse. At least *Timon of Athens* doesn't have any cannibalism."

Henry found himself grinning anew. "Come, Lady Caroline—it is only the tiniest bit of cannibalism. You don't need me to shoo Archibald Nettlethorpe-Ogilvy off your fainting couch, do you?"

"Must we discuss *Titus Andronicus*?" she snapped.

Tristan Bassingthwaighte, who had been standing near the settee, overheard, and interjected, "Indeed, Thetford, indeed. Why are you boring a pretty girl with talk of Shakespeare? Let us turn to the sorts of topics that might interest Lady Caroline. Shall we discuss last night's party, my lady? Your favorite kind of flowers? How fetching you look in that gown?"

Beside him he saw Caroline stiffen. Her smile didn't falter, but her eyes were flinty as she drew a breath through a clenched jaw.

Henry gave him a withering look. "Don't be so condescending, Bassingthwaighte. She's not an idiot. Anyone can see as much, after two minutes of conversation with her."

She smiled as if grateful but murmured, "Well, isn't this novel—you playing the part of my knight errant."

"Would you prefer that I insult you?"

"I would prefer that you go away!" she hissed.

Henry was about to reply when the butler entered the room. "Lord Graverley," he intoned.

A MURMUR WENT UP from the crowd. Apparently in addition to not dancing, Lord Graverley did not call upon eligible young ladies.

Until now.

It was the gentleman seated on Caroline's right's turn to be on the receiving end of Lady Cheltenham's fan. He surrendered his place to Graverley, who approached with his own bouquet, a mix of trailing pink, purple, and white flowers.

"How original, Lord Graverley," the countess said, "I have never seen orchids used to such exquisite effect."

Suddenly Lady Caroline was all sweetness and light, beaming at Graverley with a beautiful, empty smile. "They're stunning, my lord. I shall enjoy them tremendously."

"I thought it best to bring something unique," the marquess drawled. "For such an extraordinary beauty as Lady Caroline, it wouldn't do to bring ordinary flowers." He wrinkled his nose at Henry's primroses.

Henry covered his snort by pretending to cough. It appeared that, like Lady Caroline's forty-three other gentlemen callers, Graverley had lost his mind at the sight of her big blue eyes.

"Indeed," said Archibald Nettlethorpe-Ogilvy, who was

blessedly taking a break from his contrabassoon, "she is a diamond of the first water."

"I cannot agree with you there, sir," Graverley said. "Though she has all the beauty of a diamond, Lady Caroline could never be something so common and colorless. I think rather a rich, sparkling sapphire."

"The sapphire—it's perfect!" exclaimed the red-haired poet of the unoriginal rhyme scheme. He shuffled through his sheaf of paper for a blank sheet and began to scribble furiously.

"Well, this will give you something to look forward to," Henry murmured. "What rhymes with *sapphire*? *Quagmire*? *Ire*? *Crossfire*?"

"For Lady Caroline, *admire* and *desire* would be the obvious choices, Thetford," Graverley said.

"I'm afraid Lord Thetford has no talent for poetry," Caroline trilled. Under her breath, she added, "Or for putting words together in any sort of appropriate sequence."

"You're one to talk," Henry muttered.

Graverley frowned. "What was that, Thetford?"

"Nothing of consequence, my lord," Lady Caroline said. "La, half the time I have no idea what Lord Thetford is going on about."

"You seemed to understand me quite well when we were discussing venereal disease," Henry murmured. "Shall I return to that topic?"

"Will you *shut up*?" she hissed.

"Really, Thetford," Graverley said. "Did you bring a frog to put in her pocket? I'm half expecting you to pull her hair."

Caroline beamed at the marquess. "Of course, not every man can be as chivalrous as you."

Graverley's gaze swept over Lady Caroline's face and then drifted lower and lingered on her décolletage. "I must confess that I am not quite so gentlemanly as you imagine."

Lady Caroline made a pretense of blushing, managing to look embarrassed and pleased at the same time. She preened for a moment before saying, "I understand that you fence, Lord Graverley."

"I do indeed."

"What do you enjoy about it?"

"The strategy. Fencing is like a full-contact game of chess. It combines the mental and the physical."

"It sounds fascinating—how I wish I could try it."

Henry rolled his eyes as he was forced to endure the happy couple's attempt at conversation. "Just what we need," he muttered, "you've already captured the heart of every man in London; now you can go after our livers, too."

Graverley ignored him. "There is no reason you could not learn. My little sister Diana is an outstanding fencer. Although the footwork can be difficult to execute in a skirt."

"What a shame I cannot don trousers, as men do," Lady Caroline mused.

Graverley arched an eyebrow. "A fetching image, my lady."

Henry made a halfhearted attempt to suppress another eye roll. This was worse than the poets, a new low he wouldn't have thought possible moments ago.

Thomas Hope, who was hovering behind the settee, cleared his throat. "Lady Caroline, I have heard some news that I think will interest you."

She smiled but only half turned, as if reluctant to interrupt her conversation with Graverley. "Oh?"

"Yes," Mr. Hope said, "as you expressed a particular interest in seeing my new Eye of Ra figurine. I have learned of a new exhibit of similar items."

Henry felt every hair on his neck stand up. Items similar to an Eye of Ra figurine?

Lady Caroline spun around to face Mr. Hope. For a split

second, the coquettish mask was gone, and her eyes were intent.

She pasted on a bright smile. "How exciting, Mr. Hope. Where is it?"

"It will be opening next week at the Leverian Museum. The Eye of Ra, it is to be called. The proprietor, Mr. James Parkinson, asked if I might inspect it and give him a quotation to use in newspaper advertisements." He laughed. "Of course he wishes to have my endorsement, as there is no greater expert on Egyptian antiquities than myself."

Lady Caroline was lost in thought. "The Eye of Ra—it sounds, er, entrancing. Do you know what will be on display?"

"Do not get too excited, my lady, for it does not include any significant items, like those I will have in my Egyptian Room two weeks hence. I am given to understand that the exhibit will consist of smaller pieces—amulets and the like. But they have never before been shown for public view."

Smaller items—that was music to Henry's ears. He doubted anyone would be stupid enough to put his father's cosmetics box on display. Not only was it recently stolen, it was famous enough that every amateur Egyptologist in London would recognize it as belonging to Lord Ardingly.

Still, he could afford to leave no stone unturned.

"How eager I am to see it," Lady Caroline said.

"I should be delighted to escort you," Mr. Hope said.

"Could we go tomorrow?" she asked.

"Alas, I am busy with the final preparations to my Egyptian Room. It has proved necessary for me to oversee every stage of the work. I have been forced to complete most of the decorative painting myself. You would be shocked how difficult it is to find competent craftsmen." Mr. Hope shook his head. "Perhaps on Thursday I could take you."

Lady Caroline's face fell. "Oh, dear, I cannot go on Thursday. Mrs. Cadogan is hosting a short house party, and we have promised to attend."

"Fear not, my lady," Mr. Hope said. "I will inspect this exhibit and advise you if it is worth your time. If so, I will be most happy to escort you next week."

"You're too kind," Lady Caroline said.

"You will be attending Mrs. Cadogan's house party, Lady Caroline?" Graverley asked.

She returned her attention to the marquess. "Yes, my lord."

"Excellent," Graverley said. "I received an invitation as well." He tilted his head toward Lady Caroline's, his gaze flicking to her décolletage. "I have just decided to attend."

A redheaded maid crossed the room, snatching up a few bouquets along the way. She reached for the orchids in her mistress's lap and said in a thick Kentish accent, "Here m'lady, let me take those." As she grasped the bouquet, she stomped on Graverley's foot. He gave a sharp grunt.

"Fanny," Lady Caroline said, "do be careful."

"Beg pardon, m'lord," the maid said, already halfway across the room.

Graverley waved it off, but his voice was strangled as he said, "Think nothing of it."

"It is kind of you to say so," Lady Caroline said, "but I do hope you were not injured."

"Not at all. Although it would be worth taking any injury to receive your solicitations."

"How glad I am that you are all right." Caroline accompanied this remark with much fluttering of her eyelashes.

"Allow me to reconsider my answer," Graverley said. "If I were injured, would you nurse me?"

"La! I fear I have no talent for it, but if you are willing to submit to my fumblings, I should gladly make the attempt."

"Allow me to assure you, Lady Caroline," the marquess

said with a particularly lascivious look, "that I should be most glad to be the recipient of any of your… fumblings."

Henry could take no more. He rose to address the countess. "I beg your pardon, Lady Cheltenham. I must take my leave."

"Indeed," the countess said, rising to her feet, "look at the time. Gentlemen, thank you for coming. We must bid you all adieu but hope to see you again next week."

Most of the gentlemen were slow to depart, hoping for one final smile from Lady Caroline. Henry, on the other hand, elbowed his way through the throng and straight out the door. The poets and the contrabassoon had been bad enough, but what had been truly intolerable was watching Graverley and Lady Caroline moon over each other.

Well, at least he would never have to see that again. He did mean to apologize to her, but he would send a note round to her mother and arrange a time when there wouldn't be forty other men in the room. Then he could finally be done with it.

But that would have to wait. Right now, he needed to find out where this Leverian Museum was located.

CHAPTER 7

The hackney carriage drew to a halt on the far side of Blackfriars Bridge. Caro glanced about as she alighted. She had never been south of the river before. She had been told that the neighborhood she had just entered, Southwark, was home to a prison, two charity hospitals, a number of glue factories, and the biggest potter's field in London. But the yellow brick terrace house bearing the words *Leverian Museum* above the portico looked respectable enough.

Inside, Caro purchased tickets for herself and Fanny. "Might I speak to Mr. Parkinson?" she asked.

"Last I saw, he was with another patron, but I will see if he's available," the clerk said. "May I inform him who is calling?"

"Lady Caroline Astley."

The clerk's eyes went wide at the word *lady*, and he hurried off. Caro turned to inspect the exhibits in the entryway. Guns, guns, and more guns. Harrington would have found it interesting, but Caro couldn't have cared less. Ah— here was something different. She leaned down to inspect the bronze plate at the top of the glass case—"Remarkable Horse Shoes."

She bit down a scream of frustration. On another day, she would have found something of interest in the exhibits, even the horseshoes, but today she was too much on edge, too anxious about the possibility of finding her sister's amulet—

The rapid click of shoes on marble alerted her as an older gentleman entered the foyer. He wore his hair long, in a style more popular a few decades past, and its white color wasn't due to powder. His clothes were meticulously neat, and his posture was ramrod-straight, in spite of his advanced years.

"You must be Lady Caroline," he said, giving a cordial bow. "My apologies for having kept you waiting."

She gave him her most brilliant smile. Her plan was simple—step one: be charming, step two: ask to see the not-yet-ready-for-display amulets. "Mr. Parkinson, I believe. I have been admiring your delightful collection."

He offered his arm. "It would be my honor to give you a personal tour, my lady."

And so, with Fanny trailing behind them, she went with him around the museum, exclaiming over each room. In truth, many of the exhibits were fascinating, in particular the articles Captain Cook had brought back from his voyages around the Pacific. There were gorgeous ceremonial cloaks made from red and gold feathers. There was every variety of bow, arrow, and spear, and a little axe called a tomahawk. And there was a curious sledge used by the native peoples of the northern territories that Mr. Parkinson informed her was pulled by dogs over the snow.

Caro even enjoyed the natural history specimens, even if most of them were a bit moth-eaten. The elephant and hippopotamus were large enough that they had to be kept in the garden shed, but inside there were lions and tigers, crocodiles and alligators, a very curious animal from South

America called an anteater, a kangaroo from Australia, and even a hammer-headed shark. There was an entire room of monkeys, another of reptiles, and the room beyond which contained the "monsters." Caro walked into that room and right back out again, wishing she could unsee the strange creatures embalmed in jars.

Their tour proceeded into a skylit rotunda decorated in the style of a Grecian temple. The domed ceiling soared some fifty feet above her head, and marble columns supported a gallery ringed with a carved stone balustrade. Every square inch of wall space was lined with hundreds of varieties of stuffed birds in glass cases. Caro let her head tilt up, enjoying the view.

"How lovely this rotunda is," she said. "The light is gorgeous."

Mr. Parkinson's eyes twinkled with genuine pleasure. "It is good of you to say so, my lady. I take particular pride in this room. You see," he leaned in, "I helped design the building myself."

"Did you truly? It is magnificent. I must apologize, Mr. Parkinson—I had thought you a naturalist. I didn't realize you were an architect."

"In truth, I am neither. I am an estate steward by training, from Shrewsbury."

Caro smiled. "And how, may I ask, did an estate steward from Shrewsbury come to possess such a remarkable cabinet of curiosities?"

"Quite by accident, I assure you. The collection was assembled by Sir Ashton Lever, who decided to put it up for sale some eighteen years ago. He held a lottery. It turned out that my wife, Sarah, had purchased a ticket and never said a thing about it." His face fell a bit. "But before the drawing was held, she passed on."

Caro pressed his arm. "I'm so sorry."

"As was I, Lady Caroline. As was I." He cleared his throat. "In any case, it turned out that my wife had purchased the winning ticket. They held the drawing, and nobody came forward to claim it. It wasn't until five weeks later that I found the ticket, quite by chance, mind you, and realized that I was now the owner of a mummified hand pulled from an Irish bog, two different varieties of sloth, a polar bear from Greenland and cub, and all the rest of this lot." An expression of befuddlement crossed his face, as if even after eighteen years he still could not quite believe it. "It's strange, the twists and turns your life can take."

Caro had learned that all too well in the past week. "It is indeed, Mr. Parkinson. It is indeed."

She started, for they had entered a room containing a miniature mummy case very like the one in Thomas Hope's mansion and a selection of Egyptian urns. She hurried over to the glass case.

"Er—" Mr. Parkinson began, "I should warn you—"

"Oh!" Caro cried, jerking back. "Are those—"

"That's what a mummy looks like unwrapped," Mr. Parkinson said. "The hands and feet, in any case, and a few—ahem!—other parts."

Caro gave a nervous laugh. "I was hoping I might find some amulets. Someone told me about a new display. Something about the Eye of Ra?"

"You heard correctly, although that exhibit will not open until Saturday."

"Oh. How unfortunate." Caroline took no pains to conceal her disappointment. "I was so longing to see them."

Mr. Parkinson did not disappoint her. "Come. I would be glad to show them to you."

67

HE LED her into his office at the back of the museum, with Fanny in tow. "May I ask what interests you about this particular exhibit?"

Caro had known this question would come and had prepared an answer. "My sister recently received a gift of a beautiful Eye of Ra amulet. It is made of lapis lazuli, with some gold and ivory detail. I have been hoping to acquire something similar."

Mr. Parkinson removed a wooden box from a shelf. "I fear you will not find anything so fine in our exhibit. But there are some nice examples," he said, arranging the case on his desk. "See this turquoise-colored material? That is called faience, a form of porcelain. This one is of onyx," he said, gesturing to an elaborately carved eye the size of Caroline's palm with intricate cutouts. "This one is lapis, but as you can see, it is of a falcon-headed god, rather than the Eye of Ra."

A quick scan confirmed that Anne's amulet was not amongst the contents. Caro's heart sank, but she was careful not to let it show on her face. She took a few moments to admire the dozen or so amulets that would comprise the display. "They're lovely," she said, surprised to find that she meant it. "May I ask where you acquired them?"

"The Earl of Bessborough auctioned much of his father's collection two weeks ago. I was not the purchaser, as it happens. The winning bidder was a young man by the name of Richard Cuming, who lives nearby. He's a great devotee of the Leverian Museum, and these will make the start of his own collection. He's allowing me to display them for a few weeks."

Caro considered. These amulets had been sold at auction, and they came from an earl's private collection. They almost certainly had no connection to the thieves she was looking for. But perhaps she could learn something. "How disappointing that I missed Lord Bessborough's auction. It sounds as though I might have found what I seek."

"Do not trouble yourself, my lady. It was mostly paintings. There were few antiquities, from what I understand."

"Do you know where I might find something similar?"

He cocked his head, considering. "I am not the best man to ask. I'm not much in the acquiring business these days, as I find myself with rather more collection than I know what to do with."

"Of course," Caro said, feeling deflated. Alas, she would not learn anything of value today.

She was reaching for her reticule when Mr. Parkinson said, "Mr. Cuming, on the other hand, is interested in much the same items you are, my lady. I believe he has been in contact with some… other sources."

Caro froze. "Oh?" Mr. Parkinson said no more, so she prodded, "Might you be able to tell me? Of course, if you feel you cannot, because I would be bidding against your friend Mr. Cuming—"

He shook his head. "It's not that. Cuming can afford these, but he's the son of a tinplater. A fine piece of lapis and gold such as you described would be well beyond his means."

"Yet I sense your hesitation."

"In truth, I don't have enough information to put you in contact with his sources even if I wanted to. But you're correct, my lady. I do hesitate, and I will tell you why. When Cuming dropped these off last week, he mentioned that someone else had approached him regarding some similar items—amulets, small idols, and the like. Naturally, he asked about their provenance, and the seller said they were from Lord Bessborough's auction."

"Then they purchased them just to resell them?"

"They did not." Mr. Parkinson leaned forward over his desk. "Recall that Cuming bought his own amulets through the Bessborough auction. He went over every single lot, and he was specifically looking for Egyptian items. If the ones he was shown had been part of the Bessborough sale, he would have recognized them immediately. But he said he had never seen them before."

"How odd. Why would they lie about such a thing? Might they be counterfeits?"

"They might. Cuming thought they looked real enough, though." Mr. Parkinson paused. "Have you heard of the Rosetta Stone, Lady Caroline?"

"I have." One of Napoleon's soldiers had noticed a large slab of black granite forming part of a defensive wall at Fort Julien, near the town of Rosetta. This stone, however, was different. It was inscribed with writing in Egyptian hieroglyphics, Greek, and some sort of Coptic script. The Rosetta Stone, as it had come to be called, had generated a great deal of excitement, as it was suspected that the three blocks of text might be translations of the same message. If so, it might enable someone to unravel the mystery of Egyptian hieroglyphics, which no living person could read. "It has recently been put on display at the British Museum, has it not?" Caroline asked. "Along with the other treasures taken from the French Army?"

"Indeed, it has. But there are rumors that not everything captured from the French made its way to the British Museum. Rumors that a crate of smaller items has gone missing."

"Missing?" Caro felt the hairs on the back of her neck stand up. "Do you mean... Do you think it was stolen?"

"Well, consider this—in the hundred years leading up to the recent invasion, there have been no more than three dozen Englishmen who set foot in Egypt. The only Egyptian antiquities in the country are in their collections. And so, you should be able to trace the provenance of any Egyptian items offered for sale back to one of those men—the late Earl of Sandwich, Richard Pococke, Edward Wortley Montagu, many of whose items I have, by the by, and the like. Egypt has been a battlefield for the past three years. There is nothing coming out of there right now, except for those treasures recently brought home by the British Army. So I ask you, if there are rumors of a missing crate, and a shady character shows up peddling trinkets that look genuine but have an obviously false provenance, what is the most likely explanation?"

"That they came from that missing crate. And that they were stolen."

"Precisely, my lady."

"So, there is a group of thieves out there, peddling stolen Egyptian artifacts. That is"—*precisely what I'm looking for*—"most alarming." Caro paused, considering how to phrase her next question. "Mr. Parkinson, has anything else gone missing? Do you think these thieves might have stolen any other items?"

"I haven't heard anything, other than the rumors about that one crate. But I wouldn't be surprised. Cuming is a good man from a good family, but he's from Southwark, not Mayfair. He knows a rogue when he sees one. And his descriptor for the man who approached him was *shifty*."

Caro chose her words carefully. "Well, I must be sure to avoid these thieves. I wouldn't want to purchase a stolen item. Did Mr. Cuming give you any other description of them?"

Mr. Parkinson steepled his fingers, thinking. "Cuming said that when he questioned the provenance of their amulets, the man became defensive. He insisted that his customers included one of the most reputable collectors in England."

Caro leaned forward. Perhaps he meant Thomas Hope,

and she could ask him for a description. "Did he name the purchaser?"

"He did not. What he said was that if his amulets were good enough for a former prime minister to display beside treasures from the Emperor Hadrian's villa, then they were certainly good enough for a tinplater from Southwark."

"A former prime minister—my gracious." Well, that would rule out Mr. Hope. "Do you have any idea whom he meant?"

"I do not, my lady."

There was a knock at the door, and the clerk poked his head in. "Pardon me, Mr. Parkinson—Mr. Gilchrist is here to see you."

"Thank you, Mr. Waring." Mr. Parkinson stood, and Caro rose along with him. "I fear I must excuse myself, Lady Caroline."

"Of course. Thank you so much for your time today, Mr. Parkinson. I truly enjoyed your wonderful museum."

He offered his arm to escort her out. Caro's mind was racing. She needed to get in contact with this Richard Cuming, but on what pretext could the daughter of an earl request introduction to a tinplater from Southwark? Mr. Parkinson interrupted her reverie. "It is quite the coincidence, Lady Caroline, but you are the second visitor to ask to see the amulets today."

"Really? How curious."

"Yes, and not only that—the gentleman who came to see them this morning is a member of your set." They had made their way back to the foyer. "Oh, here he is now."

Caro felt her stomach sink. There was only one man in the room. He had his back to her, bent over the case of Remarkable Horse Shoes. He was tall and broad of shoulder, with short brown hair and an impeccably tailored blue coat. And before he even turned, somehow she knew.

Mr. Parkinson continued, as if everything was normal and she had not been thrust into the presence of her mortal enemy. *Again.* "I wonder if you might know each other? Lady Caroline, may I present Lord Thetford?"

He turned, and his bright smile was in direct opposition to her uncontainable scowl. "Why, Lady Caroline," he said with a bow, "what a delightful coincidence."

CHAPTER 8

*C*aro had her false smile in place by the time Mr. Parkinson turned to her. "You know each other, then?"

"Oh, yes," Lord Thetford said, "Lady Caroline's brother is my closest friend."

"Excellent." Mr. Parkinson bowed neatly over Caro's hand. "I will leave you in Lord Thetford's protection, then."

As soon as Mr. Parkinson was gone, Caro swept out the door, ignoring the viscount. She scanned the street. "Do you see our hack, Fanny? I believe it has left. And to think, I paid the driver a shilling to wait."

"That usually works," a deep voice intoned. The bothersome man had followed her outside. "What a shame you happened upon an unscrupulous driver."

"Well," Caro said with a brightness she did not feel, "I'm sure another one will come along presently."

"You will find that hacks are few and far between south of the river. But I would be delighted to escort you home." He gestured to a handsome high-flyer phaeton with a gold basket seat and midnight-blue velvet cushions. It was drawn by a pair of gorgeous matched greys, which were being held by his tiger, a freckle-faced boy of perhaps ten years of age. "How fortunate that we happened upon each other."

Caro glared into his smug face. "*Fortunate* is not the word I would use. And I would rather go back inside and eat that mummified hand someone pulled out of an Irish bog than get in your phaeton." She gave him her profile. "Now, if you will excuse me."

AN HOUR LATER, Caro found herself seated in Lord Thetford's phaeton.

It was rather remarkable, the series of calamities that had transpired to get her to this point. She could take a detached enough perspective to appreciate that. Things had actually gotten off to a promising start. Lord Thetford had attempted to speak with her, irritating man that he was. But Fanny, bless her, had declared that Caro "shouldn't be standing full in the sun," and had opened her parasol directly into the viscount's face. She had then proceeded to stand in front of her mistress like the three-headed dog that guarded the gates of hell.

This had spared her from having to converse with him, but, as much as it pained her to admit that he was right, more than a half hour passed without a single hackney carriage passing by. It had become clear that she needed a new plan.

Her plan had not involved getting into Lord Thetford's phaeton, however; Lady Caroline Astley was not so easily defeated as that. She had informed Fanny that they would cross Blackfriars Bridge on foot and have better luck finding a hack on the other side.

The walk had begun splendidly, if one's notion of splendidly involved hearing a string of obscenities that would have made even Harrington blush, when the drivers of two carts made for the same opening and almost collided. A fistfight ensued. Then a lecherous drunkard staggered over with arms outstretched toward Caro's bosom. She was once again saved by her indomitable maid, who stepped in front of her mistress wielding her parasol like a battle-axe, shouting, "Don't even think about it, ya buffle-headed tetaw!"

And to think that Caro had initially been disappointed not to have a fancy French maid. She made a note to take Fanny to Gunter's that afternoon. She loved the ices there.

After the drunkard, it had simply been a matter of trying not to breathe in too deeply of the rancorous malodors of the Thames and ignoring Lord Thetford's plaintive calls to give up this foolishness and get in his carriage (because of course the blasted man had followed her).

But she had ignored him and carried on. And then the end of the bridge came into sight, and she had thought she was going to make it, she truly had.

But then she had stepped in it.

Literally.

Lord Thetford grinned as he climbed up beside her. "I wonder what sort of manure that was?"

Caro did not deign to answer, but she was fairly certain the answer was pig. Her father was passionate about his herd of Gloucestershire Old Spots, so she had some degree of familiarity with the subject.

"Whatever it was, it had a remarkable case of tapeworm," he mused.

She glared silently over the waters of the Thames.

"My favorite part," he continued, "was when it sucked the slipper right off your foot, and it immediately soaked through. I don't blame you for leaving it there—"

"What a gorgeous team you have, my lord. Do you need

me to drive them for you, or are you familiar with the process?"

He glanced back to make sure Fanny and his tiger, Billy, had squeezed onto the tiny rumble seat behind them, then nudged the greys forward. Caro shifted about, scooting as close to the door as she could manage. Since making her bow, five gentlemen had taken her for a drive in Hyde Park. She knew their phaetons had been every bit as narrow as this one. But for some reason their proximity had affected her not at all.

Sitting next to Lord Thetford, on the other hand, she felt exquisitely self-conscious. The phaeton hit a bump and his shoulder nudged hers. She all but jolted out of her skin.

"Come, Lady Caroline," he said after a moment, "it is better this way." She maintained her stony silence, so he continued, "I know you wish to avoid me. But what you have failed to notice is that we are, how you say, doomed."

"Doomed. How precisely you have captured my feelings."

"First, we ran into each other over the mummified child in Thomas Hope's Egyptian Room. Today it was the Leverian Museum, with its assorted bog parts and room full of monsters. It is reaching the point of absurdity. Where will we meet next—the Hunterian Museum? They have the skeleton of an Irish giant on display. And if you thought the monsters at the Leverian were grotesque—"

"Would you like to know what I found to be the most hideous sight at the Leverian Museum?" she asked sweetly. "I will give you a hint. It was in the same room as the Remarkable Horse Shoes."

He had the temerity to laugh. "My point is, it's far better for me to get my apology over with today. Because apparently the fates have doomed us to run into each other at every crackpot's house and freak show in London until I've had my chance. And you would not believe how many freak shows there are in London."

How annoying that he was right. She gave an aggrieved sigh. "Fine. You may proceed."

~

SHE GLARED at him out of the corner of her eye. He looked nervous.

As well he should.

"Er—excellent," he began awkwardly. "Well. Four years ago, I sent you a letter. I sent you four letters, actually. Did you, um—"

"Did I cast them into the fire without even bothering to open them? Why, yes, yes I did."

Behind them, his tiger, Billy, gave a low whistle.

"I see," Lord Thetford said. "Then you are unaware of the sentiments contained therein. What I wrote was—"

"Allow me to guess," Caro said. "Seeing me standing on that balcony was one of the worst moments of your life. It was never your intention to insult me, nor to cause me any pain. You feel wretched, you are desperately sorry, and you beg my forgiveness. And so on, and so forth. Do I have the gist of it?"

"You understand me remarkably well. It's difficult for me to even find words to—" He gave her a tortured look. "Caro, I can't tell you how sorry I am. I was miserable for weeks afterwards. I still think about it every day, and I cringe, thinking how I—"

"How you said you didn't even want to dance with me? How you were *dreading* it?"

"Yes, I—oomph!" There was a loud thwacking sound, and he grunted in pain.

"Beg pardon, m'lord," Fanny said loudly, "I was just

opening me parasol."

He rubbed the back of his head. "I don't know why you even need a parasol. We're fully in the shade."

"Hmmm," Fanny returned.

"And what was it you said next?" Caro said. "Ah, yes, that you didn't want me 'following you around,' because I was a 'naive little child' without any charms, that I was 'as flat as the Salisbury Plains—'"

"Oh, that's very bad," Billy said in what he doubtlessly thought was a whisper.

"Very bad indeed," Fanny agreed.

"I mean, look at her. Is he blind?" Billy asked.

"'Tis either that or stupid," Fanny muttered.

"The problem is that he don't have any sisters," Billy continued. "Four brothers but no girls. Me, I've got three sisters, and I know full well—"

"Billy!" Lord Thetford snapped. "Your commentary is neither required nor appreciated."

"Yes, m'lord. Beg pardon, m'lord."

"And my personal favorite," Caro said, "was when you said I was 'as dull as ditchwater.'" Hearing a rustling behind her, she turned, raising a hand. "Thank you, Fanny, but there is no need to hit him again."

Fanny already had her parasol aloft. "I didn't know he said all that!"

"I told you he insulted me most terribly to his friends on the balcony."

"Ya left out a few pertinent details," Fanny grumbled.

"Returning to the matter at hand," Lord Thetford said. "Yes, that is what I said. I cannot deny it. All I can do is tell you how deeply sorry I am—"

"Sorry to have been caught," Caro scoffed.

"That is not it. That is not it at all—"

"Next you will explain how you had over-imbibed. How

your friends were goading you. How—"

"Both of which happen to be true. But those things are entirely irrelevant. I should have taken them to task. It is to my shame that I did not. No, I do not wish to make an excuse, I wish to make an apology. The only reason I said what I said is because I was a jackass."

"Based on our recent conversations, your use of the past tense seems a trifle optimistic."

"I do not blame you for being skeptical, nor do I blame you for hating me. But I have changed as a result of that day. I have," he insisted, seeing her dubious look. "I never used to consider the feelings of anyone but myself. I am far from perfect today. But at least I'm trying. I cannot honestly say that I was before. And I'm no longer friends with Arthur Nichols and Jacob Cartwright. I began to notice a mean-spiritedness to them, and I found that I did not much like the man I became in their company." He shook his head. "One good thing came out of that horrible day, because I made a brutal self-discovery. At least I'm no longer a complete cad, as I was at the age of twenty-one."

Caro gazed at the passing scenery, absorbing his words. In truth, it was a better apology than she had thought he would make. She had expected a string of excuses. She was startled to realize that he was sincere.

But there remained one problem.

"I believe you," she said. "I believe that you regret having ever said it. I even believe you are sincerely sorry for having hurt me. But"—she raised a hand as he started to interrupt —"I also believe that you meant every word you said that day."

"I... I..." His expression was plaintive, his brow furrowed in distress.

"Don't even bother to deny it," Caro said.

"The thing is, it had nothing to do with you specifically.

At the age of twenty-one, I wasn't interested in young ladies—"

Behind them Fanny gave a great snort, which she then made a very halfhearted attempt to disguise as coughing.

Lord Thetford sighed heavenward. "*Fine.* That is to say, I was not interested in *respectable* young ladies."

"That's more like it," Fanny muttered.

"Mmm-hmm," Billy concurred.

"The point is," Lord Thetford said, casting a glare over his shoulder, "the fault was entirely mine. And Billy was right earlier." He gave her a rueful half smile. "Look at you now. The most beautiful girl in London. I'm not glad to have caused you pain, but I believe the end result will be better for you in every way. You would never be interested in the likes of me." His face fell as he returned his gaze to the horses. "You'll probably be married to Lord Graverley before the month is out."

Caro wasn't so sure. She hadn't even decided whether she wanted to set her cap for Lord Graverley. And in any case, there was no appropriate response to such a remark. "Hmm," she demurred.

He drew in a breath. "I've never dared to hope you might forgive me. I never felt I could possibly deserve it. But—"

She waved this off. "Oh, I'm sure I will forgive you." He looked up, his face radiating shock and hope and… something else. Caro found it difficult to maintain eye contact when he wore such an expression. It was a bit like staring directly into the sun. "Your obvious sincerity makes it difficult to carry on hating you."

"Then do you think… Could we be friends, Caro?"

She closed her eyes for a beat. "No, my lord. I honestly do not think we ever could." She raised a hand to silence his protest. "We will see each other in the future. We run in the same circles; it cannot be avoided. I will not cut you when we do. You need never worry about that. I will nod, and I will smile. I will say good evening if the circumstances require it. But on those occasions when we meet, the kindest thing you could possibly do for me is to leave me alone."

"But… but… I will never treat you with such disrespect again. You have my word of honor upon that. And—"

"That isn't the problem. The problem is that you only wish to be my friend because you pity me."

"That is not true—"

"Your first impression of me was that I was annoying and insipid. 'As dull as ditchwater.' And ever since I overheard you on the balcony, you have thought of me as poor, pathetic Caro. Yes, you have," she said when he made to protest. "You never would have sought me out if I hadn't overheard what you said. If you had not felt sorry for me. And there is nothing, absolutely nothing I despise more than being pitied. I cannot abide it. I would much rather have the world's hatred than its condescension. It is why I have been avoiding this horrid conversation for all these years."

"But I like you," he protested.

She arched a skeptical eyebrow at him. "You didn't four years ago."

"No," he agreed. "But yesterday—that was nice, wasn't it?"

It was not ladylike to roll one's eyes, but really, who could blame her? "Allow me to clarify—your notion of *nice* involves your likening me to a pig and a cow, my calling you asinine in return, your discussion of venereal disease followed by cannibalism, and my hissing at you to shut up before someone heard the ungodly things coming out of your mouth?"

"Well, I enjoyed it," he muttered.

"I know you believe that. But the truth is, the only reason you think you like me today is because you are determined to do so. Because you feel guilty. Your true opinion of me is what you stated on the balcony four years ago."

"That is not true. I had the wrong impression of you entirely—"

"I do not believe you." He gave her that look again, the same one he had been sporting for most of the conversation. It was beseeching. Crestfallen. Pitying.

She could not *stand* it.

She glared at him. "Will you stop looking at me like that? How did we stumble into such a maudlin conversation? It is absolutely intolerable. I never imagined a context in which I might utter these words, but I preferred it when we were discussing venereal disease."

He barked out a laugh. "Truth be told, I did, too."

"How shocking, to find ourselves in agreement. Now, we're almost there. Do me a favor and say something completely obnoxious so I can go back to loathing you again. Just the first thing that springs into your mind. You have such a natural talent for it."

He was grinning at her. "Very well, I will do my best. May I speak frankly?"

"Am I to understand that our conversations up until this point have been your most polite circumspection? How very alarming."

"You, Caroline Astley, are a sham. Do any of your suitors know what an acid tongue you really have?"

"La! They do not, and I have no intention of letting them know the awful truth. At least, not until I've caught one of them in the parson's mousetrap."

He shook his head. "Have you considered that you might be going about it all wrong? That you should look for a man who appreciates your wit?"

"Such a man doesn't exist. I will sooner find a unicorn."

He looked up at her when she said that for some reason. "That's not true. Many a man would find your wit appealing."

"Spoken like a man. Trust me when I say that wit is not appreciated in a woman; indeed, it is barely tolerated. No, it is something I must conceal at all costs."

"And yet you launched into me without hesitation."

"That's because I do not care the slightest bit what you think of me." He usually grinned at her set downs, but this time he flinched. She cast her eyes heavenward. "Now this is pathetic. You cannot pretend that you are in any way deserving of my regard."

"I would be the first to agree that I am not. But we men are strange creatures. You may club me over my thick skull, and I will not be bothered in the least. But I beg you, do not wound my pride."

Caro made a show of clutching her heart. "I have three brothers. I am all too familiar with your delicate, manly pride."

"You're not so familiar as you think if you believe it to be located in the center of my chest. It resides a ways farther south—"

"Is this your notion of how to address a lady? You're lucky I'm Harrington's sister and inured to scandalous remarks. Any other woman would have fainted dead away."

"I was counting on it," he replied. They had reached Cavendish Square. "Well, Lady Caroline, this is it. You shall be rid of me at last."

Caro stood, waiting for Billy to set up the ladder so she could descend. Lord Thetford circled around to hand her down. "The ladder, Billy," he said. "Where is it?"

The young groom was distraught. "It's, it's gone, m'lord. I'm sorry, I mustn't have stowed it properly, and—"

"Never mind, Billy. We'll circle back around for it."

Well, this was going to be a problem. The phaeton was a

true high-flyer, meaning that the floorboards of the basket seat were as high as a man's head. How on earth was she to—

Lord Thetford solved this dilemma by placing his big, strong hands around her waist and lifting her down. She was unprepared for the sudden descent and started to fall as soon as her feet touched the ground. She grabbed his shoulders in the same instant he caught her in his arms.

Caroline's last coherent thought was that she was in deep trouble.

Because without giving her any time to prepare, Henry Greville, the subject of her girlhood infatuation and the only man she had ever really fancied herself in love with, was holding her in his arms.

And it felt *glorious*.

OH, God. His arms cradled her tenderly, and his body was flush against hers. She did not want this. She didn't even like him. But… why was her entire body trembling? And why was her heart about to pound right out of her chest? She was startled to realize that she had been right the other day, when she had mused that underneath his linen, he would be even more perfectly sculpted than Thomas Hope's statue. Because she had his shoulders under her hands and his broad, gorgeous chest pressed against hers, and she now knew without a single shred of doubt that every inch of him was as hard as carved marble.

She felt strangely languid, as if she couldn't have moved away from him if her life had depended upon it. She felt the slow slide of his hands moving up her back, then one of them rose to caress her neck, and she heard herself make a mewling sound she had not known herself capable of. She felt her head tipping back and her mouth falling open, and the last thing she saw before her eyes fell shut was the arc of his lips slowly descending toward hers...

And that was the instant Fanny grabbed her elbow and jerked her from his arms.

Caro was entirely befuddled. "Fanny, what—why —who—"

"You're standing in the middle of Cavendish Square," Fanny hissed. "And Araminta Grenwood is heading this way."

Oh, good gracious. Araminta Grenwood was Caro's age but had made her debut one year earlier. Caro knew Miss Grenwood; their mothers were friends, although the two girls had never grown close. Not only was Araminta Grenwood a notorious gossip, but at the start of this season, she had bragged that she would be the woman to bring Lord Graverley up to scratch.

Needless to say, the attentions Caro had received from the marquess had done nothing to endear her to Miss Grenwood.

Caro attempted a smile. "Ah, Miss Grenwood, good afternoon."

"It certainly is an interesting one," Miss Grenwood replied as she passed by. She lifted an eyebrow as she noticed that Caro was wearing only one slipper. "A very interesting afternoon, indeed."

Caro swallowed. Well, this was a disaster. She turned back to Lord Thetford, only to find he was no longer standing next to her. He was already atop his phaeton, unable to get away from her quickly enough.

She felt the mortification rising in her cheeks. She had thought he was going to kiss her, but that had been her imagination. There was some deep inner recess of her brain that could not comprehend that this man wasn't interested in her and never would be.

"Caro," he said, his breathing labored. "Wait. We need to—"

She had no intention of waiting, no desire to see the pitying look back on his face. She curtseyed. "Thank you for conveying me home. Goodbye, my lord."

Behind her, she could hear him shouting her name, but she wasn't about to stop. She was already halfway up the front steps, and if there was a merciful God in heaven, then this would be the last time she ever had to deal with the likes of Henry Greville.

CHAPTER 9

*T*hat afternoon, Caro conferred with Fanny over ices at Gunter's. They didn't discuss what had happened with Lord Thetford, but they did discuss their two potential leads in the missing amulet. Two men—Richard Cuming and some mysterious prime minister—had met with the thieves and might have additional information. The problem was, she had no idea how to get in touch with Mr. Cuming, nor did she know which prime minister it might be. As best she could count, there were five living men who had served as prime minister at one time or another.

They resolved that Fanny would ask a friend from Southwark to track down Mr. Cuming. And Caro would see if Harrington knew of a prime minister who collected Egyptian antiquities. If she could trust anyone to assist her with a hairbrained scheme, it was her scapegrace of a brother.

But when Caro poked her head inside Harrington's door that evening, she found a flurry of activity. There was a trunk open on the bed, and her brother's valet was bustling about the room, filling it. "Harrington," she said, "what's going on?"

She noticed he was dressed for riding. "Have you forgotten about the Stanhope ball? We're to leave in half an hour."

He looked sheepish. "There's been a complication."

"May I ask what sort of complication?"

"I wish you wouldn't, as it's a variety of complication entirely unfit to discuss with my little sister."

Caro crossed her arms. "It involves a woman, then?" He said nothing, so she pressed. "Harrington?"

"The thing to understand is that I did nothing wrong. It's not my fault she chose me over Markham, now is it?"

"Dare I to hope congratulations are in order?" Caro asked.

Harrington looked aghast. "Absolutely not."

"I didn't think so," Caro said, rubbing her forehead. "I take it this Markham now wants to shoot you?"

"Something like that. Look, it's going to be all right. He's a lieutenant in the navy, and I'm given to understand that he ships out in a week or two. If I can lie low until then, the whole thing will blow over."

"Hence the trunk." Caro sighed. She had been planning to tell Harrington everything. If she was going back into South-wark to interview Richard Cuming, she would prefer to do so with one of her brothers at her side. But as Harrington was leaving town, Edward was at home in Gloucestershire, and Freddie was thirteen and at Eton, that wouldn't be possible.

"So," Harrington said, "what brings you here? Other than the desire to bask in my august presence?"

"I was hoping you could help me with a riddle," she said, deciding that if Harrington wasn't going to be around, there was no point in telling him what she was up to. "Something posed to me by, er, Mr. Hope. Do you know which prime minister collects Egyptian antiquities?"

"I haven't a clue," he said, opening a leather case and

inspecting the two flintlock pistols contained therein. "But I can tell you who will know, and that's Thetford."

Caro's mouth fell open. "Lord Thetford? How would he know such a thing?"

Harrington snapped the gun case shut. "His father is mad for everything Egyptian, so he grew up surrounded by it. You can't swing a dead cat in the Greville town house without hitting, well, a jar containing a dead cat."

Caro leaned back against the doorframe, tipping her head up to the ceiling. She had the most rotten luck. Of all the people in all of London she should have to turn to for help—

"He's even going to be there tonight," Harrington said. "At the Stanhope ball. He's normally not much for that sort of thing, but he mentioned last night that his mother was forcing him to attend."

"A delightful coincidence," Caro muttered.

"Yes, well." There was a click as Harrington's valet, Andrews, fastened the latches on his trunk. Harrington picked up his case of pistols and strode through the door, pausing to drop a kiss on Caro's cheek. "I'll see you in two weeks. Make my excuses to Mother, will you? Think of something good, something that won't cause her to cut off my allowance."

"You can count on me," she replied as he started down the hall. "Try not to get shot."

"Will do," he called over his shoulder.

A FEW BLOCKS AWAY, Henry entered his parents' town house. He had come to collect his mother, whom he was to accompany to the Stanhope ball. A footman accosted him in the foyer. "Your father wishes to speak to you in the library, my lord."

He found his father pacing the room. Henry strolled over to the decanter, as it looked as if his father could use a drink. "Good evening, Father. You sent for me?"

"I did." He waved off the brandy Henry offered, so Henry sat before the desk and took a sip himself. His father took the seat opposite, tenting his fingers. "I will come straight out and say it. I received a call from the Duke of Trevissick today."

"Oh?" Henry said. That was unusual in and of itself. The duke was Lord Graverley's father and had a reputation for being something of a recluse. He rarely went out, and from what Henry understood, no visitor had set foot inside of the duke's London mansion since his wife had died almost two decades ago. Henry had never met the man, but from what he had heard, the duke was supposed to be a little bit crazy and more than a little bit cruel. "What did he want to discuss?"

"Apparently all of London is agog with the news that you took Lady Caroline Astley for a drive this afternoon."

Henry shifted in his chair. "I happened to encounter her at the Leverian Museum. Her hackney driver had abandoned her, so I offered her a ride home. It was nothing more than that."

"And the reports that you all but kissed her in the middle of Cavendish Square?"

"Those rumors are"—*entirely accurate*—"overblown. She lost her balance climbing down from the phaeton. I merely steadied her."

"That is not what is being said."

"And the rumor mill is always accurate? Come, Father. I could hardly let her fall to the curb. Why does the Duke of Trevissick care, anyways?"

"He made it clear that his son wants Lady Caroline for his future duchess."

"And he'll probably get her. He's the man everyone expects her to marry." Henry studied his father. A sheen of sweat shone upon his brow. "So Trevissick wants the way clear for his son," Henry continued. "Graverley can do his best to win her, like every other man in London. What concern is it of ours?"

His father pinched the bridge of his nose. "You recall that I told you I had taken out a loan for five thousand pounds."

"Yes. You said it was a debt of honor, to another gentleman. One that would have to be repaid." Henry heard a roaring in his ears. "Do you mean to tell me you borrowed five thousand pounds from the Mad Duke?"

"You would be wise not to call him that, considering he holds our fate in his hands," the earl snapped.

Henry sagged back in his chair, disbelieving. "I take it Trevissick threatened to ruin us."

"He threatened to expose us, which amounts to the same thing, if you come between his son and Lady Caroline. So what I need you to do is avoid the chit. I don't care if you're friends with her brother. Do not speak to her, do not dance with her, do not be seen in her company—"

Henry stood. "Very well, I will avoid her. If there is nothing else?"

His father waved him off. "So long as you understand what needs to be done."

Henry understood, all right. In truth, nothing had changed in light of his father's revelation. *The kindest thing you could possibly do for me is to leave me alone.* Ever since she uttered those words, he had accepted that this was how it was going to be. He had done enough to Caroline Astley. Of course he would honor her request. Even though…

He had known she was pretty, that she was exceptionally pretty, even. And more than that, Caroline Astley was exactly what he liked, with her big blue eyes, the body of a goddess, and especially that impish little pleased-as-punch smile she always made right before she opened her mouth to cut him to shreds. He had known all of that, but he had been unprepared for the moment her body came tumbling into his. The only thing he could liken it to was being struck by lightning. God, the feeling of her pressed against him, her lush curves against his chest, her waist beneath his hands. How could a man be expected to think when he had a girl like Caroline Astley in his arms?

In summary, that was how Henry had found himself standing in the middle of Cavendish Square, holding the woman he had just vowed to avoid for the rest of his life, sporting a raging erection.

Then she had been jerked out of his arms. He couldn't just *stand there* with his cock at full mast. He was wearing a cutaway coat, for God's sake. That maid of hers would have beaten him to death with her parasol, and he couldn't bear to have that in his obituary.

Hell, if one of Caro's brothers had happened along, they would have had to call him out. And Harrington for one was a crack shot.

So he had scrambled atop his phaeton. The seated position afforded him at least a bit of camouflage. But Caro had managed to escape. Not that he blamed her for fleeing the scene, but he wished he had gotten the chance to apologize.

A familiar theme where Caroline Astley was concerned.

Oh, well. He wondered if she would be in attendance at Lady Stanhope's ball. Probably so, as it was the premier event of the evening. But he would give her a wide berth, as she had requested.

If she was there, he would ignore her. He wouldn't go anywhere near her.

He was definitely not going to dance with her.

CHAPTER 10

*T*wo hours later, Henry reflected that, for the girl who'd been crowned the toast of London, Caroline Astley was a remarkably bad dancer.

Not that he was dancing with her.

Not intentionally, in any case.

Strictly speaking, she was dancing with Lord Graverley, and his partner was Peter Ferguson's little sister, Charlotte, whom Ferguson had asked him to lead out. It was Charlotte's first season, Ferguson had said, and she was worried about being labelled a wallflower.

But the dance was a cotillion, in which the couples arranged themselves into squares, with one couple on each side. Henry had attempted to slink into a group at the bottom of the set.

Lady Stanhope put a stop to that. "My gracious, Lord Thetford," she said, "we cannot have someone of your rank so low in the set. No, you belong right over here." And she led them straight to Caro's group. He could hardly refuse his hostess without causing a scene.

Worse than that, he and Charlotte had wound up directly

opposite Caro and Graverley, meaning that, like it or not, the figures called for him to dance with Caro almost as much as her ostensible partner. And he was doing it right under Graverley's nose.

His father was going to *kill* him.

He grimaced but didn't look down as Caro stepped on his foot. *Again.* Truth be told, she had been behaving strangely all night. When he first walked in, she had caught his eye and inclined her head to the side. She repeated this gesture seven times. Had he not known better, he would have thought she was beckoning him to come join her scrum of admirers, but that couldn't be right.

She must have had a… crick. Yes, a crick. In her neck.

But then, when he was standing with Ferguson by the refreshment table, grousing about the indignities of any occasion where knee breeches were required, Caro had broken free from her crowd of beaux and walked over to fetch her own lemonade.

What young lady fetched her own drink when she had a pack of twenty young bucks falling over themselves to perform the service for her? Henry was forced to grab Ferguson by the arm and beat a hasty retreat to the library, muttering something about going in search of stronger refreshments.

Speaking of stronger refreshments, he wondered if some young prankster had thought it a lark to pour some spirits in the punch bowl. That might explain Caro's odd behavior.

Something was clearly wrong with her. She had just elbowed him in the ribs.

The worst part of it was that he wasn't even allowed to mock her for her lack of grace. He would have enjoyed that tremendously. But no, she had asked him to leave her alone, so he stared stoically at the wall.

They went into a series of Allemandes, in which the

couples linked arms behind each other's backs and turned in a circle. It was challenging to assume the proper position without so much as glancing at one's partner, but what choice did he have? He mused that he was managing the situation as well as he possibly could, given the circumstances.

That was when she pinched him hard in the side.

"Ouch!" He glared at her and found her scowling right back up at him. "What is wrong with you?" he hissed. "You've stepped on my foot four times, and—"

The figures of the dance took them apart, and he saw her paste a bland smile on her face as she performed the Allemande with Graverley. Across the set, he caught the marquess staring at him incredulously.

At last the interminable dance ended. Caroline was all smiles, applauding the musicians and beaming at Lord Graverley. Henry bowed over Miss Charlotte's hand, preparing to beat a hasty retreat, when a familiar voice trilled, "Beg pardon, Lord Thetford. But you dropped your snuffbox."

Gad, he wasn't supposed to be talking to her, especially with Graverley looking on. "It's not mine," he said.

"I saw it fall from your pocket," Caroline said, articulating each word as if she were speaking to a particularly dimwitted child.

"I don't even take snuff—"

"Just take it, you simpleton!" she hissed, thrusting it into his hand.

Whatever she had handed him felt more like a folded piece of paper than an actual box. It felt almost like... a note. "Oh. This snuffbox," he muttered, shoving it in his pocket.

It took him some ten minutes to make his way down a deserted hall where he could read the note in private.

I need to speak with you. Meet me at the folly in the back garden during the orchestral break.

A HALF HOUR LATER, Caro waited, hidden in the shadows behind the garden folly. Lord and Lady Stanhope were holding this ball at their villa on the outskirts of London, which meant it had room for a full garden. The folly was a miniature version of a Greek temple consisting of five columns topped by an open ring, with a rustic stone bench inside.

It was a gorgeous spring night, clear but cool, with a full moon. The sounds of the party had all but faded away, leaving only the trilling of a nightingale overhead. Caro could detect the sweet fragrance of cowslips blooming nearby, reminiscent of apricots.

Then she heard it—the crunch of footsteps on the gravel path. She peeked out from behind a column and saw Lord Thetford approaching.

All at once, she was living her girlhood fantasy. And by that, she didn't mean that the situation was the sort of thing any young girl might dream up on a summer afternoon.

This was her *specific* girlhood fantasy. Midnight at a ball. A romantic folly in a garden. A bench drenched in moonlight.

And Henry Greville, stealing away from the party to meet *her*, looking… looking…

Looking so heartbreakingly handsome in his snow-white linen and coat of black superfine that it seemed impossible that he could be real.

She thought of their dance earlier that evening. Not that it had truly been their dance. He had never asked her to dance, and probably never would. But it had been so easy to pretend he was her partner in truth. It was just like when she was fifteen—even after she had accepted that he didn't feel the same way, she had longed to dance with him, just one time. It wasn't such a ridiculous hope. At a party that small, surely all of her brother's friends would have to ask her at least once.

But of course, he never had. And tonight, while they were dancing, she couldn't even get him to look at her. Not once, no matter how hard she tried to gain his attention.

And she knew that was unfair. She knew the only reason he had ignored her was because she had asked him to leave her alone. Because he thought it was what she wanted.

Still, it felt like an all-too-apt allegory for their relationship.

As he mounted the steps to the folly, Caroline stepped out from the shadows. "Thank you for meeting me."

He gave a start, then grinned. "Of course." He took a seat on the bench. "I'm curious what this is about. Here I thought you never wanted to speak to me again."

"I don't. I mean, I didn't. I mean…" She looked away, struggling to calm her nerves.

"You mean?" he prompted. She peered down the path to see if anyone was coming. "If you're worried about being discovered together," he continued, "I think we would hear someone coming. Did you not hear my footsteps?"

"You're right. I did." He gestured for her to join him on the bench, and she did so gingerly, careful to leave plenty of space between them.

She crossed her arms, hugging them close to her body, as she tried to figure out what to say. He began peeling off his coat.

She blanched. "What are you doing?"

"You're cold," he said as he freed his wrist from a sleeve.

She held her hands up, as if to protect herself from any gesture of kindness from him. "You don't have to do that."

"I know that. But what I would like, Caro, is to do something nice for you, for once in my life."

He draped the coat around her shoulders, and it was without question the most awful, most wonderful thing that had ever happened to her. It wasn't merely that his coat was so warm (which it was), or that it smelled heavenly (which it did), with hints of cinnamon, leather, a whiff of brandy, and that indefinable scent that was *Henry*.

No, the real problem was the way he was looking at her, as if he truly cared, as well as the chivalrous act of offering his coat to keep her warm. To say nothing of the unbearable tenderness those things spurred in the general vicinity of her poor, stupid heart.

She had to acknowledge that she still wanted this man. Even after he humiliated her, after spending the past four years hating him with every fiber of her being, she wanted him as intensely as she had the first time she saw him.

But that didn't mean she trusted him. If there was one thing Henry Greville had taught her, it was that hearts were fragile things. She wasn't about to risk hers again.

"Thank you," she remembered to say after a moment, wrapping his coat about her. She truly had been cold.

"You're welcome, Caro."

"You keep calling me that," she said without thinking.

"I apologize," he said quickly.

"It's not that. I was more wondering… why."

"Harrington refers to you as Caro. You were an abstraction at first, one of his many siblings whom I hadn't met. But after the incident on the balcony… I've thought of it, and therefore of you, every single day since then. And thinking about you every day… I suppose it made you feel familiar to me." He gave her a cringing smile. "Do you mind?"

She considered. "You know, I don't believe that I do."

He exhaled, relieved. "Good." He nudged her with his elbow. "You could call me Henry if you like."

How many thousands of times had she imagined calling

him precisely that? Therein lay the rub—to her, *Henry* was the man who actually asked her to dance, not once but twice (and who tried to sneak a third dance past her mother). *Henry* was the man who called on her not because he found her pathetic but because he found her enchanting. And *Henry* was the man who met her at the garden folly because he longed for a kiss, not because she had ordered him to be there.

He was not that man. And it was almost painful to think about calling him something so intimate as Henry, knowing that he felt none of the sentiments she had come to associate with the name.

"I will consider it," she said.

"Good. Now, won't you tell me what's going on?"

She swallowed. "You said that you wanted to do something nice for me. I hope you meant it."

"I assure you that I did. Why do you say so?"

She heaved a reluctant sigh, then raised her eyes to meet his. "I need your help."

FOR THE NEXT TEN MINUTES, Henry listened as Caro told him a tale that made him feel angry and excited in turns. He was furious at the thought of that cutpurse laying hands on her.

But he also saw the opportunity. Because thanks to his father, he had information, and he had connections. He could help her with this, he knew he could.

For the past four years, there was nothing he had craved more than Caroline Astley's forgiveness. And here it was, his chance to perform a great act of contrition. If he did this for her, if he helped her recover her sister's amulet, then surely, *surely* she would forgive him.

And more than that, he wanted to show her he wasn't the

cad she thought him to be. This was his chance, his only chance, most probably, to show her what kind of man he really was.

If he could do that, then maybe she would… maybe they could…

He didn't even know how to finish that thought.

He shook himself. The odds were also high that, if there was a gang of thieves out there stealing Egyptian artifacts, they might have his father's missing box. If, in helping Caro, he could also help himself, so much the better.

Something occurred to Henry.

"Describe your sister's amulet for me," he said. "You said it was in the shape of the Eye of Ra?"

"Yes. It's about this size," she said, tracing an outline against her palm. "It's dark blue, made of lapis lazuli, with ivory and onyx for the eye, and gold detailing all over."

Henry frowned. In truth, that sounded very similar to his father's missing box. "Are you familiar with faience? It's a form of porcelain and a common material for amulets. Are you certain it's not made out of faience?"

"I'm sure. I've seen some faience amulets since getting myself into this mess. This one is definitely lapis lazuli."

"And you're certain it's an amulet? It couldn't be anything else, say, a cosmetics box?"

"No, it's an amulet. I'm positive. It was flat and this thin," she said, indicating narrowly with her fingers. "In truth, I thought it a pendant. It even had a little hole at the top for me to string it on a chain."

Henry felt his shoulders relax. His father's box didn't have such a hole. Whatever similarities in design, they were talking about two different items.

"At this point," she continued, "I have two clues, in the form of two men who have been approached by the thieves offering items for purchase. One is this Richard Cuming.

Someone from Southwark is trying to locate him for me. Mr. Parkinson from the Leverian Museum hinted at the other gentleman, but he didn't know his name. I wrote it down so I would remember it precisely. It was something about... the Emperor Hadrian? Harrington said you would know to whom it referred."

She pulled out a slip of paper and held it in the shaft of moonlight penetrating the columns. Henry leaned in, eager to see if he could indeed help. "A prime minister... good enough to display beside treasures from Emperor Hadrian's villa," he read. He looked up and startled at how close they were sitting, their heads drawn together as they peered at the note. He could feel her breath ruffling his cravat, and he felt the hairs on the back of his neck stand up. God, she looked beautiful in the moonlight. Beneath his coat, she wore a simple white cotton dress, with flowers embroidered up the front in white thread. These white dresses seemed to be the prevailing fashion; half the women in attendance were wearing something similar. But the sight of Caroline in that simple white dress, and his coat, looked... looked so very...

She's not for you, he reminded himself. *Graverley wants her. The Mad Duke will ruin you.*

Not. For. You.

She glanced up and startled at their proximity. A blush rose to her cheeks as she rearranged herself on the bench so they weren't sitting so closely.

He cleared his throat. "This is Lansdowne."

"The Marquess of Lansdowne?"

"It has to be. Most of his statues are Roman, but he has a handful of Egyptian pieces. Much of his collection came from the excavation of Hadrian's villa. And, of course, he was prime minister years ago."

"What luck—Lord Lansdowne is throwing a rout tomorrow night. Mama and I are to attend."

"I will have received an invitation, too. Lansdowne and my father are… not friends, precisely, but they do like to discuss their collections. I'll plan on attending."

She bit her lip. "That won't be necessary. I don't want to put you to any trouble. Now that I know to whom I need to speak—"

"It's no trouble. And I think you'll need me there. I've known Lansdowne for my entire life. He's a difficult man. You have to know how to flatter him—"

Caro burst into laughter, and for the first time that evening, a genuine smile came over her features, distinguishable from both the bright, empty expression she wore before her beaux and the look of discomfiture she had worn these past fifteen minutes. Henry marveled that he could tell the difference, having really known her for just a few short days.

"Are you suggesting that I, of all people, do not understand how best to flatter a man? La—give me five minutes, and I'll learn all of Lord Lansdowne's darkest secrets."

"If anyone could, it would be you. I have, after all, seen you in action, adroitly managing your flock of forty-three gentlemen callers." Henry was unable to suppress a shudder.

"And what, pray tell, is wrong with my forty-three gentlemen callers? I happen to be quite fond of them."

"Clearly some parties on this bench enjoyed Archibald Nettlethorpe-Ogilvy's contrabassoon serenade more so than certain other parties on this bench."

"If you think you will trick me into casting aspersions upon Mr. Nettlethorpe-Ogilvy, then you are sorely mistaken. He is sweet in his sincerity. Besides, even if his interpretation of 'The Blue Bells of Scotland' is rather, er, singular, it's still better than most of the poetry."

"Why, Lady Caroline—I am shocked, absolutely shocked, to hear you *cast aspersions* upon the poets. What would your mother say?"

"La, if you knew my mother at all, you would know that she would heartily agree, and she would do so to their face. Whereas I am only referring to Tristan Bassingthwaighte. You yourself said he was condescending, and you weren't wrong. So you may cast as many aspersions upon him as you would like."

"I know how you can achieve the perfect revenge upon Mr. Bassingthwaighte: agree to dance with him."

Her mouth fell open in a perfect little circle before she realized he was teasing her. She poked him in the shoulder. "I will have you know I am an excellent dancer."

"My feet would beg to differ."

"I was trying to gain your attention."

"A likely story," he said, snagging her wrist when she made to poke him again. She tried the same thing with her other hand, and he captured that one as well. They were both laughing now, and she was tussling with him, trying to free her hands. He pulled the first trick a boy learned on the pitch at Eton, abruptly relaxing his arms so she would pull herself off-balance.

Of course, Caroline Astley had never set foot on the pitch at Eton, and the trick worked all too well. In the sudden absence of any resistance, she pitched backward and started to topple off the bench.

What kind of gentleman would he be if he didn't reach out and grab her about the waist, keeping her from falling?

She ended up sprawled almost in his lap, one arm looped around his neck, the other resting against his chest. He realized that when he had snatched her up, one of his hands had landed higher than he had aimed, and even now, his thumb was resting on the lower swell of her breast. She was breathing hard and fast, and her mouth was mere inches from his. Her gorgeous eyes were so blue you could make out the color even in the moonlight, and if he didn't know better, he would have said they were full of yearning.

And he wanted to kiss her. He wanted to kiss her with every fiber of his being. Without thinking, he slid one hand around her back and started to lean in.

But when he closed his eyes, an image sprang into his mind of his father glowering at him.

Not. For. You.

He exhaled with a groan, then eased her back onto the bench. As soon as she became conscious of their intimate position, she began blushing, looking everywhere but at him. She rearranged herself so there was a good foot between them.

He cleared his throat. "Regarding Lord Lansdowne... I don't doubt you could charm him. But—" An image sprang to mind, of Caro flirting with Lansdowne, that cold, predatory old goat who Henry happened to know was in the market for a third wife. Something inside of him growled in protest. He didn't like to think of it, and he was surprised to realize how much.

He continued, "I don't like for you to have to put yourself in that position. Not when there's another way."

She shrugged. "As you like."

"We have our plan, then. Come." He rose and offered his arm. "You've got to get back to the party before your absence is noted."

Soon the house came into view. Henry peeked around a large hydrangea bush. "It's clear. You head in first. I'll wait ten minutes, then follow."

"All right." She paused, her eyes grudging. "Thank you."

"You're welcome." She started toward the house, and he reached out and snagged her arm. "Aren't you forgetting something, Caro?"

A flush stained her cheeks. "What?"

"You're going to have more to explain than a fifteen-minute absence from the ballroom if you walk back in there wearing my coat."

"Oh!" She had it off in a flash. "Thank you for that, too," she said, handing it back to him.

In an instant she was gone.

He waited ten minutes, trying to ignore her sweet scent lingering on his jacket. When he rejoined the party, he was pleased to discover that his mother was ready to leave.

For the duration of the carriage ride home, he formulated his plan to deal with Lord Lansdowne.

At least, that was what he tried to focus on. But he found that his thoughts kept drifting to the image of a certain young lady sprawled across his lap and the kiss they had almost shared in the moonlight.

CHAPTER 11

*A*t Lansdowne House the following evening, Caro wasn't having any success at all.

She had tried flattering Lord Lansdowne. She had tried batting her eyes. She had even tried thrusting out her bosom.

Lord Lansdowne did glance at her bosom. What he did not do was respond to her conversational overtures.

She pasted a smile across her face and made a fourth attempt. "My lord, I understand that you collect Egyptian antiquities. Might you tell me about your—"

"Say, Waldegrave," Lord Lansdowne interjected, snagging a passing gentleman, "what's this I hear about you supporting the Duties Continuance Act?"

An argument ensued, while Caroline was ignored. Well, this was lowering. But she couldn't give up.

Lord Waldegrave extricated himself. Caro was steeling herself to try again when Lord Thetford appeared. "My lord," he said, bowing to the marquess, "I was hoping you could spare me a minute. I can't make heads or tails of this Yeomanry and Volunteers Act that's coming up for a vote. May I ask for your take on it?"

Caro withdrew but lingered within hearing range. Lord Lansdowne, who had answered her every question with a grunt, was now loquacious, lecturing Lord Thetford with great enthusiasm about the reasons the yeomanry must continue performing military drills in spite of the peace agreement reached two months ago with France. Lord Thetford did a fine job of drawing Lord Lansdowne out, hanging on his every word and peppering him with interested questions.

After about ten minutes, Lord Thetford shifted the conversation. "Excellent. Thank God I caught you, or I never would have gotten that sorted out. There was one more thing I was hoping to ask you about, at the request of my father. I imagine you already know what it is."

The ghost of a smile actually passed over Lord Lansdowne's face. "I have a fair idea."

"I hear you have some new acquisitions."

"I do. Small items, but some nice pieces. A few amulets and a statuette of a cat."

"You know I'll be in trouble with my father if I don't come back with a full description. May I have a look?"

"You may." The marquess waved, indicating he was to help himself. "They're with the rest of my Egyptian items."

"May I ask from where you acquired them? Was it the Bessborough auction?"

"They're from Bessborough's collection, although they weren't part of the auction. Apparently some of the smaller items are being disposed of through a third-party seller. That was who approached me."

"I know my father will want to get in touch with this seller. May I have his name?"

"It was Brownwood—no, Browntree—oh, I can't recall. Shortish fellow, ginger beard. I've his address written down. I'll send it round to your father."

"That would be much appreciated, my lord. I won't take up any more of your time," Henry said, bowing.

The marquess's attention had already tuned elsewhere. "Say, Stafford, what's this I hear about you supporting the Drawbacks and Bounties Act?"

Henry was heading toward the main stairs. Wait—surely he wasn't going in search of the amulets without her?

She snagged his arm. "Why, Lord Thetford, good evening. I hope you haven't forgotten your promise to fetch me a lemonade. I find I am absolutely parched."

He raised a skeptical eyebrow but led her back to the refreshment table. They took their drinks to the dining room, which had been left open so Lord Lansdowne's guests could admire the fine Roman sculptures lining the walls.

"You're going to enjoy this," she murmured as they headed for a quiet corner.

"What's that?" he asked.

"My admitting you were right. I did need your help with Lord Lansdowne."

"Lansdowne is an odd sort. He never discusses anything other than politics. You have to know exactly how to play him."

"Well, thank you. Oh!" She gestured to the bust of a young man dressed in an Egyptian headdress. "Is this his Egyptian collection?"

"Indeed, no. This statue is Roman. This is Antinous, the favorite boy-lover of the Emperor Hadrian."

Caro cast him a sideways look. "Are you quite certain you should be telling me this?"

"No, although that has never stopped me before. Antinous died while they were visiting Egypt, leaving Hadrian heartbroken. Hadrian commissioned hundreds of statues of him in the Egyptian style. But the point is, this isn't Lansdowne's Egyptian collection. He keeps that in his personal library. Where I was headed before *someone* interrupted me."

She ignored his accusation. "Excellent. When can we make our way to the library?"

"*We* will not be making our way anywhere. *I* will go up to the library and have a look around."

"Not a chance. You've never even seen my sister's amulet—"

"I can recognize it well enough based on your description."

In truth, he probably could, certainly well enough to determine if anything warranted closer inspection. But even though he had helped her tonight, she found that she still did not entirely trust him.

And more than that, something in her recoiled at the thought of handing the investigation off to someone else. This was her problem and therefore her responsibility. She needed to be doing something.

"Come on, Caro," he said, "I can be caught in Lansdowne's library without consequences. The same cannot be said for you. And if the two of us are discovered there together…"

"Then we must make sure we aren't discovered." He started to protest, but she cut him off. "My mind is set. There's no point in arguing with me. The only decision you have to make is whether you will direct me to the library, so I can slip away and meet you there, or if you will force me to wander the house in search of it, increasing my chances of being caught."

He gave a long-suffering sigh. "It's on the second floor. Meet me at the top of the landing in ten minutes."

She beamed at him. "Excellent. Thank you for the lemonade, my lord." She turned on her heel and left.

~

TEN MINUTES LATER, she made it to the top of the stairs. Henry emerged from a shadowy alcove. "We're clear. Hurry."

He led her to a room about halfway down the hall. Unlike the more formal rooms downstairs, this one had the air of a place that was used daily. On the desk, a pen sprawled across a stack of papers. The room smelled of tobacco smoke, and there were comfortable creases in the leather of the well-worn armchair before the fire.

There were also a handful of Egyptian antiquities—two life-sized statues of gods in black granite, a green basalt sphinx, and a handful of smaller statuettes.

Caro began searching the room for the amulets. Henry, on the other hand, started leafing through the papers on the desk.

"What are you doing?" she asked. "The amulets are not like to be shuffled in there."

"No, but perhaps the seller's address is around here somewhere."

They searched in silence. "Well, I don't see it," he said after checking the final stack of papers. "Which is perhaps unsurprising."

"Do you know what I found surprising?" Caro asked as she scoured the shelves of a bookcase. "Watching you charm Lord Lansdowne."

"Why did that surprise you?" he said, strolling over to inspect the bookcase next to hers.

"Suffice to say, when I think of you, *charming* is not the very first descriptor that springs to mind."

He grinned, as he always did when she insulted him. "Why, Lady Caroline, you wound me." He claimed her hand and raised it to his lips, and she felt her heart start to hammer out a military tattoo inside her chest.

He rose slightly, but kept his head angled down toward hers. His eyes were bright with mischief and with something she was too terrified to even attempt to define. He pressed her hand as he said, "Would you care for me to demonstrate just how charming I can be?"

"No!" The word burst from her reflexively. It was a bald-faced lie, but upon consideration, she decided to repeat it. "No. You would be wasting your time."

"It's not a waste of time if I enjoy it. And what fellow doesn't enjoy flirting with a beautiful woman?"

"Except you don't find me beautiful."

"I spoke with your forty-three gentlemen callers the other day. It seems I was mistaken."

"Is this your notion of charm? Informing a girl that you're flirting with her because everyone else finds her appealing?"

"No," he said, raising his hand toward her face and craning his head toward hers. "My notion of charm is telling you, my beautiful, witty Caro, that at last I have found exactly what I'm looking for."

SHE HAD FORGOTTEN how to breathe. He was leaning in, and his hand was inches from her cheek. In another second he would... he would...

He would reach past her face and pluck something from the shelf behind her, then step back, smirking. He held up a kid leather pouch. "And here it is." He bounced it in his palm, testing its weight. "About the right heft for a few amulets."

He turned toward the desk and began picking at the knot in the drawstring. Caro struggled to school her features. Just when she had felt herself softening toward him because of his help with Lord Lansdowne, he turned around and reminded her what kind of man he really was. He had never meant to kiss her, not when he handed her down from his phaeton, not last night on the bench, and not tonight, either.

This was all a joke to him. *She* was a joke to him.

And yet somehow, he was the man who invoked an animal reaction in her, one she had always been helpless to contain. She couldn't let her guard down for a single second around this man. She needed to have her armor in place at all times.

She forced an unconcerned smile to her lips, careful to take up a position on the opposite side of the desk. The knot gave way and he and poured a handful of items onto the tabletop, each wrapped in a handkerchief. "There." He reached for one. "Let's see what's in here, shall we?" He glanced up at her, then frowned.

"Don't look at me like that," he said. He dropped the small bundle on the desk, forgotten.

She smiled even harder. "I don't know what you're talking about."

"*That* is what I'm talking about. That obsequious simper you use on Graverley and the rest of them. It turns my stomach. I would much rather see you glaring at me."

She closed her eyes. "That can be arranged."

When she opened them, his brows were knotted in genuine consternation. "I say, Caro, I was only having a joke—"

"It was unkind." She was horrified to hear the tremor in her voice as she said it. She didn't want to be having this conversation, didn't want him to see the truth, that she was still vulnerable. But the words came pouring out. "You know how I felt four years ago. You know exactly. And for you to stand there and lie, to pretend that you are in any way interested in me—" She turned her head, unable to meet his eyes. "It is profoundly unkind."

She heard him come around the desk, felt him take her hand. "Caro, please. Look at me." She stared into the bookshelf. He sighed. "You put on such a good front. I know I hurt you years ago, but you're so quick to put me in my place, it honestly didn't occur to me that I could do so today."

She maintained her stony silence, so he continued, "Part of the problem is that I enjoy sparring with you so much, I tend to get carried away. But as inappropriate as my behavior was, the one thing I cannot allow you to tell yourself is that it was a lie."

She cut her eyes to him then, distrustfully. "You cannot seriously expect me to believe that."

He shifted uncomfortably but did not look away. "You're being hailed as the most beautiful woman to make her bow in a generation. Every other man in England wants you. Why would you expect me to be any different?"

"Because four years ago, you made it clear—"

"I believe we have established that, four years ago, I was a blockhead. Besides, you've changed so much since then, you might as well be a different person altogether."

She jerked her hand from his. "It does not speak well of you that the only reason you have decided I am worthy of your regard is all of this," she said, gesturing to herself from the neck down.

He scowled. "That is not what I was referring to. Although I will not deny liking 'all of this,'" he said with a wave of his hand. "I'm a man, not a bloody saint. And not one bit different from any of your other forty-three gentlemen callers, might I add. But what I meant was your wit. Four years ago, if you had spoken to me with one tenth the liveliness you do today, we would have been friends."

"Yes, it was discourteous of me to have been fifteen years old and shy. And may I gently suggest that the fault did not lie entirely with me. You would be shocked how difficult it is to establish a conversation when one's dinner companion is drunk before the first course has even been served and responds to everything you say with a disinterested grunt."

He grimaced. "I don't doubt you're right. My behavior was in every way boorish. But you raise an interesting point. You accuse me of only changing my opinion of you for superficial reasons. Well, why were you interested in me in the first place? For my wealth and my title, I would wager. You wouldn't have given me a second look if I were the second son, 'Mr. Greville,' and destined for the church."

"That had nothing to do with it!"

"You were so undone by my handsome face, then?"

"That wasn't it either." His face was a portrait of skepticism. She sighed. "Harrington is my brother, you know. He's not the best correspondent, but he did write occasionally. And over the years, I…" She trailed off.

His eyes sharpened. "Over the years, you what?"

"I felt like I got to know you, too. Harrington's letters were full of the misadventures you shared. I know all about your first day at Eton and the goat. About how you both got twenty strokes—"

"Harrington got twenty strokes. I got twenty-five."

She furrowed her brow in confusion. "But why did you receive more than him?"

"Because when the goat took a bite out of that book, I was the one who said, 'I never liked that chapter, anyways.'"

Caro felt the corners of her lips rising without her permission. It took a brief struggle to make her features stern. "Yes, well, I know all about your many misadventures. And Harrington recounted every witty remark you've made for the past thirteen years—"

"That cannot possibly be true. I make a great many witty remarks."

She smacked him in the shoulder, but there was no containing her smile this time. "I know what a fine horseman you are. I know about your disgusting tendency to put pickles on everything. I know about your terror of leeches—"

"So Harrington knows about the leeches." Henry shook his head. "I was afraid he might have guessed. And he even told you. Although I know you'll miss him, I hope you understand why I have to murder your brother."

"La! I should like to see you try. At the risk of wounding your delicate, manly pride, we both know Harrington is the superior shot. But the leeches are not the worst of it—I even know about your little incident with the peacock, the skiff, and the master of Trinity College's pince-nez—"

"*My* incident? What do you mean, my incident? That was your brother!"

She arched a skeptical eyebrow. "Really."

"Yes. One is not like to forget the sight of his best friend crossing the quadrangle of Trinity College, stark naked but for an irate peacock, which he was holding in front of his, er, wedding tackle." He huffed. "I can't believe he tried to pin that one on me."

She laughed. "It does sound like something Harrington would do. But the point is, I had been looking forward to meeting you for years. The way Harrington described you, you had this irrepressible spirit and the best sense of humor, and... I knew we were going to be friends, that we were going to have the best conversations. I honestly hadn't thought of anything beyond that before"—she lowered her gaze, unable to meet his eye—"well, before I saw you. I wouldn't have cared a whit if you were the second son. I was only disappointed that you bore no resemblance to the person I thought you would be."

His hand caressed her cheek, raising her eyes to meet his. "And what about now? Am I so different from the boy your brother described in his letters?"

She said nothing. She was terrified even to think the answer to that question, much less speak the words out loud.

At some point, he had moved closer, so that he loomed

over her. She was boxed in, her back against the shelves of a bookcase, but she had no desire to escape. She could feel his breath ruffling the little curl Fanny shaped at her temple. And then she felt something firmer, his other hand sliding up her neck, and her whole body jolted in a previously unknown combination of shock and pleasure.

"You can still decide that you hate me," he said, his eyes bright and sincere. "That you can never forgive me for what I said. That nothing I can ever say or do will be good enough. But I won't accept you thinking that this," he said, stroking his thumb along her jawline, causing her whole body to shiver, "is a lie. Do you have any idea how much I wanted to kiss you yesterday afternoon, and, *God*, last night? I have thought of nothing today but the way you felt in my arms, the way you looked at me in the moonlight. I will never lie to you, Caro. I promise you that. I wasn't lying when I told you I was sincerely sorry. And *this* is not a lie."

One arm slipped around her back, drawing her to him. His head was descending toward hers. An hour ago, she would have sworn she didn't want him to kiss her. But now she felt certain she would die if he did not. She felt her eyes fall shut and her lips fall open, and she trembled with anticipation, waiting for his kiss.

She drew in a shaky breath, tilting her head to the side.

She took another breath, then a third. What in God's name was taking him so long?

She slit her eyes open, annoyed, only to find his head raised, staring at the door.

"Do you hear that?" he whispered.

That was when she noticed it—footsteps in the hall.

Footsteps that were growing louder.

He released her so abruptly that she stumbled. "Someone's coming," he hissed. "Hide!"

CHAPTER 12

*T*hey stuffed Caroline beneath Lansdowne's desk. Henry could find no other place that offered even a chance of concealment. It was a great mahogany partners desk with thick pedestals on each side, designed to accommodate two men working across from each other. This meant there was a cavernous opening in which she could hide.

It also meant that Caro was exposed on two sides.

Henry scrambled into Lansdowne's chair. "Stay as close to this side as possible," he hissed, glancing down.

The sight of Caroline Astley kneeling at his feet, her cheeks flushed and her gorgeous blue eyes staring up at him beseechingly, was one he would never forget.

One thing was for damn sure, he was going to think about it later tonight, while he brought himself off before drifting off to sleep. For the past few days, he had thought of no one but her while accomplishing said activity.

Now wasn't the time, though. The doorknob was turning, the door swinging open, and—

God damn it, could it not be anyone but him?

"Lord Graverley," he announced, "what the devil are you doing here?"

The marquess cast him a supercilious glower suggesting his own presence was equally unwelcome. "I might ask the same of you, Thetford."

"Lord Lansdowne said I might have a look at his new Egyptian amulets," Henry, gesturing to the leather pouch. As excuses went, it was a good one; it even happened to be true. "My father will want to hear about them."

"Ah, yes, your father and his notorious fetish for jars of entrails." Graverley shuddered.

"I take it you have dined with my parents."

"I have," Graverley said, scanning the room. "I found I did not have much appetite for the turtle soup. Please don't say as much to your poor mother, though. I have never seen another human look so mortified."

"You'll be pleased to hear that I convinced my father to move his canopic jars out of the dining room."

"Splendid," Graverley muttered.

"You haven't said what you're doing here," Henry said.

"I was looking for this," Graverley said, seizing upon the decanter. He poured himself a glass, not offering one to Henry, then took a seat on the opposite side of the desk. "I needed a few minutes away from the crowd downstairs."

"Is that so?"

"Yes. A few minutes. *Alone.*"

Henry ignored the hint. He could hardly leave while Caroline was stranded under the desk, so Graverley was doomed to disappointment. "Well, let's see what Lansdowne has acquired."

He unwrapped a handkerchief and held the amulet up for Graverley to see. "A nice specimen," he narrated aloud for Caro's benefit. "A miniature mummy, in green jasper."

"Fascinating." Graverley glared across the room as he took a sip of his drink.

"Here is another fine piece—scarab beetles such as this one are very common in Egyptian decorations." The marquess didn't even bother to feign interest. Henry unwrapped the third bundle. "This last one is in the shape of the Eye of Ra. The reddish-orange stone is called carnelian. A beautiful example. My father will be envious."

"You seem to be laboring under the delusion that I give a fuck."

Beneath the desk, Caro startled at Graverley's obscenity, causing a loud thump.

Graverley gave Henry a sharp look. "What was that?"

"Er—nothing. Just an, um, leg spasm," Henry said.

"Hmm. Well, now that you have finished rhapsodizing over your little trinkets—"

"Amulets."

"—you will doubtlessly wish to rejoin the party downstairs."

"You know, that brandy looks delicious," Henry said, stalling for time. "I believe I'll have one myself."

He had to abandon his seat in order to go to the decanter, but Graverley didn't move from his place on the opposite side.

"So." Henry took his seat again, casting about for something to say. "How are you enjoying the Season so far?"

"For Christ's sake," Graverley muttered, leaning back in his chair and running a weary hand over his eyes. He froze. He must have brushed against Caro underneath the desk, because she was all but climbing into Henry's lap, trying to get as far away from Lord Graverley's side as possible. The marquess began tapping beneath the desk with his foot. "What was that?"

"That was my foot, you dimwit," Henry replied.

The marquess continued to feel around, unconvinced. "It didn't feel like a foot."

And then he scooted back his chair and bent forward to look under the desk.

~

HENRY HAD to think of something to stop him. Anything. "The reason I ask if you're enjoying the Season," he said loudly, "is because of your unusual behavior."

At least the man paused his progress beneath the desk in order to stare at him incredulously. "*You* find *my* behavior unusual?"

"Toward Lady Caroline Astley," Henry clarified. "All of London is talking about it. I should like to know what your intentions are."

Graverley sat back in his chair, narrowing his eyes at Henry. "I am not in the habit of discussing my *intentions* with a man I scarcely know. Particularly when that man constitutes the competition."

"What makes you say that?"

"Lady Cheltenham leaves nothing to chance. Two men got to sit beside Lady Caroline on the settee. Did you think I would not note the other recipient of such a coveted honor?"

"Hmm," Henry said.

"Perhaps I should ask you the same question," Graverley said. "Do you intend to propose to Lady Caroline?"

"She's far too good for the likes of me."

"I couldn't agree with you more. But that is not what I asked you."

"Perhaps I should," Henry hedged. "She'll have to accept some lucky bastard, after all. She could do worse than me."

"She could also do significantly better."

"I will be an earl one day."

"She is going to receive a better offer," Graverley said deliberately.

"How do you know that?" Henry asked, leaning forward over the desk.

Graverley's ice-cold gaze did not falter. "How do you think?"

They lapsed into silence, neither breaking eye contact. Graverley's message was inescapable. A duke outranked an earl.

The better offer would be his.

Really, there was no accounting for the lowering feeling that accompanied Graverley's pronouncement. His father had already told him the man intended to make Caro his duchess. Henry knew he had to stay away from her or else Graverley's father would ruin him.

And yet...

He swallowed, remembering how she had felt in his arms a few minutes ago.

Gad, he needed to stop thinking these thoughts. This way lay madness. He needed to stop thinking about how pretty she was, and how witty, and how much she made him laugh. He needed to stop thinking about the fact that just talking to her was fucking delightful. He needed to stop thinking about the way she not only tolerated his irreverent sense of humor, she actually seemed to enjoy it, and she could even trade barbs with him. And he definitely needed to stop thinking about the fact that for years he had been saying that was the only thing he wanted in a wife.

And he absolutely needed to stop thinking about what she had said moments ago, that the thing that had drawn her to him all those years ago had been the stories Harrington had told about him in his letters home. That the thing she had loved hadn't been his wealth (which he no longer had) or his title or even his handsome face, but his "irrepressible spirit." That the thing Caroline Astley had liked had just been... him.

He needed to stop thinking about all of those things, because she would never have him. She hated him, for good reason, and even if she didn't, now she had heard Lord Graverley, the future duke with his hundred thousand a year and his fairy-tale-prince good looks and that stupid stickpin in his cravat with a diamond the size of a quail's egg, declare that she was going to receive *a better offer*. She would never marry the likes of him even if he was still in possession of his family fortune, which he was not.

The odds were so long, there was no point in even dreaming about it. And frankly, the mere thought of confessing his financial predicament to Caro made him break out in hives. He thought of the way she had looked at him when he took her into his arms—with longing.

A terrified, knowing-full-well-this-is-a-mistake sort of longing, to be sure, but longing nonetheless.

Once Caroline Astley looked at a man that way, he could never go back. And so Henry couldn't bear to see derision— or worse, pity—in her eyes as soon as she found out he was *poor*.

"What," Graverley said, interrupting his reverie, "in God's name are you thinking about? I have seen Grimaldi on the stage many times, but I don't believe I've seen him portray half as many emotions over the years as you've gone through in the past two minutes."

Henry cleared his throat. "Yes. Well. We should head downstairs, now, shouldn't we?"

"*We?*" Graverley recoiled as if confronted with a cobra snake.

"Absolutely," Henry said. Graverley already thought he was about two currants short of a Banbury cake. If that was what he had to work with, that was what he would use. He circled round the desk and seized Graverley's arm, hauling him to his feet. "How does the saying go? Keep your friends close and your enemies closer. I'm not letting you out of my sight."

"What the devil is wrong with you—"

"Come on." He slung an arm around the marquess's shoulders. "Let's head downstairs."

Graverley had a truly impressive supercilious glower. "If you would be so kind as to unhand my person."

Henry hauled him out the door. "Ha-ha, Marcus, that's a good one!"

Now the man looked furious. "The only person on the face of this earth whom I permit to address me by my first name is my own sister."

They were halfway down the hall. "Is that so?"

"It is."

They had reached the landing. Henry released Graverley and made a show of patting his coat pockets. "Oh, dear. My snuff box must have fallen out of my pocket. I'd best go back and fetch it. You run along downstairs, and I'll join you momentarily."

Graverley, who had already descended a full story in his haste, did not deign to reply.

HENRY LINGERED at the top of the stairs long enough to make sure the coast was clear before hurrying back to the library.

"He's gone," he said as he burst through the door. "You can come out now."

Caro emerged from beneath the desk, looking immensely relieved. "Thank you for covering for me. I truly appreciate —" She bit her lip, by all appearances trying to suppress a smile.

It was contagious. "What?"

"'How are you enjoying the Season so far?'" she mimicked, and they both burst into laughter.

It took a full minute for them to return to some semblance of calm. Henry offered Caro his handkerchief, which she used to dab at her eyes. "If you could've seen me when you said that. I had to bite my glove to stay silent."

"I had to say something!"

"I don't mean to criticize," she hastened to say. "You were marvelous."

"It took me a few minutes, but I finally hit upon the one thing that will drive any sensible person away: an offer of my companionship."

"It is cruel of you to set me up like that. So many tempting responses come to mind, how am I ever to pick one?"

"Well? Let's hear them all."

She was smiling at him, her real smile, not the glossy expression she used on all the other men. She looked down and then looked back up at him. Her expression was a bit shy and a touch awestruck. It occurred to him that she hadn't looked at him in quite that way since she'd been fifteen years old.

He could definitely get used to Caroline Astley looking at him like that. In fact, he felt a sudden craving to have her look at him in just that way, every day for the rest of his life.

She's not for you, he reminded himself.

"You will hear none of them tonight," she said. "Not after you stuck your neck out like that."

"I made a proper fool of myself."

"Yes. But you did it for me."

They lapsed into silence, the faint sounds of the party below drifting into the room. Caro sighed. "We cannot linger. Someone else might come along. I take it none of the amulets were my sister's?"

125

"No, none were a match. But we have a lead—Lansdowne will be sending my father that address. Once he does, I will go 'round and—"

"*We* will go 'round. Don't even think of going without me."

"Come on, Caro. These people could be dangerous. And they know who you are, because they stole the amulet right off of you. I, at least, have some hope of going unrecognized."

Her shoulders sagged. "I hadn't thought of that. But you must notify me as soon as you receive any sort of news. And you're not to do anything without consulting me."

"I'm not sure that will be possible. Will you not be out of town for the next few days, attending that house party?"

"Gracious, I had quite forgotten about that. Well, I will have to contrive an excuse to get out of it. Nothing is more important right now than recovering my sister's amulet."

"Very well. I'll notify you as soon as I hear something. That much I am willing to promise. Now, let's see." He cracked opened the library door and peered out into the hall. "We're clear," he said, gesturing for her to follow him.

Instead of heading toward the landing, he took her farther down the dark hallway. He had to open two doors, but eventually found the servants' stairs. He dashed down two floors to make sure they were empty, then hurried back up to Caroline. "These will let you out behind the gallery. Can you brazen your way back into the party?"

"I'll manage," she said, her eyes bright. He was already turning to make for the main stairs when he felt her seize his hand.

"Henry," she said. The sound of his name on her lips washed over him like a caress. She pressed his hand, her eyes sincere. "Thank you."

Before he could reply, she released his hand and hurried down the stairs.

CHAPTER 13

*I*t turned out to be easier to get out of attending Mrs. Cadogan's house party than Caro had feared. The following morning, Fanny proved to be a magician with a pot of lip pomade and dabbed a very convincing rash on Caro's hands and feet. A hot washcloth was applied to her brow moments before the physician arrived, creating the illusion of a fever. She complained of a sore throat and a headache, as Fanny had coached her.

Her mother, who had a dread of the sickroom, hovered at the door. "Please do not fret, my lady," the physician reassured her. "Your daughter will be quite uncomfortable for a week or so, but her condition is not dangerous. It is highly contagious, however, and will spread throughout the household."

"Oh, darling," the countess said once the doctor had left, "of all the miserable luck, to come down with this on the day of the house party."

Caro strove to capture the right balance between keen disappointment and being too sick to move. "And Lord

Graverley is to be in attendance," she said, throwing her arm across her eyes in a great show of misery.

A week ago, her anguish would have been sincere. But not today. After all, it wasn't thoughts of Lord Graverley that had kept her up half the night, too happy and excited to sleep.

Lady Cheltenham turned to the footman lingering nearby. "Tell Muriel to unpack my trunk."

"Oh no, Mama, you mustn't." Caro said, making a heroic effort to rise onto one elbow. "Mrs. Cadogan is your cousin. I know how much you've been looking forward to this. And besides, you heard the doctor—this rash is contagious. It would be better for you to get out of the house for a few days so you don't catch it, too."

Her mother frowned. "I don't know, Caro. I hate to leave you here alone."

"I won't be alone. I'll have Fanny and most of the household staff to attend me. And I hardly need a chaperone. I won't be going out for a few days. Not looking like this." She raised her spotted hand ruefully.

It took another five minutes of reassurances, but her mother was eventually persuaded. And so it was that, around midmorning, Lord and Lady Cheltenham departed for the Cadogan estate two hours outside of London, and Caro found herself with the run of the family town house.

CARO KNEW she needed to maintain the pretense of being ill for at least a few days so the household staff wouldn't suspect anything. Truth be told, her social schedule since coming to London had been relentless, and the thought of lounging about for a day or two with a good book was tremendously appealing.

Not that she could settle in with a book. She found that nothing gave her more pleasure than staring off into space, daydreaming about a certain viscount.

She had come to accept that she had been wrong for the past four years. Not that her feelings had been unjustified, but she now understood that it was wrong to base her opinion of Henry solely on the worst mistake he had ever made. There was more to him than those horrible words on the balcony would suggest. She could see that now. It was her first instinct that had been correct, the one that told her they were going to be friends and that no one would have such conversations as the two of them. And then, as soon as she saw him, that they were meant to be together.

She had been right all along. They *were* meant for one another. She was falling for him all over again, with his smart mouth and his wicked smiles. And even more dangerous to her heart, the way he had thrown himself into helping her with her investigation, even at the price of his own dignity.

Yes, she was falling for him all over again. Only this time, he was falling for her, too. She felt certain that he was.

There was a knock at the door and Fanny slipped in, bearing a tea tray. It had been all too easy to convince the rest of the maids that Fanny should wait upon her mistress exclusively, in order to contain Caro's illness as best they could.

"Here you are, m'lady," Fanny said. "It's not much of a supper, but 'twas the best I could convince Cook to fix for someone who's supposed to be convalescing."

Caro inspected the tray. There was tea and broth, bread with butter, and blancmange for dessert. "This will do nicely, Fanny. Thank you."

"Now," her maid said, sitting on the edge of the bed, "I'm going to sneak out to meet with my friend tonight, to see what progress he's made toward tracking down Richard

Cuming. I'll be late. Is there anything I can bring ya now? If ya ring for anything later, everyone will notice I'm out of the house."

"I should be nicely set up for the evening, Fanny. Thank you."

Two hours later, night had fallen over London, and Caro decided to make one final attempt at her book before she went to bed. As she turned to the first page, something tapped against her window. Probably an insect, attracted to the light within. She ignored it.

A minute later, there came another tap, and then a third. This was too much of a coincidence. She climbed out of bed and peered out the window.

In the darkness below, she saw Henry lingering on the outside edges of the glowing circle cast by the carriage lamps on his phaeton. He spotted her at the window, inclined his head for her to come out, then retreated from view.

She threw on a front-lacing morning dress and dark grey pelisse and made a simple coil with her braid. Next came the matter of sneaking out of the house unnoticed. This turned out to be the easiest thing of all. Given her "contagious disease," no one was lingering in the family wing of the house.

Caro slipped into the back garden, then through the side door that led into the street. Henry hurried to her side, the elated smile on his face mirrored by her own.

He grabbed her hand and towed her toward his phaeton. "We'd best get moving before we're spotted. Let's drive around a bit, and I'll tell you my news."

Billy, who was holding the horses, laughed as she climbed up. "Well, well, well, if it isn't the lovely Lady Caroline. I see that someone managed to grovel his way back into your good graces. Dash my wig—this explains a lot."

"Good evening, Billy," Caro replied. "What does it explain?"

"Why his lordship's been in such a good mood all day," Billy replied cheekily.

Henry groaned as he climbed up next to her. "You're not supposed to tell her that, Billy. There's a code amongst men."

Billy winked at her as he headed for his seat at the back of the carriage. "Is that so? Beg pardon, m'lord."

Henry pulled the phaeton's hood up, offering some concealment. He took the reins, and they were off.

"This afternoon," he began, "Lansdowne sent my father the address of the man who sold him those amulets, as promised. It's a Mr. John Brownwood, of Montague Street."

"Montague Street—where is that?"

"Near Bedford Square."

"Bedford Square—why, that sounds positively respectable. And it's not too far from here."

"Less than a mile. I happen to be quite familiar with Bedford Square. Now, we need to formulate our plan. Tomorrow, I'll call upon this Brownwood, and—"

"*We* will call upon Mr. Brownwood."

"Caro, you know we can't do that. These are dangerous men. And they're likely to recognize you, considering they stole the amulet from right around your neck."

"*Mr.* Brownwood didn't steal the amulet. It was a little old lady posing as a flower seller."

"Who without a doubt was in league with Mr. Brownwood and his ilk. It cannot be a coincidence that, out of everyone at the party, you were the only one who was robbed. I'm sure there were other ladies wearing jewels worth as much or more as the amulet. But these people deal in Egyptian antiquities, and that's what they were looking for. Your sister's amulet isn't the only item they've stolen. In addition to the items from the British Museum, one of my father's most valuable pieces was recently stolen—a little cosmetics box, also in the shape of the Eye of Ra."

"Oh, my goodness—do you mean to say that they broke into your town house and stole it?"

Henry frowned. "You know, I'm not sure. My father didn't tell me the details. It's unlikely, though. Not only would it be difficult, but my father has packed the place with antiquities. If they did get in, they would have stolen more than one piece." He shook his head. "I imagine they picked his pocket, the same as they did to you."

"Well, this has answered one of my questions. I was wondering what you were doing at the Leverian Museum the other day. To say nothing of Thomas Hope's Egyptian Room."

"I wondered the same about you. I was up to much the same thing, as it happens—searching for my father's Eye of Ra. But returning to the thieves—they'll recognize you, Caro. That's why I need to meet with Brownwood alone."

Caro allowed herself to mope a bit. He had a point, but she didn't have to like it. "Could we at least drive past the address and have a look?"

He considered a moment. "I suppose so. It's not far, after all."

They drove through Bedford Square, then past the British Museum. "We're looking for number eight," Henry murmured as they pulled onto Montague Street.

As they approached, a door opened, and out stepped a respectably dressed man. Caro seized Henry's forearm. "There," she hissed, "number eight."

Henry slowed the horses as the man locked the door behind him. He began walking down the pavement, straight toward them. As he passed through the circle of light cast by the phaeton's torches, Caro got a look at him.

"'Shortish man, ginger beard,'" she whispered, echoing

Lord Lansdowne's description of the man who had sold him the amulets. "Henry, are you thinking what I'm thinking?"

Clearly he was, because he took the phaeton halfway down the block and turned it around. "We'll follow discreetly at a distance."

They shadowed the man to the far side of Bedford Square, then saw him turn into a narrow alleyway.

"Gresse Street," Henry said, reining in the horses. "This is a rough pocket—"

"Henry!" Caro protested. "We can't let him get away."

"It's too dangerous."

"It won't be. We're just going to drive by and see where he goes."

He shook his head. "As I said, it's a rough street. I have a duty to keep you safe—"

It was time to deploy the cannons. Caro laid her hand upon his arm and gazed up at him, her eyes beseeching. "Please, Henry?"

He looked torn. "We shouldn't—"

She swallowed, remembering what he had said last night, about how much he had wanted to kiss her. About how he had thought about nothing but the way she looked in the moonlight. *Be brave, Caro.* "Please, Henry, won't you do it?" She leaned her head against his shoulder, never breaking eye contact. "For me?"

He stared down at her, looking a bit dazed. "Fine." He gave a rueful laugh as he nudged the horses forward. "You, Caroline Astley, are dangerous."

She nudged him with her elbow. "And don't you forget it."

CHAPTER 14

*C*aro peered around the hood of the phaeton. It was remarkable how much the atmosphere deteriorated once they turned onto Gresse Street. There were no street-lamps here; the only source of light was their carriage lamps and one brightly lit house in the cul-de-sac ahead. Two women who were spilling out of their bodices stood by the front door, calling suggestively to a pair of gentlemen who approached and entered. Caro started, realizing it was a brothel. The other houses were sad and dilapidated, with crumbling bricks and boarded-up windows.

"Do you see him?" Henry whispered.

Caro squinted in the darkness, then squeezed Henry's arm. "There," she said, "by the house on the corner."

Henry drew the horses to a halt. Ahead of them lay the dead end, but an alleyway wrapped around this house, connecting to the main street. They couldn't take it, however, because the narrow lane was blocked by a wagon. Caro squinted into the darkness. The bearded man was speaking to three men who were lifting something large out of the back of the wagon. "Yer late, Brownwood," one of them said. "Now, help us with this bloody statue."

She exchanged a significant look with Henry. So this was the John Brownwood whom Lord Lansdowne had referenced in his note. And he was unloading a *statue*? She watched the four of them stagger with it through a side door leading into the house. It was difficult to see much in the darkness, but the statue looked to be almost as tall as a man, and she got the impression it was carved from some dark stone. It certainly didn't look Greek or Roman.

A few minutes later, a handful of men emerged from the building, including John Brownwood. They all climbed into the wagon save one. "We'll be back in an hour with the rest of it," the man who had admonished Brownwood said, taking a seat next to the driver. "Don't move from that room until we get back, ya hear?"

"Aye," the other man replied, disappearing through the door.

The empty cart rumbled loudly as it rolled over the cobblestones, down the alley and out of sight.

"It sounds as if he's the only one there," Caro whispered.

"It does," Henry agreed.

"How I wish we could—"

She froze at the click of a key turning in a lock. The man who had been ordered to stay in the room slipped out, locked the door behind him, then hurried toward the brightly lit house at the end of the cul-de-sac.

"Back for more, Mr. Hulston?" one of the women called.

"Aye. I've got an hour, and I don't mean to waste it." One of the women patted him on his bottom as he passed through the door and out of sight.

Caro seized Henry's arm. "Henry, this is our chance."

"No."

"But the house is empty, and—"

"No."

"But my sister's amulet is probably in there right now, with nobody watching it. We can slip right in and grab it. Don't you see? This is my chance to fix my mistake. It will be all my fault if my sister is unable to purchase her new building. Hundreds of women and children, living on the streets without a bite to eat, and it will be all my fault. I cannot bear it, Henry, I cannot!" He was staring down at her, sorrowful but unmoved. Something occurred to her. "And don't you think it's likely that your father's little box is in there, too?"

He glanced at number four, his brow knotted with indecision. "There's a lock on the door."

Caro plucked a hairpin from beneath her bonnet and held it out to him. "If only there was someone here with lock-picking skills."

He groaned. "Harrington mentioned that, too, did he?"

"He did."

He sighed but climbed down. "Fine. I will go in. *Alone.* Billy, come sit up here with Lady Caroline. Take the carriage to Bedford Square, and circle around until I—"

"Not a chance." Caro rose, hiking up her skirts and reaching a leg over the side of the phaeton. Her foot found the spoke of a wheel but slipped off, and she wound up clinging to the side of the carriage.

She felt hands reach up and grab her around the waist, lowering her to the ground. "Damn it, Caro," Henry muttered. "Could you at least try not to break your neck?"

"I'm coming with you."

"Yes, I gathered that."

Billy clambered into the driver's seat. "I'll find a safe place to keep watch, m'lord." He flicked the whip and the greys started forward.

Henry and Caro hastened to the side door, where Henry inspected the lock. "It's a double-acting tumbler."

"What does that mean?"

"It's a good lock."

"Excellent. That suggests there's something worth guarding on the other side. Can you pick it?"

He inserted her hairpin into the keyhole. "We're about to find out."

It turned out that Harrington's praise of Henry's ill-gotten skills had been well-deserved, for the lock yielded in less than a minute. Inside it was pitch-black, other than a faint glow coming from beneath a door on the far side of the room.

"Wait here," Henry whispered.

He slipped through the door, then returned seconds later. "Come on," he said, gesturing for her to be quick about it.

Caro drew in a breath and prepared to enter the thieves' lair.

IT APPEARED to be an ordinary storeroom. The floor was bare boards, the windows were boarded up, and crates were stacked all around the room. Everything was drab and unadorned.

Excepting the gleaming sarcophagus in the center of the room.

Caro wandered over, awestruck. It was a huge, imposing rectangle. It was made of wood, but to describe it as "wooden" would be a travesty. Even after thousands of years of being buried in a dusty tomb, the painted figures that covered the coffin were bright against the glossy golden wood in tones of ochre, midnight blue, and an otherworldly, glowing turquoise. Caro had no idea what the figures represented, but there was a solemn procession of strange gods, similar to the ones from Mr. Hope's drawing room.

Across the lid, a goddess spread her wings above a trio of jackal-headed gods performing rituals on a mummy. There was hardly an inch of wood that was not adorned with something—a crocodile-headed goddess, a border of scarab beetles, and row upon row of those characters no living man could read.

Henry stood beside her. "It's beautiful," she said.

"It is, isn't it? My father would kill to own this. But we haven't much time." He glanced at his pocket watch. "Let's allow ourselves no more than half an hour, in case the thieves return earlier than expected."

Together they began checking the crates. Egyptian antiquities weren't the only items the thieves were in the business of smuggling. Most of their loot was of a more conventional sort—casks of French wine, crates of tea, and what was particularly tempting for Caro, a box full of India cashmere shawls as soft as a newborn kitten.

They did find a few Egyptian artifacts, including the statue they had seen the men unloading from the wagon. It turned out to be a beautiful black stone statue of the winged goddess from the lid of the sarcophagus. There were jars with animal heads for lids that Henry said were used to hold human organs removed during the mummification process —information which caused Caro to snatch her hands away and recoil from the crate.

Henry laughed, carefully rearranging the jars inside their bed of straw. "Steady on there, Caro. There's a dearth of fainting couches in here."

They even found some amulets, including a gorgeously bejeweled scarab beetle, but not Anne's Eye of Ra. "You haven't seen your father's little box?" Caro asked.

Henry shook his head. "No sign of it." He consulted his pocket watch. "Bloody hell—it's been fifty minutes. We've got to get out of here—"

"There's just one more crate to check. Come and help me with the lid."

"Hang the last crate. We've got to go—"

"We'll be quick about it."

A vein popped out on Henry's forehead. "Caro. We're leaving."

"This would only take one minute if you would—"

From the side room through which they had entered, there came the scrape of metal on metal. The sound was soft but unmistakable.

A key, clanging against the lock as someone in the alley struggled to find the keyhole in the darkness.

Henry grabbed Caro's hand. "Out the front door," he hissed. They hurried across the room, but the door that was the room's only other exit proved to be locked.

Caro struggled to find a hairpin with trembling hands. "You've got to pick it—"

There came the ominous sound of the key turning in the lock. "There's no time," Henry hissed, scanning the room for a place to hide.

"Hulston!" a male voice shouted from the side room. "Come and help us with this load."

Oh-God-oh-God-oh-God, they were going to be discovered, because Caro couldn't see any place to hide. The crates were all stacked flush against the wall, and most of them were too heavy to move even if they had the time to shuffle them around, which they didn't, and—

"Over here." Henry seized Caro's hand and pulled her toward the center of the room.

"Over here?" Caro glanced around, but there wasn't any cover. "There's no place to hide over here."

His eyes were intense. "There's only one place we can hide in this whole entire room. Inside the sarcophagus."

CHAPTER 15

*H*er mouth fell open. "You cannot mean it."

He was already pushing the wooden lid to the side. "It's our only option."

"But—but—but—what if there's a mummy inside?" she asked, panicked.

He had the lid askew, with just enough of a gap for a person to squeeze through. "Then we're going to have one hell of a story."

She had to do it. She knew that, of course she did. But oh! How she wished she didn't. It was pitch-black in that box, and God only knew what was inside, and—

"Hulston!" an impatient voice shouted from outside. "Get yer arse out here!"

She swallowed. She was going to have to manage. She accepted Henry's proffered hand and sat down on the lip of the wooden box, then swung her feet inside. Trying to tamp down the panic rising in her chest, she closed her eyes and slid down into the coffin.

Henry was right behind her, his chest pressing against hers as they squeezed into the narrow casket. He reached up and shifted the lid back into place, and in an instant they were draped in darkness.

Really, being trapped inside a thousand-year-old sarcophagus was not nearly as horrible as everyone said it was. She would have expected it to be mustier, for one thing. It was narrow enough that she was pressed up against Henry from knees to neck, but at least it was long enough to accommodate them. And truth be told, there were worse fates than lying chest to chest with Henry Greville. She felt her heartbeat kick up a notch, and not only because the thieves were at the door.

She was also immensely relieved to find she wasn't lying on top of a mummy. Although there was something in here, some sort of rough cloth lying beneath them. Oh, God, what if it was some sort of mummy wrapping? Just because there wasn't a whole mummy in here, it didn't mean that there weren't... mummy parts.

And that was when she felt it—something hard, poking her right in the stomach. Goodness, how had she not noticed it right away? It was huge! She reached down to push it aside. The mummy shroud had bunched up between her body and Henry's, but she could feel whatever the thing was through the rough cloth. It was long, and it was hard, and she couldn't disentangle it.

"Henry!" she hissed.

"Yes?" His whisper was oddly strangled.

"There's something in here with us. It's not a whole mummy, but—I think it might be a thigh bone. Although"—she paused, feeling around—"it seems too thick for that. In any case, it's long and hard, and it's all tangled up in this cloth. I can't seem to free it. Can you—"

Her wrist was suddenly seized in an iron grip. "That is *not* a thigh bone," he hissed. "And I need for you to stop stroking it. *Immediately.*"

Comprehension dawned. "Oh. My. *Gracious!*"

"You have no idea," he muttered.

For some reason, the thought that she had been stroking his—his *wedding tackle*, sent her into a full-blown panic. "Henry, I—I—I'm sorry, I didn't mean to—"

"Shh, it's all right, Caro."

"I didn't realize that was your—your—"

"I know, darling. We've got to be quiet now."

"Yes! Quiet!" She knew he was right, but her mouth was running of its own accord. "Yes, of course we do. Quiet. I can be quiet. I can. I really, really—"

She felt rather than saw him move, as his hand groped in the darkness until it settled upon her cheek, and then his lips covered hers. For precisely seventeen beats of her frantically racing heart, she lay there, frozen with shock. Then a great shudder rippled through her body, and she arched against him. Her mouth fell open on a moan, and she felt his tongue gently trace the inside of her lips.

She had never been kissed before. She had no idea what she was doing. But feeling his tongue caress her lips, it was as if something broke inside of her. She might have known nothing about kisses, but she recognized pleasure well enough, and that was exactly what Henry was giving her. Although they were trapped against each other by the walls of the sarcophagus, her hands tugged at his coat, desperate to somehow pull him even closer. One of her slippered feet wrapped itself around his leg and began sliding up, longing for even more contact between her body and his.

Her tongue reached out tentatively, exploring the contours of his lips, and she was rewarded when he opened for her with a sound of approval. For twenty-three breath-less heartbeats, their tongues danced gingerly together. Then it was his turn to groan, and he took charge, his hand sliding into her hair to position her the way he wanted, his tongue sweeping through her mouth, his lips devouring hers.

Yes, this was what she wanted, his mouth possessive on hers. Her entire body was shaking. And why not—had she not been waiting for this moment, the moment when Henry Greville would finally kiss her, for years? One of his arms was cradling her head, but the other was working its way up her hip, across her waist, before settling on the side of her breast. An unimaginable liberty, one she wouldn't have permitted five minutes ago. But now her body gave a resounding *yes* to the question of whether or not she wanted Henry Greville's hand there, and she heard herself crying out as he worked his thumb into the tight space between their bodies in order to rub her nipple.

She pressed herself into his hand, squirming against him, wanting him to do it again, when the sound of a door banging open jolted her back into the present.

They were inside a *sarcophagus*. Surrounded by criminals.

They couldn't make a sound.

Henry gave her a silent squeeze, recalling himself in the same instant. She nodded into his neck.

Caro could hear the thieves' conversation through the walls of the sarcophagus.

"—a goddamn bloody fool, Hulston."

"Shut yer trap, Snakeface," a second voice grumbled. "It's all here. See?"

"And you're lucky that's the case, else I'd skin you alive. This room is to be guarded. One of us needs to be here, awake and alert, every minute of every day, until we've sold the last piece. That don't involve you running out to the nugging house as soon as my back's turned."

A new voice called out from the side room. "Will you two quit your yarping? It's going to take all of us to move this bloody pillar."

"Obelisk," someone said. "The term is *obelisk*."

"Do you think I give a fuck?"

The voices retreated. Caro found that her body was trembling anew, but this time it wasn't the good sort of trembling. She heard the thief's words in her mind, over and over.

The room was to be guarded. Every minute of every day.

"Henry," she whispered, "how are we going to get out?"

BESIDE HER, Henry had been thinking the same thing. If the thieves were going to guard their haul around the clock...

They were in deep, deep trouble.

There was the sound of heavy footsteps and a few scattered grunts.

"Watch the doorframe, Wallace!"

"Christ, that's heavy."

"Let's set it down here."

"In the corner, you lazy piece of shyte!"

"What's wrong with here?"

"We'll never get the statues in if we block the door, idiot."

There were a few more grunts followed by a loud thump.

"I don't see why we bothered with these big pieces," someone grumbled. "We can barely find buyers for the little stuff. Everyone wants to know whose collection it's from so they know it's not stolen. Who're we going to convince to buy all this rot?" The speaker punctuated this statement by kicking the corner of the sarcophagus in which they hid. Henry felt Caro's hands dig into his shirt, and he gave her a reassuring squeeze.

"I happen to have some news about that as of today," said a more refined voice, the same man who had insisted that the *pillar* was an *obelisk*. "I've lined up a gentleman collector to act as our liaison."

"What in seven hells is a liaison?"

"A go-between, you dolt. He'll meet with the buyers and present everything as items from his own collection."

"Well, that's a relief. At least I didn't break me back carrying that great fucking hunk of rock for nothing."

"So, if you find any potential buyers, direct them to our liaison. He's going to be waiting to transact business every Friday between two and three o'clock at the British Museum, in the same gallery as the Rosetta Stone. Tell them to look for the man wearing a lotus flower on his lapel."

"Strong work, Brownwood," the one called Snakeface said. "Now, there's three more crates and the big statues. Wallace, you—"

Out in the alleyway, a horse whinnied in fright. Henry heard the pounding of hooves and the clatter of a cart racing over cobblestones at full speed.

"What in bloody hell—" Snakeface shouted. There was a stampede of footsteps as the thieves ran for the door.

The room had fallen completely silent. They wouldn't get a better chance than this. "Hurry," Henry said, shoving the lid of the coffin askew.

He climbed out, then hauled Caro to her feet. They hurried through the side door.

Henry peered out into the alleyway. Something must have spooked the horses pulling the thieves' wagon, because they had taken off at a gallop. He could see at least five men sprinting down the alleyway. Henry seized Caro's hand and towed her in the opposite direction.

They made their way back to the main thoroughfare. "Act as if nothing is amiss," Henry whispered. Caro nodded, brushing some dust from his shoulder.

It had begun raining, lightly but steadily. After emerging from the alleyway, the horses had made a sharp right and were almost out of sight. Four men were giving chase, but they were nowhere close to catching them.

Two more men were running the other way, passing in front of Caro and Henry but on the opposite side of the street. "Come back here, you little shit!" one of them yelled. That was when Henry noticed the boy he was chasing. As the boy passed beneath a streetlamp, he turned his head to see how close his pursuers were.

Billy. Their escape had been no fortunate happenstance; his intrepid tiger had snuck up and spooked the thieves' horses, giving them their chance.

And now the thieves were after him.

He saw Billy make a sharp right turn and disappear around a corner. Henry relaxed a touch, because he knew where Billy was heading.

One more turn and Billy would be inside a mews, where horses were stabled within the city. He was likely to receive shelter there.

It was where he lived and worked, after all.

"Come on," Henry whispered, leading Caro across the street toward Bedford Square.

"What about Billy? We've got to help him."

"We will. I have a plan." The rain was picking up, and they broke into a jog.

"Henry, wait." She pulled him into a doorway. It didn't offer much shelter from the steadily increasing rain, but it was better than nothing. "What are we going to do?"

"*We* are not going to do anything. *I* am going to circle back around and make sure he made his escape."

She swallowed. "All right. I'll wait right here."

"The hell you will. Do you truly believe I would leave you in the middle of Bedford Square, *alone*, at midnight?"

"What's the alternative?"

Henry paused. "Do you trust me?"

She didn't say anything right away, and Henry found himself holding his breath. Her answer mattered to him. He was startled to realize the degree to which it did.

When she spoke, it sounded as if her response surprised even her. "You know, I think I do."

He exhaled, taking her hand. "Then come with me."

They ran through what was now a pounding rain. It soaked through his coat in an instant, but they didn't have far to go.

He led her to a town house of dark brick on the far side of the square. He pulled a key from his pocket and struggled to open the door in the driving rain.

"Henry? Where are we?"

The door gave way. This was the moment of truth, because although she had said she trusted him, she hadn't understood where he was taking her.

Henry turned to face her. "I keep a separate apartment in town. It's in here. Would you… would you like to wait inside? To get out of the rain?"

Her mouth fell open in a perfect little circle. It appeared that, for once, Caroline Astley was at a loss for words.

CHAPTER 16

*H*er command of the English language had abandoned her.

Had she hit her head as she climbed out of the sarcophagus? Because this had to be some sort of concussive dream.

At least she knew what to say just as soon as she regained her ability to speak. Because the question of whether or not she wanted to be alone with *Henry Greville* in his bachelor apartments did not require two seconds' thought.

She closed her mouth, which had been gaping open like a fish. "All right," she said, her voice emerging in a bit of a squeak.

Henry led her up a flight of stairs, then took out a key to unlock a door at the top of the first-floor landing. "There's no one home right now," he explained. "It's my valet's night off. Gibson is part of a singing club that meets Thursday nights at a local tavern. He won't be home for hours."

As she crossed the threshold, Caro peered around, unbearably curious. The room was... disappointingly ordinary, truth be told. It was decorated to a masculine taste, to be sure, with dark hardwood furnishings and midnight-blue upholstery. But instead of the den of iniquity she had imagined, it could have been the front room of any curate in England.

Henry knelt before the fireplace, filled the grate with coals, and lit them. "Billy lives in a room over the mews across the square, where I keep my horses. That was where he was headed. I imagine he found a place to hide, but I've got to make sure."

He rose to face her, then froze, his brow furrowed. "Come with me," he said after a moment's hesitation. He led her through a doorway, and her eyes went wide as saucers, because now she was in Henry Greville's *bedroom*. She didn't need a mirror to know she was blushing.

He cleared his throat as he opened a doorway that revealed a small dressing room. "You'll need something dry to change into. Help yourself to anything that looks promising." He ran a hand through his hair, scattering a few drops of rain around the tiny space. "Right, I'll be back in a trice."

And then she found herself alone. She glanced around. There were more dark wood furnishings, and the hangings and bedspread were a deep pine green. The latest issue of *The Sporting Magazine* had been tossed on the nightstand. She wandered over to snoop through his washstand. Oh—he used the same brand of tooth powder that she did. She found the bottle that contained his shaving tonic and inhaled deeply, detecting hints of cinnamon and oranges. Suddenly a picture sprang into her mind of a freshly shaven Henry standing shirtless before the long, oval mirror before her, splashing the tonic on his face. Her imaginary Henry tossed his head slowly from side to side as droplets fell upon his immaculately sculpted chest, and she felt her heartbeat ratchet up a notch.

She entered his dressing room. There, hanging next to his great coat, was his dressing gown. She gingerly reached out a hand to touch the sleeve. It was of midnight-blue satin and lined in the softest velvet she had ever touched.

Now Caro was picturing Henry climbing out of bed and slipping this gorgeous, plush, begging-to-be-stroked dressing gown over his naked body. (Why she had decided that he must sleep naked, she couldn't say, but she was panting picturing it, so she wasn't about to throw her imaginary Henry a nightshirt.)

And that was when Caro made a decision. Her hands shook so hard it was difficult to untie her laces, but she peeled off all of her wet clothes.

And she reached for that dressing gown.

HENRY KNOCKED and then waited to the count of ten before opening his own door. He wondered what he would find inside. The first thing he noticed was Caro's dress, hanging over a chair drawn close to the fire.

The next thing he noticed was her chemise and corset hanging right next to it.

He stumbled to a halt in the middle of his sitting room. If Caro wasn't wearing any of those things, it begged the question of what she *was* wearing. His mind produced several dozen fascinating possibilities.

Her head popped up over the back of the sofa that stood before the fire, and he saw that what she was wearing was his dressing gown.

Seeing Caro wearing something of his, particularly such an intimate garment, roused something primal inside of him. *Mine* was the word that sprang to mind. It was so easy to picture a thousand nights like this, nights when he would find her waiting for him in his room, clad only in his dressing gown. Her face would light up when he entered the room, he would unwrap her, and then they would pass the evening in the most enjoyable way possible.

God, he wanted that future so much he ached with it. And here it was, arrayed before him.

Except… her smile was missing. Caro wore a look of consternation. She was saying something. He made an effort to attend.

"Billy—oh, yes," he said as comprehension dawned. "He's fine. He darted into a stall, and the other grooms covered for him. He's safe in his room even as we speak."

Caro pressed a hand to her heart. "Thank God."

"Indeed." Henry realized he was dripping rainwater on the carpet. "Excuse me."

He spent the three minutes it took him to get out of his wet clothes debating the wisdom of going to sit next to Caro on his sofa. She was an innocent. She probably had no idea what an erotic picture she presented, sitting in front of a roaring fire with her golden hair tumbling down her back, wearing nothing but his satin-and-velvet dressing gown. It wasn't as if she was trying to seduce him. But given how desirable she looked, there was no possibility he could go back out there and have a single thought in his head that wasn't about seducing her.

No, what he needed to do was put on a full set of clothes and stay in his room until the rain let up, at which time he could escort her home.

Yes, that was exactly what he was going to do. He was going to stay far, far away from Caroline Astley.

No matter how much he longed to join her on the sofa.

Christ, he wanted to join her on the sofa.

No! He was a gentleman, damn it. He was going to stay

right here. He was not going back in there until the rain let up.

Of course he wasn't.

EXACTLY ONE MINUTE after telling himself these things, Henry found himself emerging from his bedroom clad only in a loose pair of trousers and a shirt open at the neck. Caro smiled and patted the sofa cushion beside her. "Sit here. It's nice and warm by the fire. I made us some tea."

She twisted to retrieve the teapot from the end table. This had the effect of causing his dressing gown to fall halfway open. God, her legs were gorgeous—he got a glimpse of slender ankles and finely sculpted calves and a tantalizing hint of her thighs.

He also ascertained that, by all appearances, she was naked beneath his dressing gown.

Holy mother of Christ.

She turned back, and her fingers brushed his as she handed him a teacup.

He took a sip, then smiled. "You know how I take my tea."

"I had occasion to prepare your cup exactly once during your visit four years ago, and I promptly committed it to memory." She looked down, her cheeks flushed. "You probably don't remember."

"I don't. I wish I did, though. I wish—" He gave a rueful laugh. "I wish I'd done a number of things differently that week."

"It's all right," she said, looking up at him. They were three simple words, but Henry felt something shift inside of him, because he could tell that she meant them. By some miracle, he'd been forgiven.

"There's something I've always wondered," he said. "If you had told Harrington what I said, you could have enjoyed my head on a platter for breakfast the next day. But you didn't say anything then, and I feel quite certain you never did. Why not?"

She sighed. "Believe me, it wasn't for your sake. It was entirely for Harrington's. Because I knew your friendship made him truly happy. And although I want to strangle him at least three times a week, I love my brother, and I want him to be happy."

"It was downright sporting of you. I remember being in a panic, knowing I was about to lose him as a friend. So even though it wasn't for my sake, I'm still grateful. After all, I need someone to have madcap misadventures with."

"I grew up on your exploits with Harrington. All the while I managed to go the first nineteen years of my life without having anything resembling a proper adventure. But here I am—your new partner in crime." She laughed. "I wouldn't have thought anything could top hiding from Lord Graverley underneath that desk. Little did I know that the very next night, I would be hiding from someone named Snakeface, inside a sarcophagus."

He reached out, tucking a curl behind her ear. "I've had some wild times with your brother over the years but nothing quite like tonight."

She seemed pleased. "No?"

"No. It will come as a shock, but I've never kissed your brother inside a sarcophagus."

She laughed, taking his teacup and placing it on the end table. She looked up at him, smiling and blushing at the same time. "That was my first kiss."

Her confession spurred a feeling of unbearable tenderness in his chest. "Was it?"

"It was. It's just that—" She gestured with her hands,

trying to make him understand. "I'm not the kind of girl who has her first kiss inside a sarcophagus."

He arched an eyebrow. "There's a kind of girl who has her first kiss inside a sarcophagus?"

And then she was laughing, and then he was laughing, and then she looped her arms around his neck, and when her lips rose to meet his, they were still curved in the shape of her smile.

There was no greater pleasure that Henry had experienced in the entirety of his twenty-five years than kissing Caroline Astley. Everything about her was pretty, and her skin felt like rose petals. Even after lying in a musty coffin and getting rained upon, she somehow smelled of honeysuckle, and her mouth was indescribably soft and sweet beneath his.

But there was something about her kiss that moved him, beyond what even the sum of her appealing parts could explain. He wasn't just kissing a beautiful girl who smelled of honeysuckle; he was kissing *Caroline*. He was well versed in the ways of lust, but this…

This was something different. Oh, but she was dangerous. He might have been a blockheaded man who thought with his cock rather than his head for twenty-three hours out of the day, but he wasn't such a fool as to tell himself she was like every other girl he'd ever wanted to bed. Caroline Astley was special.

For someone who'd just had her first kiss an hour ago, she was certainly an eager participant. She had little idea what she was doing, but her enthusiasm more than compensated for any lack of technique. She opened to him immediately and was gamely trying to kiss him back, her tongue tangling sweetly with his.

Deep down, he knew this was a terrible idea. His cock had stirred to life as soon as it warmed above freezing. It was now screaming at him to rip open that dressing gown and do something to relieve its desperate ache.

He was trying to convince himself to break off the kiss when Caro surprised him again, sinking back upon the sofa and tugging him down on top of her. Her legs had instinctively fallen open, cradling his straining erection exactly where he wanted it, right against her sex. They were separated only by a few layers of fabric, tempting him beyond reason. He knew that this way lay madness, but he couldn't bring himself to stop kissing her.

She slid her hands underneath his shirt, shyly stroking his back. He jerked in a combination of shock and arousal, unintentionally thrusting against her.

She cried out in what sounded very much like pleasure and spread her legs wider, rocking against him.

Groaning, he broke off the kiss and buried his face in the pillow next to her head.

"Henry?" she asked. "Is… is anything wrong?"

He rose up on one elbow and stroked her forehead. "Everything is right, darling, and that's precisely the problem."

Gorgeous blue eyes blinked at him in confusion. "I… I don't follow."

He rose to a seated position, drawing her up beside him, and stared into the fire. "I'm at the very limit of my control. I need to stop kissing you before I peel that dressing gown off of you and do fourteen different things you'll regret tomorrow."

He was losing his mind. Losing his goddamned fucking mind, having Caroline Astley lying beneath him in nothing but his velvet dressing gown, rubbing herself against his cock, and crying out in pleasure. How could a man be expected to think straight when all of the blood had rushed away from his head, straight down to his groin?

Because he wasn't thinking straight, not even close. That was the only explanation for what he thought he heard her say next.

He had to be dreaming. It was impossible.

Because what he thought he heard her say was, "I wouldn't regret them."

CHAPTER 17

Caroline blushed. It was more difficult than she had expected, trying to seduce a man. She had tried wearing nothing but his dressing gown. She had tried kissing him. She had even tried pulling him down on top of her. Somehow her message was not getting through.

Still, when she had announced that she wouldn't regret allowing him some… liberties, she had expected him to grin wickedly. To look excited. Lustful, perhaps.

Instead he just looked… stupefied. She suddenly recalled an afternoon many summers ago, when Harrington had taken a cricket bat upside the head. He had staggered around, befuddled, for a good three days.

That was precisely how Henry was looking at her right now.

God, but this was lowering.

"That is," she stammered into the awkward silence, "I can't get pregnant, of course. And… I'm not sure that I'm ready to lose my, my maidenhead. But… we're not likely to get many chances like this. To be alone together. And, and… aren't there some other, um, things? That we can do?"

She'd made her decision standing there in his dressing room. She wasn't prepared to give him everything. Not until he proposed, in any case. But she felt quite certain that a proposal would be forthcoming.

They were falling in love. She just knew that they were. She was halfway in love with him already, and she was sure that this time, he was falling for her, too. They weren't likely to get a better chance than this until they were man and wife, which could be months away. And it wouldn't hurt anything at all to allow a few liberties to her future husband.

Especially when her own body wanted those liberties so fiercely it left her breathless.

Henry stared at her, agog, for what felt like an eternity. "Let me be clear," he finally said. "What you are suggesting is that we will both take off all of our clothes, and then I will do"—he paused, staring at the ceiling in concentration —"eleven out of the fourteen things I have in mind, and you will not regret a single one of them?"

"Um. Yes?"

His exhale was like a benediction, and there it was—the grin she had been hoping for. It was wicked and excited and lustful, all at the same time.

Finally.

He stood, and she rose with him. "Er… shall we go to the bedroom, then?" she asked.

"No." He wandered to the far corner of the room. What was he *doing*?

He turned, a pillow in his hand. "We're going to stay right here." He proceeded to gather up cushions from all around the room, which he used to create a little pile on the carpet in front of the fire. "Perfect," he said. He took her in his arms and gently lowered her down so she was reclining against them. She felt like Cleopatra, resplendent in her repose.

He lay beside her, stroking her body through the robe.

Oh, that felt *delicious*, the feel of the soft, luxurious velvet caressing her skin.

He kissed her temple. "Do you have any idea what we're about to do?"

"Some idea," she confessed. "When I was twelve, I bribed two of the housemaids into giving me a very, um, detailed description. Of the act. And of, you know, some other acts."

The "other acts" the maids had described involved putting one's mouth on one's beloved's intimate parts, the mere thought of which had horrified her at age twelve. Now, at the age of nineteen, she was more terrified than horrified.

But if she was being honest, she was also… intrigued.

"Have you ever touched yourself?" he murmured huskily in her ear, all the while stroking her with his slow, wicked hands.

"No," she whispered.

"Then you've never climaxed." He buried his head in her neck. "God, I'm going to make this so good for you, Caro—"

"I didn't say that!" she blurted out.

He looked up, frozen. "But if you have no experience, and you've never touched yourself, then… how?"

"I had this—this dream," she stammered.

His eyes were molten. "Go on."

"It woke me up in the middle of the night, and I was, I was…"

"Yes?"

She swallowed. "I was coming. I know I was. It was exactly the way the maids said it would be. My legs were trembling, and my, my passage was squeezing over and over and over again, and it felt… it felt…"

His voice in her ear was like black licorice, dark and spicy and sweet all at once. "How did it feel, darling?"

"It felt"—she squeezed her eyes shut—"*so* good."

He gave a raspy exhale, and his hands began teasing her

breasts through the layers of his dressing gown. His caresses made the velvet rub against her nipples, which felt… gorgeous. She allowed her head to loll back.

"When was this?" he asked.

Oh, God, he would ask that, wouldn't he? "It was when—" She swallowed, drawing up her courage. "It was when I was fifteen years old."

He froze. "Fifteen years old," he said slowly. "What was your dream about?"

And there it was—the other question she didn't want to answer. She turned her head toward the fire. "Why do you ask?"

He eased her face back to him. "Because I have a feeling this will be ever so much better for both of us if you tell me."

"It was about you, Henry," she confessed.

"Oh. My. *God,*" he moaned. "What did I do in your dream, darling?"

"Well, usually you would—"

"*Usually?* Do you mean to tell me this happened more than once?"

Good Lord, her cheeks were aflame, and it had nothing to do with their proximity to the fire. "A few times that week. Perhaps a dozen times total, over the years."

His face fell. "I take it some other fortunate fellow took my place, after I said my piece on the balcony."

"No, it was always you." She shook her head. "You can't imagine how confused I was, the first time it happened after… well, you know. I didn't *want* to want you. It was as if my own body had betrayed me. Eventually I had no choice but to accept it. You have this strange effect on me. Nobody else has ever made me feel that way."

He was smiling at her so tenderly, looking so pleased by her confession that she began to relax a fraction. He rose to kneel over her. "I have good news for you, Caro."

"What's that?"

He grinned wickedly as he unfastened the tie at her waist. "I'm about to make all your wildest dreams come true."

He opened the dressing gown and froze, staring down at her. Her instinct was to close her eyes, but she forced herself to keep them open. As vulnerable as she felt, she didn't want to miss even a second of her first time with Henry. It was terrifying lying exposed before him, but then she saw his expression crystalize into a mix of longing and naked desire.

This was the way she had always dreamed Henry Greville would look at her. There was nothing to be embarrassed about. This was *right*. She was meant to be with this man, and this was going to be the best night of her whole entire life.

When he spoke, his voice held a touch of awe. "God, Caro, I never even imagined—" He swallowed. "You're so beautiful."

He helped her slide her arms out of the dressing gown's sleeves, spreading it out so that it made a velvet bed for her to lie upon. She arched her back, luxuriating in the feeling of the soft fabric beneath her and the warmth of the fire on her bare skin.

Henry stared at her, rapt. "Do that again," he growled, and she laughed as she complied.

"Sweet Jesus," he groaned. "You said you'd never touched yourself before. I don't suppose you want to start tonight?"

"It happens that I do not. I'm more interested in your promise to make all of my dreams come true."

He made to lie down next to her. "I am a man of my word."

She halted his descent with a hand to his chest. She could feel her cheeks burning, but she forced herself to say, "Then you need to take off your shirt."

He immediately divested himself of the offending

garment. Caro felt her jaw drop, and she knew she was gaping at him. She simply could not be bothered to care.

She had seen a boy without a shirt before—her older brothers and the neighborhood boys such as Michael Cranfield, swimming on a hot summer afternoon. The sight of twelve-year-old Michael Cranfield swimming shirtless had been... uninspiring, to say the least. This man, on the other hand, was a work of art. Everything that had been promised by the way he looked in his clothes was true, a hundred times over. His shoulders were broad, his waist trim. His stomach was covered by these fascinating little circles of muscle that disappeared beneath the waistband of his trousers, along with a trail of hair that started below his navel. He had a light dusting of hair over his chest, but not so very much.

His expression as he watched her watching him was one of pure masculine satisfaction. "I take it I pass muster?"

Her voice was raspy as she replied, "Yes."

He joined her on the velvet bed of cushions. "As good as your dreams?"

"Even better. I—" She paused mid-sentence. "My God, Henry. Is that your *stomach*?" Her hands had reached out to touch him of their own accord.

"Of course it is. Why do you ask?"

"It's as hard as the table." She ran her hands over him in awe.

"It's not the only part of me that's hard. I have it on good authority that I also have something long and hard, and—"

"You're awful. I can't believe I didn't realize that was your... your..."

"You're welcome to stroke it again, by the by. But first..."

And then his lips found hers, and he started touching her. She could tell he was trying to go slowly, kissing her gently, stroking her shoulders. But she was already unbearably aroused and demanded more from him from the very first kiss. Her hands were everywhere—running over his beauti-fully sculpted shoulders, tracing zigzags across his chest and down his stomach, reaching around that gorgeous, sculpted torso to pull his body to hers.

The moment her body came flush against his, all of that contact between his warm, satiny skin and hers felt so good that she broke off their kiss, crying out in pleasure. This was exactly like one of her dreams, only a thousand times more potent. A pounding pulse, almost like a second heart-beat, had sprung up between her thighs. She squirmed against him desperately, then reached around his back, needing more contact, trying to pull him down on top of her.

She mewled in protest when he didn't comply. "Caro, darling, I'm trying to go slowly. To make it good for you."

"It is good for me, Henry. It's very good. I need more. I need so much more." She was squirming against him, his warm, smooth skin caressing her front side, the cool, liquid velvet caressing her back. "I'm already so close. I want to come, Henry. I *need* to. Please, won't you help me?"

Seeing how far gone she was, he hastened to acquiesce. He rose to kneeling and drew her up so that she was kneeling in front of him, her back to his front. He spread her knees wide. She could feel his cock pressing hard and insis-tent into the small of her back through the fabric of his trousers. His voice was dark as midnight in her ear and drip-ping with sex. "Do you know how to make yourself come, Caro?"

"No. It would just… happen."

He caressed her breasts, and she groaned. Oh, *God*, that felt good…

"I'm going to show you," Henry murmured. "Do you know what men call a woman's sex?" She shook her head. One of his hands was slowly moving down her stomach, not nearly as fast as she needed it. "They call it her pussy. Would you like to know how it got that name?"

"How?" she breathed, pressing herself into his warm, clever hands.

"Because pussycats like to be pet. They arch their backs with pleasure, press themselves into your hands, begging to be stroked and stroked and stroked. And your pussy likes to be pet, too, Caro. It is begging for someone to pet you there right now. And since you've been such a good girl tonight, I'm going to do it. I'm going to show you a magic spot between your legs, and I'm going to give you a little rub. Let's see how you like it."

His hand slid between her legs then and went straight to the place that was throbbing like a heartbeat. And then he started to give her the gentlest, most teasing rub. Oh, sweet Lord, that felt good. Oh, God, she needed more, she needed more, she needed—

"You're so wet, Caro. I love that you're wet for me. What a good, good girl you are, to be so very wet just for me. I'm going to have to reward you." But he kept his hand maddeningly slow.

"Henry!" she cried. "Oh, God, I'm so close. I want to come. Please, I want to come, I—"

"Is this what you need, darling?" he asked, increasing the pace of his fingers the tiniest fraction.

But Caro couldn't answer, because suddenly she was right on the edge, she was right on the edge, and if he would just give her a little bit more, she would... she would...

Like a miracle, he understood her wordless plea, and he rubbed his fingers all light and quick and *delicious* right over that little pearl between her legs, and she found herself babbling out loud. "Oh, *God,* Henry, that feels so good, that feels *so good*, and please don't stop, please stay right there and please never, ever, ever stop, and—oh. Oh. Oh! Oh, my *God*! Henry! Yes! Yes! *Yes*!"

As she cried out, she exploded in his arms, her legs trembling wildly, her opening throbbing with a pleasure more exquisite than anything she could have ever imagined. She was out of her mind, her back arching, her head rolling to the side in ecstasy as she came and came and came and *came*. All the while he held her up, pressing her against his warm, smooth chest, somehow knowing to slow his strokes when the gorgeous sensations became too much to bear.

He laid her down upon the velvet dressing gown and came to rest beside her, cradling her head against his shoulder. She was spent, boneless, replete. He, on the other hand, was tense, every muscle flexed. She squirmed against him, loving the feeling of his skin against hers.

He groaned as if in agony and rolled on his back, loosening the falls of his trousers. "I'm sorry, Caro," he said brokenly. "I had meant to go slowly. But watching you come, I—I can't wait."

"Oh!" It felt supremely gratifying, to know that she hadn't been the only one unbearably aroused. "Can—can I help?"

He rose to kneeling above her, shoving his trousers down a few inches. He fumbled with unsteady hands to pull out his member. She felt her eyes widen. As she had predicted in the sarcophagus, it was indeed hard, and it was larger than she had imagined. Not that they were going to do it tonight, but how on earth was he going to fit—

"I want to look at you," Henry said. "Can you squirm around? The way you did earlier?"

She was all too happy to comply, and he groaned. He was pumping himself rapidly with his hand. "Oh, *fuck*, Caro, that's good. Touch your breasts for me, darling."

She could see how much Henry was stirred by the sight of her. He couldn't tear his eyes away. She found that she loved the way he was looking at her. It made her want to circle her fingers faster over her nipples.

Truth be told, it made her want to move her hands down, to caress the little spot he had shown her between her legs.

His hand slowed. "Would you..." He swallowed. "Would you mind if I spent myself on your chest?"

Caro's mouth fell open at the suggestion, but her reaction was only surprise, not disapproval. She could see by his expression how much he desired it. "All right."

He moved so he was kneeling between her legs and began stroking himself again, never taking his eyes off her. His motions soon grew frantic. His mouth fell open with a groan, and an expression came over his face that she would have assumed to be agony had she not known that it instead represented the most exquisite pleasure. And then it was his turn to call out her name. "Caro. Caro, I— God, that's good. Oh, *God*, Caro, that's so good, I—I— Oh, fuck. Oh, *fuck*, Caro... Yes! Yes! Yes!"

And then she felt it—a warm, sticky wetness, streaking up her torso and across her breasts. She could see the glassy pleasure in his eyes as he watched his essence spill across her body.

His eyes closed, his shoulders sagged, and he slumped to a seated position. After drawing a few ragged breaths, he opened his eyes and smiled at her. She found herself smiling back, and then she found herself laughing.

"What?" he asked, still smiling as he moistened a towel from the tea tray with warm water from the kettle. He gently began to sponge the stickiness from her body.

"I can't believe it," she replied. "Two hours ago, I had never even kissed a man. And now I just..."

"Made me come so hard I almost blacked out?" He tossed the towel aside and lay down, taking her in his arms. She purred as she snuggled against him.

"I don't know that I can claim any credit. I was hardly involved."

He snorted. "You almost made me spend in my trousers. I haven't been that aroused in…" He paused. "I'm not sure. Maybe ever. But if you're looking to take a more active role, you'll have the opportunity. In about three minutes."

"You mean… Are we going to do it again?" Caro asked brightly.

"You're damn right, we're going to do that again. It's as you said—who knows when we'll get another chance like this. I mean to take full advantage." He punctuated this statement by running his hand all the way down Caro's back, past the curve of her buttock, which made her shiver with anticipation.

"I wouldn't object." Truth be told, lying here next to Henry was making her feel quite eager for another go-round. She loved the feeling of his chest pressed against hers, and she wanted the full length of him. "Take these off," she ordered, tugging at his trousers.

"So demanding," he said, trying but failing to sound aggrieved.

He made quick work of the task and took her into his arms, this time with nothing separating them. "Mmmmm," Caro moaned, loving the feeling of all of that skin pressed up against hers.

"You like that," he said. "All of you pressed up against all of me."

"I do. And you like…" She trailed off, embarrassed.

He gave her a squeeze. "What?"

"Saying lecherous things out loud." She felt his chest rumble against hers.

"It's true," he said through his laughter. "Gets me all charged up." He cocked an eyebrow at her. "Whereas I could tell you didn't like it at all."

She blushed. "I suppose it was rather… stimulating."

"Speaking of stimulating," he said. His member, which had been stiffening with each passing minute, was now poking her insistently in the stomach. "I could do with a bit of stimulation right about now."

"Oh! Of course." She swallowed, gathering her courage, and reached down, fumbling to find him. "I have no idea how to do this, so you're going to have to show me—"

Her wrist was captured in a vise-like grip. "As much as I appreciate your enthusiastic participation, you're skipping steps, darling. I promised I was going to do eleven different things to you. Please don't skip directly to number ten."

He rolled her onto her back, coming to rest beside her. His hands were so warm, and he began running them all over her body, down her arms, back up her stomach, up to her neck, everywhere.

"And look what a hash I made of things the first time around," he continued, bringing his hands up to cup her breasts. "It is an absolute travesty that I have not yet kissed you here."

He slid down to remedy this oversight, kissing every inch of her right breast in a great, narrowing spiral until he reached her peaked nipple, which he proceeded to suck. His hand mirrored the motion on her other breast, and she could feel callouses on his hands, from working with his horses, no doubt. But those callouses provided the most delicious friction, and, as he gradually increased his suction over her nipple, she found her back arching up, begging him for even more. He then moved his mouth to her other breast, and she heard herself moan at the pleasure.

By the time he slid up to lie next to her, her breathing was uneven, and that curious little heartbeat of a pulse had returned in that spot between her legs. "Good?" he asked.

"Very good."

And then he was kissing her, his tongue tracing the contours of her mouth while his hands continued to rove absolutely everywhere. He ran his tongue lightly along the roof of her mouth, and her whole body shivered. She felt his member pressing eagerly into her stomach.

Once she was trembling all over and was about to go out of her mind with wanting another climax, he pulled back, a cheeky grin on his face. "Now we have reached the portion of the evening in which I tell you in explicit detail what I'm about to do to you, which will hopefully drive you mad with yearning."

"I'm already mad with yearning!"

"I can see that you are. It's doing wonders for my self-regard."

"Your self-regard needs no encouragement. I swear, Henry Greville, if you stop touching me—"

He chuckled as he lay beside her, positioning his lips at her ear. "Fear not, my darling Caro." He kissed her ear, making her groan, and stroked his hand ever so gently over her collarbone.

When he spoke in her ear, his voice was husky with desire. "So, Caro," he said, "I've showed you the magic pearl between your legs. You now know how to pleasure yourself. Will you touch yourself there? When you lie in your bed at night? When you take a bath, perhaps?"

Her breath was ragged. His hand slipped down to her breasts, and he began teasing her nipples. "Well?" he prompted. "Will you touch yourself, Caro?"

"Yes," she breathed.

"Because you want to come again."

"*Yes.*"

"And who will you think about when you do?" he asked, sliding his hand down over her belly.

"You—I'll think of you," she confessed.

"Good girl. How I will enjoy imagining you, pleasuring yourself while you are in your bath, thinking of me. I'll enjoy that so very, very much. And I mean that literally. Because I touch myself every night before I go to bed. Do you know who I've been thinking about, every single night for the last week?"

"Who?"

He kissed her neck. "You, darling. Only you." The heartbeat between her legs had grown stronger, more insistent. "And now," he said, kissing his way down her stomach, pressing her knees apart with his hands, "I am going to show you one of my very favorite items on the list of eleven things I plan to do to you tonight. Unless I am very much mistaken, you are going to enjoy this one, too."

He proceeded to kiss his way up the insides of her thighs, which were trembling. Caro had some idea what he was about to do. To be sure, the little nub between her legs was crying out for his touch. But she felt embarrassed at the mere thought of him putting his mouth... *there*. Was he sure he wanted to—

Apparently he was, because he parted her folds and ran his tongue ever so lightly over her. She froze. That felt... That felt very... He licked her again, this time teasingly moving his tongue from side to side as he passed over her.

"Henry."

"Yes, darling?" He repeated the motion.

"*Henry.*"

He teased her with a series of light, tickling passes, and she thought her hips would shoot up off the floor. "Does that feel good, Caro?"

"*Henry.* Oh, my *God.*"

"Tell me, darling."

"It feels so... so..."

"Yes?"

"I... I can't describe it."

"Should I stop, then?"

"Don't you *dare* stop, you *horrible* man—"

Chuckling, Henry put her out of her misery, sliding his hands beneath her bottom and burying his face between her legs. Oh. *Oh.* This was *exactly* what she had needed, and *oh, my God*, when he swirled his tongue over that spot, that felt... that felt... She noticed somebody moaning, quite loudly. Wait, was that her? Well, she didn't have time to be embarrassed about it right now. She was too busy feeling. What he was doing felt so good, if only he would go a little bit *faster* and just a *twinge* higher up and... and...

"Oh. Oh! Oh, my *God*, Henry. Right there. *Right* there. *That* is the spot. Just like that. Don't stop, whatever you do, *please* don't stop—"

He redoubled his efforts, swirling his tongue so fast and light and in *just* the right spot, and the entire world shattered. She knew nothing but the pleasure. Her back arched up off the cushions, and she heard herself screaming his name as the muscles deep inside of her flexed again and again and *again* in approval. He immediately gentled his tongue, prolonging her pleasure with teasing strokes, then lifted his head as she collapsed back on the cushions, boneless.

He took her in his arms, cradling her head against his shoulder. He kissed her temple. "I take it you enjoyed that."

"Mmmmm," was as much of a response as she could muster.

"God knows I enjoyed it."

"Ermmm," she said languidly.

He held her, stroking her back. After a few minutes, he said, "Er... as much as I hate to interrupt your post-orgasmic bliss, I don't suppose you might be interested in returning the favor?"

Caro looked up at him, biting her lip as she smiled. This

was it, then. She could feel his hardness pressing into her stomach. He was ready, and however anxious she felt about the prospect, she realized that she wanted to do this. She wanted to make it every bit as good for him as he had just made it for her.

She kissed him, trying to be bold, running her hands all over that gorgeous chest. She let her hands drift low over his stomach, until they were inches away from his member.

She recalled suddenly his enjoyment at talking about what they were doing, about how it seemed to excite him even more. Maybe it would please him if she tried it, too. She gathered her courage. "Oh. Oh, my, Henry. Look what we have here. You seem very, um… hard."

As she spoke, she slipped her hand around him, attempting to stroke him up and down, the way she had seen him do for himself. His eyes changed the second she started stroking him, becoming less focused. She could see the pleasure she was giving him. "I've never been harder in my life, Caro."

"I like making you hard. Making your… er… your member hard."

He grinned. "My *member*?"

"That is to say, your, uh… manhood."

Now he was laughing. "My *manhood*?"

She glared. "Don't you dare laugh at me, Henry Greville. I'm new at this. Do you want me to stop?"

"God, no. What I want is for you to keep stroking my *cock*, Caro. My shaft, my prick, my Roger, my rod, my…"

"Thank you, Henry. I get the idea."

"You certainly do. You're catching on so quickly, darling. Now, let me borrow some of these delicious juices you were thoughtful enough to make." He reached between her legs and stroked teasingly at her wetness, which he then proceeded to smear over his cock. "God, that feels glorious."

He took her hand and positioned his own over it, showing her how he liked to be stroked. "You can squeeze me tighter —yes, Caro, just like that. Go a little bit faster, darling—that's good, that's so fucking good."

He lay back on the cushions but kept his eyes fixed on her as she caressed his cock. After a few minutes, she slid down between his legs. She knew from her conversation with the maids all those years ago that a woman could use her mouth upon a man, too, but she had no idea how to go about doing it.

Seeing what she was about, Henry groaned. "God, yes, Caro. Please."

She made a tentative overture, kissing him gently right on the tip of his cock. She pressed kisses down his length and back up again.

He slid his hands into her hair and gently pulled her back. "That's lovely, darling. But do you remember how you felt during our first go-round, when I was touching you softly and you were desperate to come?"

"Yes."

"That's where I am right now."

"Oh! Um, what should I do, then?"

"Here." He positioned her hand on his cock again and helped her reestablish her rhythm. "That feels so good, darling. Now, use your mouth, too, and slide it up and down over me in the same time as your hand... Yes. *Yes*, Caro. God, that feels good. Now, I'm most sensitive right on the head of my cock. If you can keep doing what you're doing right now but also run your tongue over... Oh, *fuck*. Oh, fuck, oh—oh, my fucking *God*, Caro! I'm going to— I'm— If you don't want me to come in your mouth, you need to move right now because I— Oh, God, oh, *fuck*, oh— Yes, Caro! Yes! Yes! Yes!"

And then she tasted it—pulse after pulse of his semen, coursing into her mouth. The taste was not unpleasant, and she swallowed instinctively. His hands came to the back of her head, showing her how to gentle her strokes. After a moment, he drew her off of him and pulled her up to lie beside him. He kissed her deeply, then settled her with her head on his shoulder.

"Thank you, darling. That was magnificent."

They lay there, on his soft velvet dressing gown, before the fire. Caro mused that she had never felt more contented in her life. Being inside Henry Greville's bachelor apartment, naked in his arms—it was a situation that would have been unimaginable, even horrifying, a mere week ago.

But tonight, it felt like the most natural thing in the world. It felt… perfect.

She snuggled into his chest. She had absolutely no regrets.

CHAPTER 18

*A*n hour later, the rain had let up. As much as Caro would have loved to linger, Henry's valet was bound to return before long. And so she dressed herself in her damp gown, and they climbed into a hackney carriage to take her home.

As soon as they were settled into the carriage, holding hands, Caro laughed. "I suppose we should discuss my sister's amulet. How do you want to proceed? I think we should go to Bow Street first thing in the morning, and—"

Henry shook his head. "We can't go to Bow Street. Not yet."

"Whyever not? We saw the artifacts with our own eyes and even heard the thieves talking about their difficulties convincing people the pieces aren't stolen. Surely we have enough evidence—"

"They spoke of a new contact. The man who will be waiting at the British Museum. A gentleman, they said, who will pass their items off as pieces from his own collection."

"What about him?"

Henry sighed. "There are only a half-dozen men in all of

175

England who fit that description, and they're all friends of my father's. I know the type. They're good men, but most of them... you could say they have their heads stuck in the clouds. The sort who, in their excitement, could be easily taken in." His brow wrinkled. "It could very well be Lord Coddington. He's my godfather, Caro. I know he would never intentionally deal in stolen goods, but—"

She squeezed his hand. "Of course not. So, what should we do instead?"

"Today happens to be Friday. I'll go to the British Museum and see who this new contact is. Assuming they've been duped, I'll explain about the crate of items that went missing and see if I can get him to connect the dots. Then I can march him straight over to Bow Street, and he can be the one to turn them in."

"An excellent plan, save for a few details. First off, it's my understanding that it can take weeks to get tickets to the British Museum—"

"It can, yes." Henry grinned. "But I know a way in."

"Excellent. Which brings me to point two—what's this talk of how *you* will go to the British Museum? I believe the word you're looking for is *we*. If you think you're going to leave me behind—"

Henry laughed. "Indeed, no. You wouldn't even let me search the thieves' den by myself."

"Naturally not. And I don't see you complaining about the way the evening ended."

He raised her hand to his lips, pressing a kiss against her palm. His eyes when he raised his head were bright even in the dim interior of the carriage. "Quite the opposite."

"Good. Then you agree that I shall come, too?"

"We can hardly reveal, either to this mysterious contact or to the Bow Street runners, that we were lying together inside a sarcophagus, eavesdropping on the criminals. It would take far less than that to ruin you, Caro."

Her shoulders sagged. "A fair point. But I want to be there, to see what happens. I can bring Fanny, and we'll observe discreetly from across the gallery. And as soon as you get back from Bow Street, I want a full report."

"And you will get it. I probably shouldn't agree to this, but if it means I get to see you tomorrow…"

Caro's heart thrilled to hear him hint at feelings that echoed her own. "I feel the same way," she confessed, looking down, then back up at him again.

"Good." He squeezed her hands. "So, meet me in the gardens, not the main museum entrance. Shall we say two o'clock?"

"Two o'clock it is. There's only one remaining problem—we're to recognize our contact by the lotus flower on his lapel. I must confess, I have no idea what a lotus flower looks like."

"I do. I know exactly. They're considered to be one of the sacred symbols of Egypt, so of course my father is obsessed with them. The climate of England being nothing like the climate of Egypt, he had to have a special pond constructed inside our orangery so he could grow them."

Caro laughed. "I knew I could count on you."

The hackney drew to a halt. Caro sighed, not wanting the night to be over. She noticed Henry made no move to open the door. She leaned her head on his shoulder, enjoying the feeling of—

"We're here," the driver called. "Are ya getting out or ain't ya?"

Henry took her hand and raised it to his lips. "I would hand you down, but I probably shouldn't get out. We can't risk being seen together."

Caro sighed. "You're right. I know I need to go." She

pressed his hand. "But thank you, Henry, for tonight. For everything."

As she started to open the carriage door, she found herself hauled back into the seat. Henry kissed her, swiftly but sweetly, then nudged her back toward the door.

Caro wore an idiotic grin as she snuck back up to her room, and for long thereafter.

ACROSS TOWN, Arnold Jenner, better known as Snakeface due to his bald head and beady eyes, was in a foul mood. He'd spent the better part of two hours chasing after those fucking horses, and they hadn't caught the little shit whose idea of a joke it was to spook them. They'd finally gotten the horses calmed down and back to the alley doorway. But there was still unloading to do, and he was tired, his back was sore, and what little patience he possessed was long gone.

As he shifted a crate toward the back of the wagon, his new associate, John Brownwood, leaned out into the alleyway. "There's something you need to see."

He cursed. Brownwood was the one who had gotten them into this mess. He was an assistant to the under-librarian for God knew what kind of moldering shit at the British Museum. At least, he had been up until a month ago, when he'd been dismissed from his post. Brownwood had helped himself to a little parting gift in the form of a box of Egyptian trinkets. Then he had heard about this load coming in from the Continent, and he had approached Snakeface because he needed a place to store it and the muscle to move it.

Maybe they would make a huge haul, like Brownwood said. But it felt like far more trouble than all of these crumbling rocks were worth.

Snakeface followed Brownwood to the storage room. "What is it?"

"In our haste to stop the horses, nobody bothered to lock the door," Brownwood said.

"Shit," Snakeface replied. "Was anything stolen?"

"Nothing appears to be missing. But look at that," Brownwood said, gesturing to the sarcophagus. "It was like that when I came in."

Snakeface fell silent. The sarcophagus wasn't damaged. It sat in the center of the room, exactly where it was supposed to be.

Except that the lid was askew.

"Someone was here," Snakeface said. The whole ordeal—the horses, the boy—it was no accident, nor was it a mere prank.

One of his men staggered into the room carrying a heavy crate. "Put that back on the wagon," Snakeface ordered. He started to protest, but Snakeface pointed at the open sarcophagus. "Look at that, will you?"

The rest of their crew wandered in to see what the fuss was about.

"We've been made," Snakeface said.

CHAPTER 19

*T*he following afternoon, Henry arrived at the gardens of the British Museum a quarter-hour before the appointed time. He wandered the graveled paths in a daze, hardly seeing the exotic plants that surrounded him.

His world had shifted off its axis in the past twenty-four hours. He had known for a while now that Caroline Astley was beautiful, that she was witty, and that she made him smile until his face hurt. He had also known ever since his father informed him that the Greville family was insolvent that all of those lovely qualities came with a "but." But she hated him, but he couldn't go near her lest the Duke of Trevissick ruin them, and above all, but she would never marry him once she found out that the Greville fortune was gone.

But when he thought about last night…

Last night had been a revelation. Not just the pleasure they had shared, although that had been better than anything he'd ever known. But between the bouts of fantastic love-making, they had talked together, and they had laughed together, and Henry had felt content, more content than he could ever remember feeling. In his previous liaisons, he'd never been the slightest bit tempted to stay the night. But with Caro, he had wanted her to stay with a fierceness that startled him. He wanted to carry her through to his bed, to make love to her all night long, to wake with her in his arms. He wanted to spend all of today with her, too.

And then he wanted to repeat that process, every day for the rest of his life.

The implications were obvious: he needed to marry Caroline Astley.

To be sure, there were obstacles in his way. Insurmountable obstacles.

He was just going to have to damn well surmount them.

At least the first obstacle had fallen away—she no longer hated him. As for his other two problems, Lord Graverley and his lack of a personal fortune, they were intertwined, in that if he could solve his financial problems, then Graverley would no longer have the power to ruin him.

Other than a scant few hours of sleep, Henry had been turning the problem over in his mind. And the more he thought about it, the more a solution began to present itself.

Last year, his fledgling breeding stable had turned a profit. It was a modest fifty-two-pound, eleven-shilling, four-pence profit, but it was a profit, nonetheless. And his earnings were bound to increase, simply because he would have more horses ready for sale every year. This year he had already netted some two hundred and fifty pounds of sales, and he had sold only a quarter of his available stock. He would have to account for expenses, of course, but he estimated he would clear around five hundred pounds in profits this year, and perhaps twice that the year after.

This was nowhere near enough. But at least it was a start.

And another idea had occurred to him that morning.

While getting him dressed, his valet, Gibson, had reminded him that he had a horse race scheduled for tomorrow. Percival Thistlethwaite had challenged him to a race in the saddle, with stakes of one hundred pounds.

Having not lost a race in the past five years, Henry had a bit of a reputation. He received challenges every week from young would-be Corinthians who wanted to cement their status by beating one of the finest horsemen in England. Henry usually put them off. But it occurred to him that perhaps he shouldn't.

If he raced more often, he was bound to lose at some point. Accidents happened—horses threw shoes or came up lame. Saddles slipped. Everyone had an off day once in a while. But he was confident that he could win more than he lost, a lot more, and his winnings could take some pressure off in the short-term.

Henry hadn't yet worked out all of the details, but a plan was starting to come into focus. He might not have much in the way of conventional business acumen, but he had his own set of skills.

The one thing he could not do was tell Caro about his financial problems. She would never marry him if she knew. Hell, when she had been hiding under Lord Lansdowne's desk, she had heard Lord Graverley declare his intention to propose.

She liked him. He knew she did. But the truth was that affection counted for very little in these things, at least for the daughter of an earl. He wasn't foolish enough to believe she would put her faith in his fifty-two-pound profit, not when she had the chance to be a duchess with a hundred thousand a year.

No, he couldn't tell Caro about his current problems, not now and not ever. His father's words echoed in his head.

A man is strong. A man is stoic. A man is steadfast. A man does not burden those around him by whining about his problems. He presents a strong face to the world, never shows any weakness. He bears his troubles stoically and leaves his wife out of them.

Even once he put this unfortunate episode behind him, there was no reason for Caro to ever know about it.

≈

CARO SPIED Henry across the garden and quickened her steps. Beside her, Fanny slanted her eyes toward her mistress, wary.

"Fanny," Caro chided, "don't look at me like that."

"One night," her maid grumbled. "I leave you alone for one night, and you go off cavorting with that man."

"You're overreacting. Nothing happened." This was not entirely accurate, of course, but her maidenhead was intact, so it was near enough to the truth.

Fanny grabbed Caro's arm and hauled her behind the trunk of a pear tree as Henry came into view. Caro saw the distracted smile on his face and found herself smiling back. She recognized that expression.

It was the same one she had worn for the past twelve hours, after all.

"'Nothing,' my wig," Fanny muttered. "'Tis only one thing that will put such a shyte-eating grin on a man's face, and well do I know what it is."

"You're being ridiculous. I expect you to behave yourself. You're not to hit his lordship with your parasol."

"I most certainly will hit him! I can see plain as day he deserves it."

Caro rolled her eyes, then stepped from behind the pear tree.

Henry's face lit up. "Caro," he said, hastening to her.

"Henry." She smiled at him, and he smiled at her, and they

stood in the dappled shade of the pear tree, grinning at each other like idiots.

It was Fanny who broke the silence. "Humph," she said, her gaze traveling from Henry to Caro and back again. She tucked her parasol under her arm. "I guess that's all right, then," she muttered.

Henry gave her a quizzical look, to which Caro shrugged. She hooked her arm through his and led him to a secluded bench. "How do you like my bonnet?" she asked, gesturing to the huge flaps that all but obscured her face. "I'm in disguise," she stage-whispered. "Even so, I'd best stay off the main path as much as possible. It's unlikely I would run into an acquaintance here, but I am supposed to be sick in bed."

"I hate to tell you, but your disguise is a failure. You could wear a burlap sack, and you would still be the prettiest woman in London."

She squeezed his arm as they sat on the bench. "So, how can we get inside the museum without tickets?"

He arched an eyebrow. "Who said we need to go inside?"

"But… the contact will be waiting in the same gallery as the Rosetta Stone."

"Precisely." He gestured to a wooden shed in the corner of the gardens. "And the Rosetta Stone is right over there."

Caro started in surprise. "There? You mean to tell me the Rosetta Stone is being kept in a garden shed?"

"I do, along with everything else seized from Napoleon's army. They're out of room inside, so they had to resort to this."

Caro chuckled. "You have proven your worth yet again, Henry Greville. I would never have thought to look in the shed out back."

Henry consulted his pocket watch. "It's five after two, so I'll head in and see what's what."

"Perfect. I'll wait ten minutes, and then I'll follow." She

184

raised a hand when he started to protest. "Please don't ask me to wait any longer than that. Unless you wave me over, I will be discreet. But it's all I can do not to burst through those doors right now, to see who this mysterious liaison is."

"It shouldn't take me that long. I'll probably be back out here well before then, and there'll be no need for you to go in at all."

She laughed. "Either way, I want to go in. I would quite like to see this Rosetta Stone everyone is talking about."

"Very well. Mark my words, Caro, ten minutes from now, all of our troubles are going to be coming to an end."

IT TOOK a moment for Henry's eyes to adjust to the dim lighting of the shed. There were a handful of people admiring the priceless Egyptian antiquities, so out of place in their modest surroundings. He glanced about for the contact, ruling out a family of five, a trio who looked to be university students, and a pair of matrons admiring a sarcophagus through their quizzing glasses.

That left one man at the far end of the shed. He was a gentleman, whoever he was; Henry could tell even in the dim light that his tailoring was of the finest quality. His body was in profile to Henry, and his head was turned to speak to the under-librarian on duty, so that Henry couldn't see his face.

He did, however, have an unimpeded view of the white lotus flower tucked into the man's breast pocket.

Henry strode across the room. As a greeting rose to his lips, the man turned, and his face came into view.

"Father?" Henry sputtered. "What on earth are you doing here?"

CHAPTER 20

*T*he Earl of Ardingly regarded his eldest son coolly. "Surely you're not surprised to find me here amongst the antiquities?"

One of the matrons hailed the under-librarian, who crossed the shed to answer her question. Henry drew his father into the far corner. "I'm not surprised to find you here. I am surprised to find you here on Friday, between two and three o'clock, sporting a lotus flower on your lapel, as that takes on a significant meaning. And you know it."

His father blanched. "I—I don't know what you're talking about—"

"You're working with them!" Henry snapped. "The criminals who stole your cosmetics box. They stole a crate of items from the British Museum, did you know that? And they've gotten their hands on an even larger haul, with a sarcophagus and some statues and even more crates of items. God knows where they stole those from."

"How do you know this?" his father demanded.

"You asked me to try to recover your Eye of Ra box, and so I did. I've been working with Lady Caroline Astley, who

186

had a lead. It happened that something was stolen from her, too, a little Eye of Ra pendant she had borrowed from her sister—"

"My God, Henry. Can you really be so stupid?"

"That is uncalled for, Father. I've done a good job at this investigation. We've successfully tracked down the criminals. I know where they're storing everything—"

"That's not what I'm talking about. I'm referring to the fact that your Lady Caroline's 'pendant' is not a pendant at all. It's *my* cosmetics box. They're the same item, you fool!"

"That isn't true. I worried about the same thing at first, but they're different. Hers is lapis lazuli—"

"She thinks it's lapis because she's only seen the common turquoise form of faience, not the dark blue."

"Well, hers is no more than a quarter of an inch thick, and it has a hole in it, so you can string it on a chain—"

"That's the lid."

Henry frowned. "It would be the right thickness, but it doesn't have a hole in it."

"Oh, yes, it does. It turns on a peg that connects it to the bottom of the box. It's not obvious when the two pieces are together, but if you lift the lid off entirely, it absolutely has a hole."

"Whatever the similarities, it cannot be the same item. This is something Lord Wynters purchased months ago, as a birthday present for his wife. Are you accusing Wynters of having stolen it?"

"Of course he didn't steal it. I gave it to him."

Now Henry was completely confused. "You gave it to him? Why would you do that?"

His father sighed. "I staked it in a game of cards."

"Was this before or after you used the box as a guarantee on the Duke of Trevissick's loan?"

"After."

Henry knew he couldn't yell, but he whispered irately, "Then why in *seven hells* would you bet the very item we need to make good on the loan?"

His father had the grace to look uncomfortable. "Wynters and I used to gamble twice a week. We would go back and forth. When things got deep, he would stake this pocket watch that was a gift from his grandfather. And I would wager the box. We would give each other a chance to win back whatever we'd lost. I've lost and regained that box from him probably hundreds of times. Everything should have been fine. How could I have predicted he was going to up and die on me before I could win it back?"

Henry's patience was fraying. "Why did you not tell me the truth from the start? I promised Lady Caroline I would help her recover her sister's amulet."

"Because it didn't matter. You were supposed to be avoiding the chit anyways, remember?"

Wait until his father found out she was here right now. Henry's head was throbbing with the implications of what his father had told him. Because he needed that box. He needed it so Trevissick wouldn't tell the world that the Grevilles were insolvent, so that he could buy a little time to fix the family finances and maintain some sliver of hope he could convince Caro to marry him.

But she needed it, too. He remembered how distraught she'd been, describing her sister's starving orphans and something about a room full of sewage. He could picture the pain in her face, the guilt, as she described her predicament.

They both needed it, but only one of them could have it. And damn if Henry knew what he was going to do now.

Something occurred to him. "Why are you working with these criminals, anyways?" he asked.

"They've promised to return my Eye of Ra box if I find

buyers for the other items. That and a ten percent share of whatever is sold."

"So, this is it—the surefire plan you told me about last week. Working with known criminals, passing items that rightfully belong to king and country off as your own collection for profit."

His father huffed. "I should like to see you come up with a better solution—"

"Considering your solution hinges upon the word of honor of a man named *Snakeface*, it would be difficult to conceive of a worse one. But it happens that I do have a plan—"

Light flooded the interior of the shed, and Henry squinted. Someone had opened the door.

He glanced up and saw Caro peering around the doorframe. Any second now, she would spot him.

And she would spot the lotus flower on his father's lapel.

HENRY LUNGED for his father and ripped the lotus flower from his coat. He crushed it inside his fist, then glanced up guiltily. He saw Caro spot him, his hand still raised. He waved his fist awkwardly, and she began to cross the gallery. Henry struggled to assume a natural pose while holding his hand behind his back.

"You brought *her* here?" his father hissed. "I told you to stay away from her."

"Lord Thetford," she said, "what an unexpected pleasure."

"Lady Caroline, good afternoon. Have you been introduced to my father?" She shook her head. "May I present my father, the Earl of Ardingly? Father, this is Lady Caroline Astley, daughter of Lord Cheltenham."

Caro sank into a respectful curtsey, but his father gave

only the briefest nod. "Lady Caroline. A pleasure." His curt tone belied any warmth suggested by his words. "If you will excuse us, my son and I must take our leave."

"Oh!" Caro's gaze flew to Henry. "I had hoped, um—"

"You go on, Father," Henry said. "I would like to show Lady Caroline around the gallery."

The earl leveled a glare at him, and Henry returned the look, neither blinking. The earl flinched first. "Fine," his father bit out. "Good day," he called over his shoulder, already halfway to the door.

"Is everything all right?" Caroline asked.

"Yes! Everything is fine. Please excuse my father. He, um, he was disappointed when I told him I hadn't yet found his missing box."

"Oh. Of course." She glanced around the shed. "Have you spotted our mysterious contact?"

Henry squeezed the lotus flower clutched in his fist. "Not yet," he lied. "Perhaps he's running late."

"Oh, how disappointing. Well, let's have a look around while we wait." Caro laughed. "Having never met your father before, when I first came in, I assumed *he* must be the contact. Can you even imagine?"

Henry could imagine, all right. He could imagine far better than he would like. "My father," he said, his voice sounding strangled. "That's a good one."

"You don't much resemble your father."

"That's what I like to think," Henry muttered.

Caro's head jerked around to stare at him. "What was that, Henry?"

"Er... nothing. Nothing at all."

"I didn't mean to suggest that your father would ever be under suspicion," she hastened to add. "I didn't realize to whom you were speaking."

"No, I understand. I didn't take any offense. But of course

my father isn't serving as a criminal liaison. The very notion is ridiculous."

Of course, Henry's entire life was ridiculous right now. He really shouldn't be surprised that his father the earl's new partner in business was a man named Snakeface. That was just the kind of week he was having.

"Of course it is," Caro agreed. "Now, this must be the famous Rosetta Stone."

"Actually, let's start over there," Henry said, gesturing toward the far corner.

When Caro and Fanny turned to see what he was pointing at, he tossed the crumpled lotus flower behind a sarcophagus.

THEY TOURED the shed for a good half hour. Henry did his best to feign surprise that their contact did not appear.

They retreated to their secluded bench to regroup, with Fanny lingering ten feet away. Caro was disappointed that their investigation had stalled. "At this point," she said, "I think we should turn everything over to Bow Street."

That was the last thing Henry could do, considering the likelihood that his father would be implicated by Snakeface and his friends. "I've got to try and find this contact first."

Caro sighed. "My sister's amulet is to go up for auction the Monday after next. If we wait another week to try to rendezvous with the liaison, that will give us very little time." She looked up at him. "Could you call upon your godfather Lord Coddington? That way we could at least rule him out."

"It's a good idea. I will call on him tomorrow."

Caro beamed at him, which felt strangely bittersweet. To be sure, he felt like a king when she looked at him like that.

But she wouldn't be looking at him that way if she knew

the truth—that he had just lied to her, and he was about to go home and figure out whether to lie to her some more or to reveal that he had been lying to her for the past week because he wasn't the man she believed him to be.

"Oh, I have an additional piece of news," she said, pulling a slip of paper from her reticule. "Fanny's friend was able to track down an address for Mr. Richard Cuming. If you recall, he's friends with Mr. Parkinson over at the Leverian Museum, and Mr. Brownwood showed him the stolen amulets. It's probably no longer pertinent, as we've discovered their warehouse, but I thought I would mention it."

"No, it's good information. He'll be needed as witness for the prosecution."

"Should we try to speak with him, then?"

Henry considered. There was really no need to speak to the man, but prolonging their investigation would at least buy him some time. "I think so," he said, standing and offering his arm. "I have a horse race tomorrow morning, but perhaps we could call on him in the afternoon."

Caro beamed at him as she took his arm. "We—at last you're learning, Henry."

"May I keep this?" Henry held the slip of paper aloft. "I need to look up the address."

"Of course. So, who is the unfortunate fellow who will be losing a horse race tomorrow?"

"I hope the answer to that question is Percival Thistlethwaite and not me."

"La! I know Percival Thistlethwaite, and I suspect *I* could beat him in a horse race."

"You never know. Perhaps Mr. Thistlethwaite has hidden depths."

"I doubt it. But do be careful, Henry." She squeezed his arm, and the look in her beautiful blue eyes...

He looked away. He had to.

He shook himself. "Thank you. I will be. And I'll send Mr. Cuming a note first thing in the morning. I'll let you know as soon as I hear something back."

"Excellent."

They reached the exit. It was only one block from Henry's apartment to the British Museum, so he hadn't bothered with his phaeton.

He had, however, brought his young tiger to enjoy the gardens. "Billy," Caro exclaimed, spotting him. "There is the bravest boy in all of London."

"Oh, golly, Lady Caroline," Billy replied. "It weren't nothing."

"It absolutely was," she said. "Your quick thinking saved us. And I happen to have brought a small token of my appreciation." She dug into her reticule and pulled out some slips of paper. "Tickets to Astley's Amphitheatre."

Billy's jaw dropped, and Henry smiled. This was exactly the right gift for a ten-year-old boy. Philip Astley was a spectacularly skilled bareback trick rider; even Henry was impressed by the man's abilities. In addition to his feats of horsemanship, his shows featured a variety of other entertainments that would appeal to a young boy—acrobats, rope walkers, clowns, strongmen, and the like.

"Wait," Billy said. "You're Lady Caroline Astley. Do you mean to tell me you're kin to *Philip Astley*?"

Caro laughed. "I fear I cannot claim any connection."

"Oh," Billy said. "Of course not. I mean, you would have mentioned it straight away if you were. Philip Astley—that would really be something."

Henry mused that most people would rather be related to an earl than to the son of a cabinet maker. Clearly, however, Billy was not one of them.

Caro passed him the tickets, and Billy's jaw dropped as he counted them. "I can bring my friend Sebastian and a few more fellows, too. I'm going to be the most popular boy in the mews." He looked up at Caroline, his eyes sincere. "This is grand, m'lady. Thank you."

"You are most welcome, Billy."

Henry nudged Caroline. "If you have finished spoiling my tiger—"

"Spoiling him? I hope you're treating him well. We wouldn't have made our escape without him."

"I already gave him an entire pound of sticky toffee candies. They're his favorites."

"Good." She smiled up at him, and he smiled down at her, and he felt his heart give a squeeze, and—

"Ahem!" Fanny thumped her parasol on the ground. "The longer Lady Caroline loiters on the pavement, the higher the chances someone drives by and spots her."

Fanny was right, so Henry hailed them a hack.

Then he made the short walk home, with Billy following behind him, clutching his precious tickets.

For the rest of the afternoon, Henry contemplated what the hell he was going to do next.

By the time he fell into a listless sleep, he still hadn't figured it out.

CHAPTER 21

*I*n the end, recovering the lid to the cosmetics box turned out to be the easiest thing of all.

Henry started off the day by relieving Percival Thistlethwaite of his one hundred pounds. He then returned home to find two notes awaiting him.

The first was from Richard Cuming, inviting him to call that afternoon. It happened that Mr. Brownwood had asked to come round again, saying he had a selection of new items. So if Henry wished to meet this Brownwood fellow himself, he need only call at three o'clock.

The second note was from Caroline:

My sister, Anne, has come to nurse me today, so I must pretend to be ill. Do send me a note and let me know what happens with Lord Coddington and with Mr. Cuming. —C.A.

An idea occurred to Henry. It took a display of obsequiousness he wouldn't care to repeat, but he was able to cajole Lord Lansdowne into accompanying him to Richard Cuming's house in Southwark.

Mr. Cuming seemed nervous enough about the prospect of a viscount coming to call, and his eyes all but bugged out of his head when Henry introduced the former prime minister. But the two men were united by an interest in antiquities, which they fell into discussing while they waited for John Brownwood to arrive (at least, when Lord Lansdowne wasn't lecturing Mr. Cuming on the Post Horse Duties Act, a topic on which Mr. Cuming did not appear to have any particular knowledge or interest, but which he bore stoically).

Then Brownwood appeared, bearing a wooden box with a handle on top. He looked delighted to find two additional customers present. Henry introduced himself only as "Viscount Thetford." He had wondered if Brownwood would recognize the courtesy title for the Earl of Ardingly's heir and realize who he was. But the man smiled obliviously and set about showing them his selection of amulets.

As Brownwood came to the end of his collection, he reached for two black velvet pouches. "I seldom show these last two items because they are so dear, but such discriminating gentlemen as yourselves will no doubt appreciate them."

The item he withdrew from the first pouch was a gorgeous amulet in the shape of a scarab beetle, bejeweled in gold, lapis, carnelian, and turquoise.

The second item was the lid to his father's cosmetics box.

"Well, I'll be," Henry said, feigning surprise. "It's the lid to my father's famous Eye of Ra box. He told me it was stolen months ago. You recognize it, don't you Lord Lansdowne?"

The marquess peered at the Eye of Ra through his quizzing glass. "Indeed. It is the pride of the earl's collection. It belongs to Lord Ardingly. Unquestionably."

Under the glare of the former prime minister, there was nothing Brownwood could do but hand the lid over to Henry, sputtering an apology. "I'm terribly sorry, Lord Thetford. My associate assured me it had been procured through the Bessborough auction—"

"Impossible," Mr. Cuming said. "I went over every lot in the Bessborough auction. I would've remembered this." He turned to Lord Lansdowne. "Nor were the amulets he offered me three weeks ago from the Bessborough auction, as he claimed at the time."

Now Brownwood looked panicked. "Please, my lords, it is all a mistake. I have been misled by my partner—"

"Of course," Lord Lansdowne said with surprising gentleness. "But you will understand that we must investigate this partner of yours. Give us all of his information."

Paper and pen were provided, and Brownwood proceeded to write out the same address Henry and Caro had visited two nights before.

"Excellent," Lord Lansdowne said, taking the paper. "We will look into this Arnold Jenner." He leveled a look at Mr. Brownwood. "And you will wait in Newgate Prison while we do."

IT SHOULD HAVE FELT like a triumph, but it did not.

Hours later, long after night had fallen, Henry found himself pacing the length of his sitting room.

He knew what he should do, and that was hand the lid over to Caro. He had promised to help her retrieve it, for one. There was also the fact that by rights it belonged her sister, Lady Wynters. His father had lost it fair and square. And as far as causes went, a profligate antiquarian couldn't hold a candle to hundreds of starving orphans.

He could picture himself giving the lid to Caro. He could see the joy in her eyes, the relief. He could imagine her throwing her arms around his neck, breaking down in tears, so deep was her gratitude.

He would truly be her hero.

He would be her hero, right up until he revealed that his father had mortgaged his family's future so he could buy himself a second sarcophagus.

And then he could picture the change that would come over her face. How her features would shift from shock to disgust to pity.

He couldn't bear to see Caro look at him that way. Not after the way she had looked at him over the past three days. It didn't help his peace of mind that he could picture her here, before this very fire, lying naked upon the dressing gown that was draped about his shoulders.

And that meant there was really only one thing he could do, and that was keep the box. He wasn't about to hand it over to his father. Not until they had discussed the earl's spending habits and agreed to some limits going forward.

But there was an intricate series of maneuvers he would have to execute to have any hope of winning Caroline, and the first one involved handing the Eye of Ra box over to the Duke of Trevissick. This was the only way forward for him right now. Even if it was wrong, any other possible future was simply unthinkable.

Someday, years from now, once he had restored his family's finances, he would make a donation to Lady Wynters's charity, for the full value of the box. He would make things right.

But not right now.

And so, by the time he lay down at three in the morning, his mind was finally made up. He was going to keep the box.

God, all of that worrying, and he still had to figure out

how he was going to keep his father out of gaol and how to retrieve the bottom half of the box from the Wynters town house.

He groaned. Why couldn't catastrophes come one at a time?

CHAPTER 22

*C*aro didn't hear anything from Henry the day after their visit to the British Museum. By the following morning, the anticipation was killing her, so she sent Fanny off with a note requesting that Henry meet her midmorning in the square in front of his bachelor apartment.

Henry was nowhere to be seen when they alighted from the hackney. Only residents of the square had keys to the gate, so she and Fanny settled in to wait.

After a few minutes, who should come along but her favorite tiger, Billy, leading a gorgeous bay stallion. "Good morning, Billy," Caro said.

He smiled and drew the stallion to a halt. "Good morning, Lady Caroline."

"Is this one of Lord Thetford's horses?"

"Yes, m'lady. This is Brandywine. You can pet him if you like. He has excellent manners."

Caro stroked the stallion's neck. "Good morning, Brandywine. Aren't you a handsome fellow?" She turned to Billy. "Did you attend Astley's Amphitheatre last night?"

"Oh, yes, m'lady—it was wonderful! You wouldn't believe

the tricks Philip Astley can do in the saddle. Or I should say, out of the saddle—he didn't even need a saddle! He can stand up on the horse's back at a full canter, he can pick a handkerchief right up off the ground, he can even do a handstand—"

Caro smiled while Billy waxed on about the show, unaware that from across the square, they were being watched.

~

ARNOLD "SNAKEFACE" Jenner reflected that he never should have gone into the business of stolen antiquities. For years he had done well moving the goods he knew—drink, tobacco, and the like. He should've stuck to that.

But no, he had listened to fucking John Brownwood, and now look at the mess he was in. Brownwood had set off yesterday with all of their smaller pieces, insisting he had a customer lined up. That included their most valuable piece, the little blue and gold pendant in the shape of an eye.

Snakeface didn't know where Brownwood had gone, but he sure as shit noticed when he didn't come back. And wherever he was, he had taken several thousand pounds' worth of swag with him.

Now he was working his contacts, trying to learn if Brownwood had made off with the goods or if he'd been arrested. He suspected the latter. Brownwood thought he was so high above the rest of them, with his fancy Cambridge degree, but Snakeface knew the type well enough. John Brownwood was a white-livered cur. He didn't have the guts to strike out on his own.

And if the Charlies had him, John Brownwood was the type who would snitch. Snakeface felt sure of that.

And so he found himself making his way to his Bloomsbury flash house, to see if it was overrun with constables. That would answer his question right there.

As he skirted Bedford Square, he noticed a horse stopped along the square. It was the type of horse you couldn't help but notice—sixteen hands, perfect confirmation, glossy bay coat, four white socks, and a white blaze on his face. The kind of horse that would sell for more than a man like him would earn in a lifetime.

That bloody horse probably ate better than most of the men in England.

That was when he noticed the boy holding the lead line. Why—it was the little brat from the other night, the one who had spooked their horses. Snakeface slowed his steps.

As he passed by, he saw the reason the little shit was stopped in the middle of the street. He was talking to a woman, a real rum piece by the look of her.

And then he stopped dead in his tracks.

That wasn't just any rum piece.

That was the girl they had nicked the missing pendant off of.

He would recognize her anywhere. She wasn't the kind of girl a man was like to forget, not with those looks. Brown-wood had pointed her out as she entered that party two weeks ago, and Snakeface had arranged for someone to lift the necklace off of her as she left.

He even remembered her name—Lady Caroline Astley.

So, the boy was her groom. Suddenly it was all falling into place—the spooked horses, the coffin lid askew. Somehow this Lady Caroline had gotten wind of who had stolen her necklace, and she was looking to get it back.

The bitch probably had it back already.

But not for long.

Looking at Lady Caroline smiling at her stable boy,

Snakeface smirked, because now he had the leverage he needed.

~

BILLY RHAPSODIZED about the wonders of Astley's Amphitheatre for a good five minutes without pausing to draw breath. His reverie was interrupted by a deep voice. "How is Brandywine behaving himself this morning?"

Caro turned to find Henry approaching. Had a man ever looked so handsome in top boots, buckskin trousers, and a coat of bottle-green superfine that fit his gorgeous shoulders like a second skin? She sincerely doubted it.

"Very well, my lord," Billy replied. "Paul took him up to Hampstead for a proper gallop this morning. I've almost finished his cooldown."

"Good." Henry stroked the stallion's neck, and the horse whuffed happily and thrust his muzzle into his owner's hand. "Yes, I have something for you," Henry said, producing a lump of sugar from his pocket. He stroked the stallion's neck a few more times, looking him over. "Be sure to give him a good rubdown, Billy. I'll warrant he's earned it."

"I will, m'lord. Come along, Brandywine," Billy said, clucking to the horse. "Thank you again for the tickets, Lady Caroline."

"You're most welcome, Billy," Caro replied. She turned to Henry. "Shall we take a stroll?"

"Let's." Henry smiled at her, but only for a second. He turned and opened the gate to the green.

"As you can't get up to too much trouble here in the square, I'll give you two turtledoves a bit of rope," Fanny said. She pointed her parasol at Henry. "But know that I'll be watching." She wandered toward the far side of the green.

A chance to speak privately with Henry—this

morning kept getting better and better. Caro took Henry's arm, and they began a circuit along the square's graveled path. "So," she said, "I'm dying to know what happened yesterday. Did you claim the prize for yourself?"

Henry tripped over his own foot, then came to a dead halt in the middle of the path. His eyes were wide as saucers. "Did I... did I what?"

"The horse race," Caro said, bewildered. "I was wondering if you defeated Percival Thistlethwaite or if—"

"*The horse race*. Of course you meant the— Yes, I won."

Caro beamed up at him. "Congratulations, Henry. Not that I'm the least bit surprised."

"Thank you."

"I do want to hear all about it, but first I must know what else you learned yesterday. Did you call upon your godfather?"

"I did not."

"Oh! Was he not available?"

"Yes... unavailable... that's it. I'll, er, I'll try again today."

Was it her imagination, or was there a light sheen of sweat upon Henry's temple? How odd. The morning was pleasantly cool.

"Very good," Caro said. "How about Mr. Cuming? Were you able to call upon him?"

"Yes. I met with him. Yesterday afternoon."

She waited a few beats for him to elaborate, but he remained silent. "And what did he have to say?" she asked.

"Nothing we didn't already know," Henry said, his gaze locked on the path ahead of them. "It was a waste of time, I'm afraid."

"Oh, I'm sorry to hear that. Well, thank you for going to the trouble to track him down, all the same."

His response was a grunt. Caroline peered up at him. Not

that she had known him for so very long, but Henry wasn't acting anything like his usual self.

She drew him to a halt. "Henry, is anything the matter?"

"The matter? No. Why do you ask?"

"You're acting a bit strangely."

"I didn't sleep well last night. That's all."

Caro's brow wrinkled in consternation. He wasn't even looking her in the eye. She remembered how he had beamed at her the last time she saw him, in the garden of the British Museum. She had been so certain in that moment that he returned her feelings. That they were falling in love. Now—

Now she didn't know what to think.

"You—you're not mad at me, are you?"

"No. It's nothing like that." At least he was looking at her now, but she was struggling to read his expression. Was that sorrow? Consternation?

Unease?

She swallowed. "If there's anything I have done—"

"There's not," he insisted.

She regarded him for a few beats in silence. Perhaps it was as he said—he hadn't slept well. She shouldn't make more of it than it was.

She took his arm again and resumed their progress. "Very well, then. So, you were unable to speak with your godfather, and Mr. Cuming didn't have any new information. Were there any developments in our investigation?"

"None at all."

"How disappointing. Well, then, tell me all about the horse race. Did you ride Brandywine, or—"

She was interrupted by an explosion of yips, as a brown terrier puppy came barreling across the green. It stopped some three feet short of them, barking furiously.

"Poppy! Bad girl!" Her owner hurried over, an empty leash and collar in his hand. "I'm terribly sorry, miss. I've been trying to train her to walk on the lead, but she's a slippery little thing. She won't bite." He scooped the puppy up, then started in surprise. "Why, Lady Caroline. And Lord Thetford. Good morning."

Caro tore her gaze from the barking dog to discover that its owner was none other than James Parkinson, the proprietor of the Leverian Museum. "Mr. Parkinson," she exclaimed. "What an unexpected pleasure."

He bowed deeply. "The pleasure, my lady, is all mine. I apologize, I did not mean to interrupt—"

"Not at all," Caro said. "I believe your special exhibition on the Eye of Ra opened yesterday. Has it been well received?"

"It has, my lady, thank you for asking. We were quite busy yesterday. Mr. Cuming, the owner of the amulets, stopped in around closing time, to see how we were doing. He told me about the excitement you had yesterday, my lord—"

"Oh, dear, look at the time," Henry interjected. "Please excuse us, Mr. Parkinson—"

"Excitement? Did Mr. Cuming attend the horse race?" Caro asked, confused.

"The horse race?" Mr. Parkinson said. "I don't know anything about a horse race. What I was referring to was—"

"Come on, Caro," Henry said, tugging at her arm. "Let's go."

"Henry," Caro said, laying her hand on top of his. She couldn't imagine why he was being so rude to Mr. Parkinson, who had gone out of his way to help them both. "You were saying, Mr. Parkinson?"

"I wanted to offer my congratulations to Lord Thetford," Mr. Parkinson said. "On recovering your stolen amulet."

CHAPTER 23

*C*aro found herself unable to speak. It wasn't so much that she was having difficulty forming words as difficulty selecting a question when so many were clanging around in her head, fighting for predominance.

Why would Mr. Parkinson congratulate Henry on recovering *his* stolen amulet? Henry didn't have a stolen amulet. The one with the missing amulet was her. Henry was looking for his father's little box. And besides, Henry had told her that nothing had happened at Mr. Cuming's house.

That his visit had been a *waste of time*.

Beside her, Henry was saying something. "I believe you have been misinformed, Mr. Parkinson. I didn't recover an amulet yesterday."

Mr. Parkinson's forehead wrinkled. "But Mr. Cuming described it to me. A beautiful piece—the Eye of Ra in lapis and gold, with an ivory eye and—"

It could not be true. Caro didn't want to believe that Henry had lied to her. But that sounded exactly like her sister's amulet.

"I know the piece you're referring to," Henry said, "but it

isn't an amulet. It is the lid to a cosmetics box. And it belongs to my father."

"Perhaps I was confused," Mr. Parkinson said. "I assumed it was an amulet, because Mr. Cuming described the little hole it had at the top, so you could string it on a chain—"

Caro gasped. It had to be her sister's amulet.

"Yes," Henry said. "It is a singular design. But it was part of my father's box. Lord Lansdowne confirmed it."

Lord Lansdowne? What on earth did Lord Lansdowne have to do with any of this? None of this made sense, none of this made any sense at all—

"It must have been very exciting," Mr. Parkinson said, "when the constables came and arrested Mr. Brownwood. Have you heard anything from the British Museum yet? Are the other amulets they seized the ones that had gone missing?"

Mr. Brownwood had been there? Their primary suspect? And he had been arrested and hauled off to gaol?

This was Henry's notion of "nothing happening"?

Suddenly it was too much. Caro swayed on her feet as the world went black for a fraction of a second. Henry's hand was around her waist in an instant, steadying her. "Forgive us, Mr. Parkinson," he said. "I fear Lady Caroline is unwell."

Mr. Parkinson blanched as he took in her face. "I am the one who must beg your pardon, Lady Caroline. I should have known such a topic was unfit to discuss before a lady. My apologies." He bowed and was gone.

There was a solitary bench in the center of the green. Henry began leading her toward it. "Stop," she said.

"You need to sit," he replied, towing her along. "You're as pale as death."

She halted, jerking her arm free of his. "What I need is an explanation. Henry… what is going on? You said that nothing happened at Mr. Cuming's house. That it was a waste of time. How does that square with what Mr. Parkinson just said?"

His brow was knotted, his jaw locked. "I meant only that nothing was accomplished toward the recovery of your sister's amulet."

"Nothing was accomplished! It sounds as if not only was Mr. Brownwood there but he was taken into custody. And you recovered part of your father's box!"

"I didn't think the recovery of my father's box would concern you."

She was having none of it. "Of course it concerns me. The notion that I wouldn't be happy for you, even if my sister's amulet wasn't there, is implausible. As is the idea that I wouldn't wish to know about Mr. Brownwood's arrest." She reached out and took one of his hands, pressing it with both of hers. "Henry," she implored, "you lied to me. We both know you did. Help me to understand why. Tell me what's going on!"

"I'm sorry," he said in a clipped voice. "I should have been more forthcoming. But the only important thing for you to know is that your sister's amulet wasn't there yesterday."

"But why would you lie about all the rest of it? Why not just tell me what happened in the first place?"

He swallowed but said nothing.

"You know," she said after a beat, "when Mr. Parkinson described the lid to your father's box, I thought he was talking about my sister's amulet." He didn't reply, so she continued. "The Eye of Ra, in gold and lapis blue. He even thought it was an amulet. He described the little hole at the top—"

"It was the lid to my father's cosmetics box," Henry said through a locked jaw. "Lord Lansdowne confirmed it."

She stared up at him. She had never seen this hard look on Henry's face before.

"Then prove it," she said. "Go get it right now and show it to me."

"I can't. I gave it back to my father."

She raised her chin. "That is no impediment. Order your phaeton. We can be there in twenty minutes."

For a fraction of a second, a new emotion flashed over his face, replacing the unsmiling intractability. It came and went so quickly she couldn't be sure, but she rather thought it looked like… sorrow?

"Well?" she asked.

"No," was the only answer he gave.

IN THAT INSTANT, she knew. She knew he had her sister's amulet, and he wasn't going to give it to her. None of it made any sense. She didn't understand why he wanted it or how this whole miserable situation had come to pass, but one thing was clear.

She had trusted him.

And he had betrayed her.

Oh, God—it had all been a lie, hadn't it? Every secret smile, every touch, every kiss. Every time he had pretended to laugh at one of her witticisms, it had all been part of his act. He knew she had a weakness for him. What an easy mark she must have made. He had known that all he had to do was smile and crook his finger, and she would come running to him like a lamb to slaughter.

Nothing had changed from four years ago. He had never wanted her.

All he had wanted was her sister's amulet and the five thousand pounds it would bring, to cover some gambling debt or tailor's bill or to pay off his fancy new phaeton.

Or perhaps he needed the money to maintain his mistress...

An image sprang unbidden into her mind, of the two of them lying naked together before the fire.

He had been using her this whole time. He had never even wanted her.

And she had let him... she had let him...

Bile rose in her throat. She turned away, barely forcing the gorge back down. Now he was the one clasping her hand, shouting her name. She could not bear to even look at him.

She scoured the grassy circle. Where was Fanny? She had to leave. She had to leave *right now*. She staggered toward the gate, listing to the right, and felt Henry's arm encircle her waist.

"Caro. Look at me, Caro. It's not what you're thinking. I promise you, it's not what you're thinking—"

"Then what is it, Henry? Because it sounds like you have played me for a fool. That you've taken my sister's amulet for yourself, and—"

His eyes were desperate now, beseeching. "I need you to trust me, Caro. Don't you trust me?"

"I want to trust you. I want to so badly. It's breaking my h —" She managed to stop that thought before she humiliated herself further. She could feel tears pouring down her face and could taste a saltiness that meant her nose must be running, too. What a sad picture she must make. How sad and how pathetic. She knew she was making a fool of herself, but she couldn't stop crying. There were only a handful of people on the green at this hour of the morning, but they were all staring at her in open fascination.

Henry was oblivious. He was holding her in his arms in the middle of the grassy square, as if she were precious to him. Precious to him—what a farce! "You have it all wrong, darling," he said, his voice thick, his eyes sincere. "You're the one breaking my heart."

She had been transfixed by his eyes, but that snapped her out of it. She shoved at his chest, struggling to free herself from his embrace. "How dare you—you have the nerve to imply that I am the one in the wrong, when you have *lied* to me—"

She escaped from his arms, but he caught her hands and clung to them. "No, Caro. You aren't in the wrong, darling. I just... I need you to trust me—"

"If you want me to trust you again, it is entirely within your power. Go and get your father's box and show it to me right now."

He shook his head. "That isn't trusting me—"

"Your refusal is all the answer I need." She tried to jerk her hands free, but he wouldn't release her. "Let me go! Let me go right this instant!"

"Please, Caro. Please—"

And then, at last, Fanny came charging across the green. She shoved her way between the two of them, forcing Henry to release her hands. Fanny took up a position in front of her mistress reminiscent of the cobra snake from the Leverian Museum, primed for the strike, her parasol arched over her head like a rapier.

"What did you do to her?" Fanny shouted.

"Nothing!" Henry said. "Caro, look at me, darling—"

"Go away!"

"Should I hit him, m'lady?" Fanny asked.

"No. Thank you, Fanny, but no. I only want to go home."

She had taken all of two steps when, blinded by her tears, she stepped into a divot and went staggering. Fanny grabbed her upper arm to steady her.

Henry was on her in a flash, scooping her up in his arms

and lifting her high against his chest. He began carrying her toward the gate with rapid strides.

"Put me down," she demanded, struggling against his grasp.

"Damn it, Caro." He set her down after she managed to kick one leg free, but clung to her hands. "I know you're furious with me, but I don't want you to hurt yourself." His eyes were both miserable and sincere. "I would never let anything bad happen to you."

She reminded herself that it was all an act. That no matter how heartfelt he sounded, it was nothing but a lie. "Oh, that's rich," she said, "when the bad thing that has happened to me is you."

A look of such acute pain crossed his face that she almost took it back.

Almost. Instead she turned on her heel and strode toward the gate, with Henry clinging to her hand as he trailed after.

Fanny, who was glaring poison, had run ahead and flagged down a hackney carriage and now stood holding the door open. Henry ignored Caro's efforts to jerk her hand free and leaned inside the carriage door.

"This isn't over. I know you're upset, and I understand why. I'll give you some time. God knows I need some time, to figure out how I can explain it better. But this isn't what you think. I will call on you tomorrow, and we are going to work this out."

She managed to free her hand from his. Her voice trembled as she replied, "I never want to see you ever again."

The misery in his eyes was wrenching to see. "Caro—"

"Will you move already?" Fanny snapped, jerking Henry from the carriage. Her maid climbed in next to her, slammed the door closed, and then the carriage lurched into motion.

Caro spent the entirety of the carriage ride home sobbing

on Fanny's shoulder, and another three hours after that sobbing on her bed.

But then she got up and summoned Fanny to help put her appearance back to rights, because there was something she needed to do.

Mr. Parkinson had said that Henry had recovered an amulet, and that there had been a box of small items taken back to the British Museum.

But he had said nothing about the painted coffin and the other treasures they had encountered in the thieves' storehouse.

At this point, Caro couldn't trust Henry to do the right thing. But she knew the location of those stolen items.

It was time she paid a visit to Bow Street.

CHAPTER 24

*A*cross town, Henry stumbled back to his apartment.

He had felt terrible about lying to Caro, of course he had. But he'd only done so because that was the only way things would turn out right in the end.

They were meant to be together. If she wasn't the woman he was supposed to marry, then that woman did not exist. And she had wanted to marry him, too, before he had gone and ruined everything. He knew she had, knew she never would have allowed him the intimacies they had shared by the fireside had that not been her hope.

All he had needed was a little time to get his finances back on a steady footing. That was the only way they could have a future together.

And if he needed to lie in order to have a chance at that future, he wasn't about to apologize for it.

Still, his execution had been execrable. He could understand how it had all looked to her, for him to deny that anything of note had occurred, and then to find out that he had recovered the lid to his father's box, and John Brownwood had been arrested to boot. But Mr. Parkinson had taken him by surprise, and he hadn't had time to come up with a plausible explanation.

Now that the cat was out of the bag, he would have to tell her a bit more than he had originally planned. At least he had some time to think, so he could prepare, could figure out exactly what to say and how much to divulge.

An image sprang to mind of her face after he had refused to show her his father's box. He had never imagined that there could be something more excruciating to see than her expression out on the balcony four years ago, after he had declared that he didn't even want to dance with her.

But the face she had made this morning…

He shuddered. It had been a thousand times worse.

Well, there was only one way forward. He needed to figure out what he was going to say tomorrow when he went to prostrate himself at her feet. Something that would convince her to forgive him.

Because he knew one thing for damn sure—he wasn't giving up.

"HERE IT IS," Caro said, "number four."

She disembarked from the hackney carriage in front of the thieves' storehouse. The two Bow Street runners who had agreed to accompany her and Fanny climbed down, frowning as they examined the lock.

"How did you say you were able to get inside again, Lady Caroline?" one of the runners, Mr. Buchanan, asked.

"The thieves left the door open and unattended," Caro said. "Something spooked their horses while they were unloading some additional items, and they went chasing after the cart."

Mr. Buchanan gave a skeptical look to his fellow runner,

Mr. Ragsdale. Caro sighed. She had spent the better part of a half hour going over her story with Fanny, figuring out how to make it somewhat plausible, but she knew how farfetched it sounded.

But that didn't matter. All she had to do was convince them to enter the building. As soon as they saw all of those antiquities, she would be vindicated.

She raised her chin and strove to imitate her mother's imperious glower. "My father the earl would be grieved to hear that a thorough investigation was not undertaken. As would my sister the countess, whose property has been stolen."

Mr. Buchanan sighed. "Fine." He withdrew a set of lockpicks from a leather case and went to work. Caro couldn't help but observe that it took him more than twice as long to open the door as Henry had required, and he had been using naught but a hairpin.

She corrected herself. She would not think about him. Not right now.

Not ever.

The door yielded, and Mr. Buchanan swung it open. "Very well, Lady Caroline. Show us these stolen antiquities."

"I will," she said, striding through the door. "Everything is kept in this large room on the ground floor. Right here," she said, swinging the door open.

A silence fell over their party as they peered into the room.

Because it was completely empty.

Caro stepped into the vacant room, disbelieving. As she turned to check every corner, she caught the two runners exchanging a significant look.

"I promise you, three nights ago, it was all here. Statues and obelisks. Crates of tobacco. Casks of liquor. And here," she said, gesturing to the center of the room, "the sarcophagus." She gave a start as she noticed something on the floor. "If you look at the dust, you can even see the outline of its corners—"

"Come, Lady Caroline," Mr. Buchanan said. "We need to leave."

"But we haven't checked the other rooms yet. Perhaps there's something—"

"My lady," Mr. Ragsdale said, "the longer we stay here, the greater the chances we'll be accused of unlawful entry."

"It's not unlawful entry. The items have been moved, but you have my eyewitness testimony that they were here three days ago." She paused, taking in the two men's skeptical expressions. "You do believe me, don't you?"

Mr. Buchanan hesitated a beat too long before replying, "Of course we do, my lady." And she had her answer.

Mr. Ragsdale left to check the rest of the house. Ugh, if only she could call upon Henry to confirm her story. But that would require her to admit that they had been here together.

And then she would be ruined.

"Nothing," Mr. Ragsdale said as he returned. "As you can see, the thieves have moved on. I'm afraid there's nothing more to learn here."

"But you must question the owner of the building," Caro said. "They will have information about the leaseholder." She paused. "You will continue to investigate, won't you?"

Another significant pause before Mr. Buchanan replied, "Of course we will, my lady."

Caro could think of nothing more to say to convince them, and so a few minutes later, she climbed back into the hackney carriage, defeated. Fanny climbed up beside her; the runners had declined a ride back to Bow Street.

"You could always report a different crime to those runners," Fanny said. "Namely, the theft of your sister's amulet by Lord Thetford."

Caro sighed. "Not with Lord Lansdowne supporting him. It would be their word against Anne's. My sister may have an unimpeachable character, but I'm not sure she could prevail over a former prime minister. Besides, the only man who could say exactly how the amulet came to be in her possession is Lord Wynters, who happens to be dead. And Anne may not want to be dragged into a scandal, even with five thousand pounds in the balance."

As the hackney lurched forward, Caro stared out the carriage window despondently, wondering what she should do next.

CHAPTER 25

The following afternoon, Henry drove his phaeton to the Astley town house, ready to prostrate himself before Caroline. A gigantic bouquet of white and blue hyacinths lay on the seat next to him.

As he pulled up to Astley House, he saw an elaborate landau parked out front. Inside, he found Caro, her mother, and her sister, Lady Wynters, along with the owner of the landau, who turned out to be his favorite person in the whole entire world.

Marcus Latimer, Marquess Graverley.

Lady Cheltenham greeted him warmly. "Lord Thetford, do come in."

Caro glanced up at him, and for one second, a scowl crossed her face. She schooled her features, but not before Graverley noticed her reaction. The marquess smiled broadly.

Henry approached and presented Caroline with the bouquet. "Good afternoon, Lady Caroline. These are for you."

"Thank you, my lord," she replied, staring at the tea table instead of him.

He took a seat. "I was hoping to take you for a drive this afternoon."

She wouldn't meet his eye. "I fear I must decline, as I have promised to go for a drive with Lord Graverley."

"Oh," Lady Cheltenham said, "but we would hate for Lord Thetford to be disappointed. Did you not come in your landau, Lord Graverley? Perhaps the four of you could make up a party."

Graverley smiled sadistically. "What a splendid idea, Lady Cheltenham."

"It's settled then," Lady Cheltenham said, shepherding the party toward the door.

Lady Cheltenham, bless her, didn't realize that her daughter wanted nothing to do with him and herded them into pairs—Graverley with Lady Wynters and Caro with Henry. Caro did not deign to look at him as she accepted his arm.

As they descended the front steps, he whispered, "I need to speak with you."

She sighed. "Go away, Henry."

"I will not. Not until I've had a chance to explain—"

"I say, Thetford," Graverley interrupted, gesturing to Henry's phaeton, "where did you get those greys?"

"I bred them myself."

"Ah, that explains it. I've been looking for a pair of greys but have been unable to find one of sufficient quality. Until now. I'll buy them off you. Let us say two hundred pounds each."

Henry knew he would have to sell these two eventually, but the thought of Graverley driving his favorite team was revolting. "They're not for sale."

"They are an exceptionally matched pair, in addition to

each having perfect confirmation. Two hundred and fifty each."

"I fear you didn't hear me the first time."

"Perhaps I did not make myself clear—I have always wanted a team of greys. It is my favorite color. I'll give you seven hundred pounds for the pair."

His favorite color would be *grey*. "No."

"A thousand pounds."

Henry paused. Graverley was now bidding well above what they were likely to fetch at auction. Given his current financial circumstances, he couldn't afford to be squeamish.

Especially when this might solve all of his problems.

He looked Graverley dead in the eye. "Five thousand pounds for the pair."

He enjoyed the way the marquess's jaw fell open in shock. "Five thousand—for a pair of *horses?*"

Henry shrugged. "Take it or leave it." He turned to his tiger. "We'll be heading out in Lord Graverley's landau, Billy. Take the greys around the square a few times to keep them loose."

"Aye-aye, m'lord." Billy climbed atop the phaeton and clucked to the greys. They sprang forward with perfectly matched strides, their action gorgeous in the afternoon light. Graverley was unsuccessful at concealing the longing in his eyes.

Catching Henry regarding him, Graverley masked his features. "Alas, Thetford, I may not get your greys, but I believe there is something else with which I will have more success. Or should I say, with whom." He plucked Caro's hand off of Henry's arm and handed her up into the carriage.

Caro was uncharacteristically quiet as they departed for Hyde Park. After a few minutes of riding along in silence, her sister said, "What a handsome carriage, Lord Graverley, and how comfortable it is. I believe you are an expert on carriages and horses, Lord Thetford—do you not agree?"

Was he really expected to compliment the man's carriage? It was handsome enough, if one liked that sort of thing. But what young man didn't drive a phaeton, light and capable of top speeds, rather than a huge, hulking landau? His *father* preferred a landau. "I suppose it's fine, although some of us have a phaeton, instead of a landau, and are fully capable of driving ourselves around town."

"And others of us have three phaetons, in addition to a landau, and drive them all on a regular basis," Graverley retorted. "But these certain others of us prefer to train our eyes on something other than the backside of a horse when we know we'll have such lovely passengers."

Normally Henry would have expected Caro to make a great show of smiling and blushing at such a compliment from Graverley. But she gave no indication of having heard.

"*Lovely* is certainly an apt descriptor for the Astley sisters," Henry said. "But as I have come to know Lady Caroline, I have discovered that her true worth does not lie in her looks."

At least she looked at him then, even if it was only to narrow her eyes. "No, your uses for me have nothing to do with my looks."

"Uses for you?" her sister said. "What a curious turn of phrase. Whatever do you mean, Caro?"

"I will allow him to explain," Caro replied. "Lord Thetford, pray tell my sister what it is you have gained as a result of my acquaintance."

Henry inclined his head. "Well played, Caro. As usual."

Graverley's head snapped from Henry to Caroline. "Did he just call you *Caro*?"

"Lord Thetford presumes too much," Caro said, gazing

out the side of the landau as they entered Hyde Park. "Only my friends call me Caro."

"And I am one of those friends," Henry said, "for nobody could regard you more highly than I do."

She forced a smile. "La! Does your notion of friendship involve trading thinly veiled insults?"

"To be fair, Caro," her sister said, "there is nothing you enjoy so much as delivering a thinly veiled insult."

Caro gaped at her sister. "I should like to know whose side you are on."

"Well, it's true," Lady Wynters muttered.

"And that," Henry said, "is the key. Would you like to know the difference between you and me, Graverley?"

"A dukedom, a basic sense of decorum, and about... ninety thousand pounds a year?" Graverley guessed.

It was more than ninety thousand at this point, but Henry wasn't about to say as much. "The difference is that, unlike you, I know the real Caroline Astley. The girl who loves making a thinly veiled set down, not just the sparkling façade she shows most of the world." He looked directly into Caroline's eyes. "And I happen to think her perfect, exactly as she is."

He had hoped this might earn him a smile; instead, Caro looked more upset than ever. "Let us speak of something else," she said. "Anne, how are things at your charity?"

"Splendid, thank you for asking. I will soon be able to open a second lodging house," she explained to the gentlemen. "It has been such a joy, going through my stack of pending applications, knowing I will have a place for at least some of them. Such sad stories—there was one today from a seventy-three-year-old washerwoman who cares for her three grandchildren. It used to be four grandchildren, but the littlest one died last month. She wouldn't have even been able to afford his burial had a customer not made her a generous donation." She shook her head. "They live in the most abysmal little hovel in Wapping. I'm terrified the roof might collapse upon them at any moment."

Henry blanched. That sounded rather like his laundress, Mrs. Dakers. Gad, it probably *was* Mrs. Dakers. He felt a sudden wave of guilt. He needed the Eye of Ra box, of course he did. Caro would never marry him without it.

But it had somehow felt easier to justify keeping it when those who would suffer as a result had been people he didn't know and would never meet. As desperately as he wanted to marry Caro, he was having trouble formulating a convincing argument that he needed it more than poor Mrs. Dakers.

Lady Wynters continued, "Another application was from a woman with two children and another on the way. It's urgent that we remove her from her current situation. Her husband strikes his wife and children when he's in his cups, which I am given to understand is more often than not. Last week the four-year-old suffered a broken arm—"

Graverley scowled. "That is appalling."

"It is," Lady Wynters agreed. "It's also legal. Unless the wife has somewhere else to go, she has no recourse. And even then, the husband has the right to keep the children if he contests it."

"I did not know," Graverley said, "that your charity assisted women in those circumstances. How soon will you be able to relocate her?"

Lady Wynters sighed. "Probably not for several months hence."

"That will not do," Graverley said. "She must be removed immediately, and the children, too. Find suitable lodgings for them and send the bill to me." His face hardened. "And make it known that if the father goes anywhere near his wife or children, it will be my barrister he will be facing in court."

The countess's mouth fell open. "Nothing would please me more. Thank you, my lord," she said, her voice breaking.

"And you can expect a donation from me in the coming days," Graverley continued. "A significant one." They had reached Rotten Row, and the landau had been forced to halt due to the crowded conditions. Graverley glanced around. "Let's see, who else is here—there are Mr. and Mrs. Ellis. Are they amongst your donors?"

"They have a subscription, yes," the countess replied.

"And there is Lord St. Austell. How about him?"

"Alas, no. I have been unable to make Lord St. Austell's acquaintance."

"He owes me a favor. Don't settle for a farthing less than two hundred pounds." Graverley opened the door to the landau. "Come, I'll introduce you right now." The marquess handed a startled Lady Wynters out of the carriage.

Leaving Henry and Caroline alone.

Caro was glaring silently toward the waters of the Serpentine, refusing to so much as look at him.

Henry glanced about. Graverley and Lady Wynters were deep in conversation with Lord St. Austell.

This was his one chance. The only chance he would get to make things right.

So he took it.

ONE MINUTE LATER, they were making their way toward a secluded copse of trees on the banks of the Serpentine, one of the few places in Hyde Park that wasn't overrun with the crush of humanity who had turned out to see and be seen during the afternoon promenade.

"What. In *God's name*. Is *wrong with you?*" Caro hissed at him through a clenched smile.

"You'll have to be more specific," he murmured, which earned him an impressive glare. "Ostensibly you could be referring to the way I contrived to get you out of Graverley's carriage—"

"We can't discuss our activities of the past week before Lord Graverley's coachman, Henry. I could be ruined!"

"—or my leading you on this extremely pleasant stroll—"

"You mean this forced march to the Serpentine—"

"—although it is patently obvious that my only reasons for doing those things was so I could get the chance to speak with you, and that the root of the matter is what happened yesterday."

They had reached the banks of the river. Henry led Caro to a place where they were hidden by the copse of trees. Caro crossed her arms and glared at him. "Why don't we start there?"

Henry swallowed. It was time to have it out, then. "The first thing I need to say to you is that I'm sorry. Yesterday you accused me of lying to you, and I—I must own that it's true. I did lie to you yesterday. I didn't want to, but at the time I believed it to be the best out of a number of bad choices. I see now that it was the wrong one, and I'm sorry for it. I'm so sorry, Caro, and I want to tell you the truth, as much as I am able."

Her eyes remained wary, but at least they were no longer openly hostile. "Go on, then."

"It all started three days ago, when I encountered my father at the British Museum. That was when I found out—" He swallowed.

Caro looked grudgingly intrigued. "Found out what?"

"That your sister's Eye of Ra amulet and my father's Eye of Ra cosmetics box are one and the same. When I happened upon my father there in the shed, I gave him an update on my search for his box. I told him about your missing item, and that we had been working together. That was when he told me that his cosmetics box had been in Lord Wynters's possession."

"The Eye of Ra I borrowed from my sister was not a box," Caro said. "I'm quite certain of it. There was no compartment, and it was this thin—"

"I said the exact same thing to my father. What you thought was an amulet was the box's lid. I can see in retrospect why we didn't realize we were after the same item. The lid turns on a round peg that fits inside the hole you noted. Having never seen them apart, I honestly didn't realize it had a hole."

He slowly reached out for her, giving her the chance to rebuff him. She regarded him warily, but hope surged in his heart when she allowed him to take her hands in his. "I swear," he continued, "I had no idea before that. It wasn't a lie, not at first. I was truly trying to help you recover your sister's pendant. To be sure, I was hoping the thieves might also have my father's box, which he had told me had been stolen. But that wasn't the reason I agreed to help you. All I wanted was the chance to earn your forgiveness."

Her resolve was weakening. He could see it in her eyes. "Why didn't you tell me all of this yesterday?"

And here it was—the trickiest part of his argument. If he could convince her to accept this one point, he would win the day. "The situation is complex, but what it boils down to is this: I know how much your sister wants that box. I know how much good work she would do with it. But my father has to have the box. It's his, and he has to have it. And I regret to say that the reason he needs it so badly is the one thing I'm not at liberty to tell you. How I wish I could. I wish to God I could tell you everything, Caro. But right now, I have to ask you to trust me."

He could see the war being fought inside her eyes. They

held confusion, as well as doubt. But he could also tell that, deep down, she wanted to believe him. "Are—are you in danger?" she asked. "You or your father or—"

He sighed. "Not danger, no, but… I beg you, please don't ask me any questions. Please don't ask them of me because I can't answer them, and I don't want to lie to you again. I hated lying to you yesterday. It was horrible, and I—I never want to lie to you again."

She sighed, and he could almost see the cracks forming in her resolve. "I want to believe you, Henry. I do. I just… Can't you tell me? You're asking me to trust you. But wouldn't it be easier for you to trust me, with the truth?"

"I want nothing more than to tell you the truth. And I will one day. Someday, I'll be able to tell you everything, and we'll laugh about all of this. I swear we will. When we've been married for twenty years, and this is but a distant memory—"

Her entire body jerked, and her eyes flew to his. "When we've… *what*? What do you mean, married for twenty years? Who said anything about marriage?"

He was playing his trump card, and he knew it. He drew her into his arms, and his heart sang with victory when she didn't resist. "Of course I want to marry you, darling. I meant it when I said you were perfect exactly as you are. You were right four years ago, Caro. You saw it, and I was an idiot. We're meant for one another, and I want to spend the rest of my life with you."

A tear streaked across her cheek. "Oh, Henry," she said, burying her face in his shoulder.

He held her while she shook in his arms. "Is that a yes?" he asked softly.

She looked up at him, and he could tell how much she wanted to believe him. She laughed as she swiped at her eyes. "It's not exactly a secret that I've always wanted to marry you. I'm trying to trust you, but… I have so many questions.

You say that the box belongs to your father. How was it, then, that it came to be in Lord Wynters's possession?"

"My father let him borrow it. He was to host some Prussian diplomats for a dinner, and like so many people, they were swept up in the craze for all things Egyptian. Unfortunately, when Wynters passed away, he still had it in his possession."

Her eyes lit up. "I recall Anne mentioning the planned dinner with the Prussian diplomats and how it had to be cancelled after Lord Wynters's passing." Caro paused, then frowned. "But why did your father not simply ask my sister for its return?"

Henry froze. He thought he had gone over every scenario, every possible question she might ask.

Why hadn't he thought up an answer to such a basic query?

He saw Caro's gaze sharpen, and he knew he had hesitated a beat too long. "He didn't want to trouble your sister while she was in mourning—"

"For the first week, or even the first month after his death, that would be plausible. But Lord Wynters died last summer. My sister may not be attending balls, but she is certainly receiving callers—"

Caro gasped, and he saw the shock of realization enter her eyes. "Wait. Your father gambled with Lord Wynters. Every week, from what I understand." She glared up at him. "Your father lost it to Lord Wynters in a game of cards, didn't he?"

Henry blanched. "How did you know that they gambled together?"

She jerked herself from his arms, furious. "Because Lord Wynters was *married to my sister*, you dolt!"

"I, uh, I don't know all the details—"

"Yes, you do! It's written all over your face. You know

very well that your father staked it in a game of cards, and that by rights, that amulet belongs to my sister. And yet here you are, lying to me. *Again.*"

"Look, Caro. That box is the pride of my father's collection. He's owned it for longer than I've been alive. He did stake it when he gambled with Wynters, but only because he knew Wynters would give him a chance to win it back. They had a special arrangement. It was bad timing that Wynters died before he had the chance to do so."

"I believe there is an expression about the luck of the draw that would apply. But if your father wants it back, in a marvelously convenient twist, it's going on sale. He is welcome to bid for it next week. But by rights it belongs to my sister. And you know it!"

"It's not that simple—"

"I should like to know why not. No one wants to part with five thousand pounds, but perhaps this will teach your father the inherent risks of gambling." Henry didn't have a reply, so Caro continued, "Thanks to your mother, your family owns half of Brighton. Everyone knows that. You could buy it back. You could easily buy it back, yet you have chosen not to. You have chosen to use me, to manipulate my feelings—"

"That's not true—"

"Do you know what my mother used to tell me?" she asked, ignoring him. "That no matter how besotted they may seem, most men only want one thing from a girl. It's a standard lecture, one I'm sure most mothers give their daughters. But Mama was wrong. It was all an act with you. You didn't even want that one thing." She closed her eyes as a tear rolled down her cheek. "You did not even want it, but I gave it to you anyways."

"Caro," Henry said, genuinely shocked. "You cannot possibly believe that."

Her eyes remained closed. "Of course I believe it. What else is there to believe? You were lying to me the whole time. You never wanted me, you only wanted my sister's amulet—"

"I swear, I—"

"You knew of my infatuation with you, that I would be easy to manipulate. All you had to do was pretend an interest in me—"

"I'm not pretending!" He tried to take her hand, but she wriggled away.

"You don't care for me at all. You were only using me to steal this amulet, worth five thousand pounds—"

"Of course I care for you!"

She swiped at a tear with the back of her glove "Do you really? Five minutes ago, you said you would never lie to me again, and yet that is exactly what you proceeded to do. You were *planning* to lie to me in the same breath you pledged never to do so again. You would not have told me the truth, that your father lost the box fair and square and that it rightfully belongs to my sister, had I not caught you out. How can you expect me to believe a man who lies to me, Henry? How?"

"That's not what is important—"

"Yes, it is important! You won't even explain to me why you need it. I am left to come up with the most lurid theories. Do you need the money to cover your own gambling debts? To buy the silence of a former mistress? A current mistress?"

"I don't have a mistress," he said, managing to seize one of her hands in his. He could hear his voice quavering, but he could not have stopped the words from pouring out if his life had depended on it. "I have not so much as looked at another woman since you came back into my life. I don't want anyone but you—"

"How am I to believe you? You lied to me not five minutes

ago. If I cannot trust you in that, why should I trust you in this?"

"Because I promise—"

"Your promises are worthless. And look at what you're asking me to do. You're asking me to take the fall before my sister—"

"Your sister will forgive you—"

"That is not the point! That is not the point at all! You heard her today, talking about the grandmother who couldn't afford to bury her own grandson and the pregnant mother being beaten by her husband. Of the little boy whose arm just got broken. *They* are the point, Henry. They are the point, and do not imagine for one second that it is only those two families. I've been to my sister's lodging house—there are hundreds more with stories every bit as heartbreaking."

A tear streaked down her cheek, and she swatted at it with her glove. "I have had all of this on my conscience. The guilt has been *crushing* me. But here you are with the power to save them, the power to save me. You have the power to fix everything. Yet you won't. Instead you choose to leave me hanging in the wind."

"I hate to ask it of you, Caro. I *hate* to. But you must trust me when I say that this is the only way we can be together."

"Well, I do not. I do not trust you one iota. And why should I?"

Henry raised his hand to frame her face. Another tear streaked down Caroline's cheek. Slowly he slid his hand down her neck, to feel the pounding of her pulse at her throat. "You should trust me because of this. Don't you feel how your heart races for me?" He gently reached down and took her hand and placed it over the center of his own chest. "I feel it, too. There's no way you can tell me *this* is a lie."

She jerked her hand free and took two steps back. "I've always been stupid where you're concerned. My foolish infatuation with you is the last thing I should trust. It has never done anything but hurt me. You broke my heart four years ago, and now you have done so again. I was a fool to have ever given you another chance. Now, if you have any decency at all, you will leave me alone."

"Leave you alone?" Henry's mind refused to process the words. They made no sense. He stepped toward her, and she took a corresponding step back. "But I can't leave you alone, Caro. I know you're furious with me right now, but I asked you to marry me—"

"Well, I have refused. And I never want to see you ever again."

He blinked at her, uncomprehending. An offer of marriage was his ace of spades, and the ace of spades was the one card that couldn't be beaten.

Could it?

"Please, Caro," he sputtered, "you don't mean that—"

"Yes, I do." She gave him her profile, and her voice broke as she said, "Now go away."

He was moving to take her hand when someone emerged from behind a tree. It proved to be Caro's maid, Fanny. "Lady Caroline has had her say," Fanny said, striding toward them.

They both jerked in shock. "Fanny," Caro said, "what on earth are you doing here?"

"I followed you, of course. Did you really think I was going to let you go off for a drive with the man who's had you crying your eyes out the past two days?" Fanny snorted. "Not on your life."

"But how did you get here?" Caro asked.

"I flagged Billy down, and he drove me," Fanny replied, pointing toward the top of the rise. Henry peered around a tree, and surely enough, Billy, who was standing beside the phaeton, gave a jaunty salute. "Which is fortunate," Fanny continued, "as you'll be needing to find your own way home, my lord."

With that, she put her arm around her mistress's waist and proceeded to lead her away.

Henry watched Caro go, her words echoing in his head. *I never want to see you ever again.* He had known she was furious with him, but he had really thought he was going to win the day. Because Caroline Astley had wanted to marry him since the very first moment she ever saw him.

Just not anymore.

He saw Billy waiting for him by the pathway, and he knew he should go.

But suddenly he just... couldn't.

He sat down right on the grass and stared out over the waters of the Serpentine.

CHAPTER 26

Caro awoke the next day upon a pillow streaked with tears. After Fanny had led her back to Lord Graverley's landau, she had lied for the second time in her life about having come down with a megrim. Anne's eyebrow gave a violent twitch, as she knew full well that, for Caro, a megrim was code for *Henry Greville has just broken my heart*, but she said nothing. Lord Graverley was everything that was solicitous and understanding, raising the hood of the landau so nobody would witness her distress and conveying her home immediately. If he was surprised that Caro had happened upon her own maid in Hyde Park, he said nothing. And no one seemed disappointed by Fanny's pronouncement that Lord Thetford would be making his own way back.

There was a knock at the door, and Fanny entered with a tray. "I thought you might like breakfast in your room, m'lady."

Caro sat up. "That is exactly what I want. Thank you, Fanny." She donned her dressing gown and slippers and padded over to the little table by the window.

"How are you holding up?" Fanny asked.

"As well as can be expected, I suppose," Caro said, spreading butter and jam upon the bread Fanny had already toasted, bless her. "I still can't believe you were hiding in the trees. Did you hear everything?"

"I came up as his lordship was explaining how he never wanted to lie to you ever again." Fanny accompanied this pronouncement with a great roll of her eyes.

"Then you heard him say... you heard him say..."

"That he wanted to marry you?" Fanny asked, opening the curtains. "Aye, I did."

Caro sighed. "Really, Fanny, you might have made your presence known sooner."

Fanny gaped at her. "And interrupted that scene? Not on your life. The look on his lordship's face, when he said he didn't have a mistress, a'cause the only one he wanted was you?" Fanny made a show of fanning herself with her hand. "Jigger me tight, I may need to lay myself down."

"Surely you're not suggesting that I made the wrong decision?" Caro paused, and she heard her voice crack. "Are you?"

Fanny sighed and took the chair across the table. "What I know is that man is in love with you."

"He is not," Caro said quickly. "There was a time when I believed the same thing. But he is a good actor, a good liar—"

Fanny snorted. "He's the worst liar I have ever seen, in my whole entire life. Both times he lied to you, you figured it out within minutes."

"That was only by luck. He has a lifetime of experience at deception. I've told you about the scrapes he and Harrington would get into—"

"And doesn't every one of those stories end with the two of them getting caught and flogged?"

"Well... er... be that as it may—"

"Now, I'm not saying you did anything wrong. He lied to you, he's done the wrong thing with regards to your sister, and you've a right to be angry with him. But however much they may drone on about women being the weaker sex with the weaker brain, the good Lord knows that men are stupid creatures sometimes. Having a man isn't so different from having a puppy. You have to train them, ya see? And I think you are just the woman who can bring that man to heel."

Caro rubbed her temple. "And here I thought you of all people would take my side. I thought you would thrash him to the ground with your parasol, and that would be that."

"There was no need, m'lady. You were laying into him better than I ever could. To be sure, he needs to learn his lesson. Give him a few days to think things over and see if he won't tell you the whole truth this time."

Caro felt tears welling in her eyes. "I don't think I can bear to give him another chance, Fanny. He's broken my heart twice now. I wouldn't have thought that anything could be worse than when he did it the first time. But this..." She trailed off, a tear streaking across her cheek. "I can't go through this again. I can't bear to."

"Oh, my lady," Fanny said, rising and pressing a handkerchief into Caro's hand. "The decision is yours, of course. And if you think you would be every bit as happy with someone else, it's not as if his is the only offer you're going to receive."

"I daresay I would be very happy with Lord Graverley, should he propose," Caro said, trying to convince herself. "You should have seen him strong-arming every man in Hyde Park into making a donation to my sister's charity. I must confess, I had thought him a bit of a scoundrel. But he has hidden depths."

"In that case, you'll be pleased with the gigantic floral arrangement that came for you this morning. As soon as I have you dressed, I'll round up three footmen to stagger up the stairs with it."

"I'm sure that will cheer me considerably," Caro said, rising from the breakfast table and walking over to her dressing area. Fanny had laid out one of her favorite morning gowns, a white dress with some leafy green embroidery at the neck and hem.

"So, what do you mean to do today, m'lady?" Fanny asked as she began to get Caro dressed.

"There's only one thing for it. As there is no hope of recovery, I must tell Anne the truth about her amulet."

"I think you're right, m'lady. But cheer up—if you marry Lord Graverley, I have a feeling he would agree that a five-thousand-pound donation to your sister's charity is a small price to pay to bring a smile to his new bride's face."

"Perhaps you're right," Caro said. It hadn't occurred to her that there might be another solution to her problem, another way to come up with the five thousand pounds.

But if she married Lord Graverley…

"Perhaps you're right," she repeated.

CARO SENT a note to Anne straightaway asking when she could pay her elder sister a call, but Anne was busy all of that day and most of the next. They arranged for Caro to come for tea the following afternoon.

But the next day, as she and Fanny were preparing to depart, the note arrived that changed all of her plans and turned her previous concerns into the merest trifles:

I HAVE WHAT'S YOURS, because you have what's mine. If you want your stable boy, Billy, to live, bring the Eye of Ra to the Execution

Docks at Wapping at dusk. Bring only your ginger-pated maid. No constables, no runners, or the boy dies.

～

A HALF HOUR LATER, Caro and Fanny arrived at the offices of the Bow Street runners in a hackney carriage. Before departing, she had dashed off a note to her sister, begging her to cover for her by informing their mother that not only was Caro there, but she had decided to stay for supper. That should buy her a few hours.

They entered the offices, which contained the same crush of humanity that had greeted them three days before. Oh, God, it would take forever to find someone to assist them, and they had no time at all. Poor Billy had been taken by God knows who, and if they didn't get there by dusk—

Caro spotted a familiar face striding toward the door. "Mr. Ragsdale! Mr. Ragsdale!" she cried, hurrying over.

Recognition crossed Mr. Ragsdale's face. Recognition and annoyance. "Lady Caroline," he said, hastening toward the door.

She grabbed his arm. "Oh, Mr. Ragsdale, please, I'm in desperate need of your assistance." She unfolded the note with fingers that shook. "You will recall the theft of my sister's amulet. I received this note a half hour ago—the thieves have formed the misimpression that I have it, and now they've kidnapped a young boy—"

"What?" Mr. Ragsdale snatched the note.

"I know it says no runners," Caro said. "But I didn't know where else to turn—oh, Mr. Buchanan! Thank goodness you're here, too. As I was telling Mr. Ragsdale—"

Mr. Ragsdale handed his fellow runner the note. Mr. Buchanan scanned it quickly, and the two men exchanged a look.

Caro waited for one of them to say something, but they remained silent. "Tell me, how should we proceed?" she asked.

"Lady Caroline, there's been a triple homicide over on Ratcliffe Highway," Mr. Buchanan said.

"How marvelously convenient," Caro said. "Is that not also in Wapping? As soon as we've rescued Billy, you can head straight over to commence your investigation."

"A murder is a serious thing," Mr. Ragsdale said.

"I understand that," Caro hastened to say. "I do. But whereas those poor souls are already making their final journey, there's still a chance for Billy—"

"I know this is some sort of a game to you," Mr. Buchanan snapped. "But an actual crime has been committed. Actual people are hurting right now. The Bow Street runners do not exist to act out the titillating fantasies of young society misses—"

"It's not a fantasy! It's real, I swear it is—"

"About as real as the Egyptian treasures in that house. Come, Lady Caroline," Mr. Ragsdale said. "Meet me at the Execution Docks, or the boy dies? What Gothic novel did you take this from?"

"Now see here," Fanny said, stepping forward. "Her ladyship is telling the truth."

The two runners were halfway out the door. "Says the woman in her employ," Mr. Buchanan said. "Good day, Lady Caroline."

And then they were gone. Fanny took Caro's arm and led her back outside and into their waiting hackney carriage.

They sat in silence. "I hate to suggest it," Fanny said, "but at this point, there's only one person we can turn to."

Caro rubbed her temple. She knew it was true. There was only one person who would believe she had spent the past two weeks pursuing a gang of thieves, and that was the man who had done it all with her. He even had the ransom the thieves were demanding. She knew where she had to turn.

She just didn't want to.

Caro swallowed. It did not matter one whit what she wanted. The only thing that mattered was Billy.

She called to the driver. "Take us to Bedford Square."

CHAPTER 27

The door to Henry's rooms was opened by his valet, a middle-aged man by the name of Gibson, whose eyebrows receded almost into his hairline at the sight of a well-dressed young lady coming to call at his master's bachelor apartments.

"Please tell Lord Thetford that Lady Caroline Astley is here to see him," she said, striding past Gibson into the room. "And tell him it is a matter of grave importance."

"Yes, my lady," Gibson said, hastening toward the door Caro happened to know led into Henry's bedchamber. Gibson paused to peer back at her. "This explains so much," he said, shaking his head.

Henry burst from his bedroom scant seconds later. He looked *awful*.

At least, that was what any lady of quality would have thought. Gracious, he couldn't have so much as looked at a razor in days. He wore nothing but a pair of loose trousers and a shirt. She could see all of his neck and half of his chest. And he couldn't have been sleeping well, given his bloodshot eyes and the faint circles beneath them.

Yes, Caro should have disapproved of Henry's appearance. Although truth be told, she had never been offended by the sight of Henry Greville's bare chest. Quite the opposite, as it happened. And as for that scruff upon his jawline...

A plague upon Beau Brummel for declaring that men of fashion had to shave twice a day, because Henry Greville looked mind-numbingly handsome with a three-day beard.

And as for the look in his eyes... what girl could be expected to bear up when Henry Greville was looking at her like *that*?

"Caro!" he cried, rushing across the room to her. "Thank God!" He had her in his arms in an instant, words spilling from his lips as he buried his face in her hair. "I truly thought you would never forgive me. I was so afraid I would never see you again—"

She freed herself from his embrace and took a step back. Henry froze, the hope draining from his eyes as he took in her expression. "I am sorry to have given you false hope," she said, "but that is not why I'm here."

He looked crestfallen. "I—I see. I beg your pardon." He stepped back, running a hand through his mussed hair. "What is it, then?"

She handed him the note. "I received this perhaps an hour ago."

The room fell silent as he read it. "Gibson," he said, "I need you to run to the mews and inquire as to Billy's whereabouts."

"At once, my lord," Gibson said, calmly reaching for his hat and gloves.

"No, look at this, Gibson." Henry thrust the note before his valet's face. Gibson's eyes went wide with shock. "I need you to *run*."

Gibson didn't respond, as he was already out the door

and halfway down the stairs, waving his arms above his head as he ran.

Henry hastened into his room, where he began fastening his shirt. Caro followed, ignoring the choked sounds of disapproval coming from her maid. "I tried going to Bow Street," she explained, "but they dismissed me. Three days ago, I met with two runners and brought them to the house across the square where the thieves were storing everything. But it had been cleared out. So now they think I'm some sort of hysterical female who goes around imagining crimes for a lark."

He glanced out the window. "Dusk is in a half hour. That will give me just enough time to get down there—"

"I'm going, too."

"Absolutely not—"

"The one they'll be looking for is me. If I don't show up, they won't even come out. It's the only way."

"Damn it, Caro—"

"I can summon a hack as easily as you can. There's nothing you can do to stop me. So I suggest you reconfigure your plans so that they include me."

He glared at her in the mirror as he knotted his cravat.

"My lord!" Gibson called from the front room. They rushed out to see him hunched over, struggling to catch his breath. "No one at the stable has seen Billy since this morning."

"Thank you, Gibson," Henry said, crossing over to his desk. He pulled a knife from a drawer, slipped it into his boot, then removed a wooden case from a shelf and opened it to reveal a pair of pistols. He loaded them both.

"Right," Henry said once he was done, "let's go."

❧

THE FOUR OF them crowded into a hack. On their way to the docks, they came up with as good of a plan as could be managed on such short notice.

Henry didn't like this one bit. Especially not the first part of their plan, which involved Caro strolling down to the Execution Docks with naught but Fanny for protection. But the sun was sinking fast, and they had run out of time to think up something better.

As they had agreed, the driver let Caro and Fanny out right at the stairs to the Execution Docks, where the Royal Navy strung up pirates, mutineers, and whoever else the Admiralty decreed worthy only of death. The gallows were set right on the banks of the Thames, visible only at low tide. At high tide, the waters would rise over the freshly hung body, typically three times before it would be cut down.

For the most notorious criminals, the body could be dipped in tar, placed in a cage, and left hanging from the gallows for a year or more as a warning. Henry shuddered to think what horrors Caroline might be encountering as she descended those stairs. It was agonizing, being powerless to shield her from this.

Their driver let Henry and Gibson out two blocks farther down, and they made their way along a dock to the riverbank.

Henry dropped down over the edge of the dock, splashing into ankle-deep water. Gibson followed. The tide was coming in, and they had to wade along, hugging the sea wall that backed up to a row of raised houses and warehouses.

They jogged along for fifty yards before coming to a warehouse raised on piers that jutted right out over the river, with its own dock so cargo could be unloaded directly from ships. Henry crept beneath the dock until he came to a thick stone pillar. Gibson stole up behind him as Henry peered around the corner.

The first thing he noticed was the row of gallows lining the riverbank—all empty, thank God. And there, standing on the last dry step, was Caro, looking fresh and innocent and entirely out of place amongst the scaffolds in her crisp white dress and lilac spencer. Fanny stood beside her mistress, holding her parasol like a cudgel.

They didn't have to wait long. After a few minutes, three men descended the stairs, stopping a few steps above Caro and Fanny. The one in the middle was the beady-eyed man he had seen chasing after Billy.

"Well, well, well, if it isn't Lady Caroline Astley," he said in a voice Henry recognized as belonging to the man the others called Snakeface. "How kind of you to answer my note."

"Where's Billy?" Caro said in a voice that carried across the water.

"Where's my amulet?" Snakeface returned.

"I have it," Caro said. "Go and get Billy, and we'll make the exchange."

The three thugs began to chuckle. "That's not how this works," Snakeface said. "You have two choices. You can give me the amulet right now and trust that I'll send Billy out. Or you come with me, and we make the exchange inside."

"I don't trust you."

"Then you're not as stupid as I think you are. Not quite," Snakeface amended. "You were stupid enough to steal from me. That's a mistake you'll come to regret."

Henry had to give Caro credit—she remained uncowed. Her voice was steady as she replied, "I wouldn't expect men who stoop to kidnapping children to have any scruples. But do you know to whom the amulet belongs? It belongs to my sister."

"Another rich gentry bitch, the same as you," Snakeface said.

Caro lifted her chin. "She is the Countess of Wynters, founder of the Ladies' Society for the Relief of the Destitute. She plans to sell the amulet to establish a second lodging house. Will you deny hundreds of widows and children a roof over their heads and bread on their plates? Are you really so despicable?"

"Why, yes," Snakeface replied, grinning, "yes I am. Now, if you please, Lady Caroline, right this way." He strode up the stairs. Caro and Fanny followed, and the other two thugs circled around to bring up the rear.

God damn it—they had discussed exactly what Caro was *not* going to do, and this was it: accompany the thieves to some hidden location, where Henry might not be able to follow. He waded after them, hugging the wall, waiting until the thieves were out of sight before he mounted the stairs. He reached the street and peered around the corner, where he saw Snakeface unlocking the front door to the warehouse he had been hiding under moments ago.

"Come on," Henry said to Gibson, backtracking the way they had come. "There'll be a door for cargo on the river-facing side. We can sneak in that way."

Gibson grabbed his arm. "My Lord, is what Lady Caroline said true? About the amulet belonging to Lady Wynters?"

Henry sighed. "It is."

"Lady Wynters— I didn't realize— Then we can—" Gibson turned and began sprinting down the beach, back the way they had come.

"Gibson!" Henry hissed. "Where the devil are you going?"

"I'll be back!" he called over his shoulder.

Perfect. Now his valet had abandoned him. There was nothing for it; he was going to have to face down the criminals by himself.

Henry waded into the noxious river, for the first time in his life not giving the slightest damn about leeches, until he came to the outermost pillar. The water came up to his chest, and he had to hold his pistols aloft to keep the powder dry. He looked up, studying the structure above. The dock overhung the last pillar by a good six feet—too far to reach. But in the failing light, he spotted a pair of boards with a gap between them.

He tucked his weapons beneath his chin, shimmied up the pillar, then reached out to test the gap. It was just wide enough for him to fit his hand through. He swung out into space, using the gap to go hand over hand until he reached the edge of the dock, where he pulled himself up.

He peeled off his sodden coat and emptied his boots, then crept up to the large double doors. They were locked, as he had expected they would be. This time he had brought his lock-picking tools from his days at school. After a minute, he felt the final pin give way, and he eased the lock open.

He uttered a silent prayer as he cracked the door open and slipped inside, a gun in each hand.

Luck was on his side—the thieves' backs were turned. He counted five of them now. He also spotted Billy, gagged and bound to a chair in the corner.

The thieves hadn't spotted him, but Caro had. He caught her eye for the briefest second as he slipped behind a barrel.

He peeked out to survey the scene. The same antiquities they had last seen in the storehouse off of Bedford Square were littered throughout the room—the painted wooden sarcophagus, a sandstone obelisk so tall it had to lie on its side, and several large statues, including the one of the winged goddess. There were also dozens of crates and barrels. Fanny was standing in the corner next to Billy. She had been relieved of her parasol, which was leaning against a crate some five feet away. One of the thieves was in the process of binding her hands in front of her. The other two loomed over Caro, who was not looking nearly as intimidated as she probably should, given the circumstances. To the contrary, she was glowering at Snakeface with an expression Henry would have described as unimpressed.

"I demand that you untie my maid, and Billy, at once," she said. She pulled the velvet pouch containing the Eye of Ra from her reticule. "I have kept my side of the agreement. Now you keep yours."

Snakeface took the pouch and opened it to confirm the Eye of Ra was inside. He held it up, admiring it as it sparkled in the dim light of the room. "I thank you for that, Lady Caroline. I'm only disappointed you didn't make me search you for it." His underlings chuckled, one giving a lewd whistle.

Caro ignored them. "Our transaction is complete. Now untie Billy and let us go."

"That's not how this works," Snakeface said, grinning sadistically. "There's one more thing I'll have of you, Lady Caroline. Something you've no doubt been saving for your husband, but that's neither here nor there. Then each of my men will have a turn with you, and then perhaps I'll have another go before I put my hands around your throat and choke the last breath out of you. Then we sew your body up in a bag full of rocks and throw it into the sea." He began advancing on her. "I would bind your hands, too, but I'll enjoy this more if you fight back."

Henry had one of the pistols out, and he was trying to line up a shot. He might not be as good of a marksman as Harrington, but he shot with his friend all the time and was fully competent with a pistol.

But nothing could have prepared him for this. Hearing that lowlife threaten to lay a hand on Caro, his Caro, and seeing the terror in her eyes? And knowing that he was her only chance, that if he missed, he was going to have to watch her get raped by five men?

His hands had never shaken so hard in his life.

How the devil, Henry wondered, was he going to make this shot?

CHAPTER 28

*C*aro was terrified.

She should have listened to Henry, should have stuck to the plan. Why she had trusted someone named Snakeface to be a man of his word was now utterly beyond her. She had thought only to save Billy, but she hadn't done Billy one bit of good, now had she? Because if these men were going to rape her and kill her and throw her body to the sharks, there wasn't any chance they were going to let the witnesses go free.

Inside she was panicking, but she knew she had to put on a good front. So she clung to the only shred of hope she had left: that Henry would save her. Of course he would. In spite of the fact that he had lied to her and betrayed her, for some reason she felt confident he would do everything within his power to protect her. All she needed was to do her part and buy him some time.

And so she cocked up her chin, did her best to steady her voice, and said, "Are you so stupid as to imagine that you'll get away with this? I am the daughter of an earl. My father will tear this town apart to find you. It's a good thing there are so many gallows below. There will be enough for all of you."

Snakeface laughed, advancing on her. "By the time anyone realizes you're missing, we'll be at sea. You've made the mistake of assuming you could negotiate with a man who has nothing to lose. They've arrested Brownwood. He'll talk, if he hasn't already. We're as good as dead—if we stay in England, that is. But we've an hour or two before our ship arrives. Might as well enjoy them."

He took the final step forward, then raised his hand to grab her by the throat.

A split second before his hand touched her, the report of a gun filled the room, causing Caro to jump. The hand that had been scant inches from her neck fell, and Snakeface grabbed his shoulder, his face contorted in agony. He howled and spun toward the back of the room, searching for the source of the shot. "Someone's here!" he shouted. "Get him!"

There was a chaotic scramble. Caro dashed behind a crate. When she peered out, she saw Fanny snatch up her parasol. Her front-bound hands in no way impeded her from clubbing the nearest man repeatedly in the head. He fell to the ground, but on the fourth swing, the parasol's shaft snapped clean in two. Fanny immediately began stabbing him with the jagged remnants of the handle. The thug struggled onto his hands and knees, a murderous expression on his face. As he reached for Fanny's ankle, Billy surged to his feet, lifting the chair he was bound to with him, then came down hard, smashing the man's hand beneath one of the chair's legs. The goon screamed in agony and flopped back down onto the floor.

Caro looked around for the remaining four men. Snakeface was on the far side of the room, a red stain spreading across his shoulder, searching amongst the crates for Henry. She could see two of the other thieves, including the short man who had abandoned his watch—Hulston, that was his name—checking the wall closest to the river. But where was the last man?

A thump to her left caused her to turn, only to see the missing thief stealing up behind her, an iron crowbar raised over his head. Before Caro had time to scream, there was the crack of a second gunshot, and the man froze, a red stain spreading rapidly across the center of his shirt. He fell to the ground, dropping the iron crow. His eyes stared off into nothingness, and within seconds his body went still.

Caro snatched up the iron crow with hands that shook. Henry had only brought the two pistols, and now he had used up both of his shots. Meanwhile both Snakeface and Hulston clutched pistols in their fists, and the third man held a knife. At least Fanny and Billy had their man pinned. The final three men were closing in on the corner of the room. "He's here!" Hulston shouted.

Caro screamed as the thieves' pistols fired in unison, fearing the worst. But then she saw Henry, hurdling over a crate, landing catlike in the center of the room, knife in hand. By some miracle, both shots had missed. Henry spun to face Snakeface and Hulston, who tossed their spent pistols aside and drew knives of their own. Snakeface reached Henry first, slashing with an abandon that was surely born of pain and rage. Hulston immediately joined in the fray. Henry dodged adroitly, but that was when Caro saw the third man. He had snuck around the room and was stealing up behind Henry, lifting his knife for the strike.

Caro was across the room in a second. Uttering a silent prayer, she swung the iron crow for all she was worth. The thug never saw her coming. The metal bar took him right in the temple, and his body went limp, dropping to the floor like a puppet whose strings had been cut.

Seeing his henchman fall, Snakeface roared and threw

himself at Caro, his knife raised overhead. She tried to raise the iron crow, but it was tangled in the inert body of the man she had struck, and she couldn't pull it free.

She closed her eyes, waiting to feel the cut of the blade.

It never came. She heard a grunt and opened her eyes to see that Henry had thrown himself in front of her, taking the knife's blow in her stead. Blood poured from his face, forming rivulets across his cheek. A crimson stain began to spread across the neck of his shirt.

That made Caroline *furious.* She jerked the iron crow free and advanced on the two thugs. "How *dare* you!" she thundered.

"Caro!" Henry shouted, "Stay back!"

But she wasn't about to stay back. Something about her expression caused Hulston to take a step back, and he stumbled over the base of a statue. He regained his footing, but not before Caro smashed him over the head with her iron crow. He dropped as quickly as the first man.

She rounded on Snakeface, her eyes murderous. But Henry had the situation under control, his hands locked around Snakeface's wrists. Snakeface probably outweighed him by three stone, but Henry overpowered the wounded man easily and shoved him down onto a crate. He flipped the criminal over so he was belly down, and locked his arms behind his back.

"We did it," Caro breathed, disbelieving. "We won!"

As she said it, there came the sound of voices from the back doors, the ones that opened toward the river, followed by the click of someone fumbling with the lock. The doors swung open, and a crowd of men were silhouetted in the moonlight.

"Is the cargo ready to load, Snakeface?" one of them asked, as a group of eight sailors stepped into the light of the room.

From his position facedown on the crate, Caro saw Snakeface give an evil grin.

~

IT WASN'T FAIR. It wasn't fair, Caro mused, because they had won. They had somehow managed to fight off five men. They deserved this victory.

But now it was going to be snatched away.

"You boys arrived in the nick of time," Snakeface said from his prone position. "Seize them!"

Caro heard Fanny swearing more viciously than the sailors as two men grabbed her arms. Henry was shouting at Caro to run. Four men had seized him, but he somehow managed to surge forward, struggling frantically as he dragged the startled sailors halfway across the room, such was his desperation to reach her side. His eyes met hers for one second before he was shoved facedown onto a crate, and Caro mused that if she was about to die, at least the last thing she would ever see was Henry Greville looking at her like *that*.

The final two smugglers were advancing on her, backing her into a corner. Her hands shook, but she raised the iron crow. She was not about to go down without a fight—

From across the room, she heard the click of a pistol being cocked. She saw one of the men who had been struggling with Henry pointing a gun straight at her. "Nice try, love," the sailor said. "Now put it down."

Her shoulders slumped, and she felt her face crumple. It was all over. It was all over, and all of the horrible things Snakeface had threatened her with were about to occur—

From the doors leading out to the street, there came a deafening *thump*, as if something solid had slammed into them.

Everyone froze, turning to face the doors. In the silence, Caro could hear voices, a great many voices intermingled, and noticed a glowing light filtering around the edges of the boarded-up windows.

The *thump* sounded again, and there was a splintering sound as a crack formed in one of the doors. Goodness, if she didn't know better, she would have thought it was a battering ram.

The voices were growing louder, more irate. There came a final *thump*, and the doors burst open. And a great mob poured in, a mob of women, wielding torches and pitchforks and hatchets, but also pots and pans, broom handles, and rolling pins. The mob came streaming into the room, rushing around the wagon they had used to smash open the doors.

A mob led by Henry's valet, Gibson, and a stooped old woman who had all of four teeth.

"That's him right there!" the little old woman cried, pointing at Henry. "He's the one who helped me when I couldn't bury me grandson. Protect his lordship!"

The mob surged forward, and the smugglers and sailors were soon herded into a corner, cowering before the dozens of sharp implements pointed their way.

"Mrs. Dakers?" Henry asked incredulously.

"Good evening, m'lord," the woman replied. "I daresay ya weren't expecting to see me, now were you?"

"No. No, I was not," he replied.

Gibson handed his master a fresh handkerchief for his brow, which continued to bleed. "I apologize for having abandoned you, my lord. But I recalled that Mrs. Dakers lives in Wapping. And as soon as you said that the amulet belonged to *Lady Wynters*, I suspected that with her help, I could raise the entire neighborhood."

"I've applied to Lady Wynters's charity myself," Mrs. Dakers said. "She's like an angel come down to earth, Lady

Wynters is." She paused, shaking her head. "Ain't nothing I wouldn't do to help Lady Wynters."

A murmur of agreement went up around the crowd. Fanny stepped forward. "Well, seeing as you're all so eager to help Lady Wynters, it happens that there is something you can do." She gestured to Caro. "This right here is Lady Wynters's little sister. And if it becomes known that she was here this evening, and that she's the one responsible for clubbing those two ne'er-do-wells lying insensible on the floor upside the head with that there iron crow, she'll be ruined in the eyes of the fancy folk."

An admiring rumble passed through the crowd. "You did that?" Mrs. Dakers asked, nudging Caro with her elbow.

"I did," Caro confirmed.

"I like me a girl with some pluck," Mrs. Dakers said.

"So," Fanny continued, "when the magistrates show up, no matter what tale those good-for-nothing bastards who tried to steal from Lady Wynters might tell, we'll need about fifty eyewitnesses to insist that Lady Caroline wasn't here, and neither was I. That Lord Thetford was here alone, holding his own against those thugs when ya burst through the doors. Can ya do that?"

The sound of genial agreement filled the room.

"Thank you," Caro said. "Thank you, truly."

"Come, m'lady," Fanny said, towing her toward the door. "We've got to get you home before you're missed. Leave that here," she added, plucking the iron crow from Caro's grasp and laying it aside.

As Fanny led her into the street in search of a hack, Caro caught Henry's eye, but there was no chance to say anything or even to see how serious his injuries were.

And truth be told, she now had no idea what she wanted to say to him.

CHAPTER 29

$\mathcal{A}$s the clock struck midnight, Caro mused that she had become quite skilled at sneaking out of the Astley town house.

She hailed a hack and settled back for the short ride. She had been so lucky today. They had survived their encounter with the thieves and rescued Billy. Anne had covered for her by sending a note to their mother, and when she and Fanny had walked through the door, her mother had assumed she was returning from nothing more exciting than supper with her sister. No magistrate had showed up at the Astley town house to question Caro about a strange story being told by a group of criminals.

And she had finally decided what she needed to do about one Henry Greville.

After the hack dropped her off on Bedford Square, she climbed the stairs to his apartments and knocked at the door. Once again, Gibson's eyebrows shot up at the sight of Lady Caroline Astley standing on his master's doorstep, this time in the dead of night.

"Good evening, Gibson," she said, gliding into the room.

"Good evening, Lady Caroline," he sputtered.

The sound of her voice must have reached the bedroom, because Henry appeared in the doorway, dressed in a shirt open at the neck, some loose trousers, and his dressing gown. There was a great gauze bandage wrapped around his forehead, sloping toward his ear. The sight of his battered face made her heart squeeze, as did his eyes, which held more resignation than hope.

"You are dismissed for the evening, Gibson," Caro said. "I will see to your master."

"Yes, my lady," Gibson said, hastening out the door.

A silence fell, as Caro and Henry stood regarding each other across his sitting room. "How is your head?" Caro asked.

"It's fine. He sliced open my eyebrow and across my temple," he said, tracing the path the knife had taken over the bandage. "Nothing a few stitches couldn't fix. Head wounds bleed like the dickens, so it looked worse than it was."

Caro strolled over to inspect the bandage. "A hair lower, and you would have lost your eye. If you survived, that is."

He shrugged. "I didn't."

"But you could have."

"It's all right."

"Hmm." She crossed the room and sat upon the sofa before the fire, the site of their previous lovemaking. She patted the cushion for him to join her. He did so, careful to leave plenty of space between them. "So," she said, "what happened after I left?"

"It turns out that there were two Bow Street runners nearby, investigating a murder near Ratcliff Highway. Someone ran to fetch them while the surgeon stitched me up. Buchanan and Ragsdale were their names—"

"Humph. I'm all too familiar with Mr. Buchanan and Mr.

Ragsdale. They were the pair who refused to help me, who accused me of having made the whole thing up as a lark."

"I would have throttled them had I known that."

"I appreciate that. But what I regret is that I wasn't there when they walked through the door to find a roomful of Egyptian artifacts. You cannot imagine how smug and condescending I would have been."

A ghost of a smile crossed Henry's face for the first time. "I would've liked to have seen that. I'm quite partial to your condescending glower."

"I know you are. So, what happened from there?"

"Snakeface and his friends were taken into custody. Night watchmen are guarding the artifacts even as we speak. I'm to go back down there tomorrow morning and meet with the runners again."

"Oh?" Caro asked, surprised. "What more do they need from you?"

"I figured something out after the fact. I realized who the rightful owner of the sarcophagus, and the other stolen antiquities, must be. He'll bring the paperwork tomorrow and officially claim them."

"Ah. I see."

They lapsed into silence. After a moment, Henry said, "Was there anything else you wanted to ask? If not, I would be glad to escort you home—"

"There is one more thing I was hoping to discuss."

"What's that?"

She drew a deep breath. "I couldn't help but notice something, Henry. When Snakeface was looming over me with that knife, I felt certain I was going to die. But then you stepped right in front of me. Right into the path of the knife."

"It was nothing—"

"And although you seem determined to minimize it, you came a hairsbreadth away from being stabbed in the eye."

He shrugged, staring at the carpet.

She reached over and took his hand. "You were willing to die for me."

He glanced up at her, his eyes full of sadness, and gave a slight nod.

She stood, drawing him to his feet and leading him across the room.

"Caro?" he asked. "What are you—"

She didn't stop but opened the door to his bedchamber and led him through, halting only when they both stood at the foot of the bed.

"I don't understand," he said.

She looked him in the eye. "I realized something tonight. When they threatened to rape me—"

He squeezed his eyes closed. "Please don't talk about that. I can't even bear to think about it—"

"—I realized that I regretted not making love to you when I had the chance."

His eyes flew open, confused. "What—what do you mean?"

She summoned all of her courage. "What I mean is that whatever happens in the future, my first time should be with the man I love." She looped her arms around his neck. "And that is why I've come here tonight."

HENRY STARED AT CARO, struggling to process what she had said. He hardly dared to allow himself to hope, but…

"Caro," he said, "are you saying you'll marry me?"

"I cannot marry a man who lies to me. Who won't tell me the truth."

"Oh." He must have allowed himself to hope, because now he felt deflated. "I see."

"Henry," she cajoled, "why can't you just tell me?" He tried to look away, but she reached up and caressed his uninjured cheek, turning him back to her. "I'm so confused—it's as if you prefer death to telling me the truth."

Henry gave a bleak chuckle. "You understand me at last, Caro." Because that was the way it was with men. Physical acts of courage were part and parcel. They were *expected*.

Whereas admitting your troubles, your weaknesses? That was anathema.

"Should it not be the other way around?" Caro asked.

"Probably it should, darling, but that's not the world we live in."

She made a frustrated sound. "The thing is—I do trust you. I trust you when you say you want to marry me. I trust you when you say that the only one you want is me. And I can tell it's eating you up not to tell me the truth, so you must have a very compelling reason to do so."

He gave a faint nod, and she continued. "I believe you. I believe you, Henry. Because I know what kind of man you are. You're brave, and you're honorable. You're the man who stepped in front of a knife for me. I know you would never hurt me. I—I love you, Henry. Can you not trust me and tell me the truth?"

Oh, but this was agony. The words *I love you* on Caro's lips were like balm for his recently battered sense of worth. He wanted to close his eyes and revel in them, to let them echo around all the empty places inside of him, to see if they could fill the holes that only he knew lay beneath the strong front he had to show the world.

Most alarmingly, there was a part of him that very much wanted to say those words right back.

But he knew better than to take comfort in words he knew to be a lie. Not that Caro was to blame. He could see the sincerity in her eyes. She truly believed that she loved

him. But she also thought he was *honorable*. She didn't understand that he had been lying to her this whole time by
allowing her to believe he was a man who was capable of
supporting her. That he ranked amongst the men she would
even consider marrying.

And he wasn't about to enlighten her. To tell her what a
failure he was. To confess how deep his lies had gone. To tell
her he wasn't the man she thought he was.

Because there was no way she would still love him if he
told her all of that.

So what he said was, "That's the problem, darling. Right
now you're looking at me exactly the way I need for you to
look at me. But if I tell you the truth—"

"I *love* you, Henry. I love you so much. Nothing you could
tell me will change that—"

"You say that now. But you wouldn't love me if you knew
the truth. You would never even consider marrying me. And
I can't bear to see the scorn in your eyes, the derision, when
you find out."

"I won't. I promise I'll look at you precisely the same way.
Can't you trust me?"

"I'm sorry, Caro. I—I'm a coward."

"I will not countenance such talk. Not about the man who
was willing to give his life for me."

He bowed his head, unable to look her in the eyes. He felt
her release his hands. "I understand you won't want anything
more to do with me," he said. "But please allow me to see you
safely home."

He heard a rustling sound, followed by one soft thump,
then another. "Caro?" he asked, confused. He raised his head.

What he saw caused his heart to stammer in his chest. She
was kneeling on his bed in her stockinged feet; the two
thumping sounds had been her slippers hitting the floor. She
was peeling off her spencer, which soon floated down to join

the slippers. She reached behind her back, struggling to reach the ties of her gown.

She looked up at him and smiled. "I could use some assistance."

He came to her side, sitting down upon the bed, but only to seize her hands, stilling them. "Caro, you don't have to do this."

"I want to do this. I told you, I want my first time to be with the man I love."

God, she was killing him. "But I told you, I'm unworthy—"

She stopped him with a hand to his mouth. "I will be the judge of whether or not you're unworthy. The only thing I want to know right now is whether or not you're unwilling."

He laughed blackly. "Of all the ridiculous questions. There's nothing in the world I would rather do than make love to you, Caro."

Her smile was tender. "Excellent."

And then she looped her arms around his neck and kissed him.

$\mathcal{T}$hings were ever so much better, Caro reflected, now that Henry was kissing her.

He had been slow enough to get started, erroneously believing that the nobler course was to refuse her.

But he hadn't lasted long under her onslaught of kisses, particularly when she pulled his bottom lip between her own and started to suck. This elicited a groan, and then he began kissing her demandingly, burying his hands in her hair.

That started her body humming in all the right places, but when she shoved his dressing gown down his arms, then pushed it in a heap onto the floor, he tore his mouth from hers with a ragged breath.

"You're certain about this, Caro?"

She tugged his shirt free from his trousers and began pushing it up his magnificent torso. "Absolutely certain," she breathed.

Turning over the problem again and again after leaving the warehouse, she finally realized that Henry was too afraid of her rejection to trust her with whatever dark secret he was harboring. What she needed to do was find a way to show

269

him that she believed in him unconditionally. That she was willing to stake absolutely everything on him.

The only way she could do that was by giving him the one thing she could never take back.

And she knew this might very well mean her ruination. That was a chance she was willing to take.

Because she knew with complete certainty that this was the man she wanted to spend the rest of her life with. If she couldn't marry Henry Greville and have the kind of honest marriage she wanted to have with him, she would rather die a spinster, banished to some remote cottage in the country, than marry someone else.

Henry was speaking. "Because—" He made a muffled sound of protest as she pulled the shirt up over his head mid-sentence. As it went fluttering toward the floor, he continued, "Because once I get you out of that dress, I will be *very* disappointed if I have to stop."

She ran her hands over his chest, purring in delight. God, his body was gorgeous. "I would be just as disappointed."

He lay down beside her then, his lips going to her ear. "I'm glad to hear it," he murmured. And then he was kissing her there.

Gad, who would have thought an ear could be so sensitive? His kiss sent shivers throughout her body, and she felt her breasts tighten into peaks. It was wonderful that she had taken his shirt off, wonderful to have all of that warm, satiny skin beneath her hands, but for God's sake, why was there still so much fabric separating her from Henry?

They were of one mind on this subject, for Caroline was pleased to see that he had somehow managed to loosen the ties of her dress and was now tugging it down her arms. He loosened the tie at the neck of her chemise and pushed her breasts up out of the short stays she wore. And then his hands were on her breasts and then his *mouth* was on her breasts and suddenly she was arching her back so hard that she lifted them both off the bed, and who was making that very loud mewling sound? Oh, was that her? Doubtlessly that particular sound wasn't considered to be ladylike, but who could be bothered to care when Henry was sucking her nipple like that? It was like there was a sinew that connected her nipple to the place right between her legs, because *that* was what had started to throb, and *why* was he not touching her there, and *how* could she get him to start?

She gave a shriek of frustration and shoved her crumpled gown down over her hips, then kicked it onto the floor in a heap. He was laughing at her, but at least he made good use of his hands, unlacing her stays and helping her to remove them and her shift in rapid succession.

This left her in nothing but her stockings and garters. He groaned as her body came into view, his hands stroking from her hips across her stomach and up to cup her breasts. She reached down and began to untie a garter. "You could leave those on," he suggested, drinking her in with his eyes.

She gave him a quick kiss on the lips. "Another time. Right now I want all of me pressed up against all of you."

Having made quick work of her stockings, she reached for the placket of his trousers, but his hand shot out, capturing her wrist.

"Slow down, minx," he said.

"There's no need to slow down, Henry. I—I'm ready."

"*I* need to slow down. Those trousers are the only thing reminding me not to fall on you like a starving animal."

"Mmm." She ran her hands over the planes of his chest. "That doesn't sound so very awful."

He groaned, burying his face in the pillow beside hers. When he looked up, his eyes were tender. "Your first time is going to hurt, Caro."

"I know that."

"I hope I can still make it good for you. That the pleasure will outweigh the pain. But I can't be sure. So, what I would very much like," he said, stroking his hand along her cheek, "is to pleasure you first."

She sighed dramatically, as if aggrieved. "If you insist."

Henry was grinning as he rolled on top of her. He kissed her deeply, lingeringly. After a minute, he began to work his way down her body, starting with her neck and then pausing to suckle her exquisitely sensitive breasts. His hands were everywhere, which was exactly where she wanted them— skimming up her sides, over her shoulders, down her arms, and then teasing their way across her stomach and down to her hips. His mouth continued its path downward, as he nibbled his way across her stomach, pausing to tongue her belly button. Oh, it wasn't that it didn't feel good. What he was doing felt divine, truth be told. But his ministrations were making her acutely aware of how much she wanted his hands and mouth in a different location.

She noticed that he was laughing at her again, the vile man! And what was that thumping sound? Oh, were those her own hips, bucking up and down on the bed, demanding some of Henry's attentions be directed between her legs? Well, so what if they were? He knew what she wanted, so why in God's name was he not giving it to her? She mewled in protest.

"Are you needing something, Caro?" he asked.

"You know full well what I'm needing, you scoundrel!"

"Oh, were you wanting some of this?" he asked, putting her out of her misery by gently swirling his thumb over the tender nub of flesh between her legs. She cooed in approval, which caused him to chuckle. Well! She was beyond caring if he wanted to laugh at her, now that she was *finally* getting what she wanted. Oh, *Gods*, that felt good! If only he would go the tiniest bit *faster…*

Henry was kissing his way down her stomach again, until she felt warm breath between her legs. She squirmed in anticipation. This time he didn't make her beg, he just parted her folds, and she felt his tongue, right on the center of her, and oh, *good Lord*, that felt *divine*.

He kept his hands busy while he swirled his tongue over that magical little spot between her thighs, caressing her legs, her sides, her breasts. God, everything felt so good, but especially his tongue stroking her so light and wet and quick. She was exquisitely aroused, and the pleasure was incandescent. If only he would *never* stop. If only he would never, never, never, ever stop. Oh, *God*, she was so close, if only he would stroke her just like that, just like that, *just like*—

Her peak came hard and fast, catching her off guard. One minute she was lying back, relishing the mind-numbing pleasure Henry was giving her, and the next thing she knew, the sparks that had been coursing throughout her body seemed to ignite, and she felt her eyes squeeze shut as her whole body was wracked with convulsions.

When the world stopped shaking, she opened her eyes to see Henry regarding her with a smug smile. "Again," he said, caressing her thighs.

"Again?" she asked in disbelief.

"Again," he answered firmly and lowered his head back between her legs. Caro's every nerve was on fire. She would have said she was too sensitive, but Henry was stroking her so softly and so gently with his tongue, and actually... actually... actually, that did feel quite nice, and oh! That little swirly circle he was making was in precisely the right spot. That made her back arch and her toes curl and... and... and now that she thought about it, he could go a little bit faster, give her a little bit more, because it appeared that Henry had been right, she wasn't too sensitive, not at all...

It was fortunate that Henry was fluent in the wordless

language of Caro's moans and bucking hips, because she had lost the ability to string words into actual English sentences. But he somehow knew exactly what her body wanted, even if she couldn't have told him what that was had her life depended on it. She was building toward her peak again. She now understood enough to know what was coming. And right when she thought it wasn't possible to feel any better, he slipped a finger inside her, and that spot he was rubbing, that felt… very interesting. The pleasure wasn't so intense as what he was giving her by caressing the little rosebud between her legs, but it was intriguing, and it made her feel terribly *curious…*

And then the beautiful sensations stopped. Caro cracked open her eyes to protest, only to see Henry unfastening his trousers. He cast them aside, then crawled right on top of her, and oh, the weight of him, pressing her into the bed, the feeling of him warm and naked and on top of her, was absolutely divine.

He was raining kisses all over her face. "It's time, darling," he said. "You're as ready as it's possible to be."

"Yes, Henry. *Yes.*"

His face tightened in concentration, as he reached down and positioned himself at her entrance. And then she felt pressure between her legs as he inched forward, and as her body started to resist him, she felt doubts start to creep in. Oh, God, this was never going to work. Just look at the size of him! How could that thing be expected to fit inside of her? And then the pressure gave way to a tearing pain, and she knew that had to be her maidenhead. She tried to bite down her cry of pain but was unable to conceal it completely.

She peered at Henry, who was frozen above her. His brows were knotted in concentration, his jaw locked. He studied her carefully, stroking her face with one hand.

"Is it terribly painful, darling?" he asked.

Caro swallowed. "It... it does hurt."

He swallowed. "I'm sorry. I won't move again until you're ready."

Something about his eyes in that moment... They were so warm and filled with tender concern... they brought back a little bit of the glow she'd been experiencing a few minutes before. She gave an experimental wiggle of her hips. It did still hurt, but her motion made him groan. His neck was knotted up so tightly she could see his pulse leaping at the side of his throat. And seeing the solicitude in his eyes, and his determination not to hurt her... suddenly the pain didn't matter so much. All that mattered was that she was experiencing one of the most beautiful moments of her life, one that she would treasure always, and she knew with absolute certainty that she had picked the right man to share it with.

She kissed his neck, causing him to shudder. "You can go ahead," she said.

He hesitated, peering down at her with a knotted brow. "Are... are you sure?"

"Yes, darling."

He groaned and buried his head in her neck, and then slowly, slowly, *slowly*, he started sliding within her. After a few minutes, he had settled into a moderate pace. She still felt a stinging pain with every thrust. There was probably no way to avoid that her first time. But she found herself quite swept up in the closeness she felt with Henry, feeling him on top of her, *inside* her, holding him in her arms as he took such obvious pleasure in her body, that she truly didn't mind. She thought her heart might burst, so poignant was the moment.

Suddenly he straightened his arms, lifting his torso up off the bed. He continued thrusting into her, but he reached one hand down to the place where their bodies were joined. His clever fingers sifted through her curls until he found that magical spot between her legs.

And then he began to rub her there.

The pleasure was different this time. Her emotions were so close to the surface—tenderness, intimacy, vulnerability, love—and they spilled over, hastening her physical unraveling. Given the pain she was feeling, the immediacy of her response startled her. Because as soon as his fingers found her core, her legs began to tremble.

Of course Henry knew exactly what she liked, knew exactly how to touch her. But she rather thought it was the way he was looking at her that was her true undoing. Never would she have thought that Henry Greville, who was surely the most sardonic, the most flippant, the most facetious man in all of England, could look at her with such sincerity, such tenderness, such *yearning*.

The effect was devastating. Almost immediately she was awash in the pleasure, rapidly hurtling toward climax. A small part of her wanted to look away, to close her eyes with embarrassment. But closing her eyes would mean looking away from his expression, from the look that told her that she meant everything to him, even if he would never say the words. And she needed to see his eyes, needed to relish every second she could of them, because after tonight, who knew if Henry would ever look at her that way again?

And so she looked him in the eyes as the pleasure swept over her. "Henry... oh, my God, *Henry*, that's so good, that's... that's..." She cried out as she almost went over the edge. "You're going to make me come."

"Yes, Caro. *Yes*. Come for me, darling. I want to feel it. I want to feel you around me when you take your pleasure."

"Oh, God, I'm so close! I'm so close I—" Henry responded to this pronouncement by shaking his wrist, which gave her some light, rapid strokes just where she needed them. And then she felt it, the unadulterated ecstasy when she was right on the brink. Her hips were bucking up off the bed, and she was screaming, so intense was the pleasure. "Henry! Oh, God, oh… *Yes*, that's so good, Henry! That's so good, Henry! Yes! Yes! *Yes!*"

She looked him in the eyes as she came, loving his expression as he watched her take her pleasure. His own thrusts had become frantic, and she reveled in seeing him so out of control for her.

And then, just as her own pleasure started to wane, she felt him withdraw from her, and his body was wracked with convulsions. And then it was his turn to look her in the eye as he cried out her name, and she felt a warm wetness as he spent himself onto her stomach.

He came to rest on top of her, his face buried in the pillow next to hers, his breathing hard. A deep contentment settled over her.

And she knew they still had problems. She knew she had work to do, to somehow convince him to trust her, to tell her the truth.

But lying in his arms, it was very easy to believe that everything was going to work out. They were perfect for one another, and there was no price that was not worth paying for them to be together. Surely he was feeling it, too.

Snuggling into Henry's chest, Caro drifted off into a contented sleep.

CHAPTER 31

After his climax, Henry collapsed on top of Caro like a beached whale; there was no point in lying to himself and pretending the maneuver had been executed with anything resembling grace or aplomb.

Tonight had been the most wonderful, most excruciating night of his life. Wonderful for obvious reasons—he had made love to Caro, *his* Caro.

Excruciating because this would be the only night he got to make love to her.

Every time his mind had started down that path, the agony that rushed to greet him was consuming. He would not have thought it possible to feel complete happiness and abject misery in equal measures.

But then Caro would smile at him, would say one of her characteristic coy remarks, and he couldn't help but smile back. And he had finally realized something.

The important thing tonight wasn't him. It was her.

This was Caro, the most sparkling, magnificent girl in the whole entire world.

And Caroline Astley deserved for her first time to be

magical. Damn if he was going to fail her by moping all night and obsessing over his own pain when he should have been focused on her pleasure.

Triumph had swept over him when he felt her exploding beneath him. He had never felt so gratified in his entire life as the moment he heard *his woman* screaming his name, the moment he felt *his Caroline* come apart around him. He would never forget the look in her eyes as she had reached her pleasure. Never. It had been better than his own climax, which had been more powerful than anything he had ever known.

He sighed. He wanted nothing more than to stay exactly where he was forever. But of course, that wasn't possible.

"I must be crushing you," he said.

"Mmmm," Caro replied, holding him tighter.

He smiled. "I'll get up soon, I promise."

They lapsed back into a contented silence. After a few more minutes of reveling in the feeling of Caroline beneath him, Henry rolled off of her.

What he saw made his heart all but burst with tenderness. She was asleep, looking completely replete, relaxed, and... well pleasured.

She made a wordless sound of protest at the rush of cold air when he left her, but she didn't even awaken at the touch of the damp cloth from his washstand, sponging the stickiness from her chest and belly.

Henry wanted nothing more than to climb back into bed with her then and spend however many minutes they had left together holding her in his arms.

But there was one thing he needed to do first.

A half hour later, his task was complete, and he slipped beneath the covers, taking Caro in his arms. After a while, he, too, drifted off to sleep.

HENRY WAS HAVING the most *wonderful* dream.

He was naked in his bed, and *Caro* was naked in his bed with him. And she was kissing his neck and running her hands all over his chest, right down across his stomach to his rock-hard—

Henry came awake with a start, to discover that his dream was not, in fact, a dream.

Oh, no, this was reality. Glorious, glorious reality!

He would have liked to say that, upon waking, he greeted Caroline charmingly. That he stroked a hand along her cheek and whispered, "Good morning, darling."

But in the spirit of honesty, he was forced to acknowledge that there was little sophistication in the feral groan that emerged from his mouth when he awoke to find her soft, sweet hands stroking up and down his cock.

A few words he would not normally have uttered in the presence of a lady might have emerged from his mouth. He really should apologize. And he would. He would do so… very soon. But it was so hard to concentrate when she was… when she was…

Gads, he needed to pull himself together. He opened his mouth to issue the appropriate words of regret, and… *Oh, God*, she swirled her thumb right over the head of his cock, where it felt *so* good…

"*Fuck, Caro…*" Somehow, in spite of his best intentions, those were the only words he was able to manage.

His profanity was met with a bright giggle. He opened his eyes a slit.

They'd only gotten about four hours of sleep, and it showed. Caro had faint shadows beneath her eyes, and she lacked her usual rosy glow. She had fallen asleep with her hair unbound, and it now formed a tangled clump on the side of her head.

None of that mattered. The sight of her smiling at him was the most gorgeous thing he had ever seen in his twenty-five years.

One unruly curl fell across her eyes. She rose to one elbow to push it out of the way and lost her balance, landing with an inelegant thump beside him on the bed.

Then they were both laughing. Henry rolled on top of her and kissed her deeply. She spread her legs for him, giving an enthusiastic wiggle of her hips.

This gave Henry no small amount of masculine satisfaction. Not that his cock needed any encouragement to rise to the occasion. He'd never been harder in his life. He reached down, positioning himself at her entrance. It would be his absolute pleasure to give her exactly what she wanted...

Except... there was something he needed to remember... from some dark, hazy corner of his brain, a thought emerged.

Virgin. Maidenhead.

Just. Last. Night.

Oh, hell...

So instead of thrusting into her, he brought his hand up to stroke her cheek. "Good morning, darling."

"Good morning, Henry."

He glanced at the window. The first hint of light was creeping its way around the edges of the curtains.

He would need to take her home, and soon.

He pressed a kiss to her temple. "I would like to make love to you again before I have to take you home. But not if you're too sore."

"I'm not too sore, Henry. I—I want to make love with you, too."

"Good." He kissed her again, and she was right there with

him, eagerly kissing him back. Her hands were everywhere, stroking over his shoulders, down his arms, across his stomach, and back up his chest. She seemed very enthusiastic, and he reached between her legs to see if she was ready.

He teased her little pearl. "You're wet," he said with a satisfied smile.

"Oooooooh, mmmmmmmm," was as much of a response as she was able to manage.

"I made you wet," he said smugly, his thumb circling gently on her nub. She began to buck her hips against his hand, desperate for more friction.

But when he slipped a finger inside of her, she flinched and was unable to mask the pain that flashed across her face. Henry removed his hand immediately.

"No," Caro protested. "Come back. I want to make love to you."

"I do, too, Caro. You know I do. But I wouldn't hurt you for the world."

"I'm only a little sore. It'll be all right. And we have to make love. Because what if—"

She broke off, unable to finish the sentence, but Henry knew what she was going to say.

What if this was the last chance they would ever have?

He pressed his forehead against hers. "If you're sure—"

"I am," she insisted.

"Very well, then," he said. An idea was fermenting in his head. He rose from the bed.

"Henry? Where are you going?" Caro sat up in bed, looking adorably befuddled.

Henry took a chair from the corner and brought it to the center of the room. He sat down and held his hand out for Caro to join him. "Come here."

She rose from the bed and approached. "What—what are we doing?"

He helped her climb into his lap, straddling him. "You'll have more control this way, darling. You'll be able to set the pace, choose the angle. If anything feels uncomfortable, you can stop right away."

"Oh!" she said, comprehension dawning as she glanced down at his straining cock. "You mean, I can…"

"You can. Whenever you're ready, darling."

She was already rising onto her toes in order to sink down onto his cock. She did so hesitantly, her brow furled in concentration.

Henry studied her. "All right?"

She slid up and down his length experimentally. "Yes, I—I think so. I'm only the slightest bit sore."

"Good." She soon settled into a rhythm. Christ, she felt so good. She was so wet and so tight. *God*, he wanted to come. The tantalizing view he had from this angle, of her breasts bouncing up and down with each stroke, was arousing beyond measure. He realized he wasn't going to last long, and by the look of things, Caro wasn't progressing nearly as quickly as he was. Which was unsurprising, given that this was her second time making love. He needed to do something more for her, so as she came down, he flexed his hips, giving the sweet little rosebud between her legs a little nudge with his pelvis.

"Oh!" she cried. Her eyes shot open in surprise, and she lost her rhythm. When she resumed, he did it again, and again she cried out, stopping what she was doing to grind against him.

He caught sight of the two of them in his dressing mirror, which was standing to the side of the chair. Seeing the direction of his gaze, Caro turned her head, her mouth falling open at the sight of the two of them joined together.

"Oh, Henry," she moaned, unable to tear her gaze away from the image in the mirror.

"You like that, don't you?" he asked, careful to make sure he was rubbing against her pearl with each stroke. She nodded, never taking her eyes from the mirror. "Seeing us together?"

"Yes," she breathed.

"Watching me fuck you?"

"*Yes!*" she cried as he gave her another nudge with his pelvis. Her eyes had gone glassy with pleasure.

She mewled in protest when he lifted her off of his cock and set her aside, but only for as long as it took to reposition the chair so it was facing the mirror. He quickly scooped her back into his lap, this time so her back was facing his front. "Then you're going to like this even better," he whispered.

Her gaze was locked on the mirror, on the same sight Henry could see—him kissing her neck, his hands tan against her porcelain skin as he caressed her arms, teased her breasts, and then lifted her hips to settle her back over his cock. She had to lean forward to take him, but he wrapped an arm around her torso, supporting her weight. She had soon reestablished her rhythm, her eyes never wavering from the sight of the two of them together.

"And best of all," Henry murmured, "from this angle, I can do this." In the mirror, they both watched as he reached his hand between her legs, giving her a teasing rub right where she needed it.

She cried out and quickened her pace. He kept rubbing her all the while. God, that felt good. Feeling her and seeing her in the mirror... *God*, it made him want to come. He was right on the brink, fighting to hold back. He knew he needed to think about something else or he would come too soon, but there was no way he could tear his eyes away from the most beautiful, erotic sight he had ever seen.

Thankfully, it appeared that Caroline was right there with him, because right when he thought he was either going to explode or he was going to die, he felt her go tense in his arms, and her back flexed like a bow, and then she was coming, coming hard by the looks of it.

"Henry—oh, my *God*, that's so good. Yes, Henry! Yes! Yes! *Yes!*"

And then her whole body started shaking and her passage was spasming so hard around his cock that he could feel it squeezing him deliciously with every frantic pulse of her delight.

That was all it took. The sight of her pleasure sent him hurtling straight for the edge. In the back of his mind, he knew he needed to withdraw, needed to withdraw right now, because he knew he was about to come, too, but he just wanted a few more strokes, he just wanted a few more thrusts because that felt so good, *fuck*, that felt so good, that felt so, so good, and... oh, God, oh, *God*, oh, *fuck*—

Everything went hazy and the room disappeared as he was overwhelmed by the mind-bending pleasure of his orgasm. He became aware of a hand stroking through his hair, and he squeezed his eyes open. And what a welcome sight greeted him—Caroline Astley, naked in his lap, smiling at him and looking very well-pleasured. He saw his reflection smile back at her in the mirror and bend to kiss her neck.

He buried his face in her hair, overwhelmed and needing a chance to collect himself. He was relieved to see that, based on the arc of semen that streaked up her back, he had somehow managed to withdraw in time. How, he had no idea, but he thanked the Lord for this small miracle.

Once he had gained some measure of control, he looked up again, to see that Caroline was still smiling at him. She turned herself around so that she was facing him and looped her arms around her neck.

"Sorry about that," he said. "The room was spinning."

She laughed. "I know exactly what you mean."

He played with a lock of her hair. "Well, that's gratifying. At least I made the room spin for you, too."

She kissed his cheek. "You certainly did. That was... I could say it was magical. Earth-shattering. Magnificent. And it would all be true. But somehow... it's not enough. My very best words pale in comparison to the way you made me feel."

"I understand," he replied, stroking her cheek. "There are no words. For me either, Caro."

She smiled and leaned in to kiss him, and he kissed her back, and the moment felt so beautiful, all he wanted was to stay there forever.

There was a rap at the door. "My lord," Gibson called from the other side, "it's half five. The city is stirring."

But they couldn't stay there forever.

His time with Caroline Astley was all but over. He only had the scant minutes it would take for them to dress, and the carriage ride to Cavendish Square, to have her in his life.

One last chance to get things right.

hey were silent as the hackney carriage conveyed them the short distance to Cavendish Square. Caro reflected that this was inevitable. When one had so much to say, sometimes the only course was to say nothing at all.

But given what had passed over the last twelve hours, and the way Henry was looking at her, he knew. She felt certain that he knew.

All too soon, they reached the Astley town house. So this was it. Caro attempted a smile, only to feel her face crumple. Oh, but this was not what she wanted. She didn't want him to remember her like this, red-faced and pathetic, with her nose running like a spigot. "I'm sorry," she said, struggling to control her shaking voice. "I didn't want to cry. But thank you, Henry." She could hear the sincerity in her voice, even as it broke. "Thank you for everything."

She pulled the door open and stumbled down onto the pavement, trying to locate the door that led into the back garden through her tears.

But then she felt it—Henry taking her elbow and spinning her back around.

"Henry?" she asked.

"Beg pardon, Lady Caroline. But you dropped your snuffbox," he said, his eyes warm and his own voice a trifle unsteady.

"My—my what?" she asked, flummoxed. "I don't have a snuffbox—"

"Just take it, you simpleton," he whispered, pressing something into her hand, his insult offset by the tenderness in his gaze and the adoring hand he used to frame her face.

He kissed her once then—firmly, tenderly, *finally*—then stepped back.

"Please don't cast this one into the fire," he said.

He turned and climbed back into the hackney carriage. And just like that, he was gone, leaving Caro standing alone in the middle of the pavement, staring down at the thick letter Henry had thrust into her hand.

A letter with something hard and flat tucked inside.

An hour later, Caro was sitting up in bed, reading Henry's letter for the fifth time, when Fanny slipped into her room.

"Good morning, m'lady." Caro had opened the curtains of one window so that a shaft of light fell across her bed. Fanny began crossing the room to open the rest of them. "I didn't think to find you up this early."

"Indeed," Caro said, setting the letter aside. "It has been an eventful morning already."

That was when Fanny noticed the badly crumpled gown Caro had draped over a chair. She came staggering to a halt in the middle of the room and rounded on her mistress, hands on her hips. "I can see that it has. Tell me you haven't been out running around with that scapegrace Henry Grev—oh, my gracious!" Fanny broke off mid-sentence, rushing across the room to peer at the blue and gold object lying atop the counterpane. "Is that what I think it is?"

Caro picked up the Eye of Ra amulet... or cosmetics box lid... or whatever it was. "It is indeed. That scapegrace, Henry Greville, finally did the right thing and returned it to me. And he wrote me this letter," she said, gesturing to the five sheets of foolscap littering the bed. "At last, I understand everything."

Fanny sat upon the corner of the bed. "Does this mean... Are you going to marry him, m'lady?"

Caro sighed. "For me to be able to marry him will require an act of manipulation so cunning, so underhanded, so devious, that there are perhaps only two women in all of England who could even dream of pulling it off."

"Two women. Let me guess, that would be you and your lady mother."

"Precisely." Caro smiled. "I learned from the master. Now," she said, rising from the bed, "let's get me dressed. There's so much to do before tonight. First, I must send a note to Anne. I need to see her immediately." Caro shook her head. "Truth be told, this is going to be a challenge. I hope I can pull it off."

Fanny snorted. "That man doesn't stand a chance."

ACROSS TOWN, that man was ensconced in the Greville family carriage with his father, who was peering out the window. His nose wrinkled as he took in the run-down neighborhood. "Where did you say we were going again, Henry?" the earl asked.

"Wapping," Henry replied cheerfully.

"Wapping? What the devil is in Wapping?"

"The Execution Docks."

His father pinched the bridge of his nose. "Don't tell me that you dragged me from my bed at this ungodly hour in order to witness a hanging."

"No, the hanging's not today. That will be a few weeks hence. They have to hold the trial first. Ah, here we are."

"Trial? What trial? What are you talking about?"

Henry alighted from the carriage and held the door for his father. "Your new business associate, Arnold Jenner. Or Snakeface, as he's usually called. He and his henchmen will be going on trial soon."

"Do you mean—" The earl grabbed his arm, dropping his voice to a whisper. "Jenner has been arrested? You don't think... You don't think he mentioned my involvement. Do you?"

"He most certainly did. Do you have the papers I asked you to bring? The Bow Street runners will need to see them."

"What do you mean, the Bow Street runners? I cannot meet with the Bow Street runners! I am in a—a delicate situation, as well you know. And how do you know that Snakeface mentioned my name?"

"I was there when they questioned him. Brownwood actually ratted you out five days ago. The magistrates have been preparing to arrest you." His father sputtered in alarm, but Henry continued. "It's a long story, Father, but the short version is that I shot Snakeface, then he almost stabbed me in the eye—not sure if you noticed this rather large bandage obscuring half my face—then the angry mob fetched the Bow Street runners, and I have brought you here to clear your name."

"Clear my name? But how am I to do that?" His father looked genuinely panicked.

Henry clasped his shoulder. "Don't worry, Father. I have everything under control."

He threw open the doors to the dockside warehouse, and his father fell silent. Because his father, being his father, could think of nothing but the beautiful Egyptian treasures arrayed before him, even when he was on the brink of being arrested for conspiring to steal from the Crown.

"Oh, how glorious!" the earl said, hurrying across the room to examine the cedarwood sarcophagus. "Look at the colors and the detail. Never have I seen something so magnificent."

From across the room came the sound of a man clearing his throat. "As much as I hate to interrupt, Lord Ardingly," Mr. Ragsdale, the Bow Street runner, said, "we have some questions you need to answer." He gestured for Henry and his father to take the two chairs across the table.

The earl blanched as he and Henry sat. "Of—of course. This is all a misunderstanding, you see. You don't trust the word of a man named Snakeface, do you?"

"So, you admit to knowing Jenner," Mr. Buchanan said conversationally. "Tell me, how did the two of you meet?"

"I... er... that is..." The earl trailed off, then looked at Henry, panicked.

"Allow me to explain," Henry said. "Four years ago, my father purchased a shipment of Egyptian antiquities through his agent in Cairo. Unfortunately, this was right when Napoleon made his unexpected invasion of Egypt, and the ship was captured. My father never received the cargo."

Mr. Ragsdale leaned back in his chair and crossed his arms. "And what does this have to do with his working with Arnold Jenner?"

"A few weeks ago, rumors arose of some new Egyptian treasures appearing on the black market," Henry continued.

"My father immediately recognized them for what they were. Do you have the cargo manifest, Father?"

"What? Oh, yes," Lord Ardingly said, removing an envelope from his breast pocket. Henry passed it to the two runners.

"This is an interesting tale," Mr. Buchanan said. "But it doesn't excuse him for attempting to pass on stolen goods—"

"Look at the cargo manifest," Henry said. "'An obelisk of sandstone, carved with hieroglyphs.' 'A painted cedarwood sarcophagus, with lid.' 'A statue of the winged goddess Isis, in black basalt.' 'A scarab beetle, bejeweled in gold, lapis, carnelian, and turquoise.' Now look around the room, gentlemen. I ask you, is it a crime for a man to try to recover what is rightfully his?"

"You mean—" his father sputtered, "you mean all of these glorious treasures are *mine*?"

Henry kicked his father under the table, and the earl schooled his features. "That is to say, of course they're mine. You will excuse my enthusiasm, gentlemen. I had never actually seen my new acquisitions before today. After all these years, it is, erm, hard to believe."

"So you see," Henry said, "my father the earl was not working with those rogues to steal from the Crown. What an absurd notion! He *infiltrated* their criminal ring, in order to recover what is rightfully his."

Mr. Ragsdale looked skeptical. "That's not what Brownwood said. He said your father was going to pass off these items as part of his own collection, including a crate of treasures stolen from the British Museum."

"Well, he could hardly tell Brownwood what he was really about, now could he? And my father knew nothing about a crate of items from the British Museum. Isn't that right, Father?"

"What?" The earl had been turned in his chair, gazing at the sarcophagus. "Yes, exactly right."

"After all," Henry continued, "Brownwood was peddling the items from the British Museum himself. I should know. He tried to sell them to me and to a man named Richard Cuming." He leaned forward and gave the runners a hard look. "And also to Lord Lansdowne, who will confirm all of this."

The two runners exchanged a look. Mr. Ragsdale, who had been poring over the cargo manifest, nodded.

Mr. Buchanan stood. "My apologies, Lord Ardingly, for having even suggested that you were involved. You understand it is our job to ask questions when an accusation is made—"

"Of course, of course," Henry said, also rising to his feet. "I trust, however, that there are some accusations so absurd, and so potentially harmful, that they will be handled with the utmost discretion. I refer, of course, to Mr. Jenner's ludicrous suggestion that Lady Caroline Astley was in any way involved. Although"—Henry stroked his chin thoughtfully —"Lady Caroline was tangentially involved, in that she was the one to summon me after you two refused to assist her."

"If you would be so kind," Mr. Ragsdale said, "as to convey our most abject apologies to Lady Caroline—"

"I will. An apology to me wouldn't be entirely out of place, either. I was the one who got knifed in the head because you two refused to do your job."

"We are horrifically sorry for that as well, Lord Thetford," Mr. Buchanan hastened to say.

Henry smiled magnanimously. "Apology accepted, gentlemen. And your superiors won't hear one word about it. Provided," he added, his voice hard as iron, "that Lady Caroline and my father are not mentioned in this sordid business."

"You have our utmost assurances that Lady Caroline's name will never come up," Mr. Ragsdale said. "And as for your father, his only involvement will be as witness for the Crown."

"Excellent." Henry turned to the earl. "Come, Father. Let's round up a few wagons. Your treasures are coming home."

CHAPTER 33

*I*t took the better part of four hours to secure enough wagons to transport the earl's new acquisitions and to get them loaded up. It was midafternoon when they made their way back to the Greville town house on Hanover Square.

His father had spent the entire time babbling delightedly about his new treasures, rhapsodizing over their most minute details, and telling Henry more details about the mummification process than he frankly cared to know.

After four hours of such chatter, he was only half attending when his father shifted the conversation. "It was well done of you, son. What you did back there."

Henry blinked. "You mean the strategy I devised to keep you out of gaol?"

"That, too," his father hastened to add. "I was more thinking of how you were able to recover my antiquities."

It took every ounce of filial piety Henry possessed to stop himself from rolling his eyes.

"I must confess, I've never quite understood you, Henry," his father continued. "I was always more bookish, whereas you aren't bookish at all. But what those runners described—the way you broke into that warehouse, shot two men, fought off three more, got stabbed in the face but kept going, and rescued Billy—" His father paused, shaking his head. "I could never have done all that. Sometimes the situation calls for a man of action." He met Henry's eyes. "That's the kind of son I have. And that is something to be proud of."

Henry smiled. "Thank you, Father."

The carriage came to a halt, and the earl scrambled out, giving directions for the unloading of his new acquisitions.

Henry went inside to check on his mother. The rout she had been planning for weeks was to be held that evening, and he thought he would see how the preparations were going.

Behind him, he could hear his father barking out instructions. "You there, don't take the new sarcophagus through the front door. It will never fit. Take it back to the orangery."

Henry sighed. He was glad to see his father achieve his heart's desire.

Even if his own heart's desire was now forever out of reach.

By now, Caro would have read his letter. That meant she knew the awful truth. He felt his shoulders sag. She would want nothing to do with him now.

He would probably never see her again.

The door to the green parlor opened, and out walked... Caro? She had her arm around his mother's waist, and he saw that his mother was quietly weeping.

"There, there, Lady Ardingly," Caro said, pressing a handkerchief into his mother's hand. "Everything will be all right. You'll see."

"It will be," his mother said. "I will make sure of it. I cannot believe that he—" His mother broke off, noticing two footmen staggering by with a statue of a jackal. "What on earth is that? Don't tell me he's gone and purchased even more of this... this *junk!*" A look of fury Henry had never seen before swept over his mother's face. "Phillip!" she shouted. "You get in here *right now!*" She stalked off toward the entryway.

"Good afternoon, Henry," Caro said cheerfully, taking his arm.

Henry was blinking at her in confusion. "What—what are you doing here?"

"Saving the day, of course." She towed him down the hall toward the shouting coming from the foyer. "Why did you not tell your mother immediately? About your father's financial missteps, I mean."

"My father said it was for the best. That it was beyond her capacity to fix the situation and telling her would only distress her."

Caro snorted. "Oh, yes, the poor, helpless little lamb."

They had reached the foyer, where his mother was glaring murderously at his father over the top of the sarcophagus. "How dare you! Those terrace houses were *my dowry!*"

"And as your husband, they became my property, to dispose of as I saw fit."

"My father intended those houses to be for our children. And you know it! Just wait until Papa hears about this."

The earl blanched. "You are not to tell the duke!"

"I most certainly will tell him!" the countess thundered.

Caro leaned up to whisper in his ear. "Your first mistake was that you failed to deploy your cavalry. By keeping your father's secret, you deprived yourself of your natural allies. Your mother. Your grandfather the duke. Your brothers, who don't want your mother to sink into poverty any more than you do. And your most important ally. *Me.*"

The earl noticed the two of them standing there. "Henry," he said, "there's one item I haven't been able to find amongst the crates. Have you seen my Eye of Ra cosmetics box?"

"I have. I gave it to Lady Caroline, to return to its rightful owner, her sister."

"Henry!" his father protested. "How could you?"

There was a knock at the front door, and the butler moved to answer it. Caro consulted a little pocket watch which she pulled from her reticule and smiled. "Ah! Unless I am very much mistaken, this should be another one of your allies, arriving just in time."

"Lady Wynters," the butler announced.

HENRY WATCHED as Caro's sister entered the foyer. "Lady Ardingly," she said, "how lovely to see you, as always."

"Lady Wynters, good afternoon," his mother returned, as the two countesses curtsied to each other gracefully.

"And Lord Ardingly." Lady Wynters made another very polite curtsey, then drew herself up to her full height. The countess was statuesque, and only perhaps an inch shorter than his father. The earl's shoulders slumped, and he physically shrank before her unwavering gaze.

"I had the most fascinating conversation with my sister this morning," Lady Wynters began.

His father blanched. "I—I can explain—"

"No, my lord, I do not believe that you can," the countess said, turning to Henry. "But how kind of you, Lord Thetford, to make the recommendation that we search for the bottom portion of the box. We found it this morning—it had somehow become wedged in the back of my late husband's dressing table so that when his valet went to clean it out, he found only the lid. I'm sure its being complete will increase the sales price considerably."

"Lady Wynters," his father said, "I beg you. That box is the jewel of my collection—"

"It's gorgeous, I agree. And I am given to understand that it will fetch such a price that it will provide food and housing for two hundred some-odd women and children."

"But everyone knows it is mine," the earl protested. "If you put it up for auction, then they'll all know that I lost it at the card table," he added, bowing his head.

"It happens that my sister and I have hit upon the perfect solution. We will say that you gave it to my society as a dona-tion, out of tender feeling for the widows and orphans we assist. Who could assail such a noble impulse?"

"But... but..." his father started to protest.

"Unless," Lady Wynters continued, "there's another story you would prefer for me to put about?" The countess's smile remained serene, but her eyes were keen. "Because we both know there's another story I could tell. Isn't there, Lord Ardingly?"

His father swallowed. "If you would be so kind as to say it was a donation."

Lady Wynters beamed. "I will gladly do so. Well, I pray you will excuse me, but I have a few matters to attend to. You'll be pleased to hear, Lord Thetford, that there's been a vacancy at my lodging house, and I will be able to offer a room to your intrepid laundress, Mrs. Dakers, effective immediately. I must hie myself over to Wapping to tell her the good news."

"I am gratified to hear it," Henry said. "Thank you so much for assisting her."

"It is my pleasure. Lord Ardingly, Lady Ardingly," Lady Wynters said, inclining her head, as regal as a queen.

His mother stepped forward. "Please allow me to accom-pany you to your carriage, Lady Wynters." The two count-esses linked arms. "I cannot apologize enough for Lord

Ardingly. What can I say, husbands are troublesome creatures sometimes."

"I understand completely," Lady Wynters replied as they stepped outside. "I had one myself until very recently."

"Thank God that's over," his father said, running a hand over his face.

Caro stepped forward, smiling brightly. "Indeed. Now we can move on to the next stage."

"The next stage?" the earl sputtered. "What do you mean, the next stage?"

"Well," Caro said, "I know you don't wish to see your wife humiliated before all of society, unable to live in the style she deserves, and worried about how she will survive in her dotage?"

His father had the grace to look shamefaced. "Of course not."

"And," Caro continued, "thanks to your son's quick thinking, the size of your antiquities collection has doubled overnight. La, you don't even have room to house everything! Some of it must go, and so it is time to hold a sale."

His father bristled. "Surely you're not suggesting that I sell half of my collection?"

His mother had reentered the foyer and took up a position right beside Caroline. "Sell half of your collection—gracious, no," Caro said with a laugh.

"Good—"

"I am suggesting that you sell *at least* three quarters of your collection," Caro said. "Closer to ninety percent, assuming we can get the prices I want."

"Ninety percent!" his father said. "Don't be absurd. Ninety percent—"

"Phillip," his mother growled.

"They're mine," his father said. "Those antiquities are mine, and you cannot force me to sell them—"

His mother crossed her arms. "Shall I summon my father, then?"

"But... but..." Lord Ardingly trailed off, seeing that everyone was against him. "But I haven't even had the chance to enjoy my new sarcophagus," he said, pouting.

"I promise not to sell the new sarcophagus," Caro said.

"Thank you—"

"Leastwise, not for a penny less than five thousand pounds," Caro said, pulling a pencil and a tiny notebook from her reticule. "Now, Lord Ardingly," she said, taking the earl's arm, "why don't you tell me all about these fascinating antiquities? And exactly how much you paid for each one."

His father gave Henry a beseeching look. Henry grinned cheerfully in return. With a resigned sigh, the earl led Caro toward the library.

CHAPTER 34

That evening, Henry found himself back at his parents' town house, this time dressed in his evening kit. His head wound had closed sufficiently that he was able to leave off the bandage. The stitches were visible, but they were less conspicuous.

The house was in a flurry with the final preparations for his mother's rout. Henry saw that someone had thought to place candles inside the white alabaster sarcophagus in the foyer. The glowing translucent stone was the only source of light in the entryway, and the effect was eerily sublime.

His mother entered the foyer, giving final instructions to the butler. Henry bent to give her a kiss on the cheek. "Whose idea was that?" Henry asked, gesturing to the sarcophagus.

"Lady Caroline's," his mother replied. "Speaking of whom."

Henry turned to see Caro striding through the front door. "Oh, that turned out even better than I imagined!" she exclaimed, gesturing to the sarcophagus. She curtseyed to his mother. "Good evening, Lady Ardingly. Is everything in readiness?"

"I believe so," his mother replied. "My father arrived an hour ago. He has been having a rather forceful conversation with Lord Ardingly. He had thought the Brighton terraces were added to the entail."

"Really?" Henry said. "Then how was Father able to sell them?"

"Supposedly the paperwork was not executed properly," his mother said. "Papa disagrees. He maintains the sale was illegal and has already threatened to sue the buyer in court. He has terrified them sufficiently that they now wish the deal had never happened. They've offered to let us buy them back. The only catch is that we will have to come up with the full original sales price."

Henry felt his shoulders slump. "That won't be possible. You see, the antiquities weren't the only things Father purchased. He also bought a ship to carry them. And the ship has been lost."

"Indeed," his mother agreed. "I went over the numbers, and we would have to sell everything at more than six times the price your father originally paid for it." The countess shook her head. "Well, we will do the best we can. Ah, Lady Cheltenham, good evening."

His mother drifted across the room to greet Caro's mother. Henry turned back to Caro. "It's kind of you to try to help me get my financial house back in order."

"Kind?" Caro asked, laughing. "I wouldn't say I'm doing it out of kindness, precisely."

So she was helping him out of pity. *Splendid*. "Well, I appreciate it, nevertheless. The fact that you were able to coerce my father into selling his collection is more than I was able to do."

Caro snagged a glass of champagne from a passing tray.

"Of course you are welcome, Henry. But what excellent news from your mother. If we can manage to raise the capital, you'll be able to buy back those terraces."

"There is little hope of that. You heard my mother—we would somehow have to sell everything for six times its original sales price. And I've no doubt my father overpaid horribly to begin with. He's not exactly a model of financial prudence."

Caro took a sip of her champagne and regarded her glass with interest. "That is delicious."

"Caro! Are you even attending?"

"I must ask your mother where she procured it. And yes, I am attending. So it will be a bit of a challenge. What of it?"

"A bit of a challenge? The odds are insurmountable. After all," he said, looking around, "how are we going to convince anyone to buy all of this junk?"

There was a gust of cool air as the front door opened. The first guests had arrived.

Caro smiled up at him, her eyes shining with laughter. "Be a dear, Henry, and hold this for me," she said, pressing her champagne glass into his hand.

He saw her paste on her fake smile as she turned toward the door. "Mr. Hope," she said, crossing the foyer to take his arm. "How good of you to come on such short notice."

HENRY SPENT the next three hours watching Caro with amusement.

He had to admit, she was good. She worked Thomas Hope over good and proper, narrating the dramatic recovery of his father's new treasures. "And what is even more exciting, because Lord Ardingly now has far more antiquities than he has room for, he has decided to sell a few pieces. Not that you would be interested, of course," she said, laughing. "Everyone knows you have the finest collection of Egyptian antiquities in all of Britain. I can't even imagine how large your collection must be, to eclipse Lord Ardingly's. I cannot wait to see it at your rout—it's tomorrow night, is it not? La, it will be all anyone can speak of, comparing your collection with that of the earl."

Mr. Hope's face took on a slightly greenish hue, and Henry didn't blame him. Henry had seen the Egyptian Room Mr. Hope had been bragging about for the better part of four months, and, as fine as it was, he didn't have a tenth as many genuine Egyptian items as his father. "Lord Ardingly is willing to sell a few pieces? Really?" Mr. Hope asked, tugging at his cravat.

"Indeed," Caro said brightly. "Here, let me show you the library."

And Thomas Hope wasn't the only guest to make a purchase. With Caro rhapsodizing about her fascination with everything Egyptian, every young buck in London shelled out for an amulet or a small statue.

His father was not enjoying the party. Henry found him in the library standing next to his mother, his arms crossed. "I should like to know who invited Thomas Hope," his father huffed.

"I did," his mother said. "Along with the Nettlethorpe-Ogilvys and several others. All at Lady Caroline's suggestion."

"He isn't welcome," his father grumbled. "And the Nettlethorpe-Ogilvys are *industrialists*." His father shuddered as he glared across the room at the couple, who were the parents of Henry's contrabassoon-playing contemporary.

"I don't care if they're circus freaks," his mother said. "If they're willing to pay good money to remove that eyesore of a sarcophagus from my foyer, then they are heartily welcome."

The earl narrowed his eyes at his wife.

"If it makes you feel better, Father," Henry said, "Thomas Hope has spent the last three hours rhapsodizing over your collection. He's bought a good quarter of it, so fearful is he that his own will suffer by comparison at his rout tomorrow. Is that not what you've been wanting?"

His father did not look mollified. "It will have to serve," he grumbled, wandering off. His mother winked at Henry before trailing after her husband.

Henry leaned against a column. He found he was enjoying the party. He had lost track of Caro while speaking to his parents.

As he was in the library, Henry decided to help himself to a brandy before going in search of Caro. As he took a sip, a familiar voice murmured in his ear, "You will not believe how much I just convinced the Nettlethorpe-Ogilvys to pay for the Arse of Anubis."

Henry had to clap his hand over his mouth to stop himself from spewing brandy across the room.

"My gracious, Henry," Caro said once he stopped coughing. "Are you all right? And where is my glass? Did I not ask you to look after my champagne?"

He reached into an alcove and retrieved the glass from behind a floral arrangement. "I would never fail you."

"Excellent," she said, accepting her drink, "because a toast is in order. To your father's collection. His much *smaller* collection."

Henry clinked his glass to hers. "I'll drink to that."

A gentleman approached. "Ah, Mr. Nettlethorpe-Ogilvy," Caro said warmly. "Good evening."

It was the younger Nettlethorpe-Ogilvy, Archibald, who approached, newly arrived to the party. "Good evening, Lady

Caroline. I apologize for being late, Thetford. There were a few matters of business that required my attention." He gestured to the crowds clustered around the antiquities in the library. "Everyone is so excited about your father's sale. I must be the only one here tonight who hasn't made a purchase."

"You just might be," Caro said. "But don't fear, you will be able to enjoy your parents' acquisition."

"Ah, and what might that be?" Mr. Nettlethorpe-Ogilvy asked.

"It is just there," Caro said, gesturing across the room. "The stunning torso fragment from a statue of Anubis, in black granite."

"Wait—" Mr. Nettlethorpe-Ogilvy said, blanching. "You don't mean that huge statue of a man's ars—" He managed to stop himself halfway through the word, glancing at Caro in mortification. He followed this with a rather unconvincing attempt to cover what he had been about to say with coughing.

Caro beamed at him. "Isn't it magnificent? Oh, dear, you seem to have something caught in your throat. Let us get you a glass of this excellent champagne."

"I believe Mr. Nettlethorpe-Ogilvy will be wanting something stronger," Henry said, pouring him a good four fingers of brandy.

"Thank you," Mr. Nettlethorpe-Ogilvy said. He proceeded to swallow the brandy in one gulp. "Speaking of my parents, I don't suppose you know where they are?"

"You might check the foyer," Caro said. "Last I saw, they were engaged in a bidding war with Mr. Hope, over the large alabaster sarcophagus you doubtlessly noticed upon entering."

"They're *what*?" Mr. Nettlethorpe-Ogilvy peered out into the hall. Whatever he saw there caused his eyes to go wide. "Dear God. Pray excuse me, Lady Caroline, Lord Thetford."

"Oh, dear," Caro said once he had taken his leave, her eyes twinkling up at Henry, "I'm not sure if Mr. Nettlethorpe-Ogilvy is enjoying the party."

Henry grinned. "I cannot imagine why not."

They were interrupted by the sound of someone clearing his throat. It turned out to be Lord Graverley. "Good evening, Lady Caroline," Graverley said, bowing over her hand. He extended a piece of paper toward Henry. "This is for you, Thetford."

Henry unfolded it to reveal a bank draft for five thousand pounds. Caro leaned in and peered at it. "Oh, dear, Lord Graverley," she said, "I believe the bidding for the sarcophagus is already up around seven thousand some-odd pounds. But it isn't necessary to produce the money tonight."

"I'm not interested in the sarcophagus," Graverley said.

"Perhaps you would prefer my father's canopic jars?" Henry suggested, gesturing toward the mantelpiece.

Graverley narrowed his eyes. "It's for your horses."

"Ah!" Caro said, scrunching her nose at Henry in delight before turning back to the marquess. "I daresay you will be quite pleased with them."

"For five thousand pounds, I had better be," Graverley muttered.

"As it happens," Henry said, "my father owes a debt to your father to the tune of five thousand pounds."

Graverley frowned. "Really? How did that come about?"

"Who knows?" Henry said. "Probably cards or some such." He handed the bank draft back to the marquess. "So this won't be necessary, but if you would be so good as to inform your father that the debt has been discharged."

Graverley shrugged. "As you like."

"I'll send the greys 'round first thing tomorrow morning."

Henry paused. "Are you certain I cannot interest you in the canopic jars? I would let you have them for a very reasonable price."

"Alas," Caro said, "Mr. Hope has already purchased the jars."

"A pity," Graverley said dryly. "Now, if you will excuse me, I must take my leave." He glanced about, shuddering. "This room always makes me feel as if I am on the cusp of being stricken with some biblical plague."

Once the marquess was gone, Caro nudged Henry with her elbow. "Five thousand pounds! Congratulations, Henry. I hope you won't miss your greys too terribly."

Henry sighed. "I will, of course. But I have a few other pairs coming up. I'm sure I can find one that will serve."

"Excellent." Caro peered out into the hall. "Oh, dear, I must be off. It appears that Mr. Nettlethorpe-Ogilvy was able to talk some sense into his parents. Perhaps I can persuade Lord Graverley to take their place in the bidding war against Mr. Hope."

She sailed down the hall. Henry saw her take Lord Graverley's arm and whisper something in his ear. He arched an eyebrow as he said something in return, and she responded with something that made him throw his head back and laugh.

Henry felt his heart splitting in two.

Caro was perfect for him. *Perfect.* She was everything he had ever wanted. Just speaking to her for the past three minutes had made him feel incandescently happy.

Oh, who did he think he was fooling? Telling himself he didn't love her—

No. No, he wasn't even going to *think* that thought.

Because she might be helping him tonight, but raising a few thousand pounds wouldn't be enough to restore his fortune. And a girl like Caroline Astley did not go marrying a man who was scraping by, not when she had the richest future duke in England on a string.

And if the love of his life went and married someone else, that would break him in ways from which he would never recover.

And so, as he watched Caro stroll toward the sarcophagus on Lord Graverley's arm, their golden heads bent together, he told himself that he didn't love Caroline Astley. He was… attracted to her. Infatuated with her, even. Not so very different from half the men in London.

But he wasn't *in love* with her.

Of course he wasn't.

He couldn't be.

God, he needed another drink. He reached for the decanter, suddenly not enjoying the party so much after all.

CHAPTER 35

*H*ours later, long after the party had ended, Caro snuck out of her family's town house and summoned a hack to take her to Bedford Square.

She felt almost giddy as she climbed the stairs to Henry's apartment. Because she had spent the last two hours going over the numbers (and waiting for everyone in her own household to turn in for the night), and even if the sale hadn't generated enough to repurchase all of the Grevilles' terrace houses, she had a plan.

This time Gibson didn't look the least bit surprised to see her. "Lady Caroline," he said, bowing deeply. "A pleasure. If you will excuse me," he said, leaving the apartment and closing the door behind him.

Henry appeared silhouetted in the doorway to his bedroom. He had removed his evening kit and was wearing his dressing gown over a shirt and trousers. He looked befuddled. "Caro? What on earth are you doing here?"

She rolled her eyes. "What am I doing here? What do you think I'm doing here, Henry? I'm here to go over the numbers." She strolled over to the sofa and took a seat, pulling her notebook from her reticule. "Now, as you can see —" She glanced up to see Henry still gaping at her from the doorway. "Are you coming or not?" she asked, exasperated.

He hastened over and took a seat beside her on the sofa. She went page by page in her notebook, detailing the sums raised from his father's artifacts.

Once she ticked off the last item, she rose, full of excited energy, and began pacing before the fire. "So as you can see, although we didn't achieve our goal of six times what your father spent, we did raise three times the purchase price. Which should enable us to buy back half of the terrace houses—"

"Us?" Henry said. "What do you mean, us?"

She narrowed her eyes at him. "Of course I expect to be involved in these decisions. I believe I made it obvious tonight that I can be of use to you. Which brings me to the matter of your breeding stable. Honestly, Henry, I know the Brighton terraces are a brilliant investment, but I think we would do better to use some of the money to expand your operation. Once word gets out that Lord Graverley paid five thousand pounds for a pair of your horses, you'll be able to name your price—"

"Caro, what—"

"—and I will be able to help you with the sales of your horses, as I did tonight. I have it all planned out—tomorrow I will spend all morning making the rounds with Mama, gossiping about how much Lord Graverley paid for your team. And then you and I will take your two finest mounts out for the afternoon promenade in Hyde Park. That will set the fashion. So if you are in need of funds to maximize your operation—more broodmares, more stabling, or whatever it is—I feel we should fully fund that first, and only then look at repurchasing the Brighton terraces."

He looked baffled. "I will consider your advice, but why did you—"

"Oh, and we're forgetting something significant. My dowry is thirty-five thousand pounds. Which isn't enough to buy the rest of the terraces, but it isn't nothing. So we can add that in with our assets—"

Caro found her hand seized in an iron grip as she paced past the sofa. Henry rose slowly to his feet. "Your dowry? What do you mean, your dowry?"

She laughed. "Of course I have a dowry, Henry."

"I know that. But your dowry will be going to your husband." Seeing her confused expression, he clarified, "To Lord Graverley. Not to me." He dropped his head and stared into the fire.

She absorbed the truth like a blow. "Oh," she said, crumpling onto the sofa. "You didn't mean it. I thought when you said you wanted to marry me, you truly—" Her voice broke, and she was unable to speak.

Henry sank beside her on the sofa. She couldn't bear to meet his eyes. She heard him say, "Of course I meant it, Caro."

"Then what's all this talk of my dowry going to Lord Graverley?"

"There is the fact that you refused me," he said. She glanced up at him then, and his eyes held an intoxicating blend of nervousness and hope.

"But as I said at the time, the only reason I refused you was because you wouldn't tell me the truth. But then you did. You told me everything in your letter, and in doing so, you removed my only objection—"

He tore his gaze from hers with a sound of despair. "Yes, I removed that objection, by raising one even worse. That I was no longer in a position to support you."

She regarded his profile, saw the shame and how heavily

it weighed on him. At last she understood. And her heart broke for him, that he had thought he had to carry this alone.

She tried to make her voice teasing, but heard it quaver as she said, "Which part of *I love you* taxed your understanding?"

He shook his head. "I won't hold you to that. I know you don't love me anymore. Not now that you know the truth."

"Henry," she said, taking his hands in hers. "Look at me."

THE PROSPECT TERRIFIED HENRY, but he forced himself to turn toward Caroline and squeeze his eyes open a fraction.

What he saw caused him to squeeze them right back shut again.

Because, unless he was losing his mind, Caroline Astley was positively beaming at him. Her eyes held such love, such adoration, such affection, that—

That he was clearly losing his mind.

He opened his eyes again, just for a second. She was still smiling at him.

He did it one more time. Still smiling.

"Caro," he sputtered, "you—you don't hate me."

"No," she said, squeezing his hands.

"You don't think I'm pathetic or despicable or—"

"Of course I don't, darling."

"You—you love me!"

"I do," she said, looping her arms around his neck. "I love you so much, Henry. Do you understand now?"

He wrapped his arms around her. "I do. I—I can't believe it." He buried his face in her hair, his whole body shaking with relief.

"I know you're having difficulties right now. But they're not of your making. Much to the contrary, you're the one

314

fixing your father's problems. You are the man who pressed his last fifty pounds into his mother's hands, to save her from embarrassment. My opinion of you has not changed in the slightest. I love you, and the only thing I want is to spend the rest of my life with you."

"I love you, Caro." The words came pouring out of him like a flood. "I love you so much." He lifted his head to look her in the eye. "I think I fell in love with you the moment you called me *asinine*."

She laughed. "These sweet romantic nothings we whisper to one another. Would that I had known to say that when I was fifteen."

He hesitated. "Do you really think we should expand my breeding stable? Instead of buying as many of the terrace houses as we can?"

"I do. I have seen your horses. It's not merely their confirmation which sets them apart but their training. Your breeding program is going to be a magnificent success, and we must do everything we can to support it." She studied him for a beat, her brows wrinkling in confusion. "What is it?"

"It's nothing. It's only—" He glanced up at her then, feeling bashful and hopeful in equal measures. "You believe in me."

She gave him a quizzical look. "Of course I do. Does this come as a surprise?"

"I'm afraid it does. My father has never believed in me, after all."

She looked irate on his behalf. "At the risk of disparaging my future father-in-law, I would not put too much stock in the opinion of a man who spent"—she paused in order to page through her notebook—"one hundred and fifty-three pounds on a two-thousand-year-old statue of a man's arse."

"Technically it's not a man's arse. That is the arse of a god."

Caro's smile was mischievous. "Trust me, because I am in a position to know—there was only one godlike arse in your parents' library last night, and it is right here," she said, pinching it.

Henry laughed, delighted. "In any case, I could certainly get used to it. Someone believing in me, that is."

"You will get used to it, because from this day forth, you will always have me." Her face suddenly turned somber. "There's only one concern I have. I understand now why you did it. But you must never lie to me again. Not even to spare me from worry. Whatever troubles the future might hold, we will face them together."

"I promise you, my darling Caro, I will never do so. Those were the worst moments of my life, too. Seeing you cry, knowing I had done that to you—" He shuddered.

She squeezed his hands. "I forgive you. But never again."

"Never again," he vowed. "I have a concern of my own."

"Oh? And what's that?"

He scooped Caro up and settled her on his lap. "I'm wondering if you intend to manage me in the same flagrant manner you manipulated all those poor sods at my mother's party."

Caro laughed. "Oh, Henry, of course not. Don't be ridiculous."

He smiled. "Good."

"No, I will have much more effective methods for managing you." She looped her arms around his neck. "Would you care for me to demonstrate?"

"That depends," he said, stroking his jaw as if deep in thought. "Do these methods involve both of us removing every last stitch of our clothing?"

"How did you know?"

"Well, then. Let's see how you do."

THEY LAUGHED as they undressed each other, their garments ending up strewn across various pieces of furniture. Caro shoved Henry's dressing gown down his arms and tossed it to the floor, but Henry immediately reached down and grabbed it, moving it away from the fire.

"We must be careful with that dressing gown, darling. You cannot imagine the things I'm going to do to you while you're wearing it. It needs to last for decades to come."

She did rather like the sound of that, even if she didn't care for anything that slowed her progress in getting Henry out of his clothes. She yanked his shirt up over his head, then purred as she ran her hands over his beautiful chest.

When he had stripped her to her shift, Henry scooped Caro up in his arms and carried her through to his bedchamber. They both laughed as he rolled back onto the bed so that Caro ended up in a heap on top of him.

Caro sat up to take in the view. Henry was half reclining on the bed, leaning back on his elbows, naked to the waist. His brown hair was adorably mussed, and his torso was tan and lean and deliciously muscled. There was a very prominent bulge in the front of his trousers. The look in his eyes she would describe as… famished.

The sight of him made her want to crawl on top of him and do naughty things, so that was exactly what she decided she would do. She slithered her way up his body and came to rest straddling him, her legs astride the delicious bulge that she knew was all for her. He straightened his arms and sat up. She couldn't resist touching him, and she found her hands roaming over his chest, his shoulders, his neck. She found that her hips had begun to wiggle of their own accord, rubbing against him.

She was dressed in nothing but her chemise, which, being

the very finest quality, was of such fine white linen it was practically transparent. She could see the rosy circles of her nipples through the thin fabric, and she saw Henry swallow as he took in the sight.

Apparently mere looking was insufficient, because he began kissing her breasts right through the fabric. Caro wouldn't have thought to do such a thing, but the linen provided just a little bit of additional friction over her peaked nipples that felt... that felt so very... so very, very wonderful, and... she needed more. More of... everything. Now her hips were bucking hard against him, and she felt her fingernails dig into the muscles on his back, and do you know what? That was delightful, what he was doing to her breasts, absolutely delightful, but what would be even more delightful would be if there was no fabric separating them at all, and she heard herself crying out in frustration and desperation and arousal, as her hands came up and pulled the chemise up over her own head and hurled it to the floor.

She was pulled out of her erotic reverie by the sound of male laughter. "What?" she demanded.

"You're a bit eager," Henry said, groaning as he filled his hands with her bare breasts.

"As opposed to you, who are not eager at all," Caro said, rocking pointedly against the bulge in his trousers. "Is that a complaint?"

His eyes were molten as he replied. "Not in the least. I like you eager."

"How fortunate, because there are a few things I would like to try." Caro pushed him onto his back. She lined herself up just where she wanted to be and started rocking against his straining cock, moaning at the delicious sensations. Continuing that motion, she let her hands rove unchecked across his body as she leaned forward to kiss him. This had exactly the effect she desired. Within seconds she had him groaning beneath her, every muscle in his body taut with anticipation. She began to kiss her way down his neck and across his chest, pausing to suck each of his nipples. As she descended, she worked her hands down his body, too, massaging him everywhere except for where he wanted it the most.

She laved his belly button with her tongue and pressed her breasts against the rock-hard bulge in his trousers, giving an experimental wiggle. She noted with satisfaction a vein popping out in his neck. She decided to put him out of his misery and placed her hands right on his cock. Very gently, she began to caress him through his trousers.

He swore, and his hips shot up off the bed as he tore the trousers from his body; Caro actually heard the fabric rending. "I thought we were having a care for our garments," she teased.

He was breathing hard. "Goddamn it, woman! As if I give a damn about my goddamn bloody fucking trousers right now!"

Caro was expecting him to roll her underneath him and drive into her right away, as he looked to be at the point of desperation. But he surprised her by lying back and pulling her down on top of him. Now it was his hands' turn to roam unchecked, which they did, over her breasts and down her ribs and over her stomach, their warmth delicious on her cool skin. And then his hands trailed lower, and his fingers finally made their way to the place where she wanted them.

Turnabout was fair play, because his touch was deliberately gentle.

She cried out in frustration. "Oh, God, Henry! Please! I want to come!"

He chuckled. "Don't worry, darling, you're going to." He eased her back a few inches so he was perfectly in line with her entrance. "But when you do, it's going to be on my cock."

As always, his filthy mouth increased her arousal tenfold. His suggestion suddenly sounded rather appealing, and since his cock was right there, she went ahead and sank down on it a few inches. She realized that, in the back of her mind, she had hesitated, wondering if she was going to feel any pain, any rawness, as she had her first time. But this time there was no pain as she took him in. She closed her eyes and moved experimentally, testing several different angles.

She found one that actually felt rather nice, and she settled into a rhythm. Yes, that did feel quite nice, and although the pleasure wasn't as acute as when Henry caressed her at the juncture of her thighs, she found that the pleasant sensations were slowly building as she continued riding him.

Then she felt Henry's hand right at her entrance where they were joined, and oh! He was *rubbing* her, he was *rubbing* that little nub right at her entrance, and *God*, that felt good! She opened her eyes, and what a sight greeted her. Henry, her Henry, with his big, beautiful body splayed naked beneath her. And the way he was looking at her—the most wonderful combination of adoration and desire.

And as her eyes met his and she thought her heart might actually burst from the purest, most unadulterated happiness she had ever experienced in her whole entire life, she felt her climax building. "Oh, God, Henry," she cried out, "Oh, God, that feels good! Please, Henry, please!"

He knew exactly what her body needed, quickening the speed of his hand and giving her a few nice hard thrusts for good measure, and then the pleasure was almost upon her. It was delicious, it was delectable, it was indescribable, it was —"Oh, God, oh, Henry! Yes! Yes! *Yes!*"

And then her whole body was shaking, and she felt her back arching like a bow, and she heard herself screaming his name over and over as she throbbed and throbbed and *throbbed* around his cock. And then she felt every muscle in his body go hard as a rock beneath her, and his hands seized her hips in an iron grip as he gave her a few more hard thrusts. And then it was his turn to call out her name and throw his head back, and she felt his cock spasm inside her.

His hands guided her down as she collapsed on top of him, his cock still buried within her. Her head was on his shoulder, and his hands were gently stroking over her back. "I love you, Caro," he murmured in her ear.

"I love you, too, Henry," she replied.

And Caroline was sure, more sure than she had ever been about anything, that this was the most perfect moment of her whole entire life.

The last thing she heard before drifting off to sleep was Henry's whisper in her ear. "You know, that just might work." She fell asleep with a smile on her lips.

EPILOGUE

$\mathcal{U}$nfortunately for Caroline, this time when she attempted to sneak back into her bedroom, she found her mother waiting for her.

"You, young lady," the countess said, rising from her chair, "are in deep trouble."

Caro had no choice but to explain where she had been. In short order, Henry was summoned to the Astley town house, where Lord and Lady Cheltenham informed him that he would be marrying their daughter. "This afternoon?" he asked hopefully.

This earned him a glare from his future mother-in-law. "From what my daughter tells me, we should know in approximately one week if an expeditious wedding will be necessary. Assuming it is not, you will be having a respectable eight-week engagement, during which time the two of you will be *very* closely chaperoned."

Lord Ardingly was horrified that the managing young lady who had orchestrated the departure of his antiquities was going to be his daughter-in-law. But Henry's mother was delighted. When Caro invited Lady Ardingly to accompany the Astley ladies to the dressmaker to design Caro's gown for their engagement ball, Henry's mother burst into tears. "Five sons," she said as she accepted Henry's handkerchief. "I have five sons, you see, but no girls." She gave Caro a smile that was sincerely joyful, for all that she was crying. "I'm finally getting a daughter. And my son couldn't have chosen me a better one."

As Caro had planned, she and Henry put in regular appearances during the afternoon promenade in Hyde Park. The first one in particular caused a stir, because Henry mounted Caro upon Brandywine. Admiring whispers followed them throughout the park. Between that and rumors of the price Lord Graverley had paid for Henry's team, he was able to make some extremely profitable sales.

Henry's financial situation received an additional boost when his grandfather the duke announced that he would make them an interest-free loan so they could repurchase all of the terraces houses his father had sold, in addition to funding Henry's stable. It would take almost twenty years to repay the loan in full, but the important thing was that those properties would be staying in the family.

Although they had gotten off to a rough start, Henry was eventually able to win over his future father-in-law. Seeing Henry's determination to do a better job managing his estate than his father had done, Lord Cheltenham summoned his eldest son, Edward, Viscount Fauconbridge, from the family seat in Gloucestershire. As he was Harrington's older brother, Henry already knew Fauconbridge fairly well from their years at Eton. Ever since being named Senior Wrangler, the highest honor given at Cambridge University denoting the top student in mathematics, the brilliant Lord Fauconbridge had taken over the running of his own family's estate. He now spent several hours a day sequestered with Henry in the library, showing him how to read an account book, how to evaluate an investment, and discussing the latest advances in agriculture.

"You would not believe," Henry told Caro, "how much I now know about mangel-wurzels. Far more than I realized there was to know about mangel-wurzels."

"Mangel-wurzels," Caro replied. "You don't say."

For weeks Lord Cheltenham contrived an excuse to loiter in the library, eavesdropping on Henry's tutoring sessions. Seeing how determined Henry was to learn everything Fauconbridge could teach him about managing an estate, coupled with his obvious devotion to his daughter, the earl eventually decided that young Lord Thetford would do after all.

The very day after Henry's father sold him many of his antiquities, Thomas Hope threw his own rout, in which he debuted several newly designed rooms. This included his new Egyptian Room, which was enhanced by a significant portion of Lord Ardingly's collection. Almost a thousand guests attended, including the Prince of Wales. The crush was unimaginable, and Henry and Caro took great delight in strolling arm in arm through the house, loudly feigning surprise at the rooms that were new to everyone but them.

Two weeks after that, Lady Cheltenham threw a ball to celebrate their engagement. Harrington had just returned from hiding, and Henry found himself standing on the back terrace of the Astley town house with his best and oldest friend, enjoying a drink while they waited for the ball to begin.

Harrington was one of the few people they had told the truth regarding Caro's role in rescuing Billy from Snakeface and his friends, and he had requested yet another retelling of their clash with the thieves.

"I lined up my shot," Henry said. "And just as Snakeface

was reaching for her, I pulled the trigger, taking him square in the shoulder."

"May I ask why you didn't aim for his head?" Harrington asked. "If he was in profile to you, you could have gone for the kill shot."

Henry paused. The truthful answer to that question wasn't something he would have even considered admitting to his friend a few weeks ago. Real men didn't have any fears, nor any weaknesses, and if they did, they certainly didn't talk about them.

Fuck that, Henry decided. Not that he was about to start spilling his guts to every stranger on the street.

But he didn't want to spend his entire life pretending to be made of stone. That had never done anything but make him miserable.

Besides, this was Harrington.

The words came pouring out, even as he questioned his own judgment. "The truth is, my hands were shaking so hard, seeing Caro in danger, that I didn't trust myself to make the head shot. I thought the body shot was a safer bet, being a larger target area."

A silence fell. Harrington was staring at him with his mouth gaping open.

Oh, but this had been a mistake. Henry grimaced. "You're probably thinking I'm the last man you want to marry your sister—"

"You really love her," Harrington interrupted. "That's absolutely *brilliant*. You are *exactly* the man I want to marry my sister."

Henry exhaled with relief. "I do love her," he admitted, a bit stiffly. "Madly, as it happens." He leaned in. "Do you want proof?"

"Do tell."

Henry glanced about to make sure the balcony was

deserted. "In order to reach the back door of the warehouse, I had to wade chest-deep into the Thames."

Harrington froze. "Wait. *You* waded *chest-deep into the Thames?*"

Henry nodded. "Didn't even hesitate."

"Were there—"

"*Leeches*," Henry confirmed, shuddering. "I found three of them on me afterwards." He shook his head. "That's some true love, right there."

Harrington threw back his head and laughed. "It certainly is." He raised his glass. "To true love!"

Henry clinked his glass against Harrington's. "To true love," he agreed.

"I always knew she was perfect for you," Harrington said after sipping from his glass. "She has the same irreverent sense of humor. Every time I came home from school, she would pester me for stories about you."

"She is perfect for me; she really is. Not to get all sappy on you, but she's everything I've ever wanted. She's smart—smarter than me, but don't tell her I said that. And she's funny, and she's so quick, and being around her..." He waved his hand, struggling to explain. "She just... makes me so fucking *happy*. She's obviously gorgeous, and she... she has the best heart. The best heart in the whole entire world. I wish I could marry her right this second. I don't know how I'm going to survive another six weeks—"

Harrington's gaze focused on something behind Henry's shoulder. "Oh, good evening, Caro."

Henry turned and saw his betrothed.

It was a familiar sight, Caro standing on a balcony, struggling not to cry.

At least this time she was doing it with the biggest smile on her face.

"Caro," Henry said, hurrying over to take her hands, "don't cry, darling."

"I know," she said, laughing through her tears, "I can't have puffy eyes at my own engagement ball."

Harrington cleared his throat as Henry took Caro in his arms. "I am going to stare out over the back gardens for precisely ten seconds. I trust that when I turn back, any displays which an older brother would not wish to see will have concluded."

Henry gave Caro a quick kiss. "How long were you standing there?"

"Ever since the bit about the leeches."

"At least my balcony soliloquies are improving."

She looped her arms around his neck as she leaned in for another kiss. "They certainly are."

They were still kissing when Harrington turned. "Ugh," he said. "I know you're going to marry her, but I still could have done without seeing *that*. Which brings me to something else—did you really have to go and compromise my little sister?"

"It wasn't Henry's fault," Caro protested. "I was the one who showed up at his rooms in the middle of the night."

Henry smiled sheepishly. "I'm not a bloody saint. As well you know."

"Hmm," Harrington said. After a beat of silence, he added, "And how, exactly, did she know the address of your bachelor apartments?"

Caro and Henry froze, exchanging a guilty look. Henry cleared his throat. "Our friendship will not survive my answering that question."

"You absolute *codpiece*," Harrington said, lunging for his best friend's neck.

"Hey now, I'm marrying her!" Henry protested.

After the scuffle concluded, Harrington turned to his sister. "So, what brings you out here, Caro?"

"Mama sent me to fetch you two." She turned to Henry. "We are needed to open the dancing."

Henry offered his arm. "In that case, may I have the pleasure of this dance, my darling Caroline?"

She gave a dreamy sigh. "I have been waiting so long to hear you say that."

She smiled at him, and he smiled at her. Then Henry led her inside, and the dance began.

Afterwards, those who were present would confirm it was a strange dance. Lady Caroline, who up until that point had been widely regarded as one of the most graceful dancing partners in all of London, stepped on Lord Thetford's foot three times. And stranger still, each time she did it, they both burst into laughter.

The future bride and groom were rather obviously besotted with each other, and there were some who agreed with Lord Graverley's assertion that this was "gauche."

But there were even more who seconded Lady Cheltenham's opinion, stated loudly enough for all to hear, that any couple who possessed such an obvious affection was bound to live happily ever after.

Which is exactly what they did.

KEEP READING for a special preview of Book Two in the Astley Chronicles, *What's an Earl Gotta Do?*

Thank you so much for reading my debut novel! I truly appreciate it, and I hope you enjoyed seeing how Caro and Henry got to their happily ever after. If you would be willing to take a few minutes to leave a review on the site from which you purchased it, that is a great help to me as a new author.

∾

Would you like to find out what life looks like for Caro and Henry fifteen years after their wedding? All subscribers to my newsletter will receive a **free short story**, along with Regency fun, exclusive sneak peaks, and videos of me almost burning my house down whilst attempting to make a traditional Christmas pudding!

Visit www.courtneymccaskill.com to sign up.

∾

Coming Soon: The Astley Chronicles, Book Two: *What's an Earl Gotta Do?*

A widow at the age of twenty-three, Anne Northcote, the Countess of Wynters, is steeling herself for another trip 'round the Marriage Mart. Can she make a love match this time? Read on for a special preview of Book Two in The Astley Chronicles, *What's an Earl Gotta Do?*

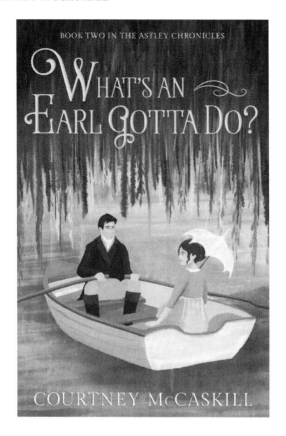

PREVIEW: WHAT'S AN EARL
GOTTA DO?

*L*ondon, England
March 1798

MICHAEL CRANFIELD LEAPT from the carriage before it had even come to a full stop. His legs, cramped from the overnight journey, were unprepared for this sudden exertion, and he almost went sprawling onto the pavement. He managed to keep his feet and sprinted toward the Astley town house, taking the stairs two at a time and ignoring the footman's expression of bewilderment.

"Is Anne here?" he said, panting as he crossed the threshold. "I must speak to her right away."

An older man with a butlerish look about him, between his ramrod-straight posture and air of silent disapproval, raised a single eyebrow. His expression was that of a man who had smelled something exceptionally unpleasant, and he seemed to be pondering which was the graver offense, the fact that Michael looked every bit as rumpled and dusty as one would expect after eighteen hours spent on the road, or that he'd had the audacity to refer to the Earl of Cheltenham's daughter by her first name. He lifted his chin high enough that Michael could see right up his nose. "Could you possibly be referring to *Lady* Anne?"

"Yes—Lady Anne, of course. It's just—I've known her all my life, so I—" Michael swallowed. He didn't have time to explain. "Is she here? I need to speak with her. Urgently."

"She is not. Perhaps you could leave your card, Mr.—"

Oh, God. The most important conversation of his life, and he was going to miss her. "There isn't time for that. Where did she go?"

The butler puffed out his chest. "This is most irregular, sir. You may leave your card. *If* Lady Anne wishes to receive you—"

"In two hours, there is a ship leaving for Canada, and I must be on it," Michael bit out.

The butler looked him up and down. "Rather urgent business for a man of your years. Do tell what it might be."

"I am not at liberty to disclose it. But the matter is urgent enough that my father just pulled me out of Oxford." Michael detected the tiniest sliver of interest in the butler's stony expression. "Please, sir," he begged. "I have to be on that ship, and I must speak to Anne before I go. I could be gone a full year, and I—I've never told her that I—" He swallowed, unable to believe what he was admitting, and to a complete stranger. "I mean, I'm fairly certain she already knows, but—" Lord, this was mortifying. The butler's mouth was hanging open in a most unbutler-like fashion. But Michael ploughed on, because he had to convince the man somehow. "But I haven't actually asked her to—to be my—"

The butler's eyes sharpened. "You are *Lord Morsley*."

"Yes. Yes, I am." Michael felt his face reddening, all the way to his large, sticky-outy ears. He shouldn't be surprised. Everyone back home in Gloucestershire seemed to know he was hopelessly in love with his best friend, that he had been for years.

But it was lowering to discover that his feelings were so openly discussed that this man whom he had never met, who lived a hundred miles away, was privy to them.

At least his confession had the desired effect. "A thousand apologies, my lord. Carter!" the butler snapped at the man posted at the door. "I want every single footman in this house standing before me in one minute, as well as Lady Anne's and Lady Cheltenham's maids."

"Yes, sir!" Carter said, already sprinting toward the back of the house.

It was quickly ascertained that Anne and her mother had gone out to pay a round of social calls. Nobody knew their precise itinerary, although between Yarwood (this proved to be the butler's name) and the ladies' maids, they were able to put together a list of several dozen possibilities.

Footmen were dispatched at a run to inquire at the houses on the list. Michael was pacing past a drawing room when a gentleman with short brown hair peppered with flecks of grey appeared in the doorway. Michael started, and the man laughed.

"I'm sorry. Probably I should have made myself known earlier. I've been waiting for Lord Cheltenham." He extended a hand. "I'm the Earl of Wynters."

"Lord Wynters." Michael pumped his hand. "I am the Earl of Morsley."

"Come, sit," Lord Wynters said, gesturing to a chair before the fire. He strolled over to a decanter in the corner and filled two glasses. "I daresay you could use a spot of this," he said, handing one to Michael.

Michael was just starting to take a sip when a great clattering sound made him all but jump out of his skin. It proved to be Lord Wynters's walking stick, which he had knocked over as he resumed his seat on the sofa. As the earl leaned it against the couch once more, Michael noticed that the shiny black lacquered stick had a silver handle shaped like an icicle. "I could not help but overhear your predicament," Lord Wynters said.

Michael cringed. "I, er—"

The earl laughed. "Come now, there's no need to feel embarrassed. I, too, was once"—he paused, studying Michael assessingly—"seventeen?"

"Nineteen," Michael said, unable to keep a hint of defensiveness from his voice.

"Nineteen. My apologies." Lord Wynters sipped his drink. "Lord Morsley—that'd make you Redditch's heir."

"Yes, sir."

"Then you've nothing to worry about. Your father is tall, as was your mother, God rest her soul. I'll wager that, within the next year, you'll grow into those hands and feet."

"Thank you," Michael muttered, even though he felt the opposite of grateful. He was all too aware that, unlike his friends, who had shot up dramatically in the last few years, Michael remained on the shorter side of average. Not only that, he was scrawny and *terrifically* awkward, with hands and feet so large they looked like they could not possibly go with the rest of his body.

Throw in his gigantic ears, and he wasn't exactly a fairy-tale prince.

But Anne wasn't shallow. She didn't care about things like that.

At least, he hoped to God she didn't.

The earl was shaking his head, looking amused. "You remind me very much of myself when I was not too much older, when I began courting my first wife. You've chosen well for yourself, if you don't mind my saying so. Lady Anne actually bears a striking resemblance to my Clara."

"I see," Michael said. He was so anxious, it was difficult to attend to what the man was saying, but he was trying not to be rude.

There was a rush of footsteps in the foyer as the first footman returned. "Excuse me," Michael said, already halfway across the room.

"They were at Lady Grenwood's house earlier," the footman said, hands on his knees, breath coming in gasps. "But they left a half hour ago, and her ladyship didn't know where else they were heading."

Yarwood gave the man no quarter, handing him another slip of paper. "We've thought of three more houses."

"Yes, sir!" the footman said, hauling in one last breath before rushing out the door.

Time passed both agonizingly slowly and all too quickly. Somehow every time Michael checked his pocket watch, another five minutes had disappeared. Soon all of the footmen but two had returned, and still there was no news.

Michael sighed and turned to Yarwood. "If I am to make my ship, I must depart in ten minutes. As much as I hate to convey such a message in a letter, it appears it has come to that."

"I believe you are right, my lord," Yarwood said, leading Michael back into the drawing room, where the earl was still waiting before the fire. Yarwood opened a writing desk and gestured for Michael to sit.

Over the years, Michael had imagined proposing to Anne in hundreds of different ways—on the balcony at a ball. In the Greek folly behind her house. On the pond where, years ago, they had whiled away many an hour playing pirates (Michael had quickly rejected that one. They were prone enough to overturning the skiff without anyone attempting to go down on one knee.)

But he had finally decided that he would propose in the

meadow next to Cranfield Castle, the glorious old ruin that had been in his family for almost five hundred years. This happened to be the spot they had been picnicking the summer they had both been fifteen, when Michael had come oh so close to kissing her.

And so proposing in a letter tasted like the bitterness of defeat, and what Michael was able to compose in the space of ten minutes left much to be desired. But at least he was able to cover the essentials—that he loved Anne, that he had for years; that he wanted no one but her for his wife; that he never wanted to be parted from her; and that if she would but wait for him, he would rush back to her side just as soon as he had completed the task his father had set before him.

"There," he said, putting a final crease in the paper and rising to his feet. He consulted his pocket watch and was dismayed to discover that he should have left five minutes ago. "I must hurry."

"I will ensure that Lady Anne receives it," Yarwood promised.

"Thank you, Yarwood," Michael said with feeling. "For everything."

The earl had crossed the room to shake Michael's hand. "Good luck to you, young man."

Michael accepted his hand. Plague take it—he was in such a state he had entirely forgotten the man's name. "Thank you, my lord," he said.

And so Michael hurried down the steps as quickly as he had rushed up them, anxious for Anne's answer, and knowing he would have to wait months to learn what that answer might be.

LORD WYNTERS GLANCED about the drawing room. The house was still aflutter following the excitement caused by young Lord Morsley's unexpected arrival. The footmen were chattering amongst themselves in the foyer.

Lord Wynters noted that Yarwood had taken up a position just outside the door, the only one who seemed to recall that they still had a guest.

"Yarwood," Lord Wynters called, "I suppose I won't wait any longer. But I wonder if I might ask a favor before I go."

"Certainly, my lord."

He raised his empty glass. "I happen to know that Cheltenham keeps a bottle of Martell up in the library. Would you mind fetching me a glass?"

"At once, my lord."

As soon as the butler was out of the way, Wynters crossed to the writing desk and seized Lord Morsley's letter. He didn't bother to open it; he knew well enough what it said.

He threw it straight into the fire.

He then scrawled a quick note of his own, which he positioned on the desk at the precise angle of Lord Morsley's missive.

By the time Yarwood returned with his drink, Wynters was back in his seat, arm draped across the back of the sofa, looking for all the world as if he had never moved.

ABOUT THE AUTHOR

After reading *Black Beauty* for the 1,497th time, Courtney McCaskill was inspired to write her own stories. Reviews of her early work were mixed, with her fourth-grade teacher, Ms. Compton, saying, "Please stop writing all of your assignments from the point of view of a horse."

Today, Courtney lives in Austin, Texas with the hero of her own story, who holds the distinction of being the world's most sarcastic pediatrician. She is reliably informed by her six-year-old son that she gives THE BEST hugs, "because you're so squishy, Mommy." When she's not busy almost burning her house down while attempting to make a traditional Christmas pudding, she enjoys playing the piano, learning everything there is to know about Kodiak bears, and of course, curling up with a great book. Visit her online at www.courtneymccaskill.com.

ACKNOWLEDGMENTS

I would first like to thank my mom, Susan, who is exquisitely beautiful inside and out, for encouraging me to write what I really wanted to write, which was a romance novel, and for telling me not feel embarrassed about it.

I would also like to thank my father, Gordon, for being the world's best dad; my sister, Gennie, for being my lifelong partner in crime; and my son for being the joy in my life.

Many thanks to everyone who read some version of this story and offered me feedback, including Amy, Erica, Karen, Lisa, Eva, Susan, Kitty, Carlos, and Tracie, as well as the members of my critique group, Rose, Cat, Darci, and Amanda. I am so grateful to my wonderful editors, Caroline Tolley and Amy Knupp, and my fabulous cover designer, Bailey McGinn. I would also like to thank the University of Texas Libraries for saving me approximately four gajillion dollars on research books, and all of the fabulous writing friends I've made along the way, without whom I would never have made it this far!

This book is dedicated to my wonderful husband. I wrote

something really sappy enumerating the many reasons why, and he absolutely refused to let me put it here.

But I made him read it. So he knows.

Printed in Great Britain
by Amazon